Expiration Friday

Expiration Friday

Percy Stone

ISBN: 979-8-9855571-3-8

This is a work of fiction. Names, businesses, characters and events are entirely imaginary. Any similarity to actual persons, living or dead, or actual events is purely coincidental. Certain long-standing institutions, agencies and public offices are incorporated into the story, as are actual historical events and public figures associated with those events.

Front cover image by Percy Stone

Published by Percy Stone LLC

Contents

Prelude

The following happened over one week in 2007. Most of the world never knew what actually transpired in those six days. The events and their details remain strictly classified to this day. But evidence has emerged in the years since that has allowed investigators to assemble a picture of that terrifying week. This is an accounting of those events...

Sunday, September 16, 2007

Yongbyon Nuclear Scientific Research Center, North Korea

Rains beat down on the sprawling Yongbyon nuclear complex with its menacing concertina wire coiled atop the outer walls. The center was cloaked in nighttime darkness, save for the spent yellow glow cast in bubbles by watchtower lights dimly illuminating the compound's two-story entrance gate. Ghosts leapt across the access road from magnified raindrops striking the floodlights.

A shrill blast from a tinny horn broke the rain's rhythm. The tapping sound resumed only briefly before there was a groan and a screech of rusty metal on metal as the pair of towering steel entrance doors rumbled open in outward arcs.

Eight uniformed North Korean Special Operation Force sentries marched out of the gate clutching AK-74 rifles at their waists. Expressionless, they dispersed in pairs, lining up on either side of the entrance, slinging the AKs over their shoulders once in position. They stood still as cement, with their unblinking eyes under protruding army caps as the rains continued to pelt their faces.

Moments later, a pair of headlights peered out from the darkness of the complex. An engine revved, and a lead guard vehicle, a Russian-made UAZ-469 light utility truck, similar to an American covered jeep, edged out onto the gravel road, crept forward a hundred meters, and braked to a stop.

The passenger-side door flung open, and an officer emerged, gripping a handheld spotlight. He switched on a sharp corridor of blue-white light that pierced the night and exposed the hidden countryside surrounding them.

The officer swept the beam in a 180-degree arc before him. He whisked the wet cement walls of the compound, followed by the drenched roadside shrubs, and then the road itself. Finally, he stretched the light in a path over the adjacent farmland. The spotlight revealed no movement or life at all. It was desolate.

Satisfied, he switched off the spotter, sucking the beam back into the flashlight and restoring the area to the rainy, amber-lit night. The officer signaled to the eight sentries with a quick wave and slid back into his UAZ. The soldiers relayed his command, beckoning those waiting inside the complex.

In hurried succession, seven more vehicles crested the entrance, drove onto the access road, and lined up behind the UAZ. The sentries hustled into the compound, and the steel gates rolled shut to the horn blast. The motorcade wasted no time and sped out onto the regional freeway, the sole vehicles on the road.

Only the pacer UAZ shone its headlights, the rest rode un-lamped. The second vehicle in the convoy was an armored truck with a mounted heavy machine gun and gunner atop the driver's cab. Following that was a troop carrier, inside of which sat ten helmeted NK soldiers in an uncovered bay, their rifles at the ready.

The next three vehicles were the cargo trucks. Sturdy, eight-wheeled heavy-utility carriers, they were North Korean knockoffs of the Russian-made KamAZ-6350. Each truck had a two-person cab in front of a long cargo bay that was covered with a tightly stretched black tarp to conceal its contents. The trucks were chased by a second machine-gunner, and the convoy was anchored by another UAZ jeep.

Inside the cab of the third cargo truck, the driver, an NK soldier, steered the wheel with his right hand while he smoked a cigarette with his left, extending it out of the window in between drags. The passenger riding next to him reached over and flicked the cigarette out of the driver's hand, who shot him a cold look of death. But the passenger was not deterred. He simply responded with a head check motioning behind them toward the cargo bay's contents. The driver had no choice but to acknowledge.

This rider was not dressed like a soldier. In fact, he wasn't wearing a uniform at all. Outfitted in scientist togs, Sohn Tae Jae was a gaunt man with rimless glasses, a radiochemist for the Yongbyon Radiochemical Laboratory at the complex. He had worked in the North Korean nuclear weapons program since the mid-1990s.

Sohn removed his glasses and wiped the condensation from the lenses. He saw outside the rains were finally letting up, and, absently, his gaze moved to the cargo truck in front of them. In his mind's eye, he could almost see through the covering tarp into its contents. He knew well what was being transported, having inventoried the modules personally. It was his duty.

Each cargo truck carried the complete set of components for two plutonium-based nuclear warheads. This included the explosive wrap, or lenses; the neutron initiators; the casings; and their plutonium pits. Assembled, each had an explosive yield, or throw weight, of twenty to thirty kilotons, or about twice the size of the Hiroshima Little Boy bomb. Six warheads in total were being moved.

They were headed to a location about thirty kilometers from Kusong, a small northern town nestled among sylvan foothills that hid a secret underground missile production factory. There, the warheads would be assembled and mated with intermediate-range ballistic missiles—birds that could fly a thousand kilometers and deliver a nuclear blast.

Sohn rolled down his window to let some air blow inside. He stared into the chilly, quiet night in thought. His mind was preoccupied with that night's transport. There was one detail about their trip that troubled him.

The run itself wasn't unusual. Since last year's nuclear test—the nation's first detonation of a working nuclear device, internally known as the Great Bang—their military commanders had ordered missile assemblies with increasing frequency. The Dear Leader had become paranoid that the Americans would bomb Yongbyon and didn't want his precious fissile material inventory sitting vulnerable at the site.

Like clockwork, as soon as the reactor had produced enough plutonium for new warheads, they were sent on another delivery to Kusong. Since the Great Bang, Sohn had shuttled bomb components to Kusong four times already, so he was quite familiar with the trip and its route.

What troubled Sohn this time, however, was the materials accounting. Anytime fissile material was touched, it had to follow a very strict procedure. And for this trip, the chain-of-custody ledger had deviated from that protocol.

The expected process was to have a single set of records corresponding to each delivery. But on this run, they had *two* sets of documents. His Yongbyon team had processed five bombs under one account, and a sixth warhead with separate paperwork, as if it were meant for another destination, altogether.

Sohn had approved both transport bills, but he also *hadn't* raised any objection with his superior, Colonel Cho, who was riding with them in the first KamAZ truck, mostly because he didn't want to appear insubordinate or question the colonel's authority. But now as he went over it in his mind, it was all deeply troubling to him.

Sohn stared out of his window as they rode. In the pitch darkness, he could barely make out the edges of the roadside trees and the foothills surrounding Kusong. Their convoy was beginning to wind up a narrow course, climbing into the forested hills.

His mind returned to the inventory separation issue as their vehicles labored up the incline. Dividing the bomb accounts also raised operational risk that a mistake could occur, he worried, one that could get him discharged or, worse, accused and then jailed and tortured.

Their truck lurched to a stop. The driver cursed as he slammed the brakes and they were both thrown into the dash. After recovering, they craned their necks to discern what might be going on ahead of them. It appeared the entire convoy had braked. Sohn regarded the driver, whose expression was one of irritation, but he didn't say anything.

Sohn puzzled as to why they had stopped. A mechanical issue, most likely, he thought. These were frequent, as maintenance on their vehicles was poor, and engines often broke down. Add to that, the roads were even worse, replete with potholes. It was likely one of the vehicles needed a wheel change. Sohn rolled down his window further. The driver shot him a scolding look, so Sohn stopped it halfway and furtively peeked through the opening to spy on what he could.

He saw that all the vehicles had halted at a fork in the road where one branch continued uphill toward the missile factory, and the other wound back downhill toward the shoreline of the north Yellow Sea. Sohn could hear vehicle doors opening and shutting. He heard the colonel's voice with the intonation of snapping orders but couldn't make out the specific words. Then he heard the clang of a tire iron, or something metallic on the road. This relieved him as it confirmed his suspicion that the convoy's abrupt halt was most likely due to a punctured tire, and that they would shortly be on their way.

The relieving moment lasted only a few seconds before it dawned on Sohn that if the crippled vehicle was one of the KamAZ trucks, it could be gravely dangerous. Transporting the high-explosive lenses for the warheads was always hazardous, but if the truck overturned or crashed, it could set off the explosives. Even though an explosion couldn't detonate the nuclear materials, as the plutonium pits were separated from the explosives themselves, it would still kill them all and shred the plutonium to bits, scattering radioactive debris all over the hills. That they'd be killed in such an event was the easy way out, Sohn internally chuckled, as surviving a brainless failure like that and then having to confront the authorities would be far worse. State recourse would certainly mean a sentence of torture and family enslavement for three generations.

Sohn exhaled in a mix of worry and impatience. He stretched to get a better look through the window, again, to the annoyance of his driver. Sohn felt the vibration of their own truck being opened at the back, and the covering tarp being unfurled. He glanced in his side mirror but couldn't see what was happening. His driver also glanced into his, and then eyed Sohn, monitoring him as if he were taking too much interest.

Sohn removed his glasses to distract the driver. It felt to him like something was being loaded onto their truck. This alarmed him. Were they moving components? Had something been damaged? Such a transfer was strictly forbidden during a delivery. Sohn wanted to get out to see what was going on, but he wasn't permitted. This was forbidden, too.

But Sohn couldn't help himself. He placed his hand on the inside door handle, about to pull it open.

"You stay inside!" warned the driver, sharply, his hand gripping his sidearm.

Sohn gave a sideways glance at his driver's pistol and relented. He fit his glasses back on and kept still. He rolled his window back up to appear obedient, but he concentrated on the movements and paid close attention for any clues.

After a few more minutes, Sohn heard footsteps at the rear of their truck, and felt more rocking from their rear bay. He gasped. His driver, who was peering out his own window, started up their truck's engine. And Sohn heard the other vehicles fire up as well. What was going on? What had happened?

Their truck jogged forward, and they resumed moving. Sohn eyed his driver, who rebuked him by pushing Sohn's head back to its forward-looking position. But in that brief moment, Sohn caught a glimpse of one of the three KamAZ trucks peeling away from their convoy—and turning down the road branch that led toward the sea.

Sohn's heart beat faster. Something was wrong. He paid attention to when they curved around a turn, and he counted the vehicles remaining in their convoy.

In the forested darkness, it was difficult to see anything, but there was a half-moon emerging, after the rains, which provided enough glint on their vehicles so that he could differentiate them. Seven, he counted; there were seven! Only that single KamAZ truck had split off from their group... *Why?* Did it still have its bombs on it? Were they transferred? Is that what he'd felt a few moments ago? If there had been a fatal mechanical issue, the truck would not have been able to drive on, Sohn theorized.

A sickening feeling grew in his gut. He tried to suppress his noticeable panting. Where was the colonel? That was the colonel's truck. Did he remain with it? Sohn now worried he was going to arrive at Kusong missing bomb components. It was his duty to provide the accounting. If he arrived with a short inventory count, he would be arrested at once, tried, and then quickly disappeared.

Sohn had good family origins in the party, he reassured himself. His father was a regional secretary of the Workers' Party, which was how he had received a good technical education, trained as a radiochemist and got invited onto the bomb program, a special privilege only given to those from exceedingly loyal families. Maybe that would save him from being shot, he hoped. Maybe they would sentence him to the work prisons, instead. Sohn began to sweat. He tried to conceal this, too, from his driver, and pretended again to fidget with his glasses while he wiped the sweat from his temples.

In a moment, though, it struck him, as sharply as fists beating on his chest. Sohn connected the separate accounting in the paperwork, one plus five warheads, with the third KamAZ truck that had just separated from them. His mind added it all up as fast as a calculator. Sohn's convoy was now transporting five bombs, driving to their original destination, the Kusong missile factory. And the sixth bomb, in the single KamAZ truck, was heading to the sea…or to someplace else.

He realized that because the paperwork had been divided this way, he would arrive at Kusong with a perfectly reconciled inventory. He would not get into trouble after all. It also occurred to him that the colonel had probably orchestrated things in this way to protect him. *What* was the colonel protecting him from? *Where* was he going? It was clear, a warhead had been secretly diverted, but *why*?

Sohn's mind raced. He cracked his window to get some air, not caring this time what his driver thought. He was stressing about Colonel Cho. Had he accompanied that breakaway KamAZ? Was he operating under orders? Was it a secret directive from the Dear Leader himself?

That KamAZ truck was not heading toward any approved bomb destination. There were no military ports that could properly handle the carriage of a nuclear weapon. There were only fishing villages along that part of the Yellow Sea coastline. And unless the KamAZ doubled back, which would be very strange, given that it was unguarded and without any escort, the truck's heading didn't make any sense at all.

Sohn rubbed his sweaty hands on his trousers. They would shortly arrive at the missile factory in fifteen minutes, he figured. Their truck leaned into a curve as they bent around a narrow turn. It was a part of the road that he knew well. Off that particular hillside edge, there was a steep drop, about twenty meters, densely filled with conifers. Sohn looked up at the KamAZ in front of him, slanting with the turn. He drummed his fingers on his knees. And he took a deep breath.

In a single move, with the KamAZ in motion, Sohn forced open his door and jumped out. He leapt into the darkness below and over the edge of the road and fell into the thick underbrush on the steep slope, sliding uncontrollably for twenty, thirty, forty, meters, tumbling to the lower grade where his plunge was finally broken by a copse of baby pines. He came to a rest and lay still for a moment, bruised, and stunned, but also half listening.

Back atop the road, the convoy screeched to a halt. The officer in the front guard vehicle sprang out and ran to the KamAZ with its swinging passenger door. Sohn's driver was shouting, hands waving, pointing over the edge and at the wide-open passenger-side door. The lead officer gawked at the empty seat, and then peered over the ledge of the bend into the trees. Alarmed, he ran along the line of trucks, banging the side rails of the troop carrier.

"Get him! Get him!" he yelled at the soldiers, who streamed out of the back like a snake. Rifles leveled, they jogged to the edge of the turn and began shooting indiscriminately downward at a terrible angle. Their bullets only vanished into the dense combination of night and thick, wooded trunks. The lead officer reappeared with his spotlight and saw the futility of the soldiers' efforts.

"Stop shooting! Stop shooting," he shouted. The crackle of gunfire ceased. The officer flicked on his flashlight and pointed the beam into the overgrowth. As bright as the lucent spotter was, it disappeared after about five meters in the swallowing darkness. Little was visible except for the immediate brush and branches. He handed the light to one of the soldiers, grabbed him by the arm, and forced him to the aspect where he wanted him.

"Point it down there," the officer berated him, as he clutched two more soldiers by a handful of their vests and shoved them toward the rim, too.

"Climb down after him. Shoot him when you see him," he ordered. The two soldiers nervously surveyed the thick woods and blackness below them. They slung their rifles over their shoulders and stepped over the side, like they were dropping into water for a dive, reaching out for anything they could to steady themselves down the slope.

The lead officer jogged back to the open KamAZ truck. He reproved the driver to restart the engine, and he shut its door. Everyone returned to their vehicles, and in moments, the convoy had resumed and vanished beyond the bend.

At the bottom of the slope, Sohn shook off his daze and unsteadily rose to his feet. He stared upward through the trees toward the top of the ridge where the road was. He couldn't see it directly, but he heard the shouting and rifle fire. And he saw the strobing of the light as it swept through the trees. Sohn knew they were after him.

Clutching the saplings, he pulled himself to a start and dashed forward, spurred by a lightning fear in his chest. Sohn sprinted across the wooded slope, dodging tree trunks and brush, and stumbling over uneven ground. Darkness was his best friend at that moment. And as long as there was tree cover, he could evade them, he thought, at least for a short while. Behind him, he heard a rifle shot ring out, and then another. Sohn ran as fast as he could.

The low-level soldiers weren't his problem, he knew. They would soon give up and return to the road. It was what followed that filled Sohn with fear. Once the convoy arrived at Kusong, the commanding officer would immediately report Sohn and dispatch the hunters—elite soldiers who stalked and killed deserters or defectors—*they* were his problem. Sohn knew he had only a few hours, at best. The hunters were tireless predators and would pursue him with their night-seeing glasses and their dogs.

The Yalu River was about twenty kilometers to the north, he estimated. Over this terrain, it would take him several hours. Sohn's only chance was to make it to the Yalu and try to cross to the Chinese bank. But once he arrived at the river valley, he would be at much greater risk. There were fewer areas to hide, and the special forces, *and* the border guards, were everywhere around the river. Even if he made it past all that opposition, he still had the thick and swift Yalu River to cross. The Yalu devoured many a defector.

Sohn's heart beat like a bird's flapping wings. His legs were sore and rubbery. He needed to regain some strength. He was exhausted but reminded himself to stay alert, especially when he arrived at the Yalu. Sohn pressed on. He projected to where the best—easiest—part of the Yalu was where he could cross. There was a segment of the river that narrowed considerably west of the PetroChina station, he remembered. It was thinner there, but that also meant the currents were swifter. And he needed to get there quickly. He had to cross under darkness. He knew once dawn appeared, he was dead...

Upper Atmosphere, 720 Kilometers above North Pacific, Western Orbital Plane, at Night

Arcing across the earth's atmosphere over North Korea in a sun-synchronous orbit, a US Onyx radar imaging reconnaissance satellite blanketed the ground below with millions of high-powered radar pulses. The pulses, each a tiny duration of ten to fifteen microseconds, raked the Yongbyon Nuclear Scientific Research Center and all its buildings, structures, vehicles, land, trees, cows, and every other object in the surrounding area. This radar energy scattered in all directions, with some of it being reflected to space and into the gold receiver dish on the Onyx.

Computational units onboard the spy satellite sucked in and processed the returning beams. The calculations were exacting as the processors accounted for the satellite's location to within centimeters, its orbital velocity, and the subtle, doppler-effect lengthening of the reflected energy. And since radar waves traveled at the speed of light, the CPUs could also calculate, precisely, their return time, which meant the height of any object could be resolved to within ten centimeters. It was a marvel of engineering.

The NRO, the National Reconnaissance Office, operated this Onyx unit, along with the dozens of other eyes in the sky. North Korea's 2006 atomic test had surprised and alarmed Washington, and the Bush administration, which had been so focused on the action in the Middle East that North Korea had fallen in priority. This bird had been reassigned to the NE Asian theater following that baleful event.

The satellite hurtled through space. Its eyes trained on the North Korean targets in miniature far below it. As the eight-vehicle convoy exited Yongbyon and snaked through the North Korean hills to the Kusong missile factory, its officers and soldiers had no idea of, nor could they physically feel, the rain shower of tiny light waves painting them and their actions from above.

The Onyx furtively swept its targets, processing the copious data funneled to it, and relayed the imagery to the Tracking and Data Relay Satellite System (TDRSS) ground station at White Sands, New Mexico. The station then streamed the data to subject matter experts at different intelligence agencies in Washington, where it awaited their analyses…

Honggon-do Island, North Korea

A long wooden dock levitated over an oily marsh amid a retreating fog. Moored to the dock, a lone eighteen-meter fishing trawler creaked with a pendulum rhythm in the darkness.

A runtish Syrian cur of a man stood on the south side of the pier, smoking a cigarette, and staring out into the mire. Impatient, he stepped from the edge and flicked his half-finished stub into the water. He tilted his wrist and eyed his watch.

"Three-thirty. They're late," he complained as he glanced, upset, at a taller, wiry Syrian partner of his, another cur-like figure who was leaning against a stack of empty cargo palettes, smoking a cigarette himself. He didn't respond to his shorter companion. He simply took a long drag and watched his broadening exhale swirl and disappear into the mist.

"This place is a soiled hell," the short one scoffed, sneering at the boat behind them. The taller one delayed his acknowledgment, and after a few moments regarded his shorter partner and then the trawler. He still didn't say anything, just took another drag.

Honggon-do was an island in the northern crook of the Yellow Sea, part of the Banseong Archipelago. To the immediate west lay Chinese territorial waters—waters that were in continuous dispute between Chinese and North Korean fishermen. That was the life there. Most of these islands were jutted with shaky docks from which hung scores of deteriorating wooden fishing skiffs. It was a forlorn region, with little military presence, and many kilometers of poorly mapped marshes, perfectly formed for smuggling.

The deep bass grumble of an approaching truck awoke the Syrians from their spell. The taller Syrian doused his cigarette and grabbed a backpack that was propped against a cargo palette. He unzipped it and removed a pair of handheld devices. The first device appeared to be a cell phone; the other was larger, the size of a paperback novel. It was dark plastic or metal with a circular brass wire-screen window on its front.

The approaching vehicle shone its headlights and cast the pier in a bright haze as the beams diffused in the mist. The shorter cur shot his partner an annoyed glance at the conspicuous gleam.

A moment later, a single KamAZ truck—the one from the convoy—nosed forward out of the fog, hesitantly rolling onto the pier. It cut its lights and shut its engine. Both cab doors swung open. The riders climbed down and landed with a thud on the pier's wooden planks. The shorter cur put his hand on his pistol inside his jacket. He warily eyed the approaching figures.

Emerging from the truck, Colonel Cho stopped before the Syrians. He gave a short, stiff bow to them, and spoke awkwardly in broken English.

"My eldest son is healthy and well," he offered in a rehearsed-sounding tone. His eyes widened as he studied the Syrians for their response. The taller Syrian cleared his throat and then spoke in smoother English.

"Perhaps your son should meet our daughter," he replied. There was a long, difficult pause, and finally, Colonel Cho removed a cell phone from his topcoat pocket. He flipped it open, and the display screen lit up with a purplish glow of a partial image of a soccer ball, the left hemisphere.

The tall Syrian eyed it and flipped open his own cell phone. Clicking the scroll button a few times he revealed the image on the phone's display—a similar image of a soccer ball—the right hemisphere of the same ball. Colonel Cho passed his phone to the Syrian, who held the screens next to each other, forming a complete image of the soccer ball, perfectly aligning the black-and-white hexagon pattern. The tall Syrian nodded to the colonel and returned his phone. The shorter Syrian watched them closely, still cautious, but withdrew his hand from his pistol.

The four walked to the rear of the KamAZ. Uncovering the tarp, Colonel Cho waved his hand over a set of crates and the components within them. The driver hung a small lantern from the rear frame of the truck to give them some light.

"Everything, as agreed," Colonel Cho presented. He pried the wooden lids off of two of the three crates. The taller Syrian explored the contents. He raised his other handheld device, the larger one with the brass wire screen, over the crates. The device began to stutter with a series of piezoelectric chirps.

Colonel Cho, realizing his intention, motioned to a hardened plastic case among the components, and unlatched its lid. Inside, there was a dull-metal ball, the color of pewter or lead, about the size of a grapefruit. The Syrian held the device above the metal ball, and the beeps accelerated into a rapid cackle. He and the colonel exchanged nods.

Several fishermen emerged from the trawler. Colonel Cho signaled for them to remove the components, and the fishermen began to hoist the crates and transfer them to the boat.

"Slowly, be careful," the shorter Syrian barked at them, after which he and his partner joined the crew in relaying the cargo onto the craft. When all crates had been removed, the taller Syrian lit up another cigarette, and shook the colonel's hand. The Syrians abruptly turned to the trawler, and Colonel Cho and his driver returned to their truck. The KamAZ reversed off the pier, and the remaining fog closed around it like a set of curtains.

The crewmen unlashed the boat's mooring ropes from the pier, and the Syrians climbed the rickety gangway onto the vessel. A puff of choking black smoke enveloped them as the engines coughed to a low roll. The trawler fell backward into the swampy waters and vanished into the remaining night.

Bank of Yalu River, North Korea

Sohn peered out from behind the cover of a dense thicket on a ridge overlooking the south bank of the Yalu River. The Yalu coursed smoothly at this bend, its flat surface mirroring a sheen from the white moonlight above. Here was a good place to cross, but he knew it masked dangers and death beneath its polished appearance. Light would shortly arrive, and he had precious little time to exploit the remaining darkness, which would be his only cover once he was exposed.

Sohn looked behind him through the depleting woods from where he had come. A momentary thought urged him to retreat inside, back into the safety of the concealing forests, and to give up on this whole thing. *Turn around and go back,* he thought. *Explain to your superiors that you had panicked, apologize to them and to the Dear Leader, and accept whatever punishment they mete out,* he proposed to himself. As soon as he started down the hill before him, there was no returning. The hunters would be on him.

Across the river, Sohn could barely identify the outlines, the edges of what might be a riverside road, some ten meters above the riverbank. He surveyed a few kilometers upstream. He saw what he believed was a power station, or a factory. On the other side, there was life, civilization.

The wind started up with regular gusts from the hills behind him and rolled down the banks toward the Yalu and the Chinese towns across it. Sohn thought this was a favorable distraction, a momentary window he could seize. He waited and followed the wind's cadence as it died down and picked up again. And with a sudden burst, he ran.

His ears filled with the roar of rushing air. He sized up the fast-approaching Yalu in front of him. The river was flat and glossy, extending out from the muddy banks. Closer to the middle, it became angrier with savage rocks and currents. He could hear the clatter of those midriver torrents as he neared.

17

Sohn forced himself forward, wading into the mushy river, his shoes filling with freezing water, and his skin burning from its icy sting. The river deepened, and Sohn let go of the bottom, floating with the waters, cleaving them silently as he thrust ahead. He paddled toward the flow of the rocky currents, keeping his arms and legs below the surface, and only his head above, minimizing his profile and protecting his glasses for as long as he could.

He reached a central sandbar where the waters became shallower, and he could stand again. The riverbed was uneven and rocky, and he struggled in the stronger currents to grip the bottom with his feet. Sohn lost his balance and plunged into the water, his arms threshing to try to catch himself. He wrestled toward the rapids, pushing off rocks below and dog-paddling to propel himself.

A muffled report interrupted the river swell and pierced the whoosh of the wind. Sohn rotated to the source of the sound, behind him. In silhouettes against the rising hill on the North Korean bank, he glimpsed movement, human forms, a dozen of them. Sohn froze. There they were, the commandos, cascading down the hill after him, rifles in their grips.

Another shot rang out. He heard it clip the water and smack a rock ahead of him. He hastened his crossing, kicking and pushing against anything his feet could find just to get farther across. He strove for the central rapids, where he could use the rocks as cover.

The commandos streamed to the river's edge. Their eyes acquired the small shape with the tuft of black hair flailing. One commando shouldered his AK and braced for an anchored aim. He rattled off a burst of tracer rounds that followed like lasers into the river after Sohn.

Sohn heard the louder, automatic weapons fire and flattened himself down into the water. His peripheral sight picked up the lit rounds tunneling into the dark waters, glowing in straight lines. He tried to remain submerged within the currents, but his thigh struck a boulder. He was twisted around, pushed upward, and suddenly faced the commandos on the bank. The surging waters held him up, suspending his head and torso in the air, exposed to the eyes tracking him.

From the flat of the bank, a commando, lying prone with a sniper rifle, squeezed his trigger, followed again by a second and third shot.

Sohn was struck in the shoulder. The bullet cut a path clean through him, exiting out his back and dinging off a rock behind him. The force spun him around, and a second shot shattered his left forearm, casting him backward into the whitewater. Sohn was pulled under. He struggled, his other arm lashing out for anything, his legs flailing. The bitter cold water was now a strange ally, as it numbed his wounds, and he did not notice the agonizing pain. He knew his left arm was dead, but he managed to paddle, one-handed, for a few strokes.

Wounded, and crippled, Sohn resurfaced in the central rapids. He clung to a rock as the currents thrashed around him, peeling away his tenuous grip. He extended to the next rock, thrusting off a slab underneath him and finding some solid footing. He stretched for the security of a large boulder, his good arm hugging it tightly.

Sohn paused and peeked at the bank. He realized then his glasses were lost. All he could see were smeared forms. The commandos were closer. He heard more rifle shots and AK fire sound off like whip cracks, even over the torrent of the river. He knew they must have waded into the shallows and were firing on him.

18

His wounds bleeding, his left side numb and limp, he dragged himself into an eddy. He was navigating only by sound. If he could make it past the loudest rolling, he was beyond the center, and he could swim to the other bank, he thought. He reached for a pile of rocks but misjudged its distance.

A rock gave way, and Sohn fell into the strongest channel of currents, water foaming and bubbling, engorging him. The river swallowed him. He was sucked under again. Sohn caromed off a moss-covered boulder underneath, and his head struck the edge of it. The Yalu was in command. He felt himself thrown outward, into the air, and the world went dark.

Moments later, his eyes flew open. He gasped for air. In his panic for survival, he caught a glimpse of stars above him and the emerging dawn. He realized he was floating on his back, drifting in a quieter part of the river but also flowing swiftly downstream.

Sohn tilted his head up, chin to chest to look toward the commandos. They were much farther away now, on the opposite bank, upriver. He could only tell where they were by the occasional flashes of their tracer fire. He realized they hadn't seen him fall and disappear below the rapids.

Sohn let himself quietly drift for some distance. He knew he was invisible, floating on his back, unmoving. He worked his right foot to edge himself toward the Chinese bank as he coursed downstream.

After much kicking, the back of his neck felt something brush against it. He smelled the scent of mud and clay. Sohn rolled over, and his right leg found the bottom. It was soft and spongy and didn't offer much support. Still, he dug into the muck and battled along. Through twenty meters of mud, he emerged from the waters and hauled himself onto a narrow strand of riverbank.

Finally, out of the river, he lay panting, coughing up water and blood. He was wet and cold and felt his eyes close. He wanted to drift into a slumber—*danger*—but he caught himself. Retreating from the edge of unconsciousness, Sohn summoned remnants of reserve strength.

Lifting onto his hands and knees, he started to climb, scratching up the muddy slope, his feet rucking the sandy clay behind him. His working hand found the tree roots of a fir sapling, and he gripped them with his remaining muscle and strained himself up to the crown of the grade. Sohn climbed another two meters of bank and was at last on level ground. Weaving through briars and shrubs, he found that single-lane dirt road.

A stuttering of gunfire erupted. Sohn felt the power of a sledgehammer hit his ribs. His chest burst open with a spigot of blood. He gasped, looking down at himself, his right arm clutching at the wound. Sohn collapsed onto the dirt. Through tears, he saw dark figures—North Korean commandos—they had crossed the river! They encircled him.

One commando closed in and whipped out a gravity knife, the blade shine catching the earliest light. The commando leapt at him. Sohn knew he was about to have his throat cut. Sohn's eyes, sallow, with what little remaining life he had left, awaited the job to be finished when a thundering series of *cracks* sounded. The commando's skull exploded, dowsing Sohn, with the limp body buckling onto him. Shouts and more gunfire spread.

Sohn was underneath the dead commando, not knowing what had just happened. He saw the remaining hunters flee as sharper rifle fire pursued them. He saw a blur of shiny boots. They were uniformed PLA, Chinese People's Liberation Border Police.

The gunfire ceased. He heard yelling in Mandarin. One of the PLA officers shoved the dead commando off of Sohn. Two more guards approached, and stood looming over, appraising Sohn. One of them felt for his pulse and yelled over to the other PLA police. Sohn wafted in and out of consciousness. His eyelids dropped, and he let go. Sohn fell into blackness.

Sohn awoke, his eyes blinking with a fog. He struggled to breathe. He could taste blood. He didn't know where he was. He didn't know what had happened. He moved the fingers on his working hand and felt what was underneath him.

He was on a cold metal table in a bare room with gray-painted walls. There was a dim incandescent light source in the corner. He saw an IV was in his arm. A voice in a mix of textbook Korean with Mandarin came to his ear.

"What is your name and rank?" the voice demanded. Sohn didn't respond.

"What is your *name and rank*?" the voice shouted again.

Sohn managed with some effort to turn to his side. He saw the man of the voice, not a PLA soldier. And there was a second man, who was quiet, standing behind him in the corner. He was not in a uniform, either. These men were something different, not soldiers. They both wore buttoned, collared shirts with pressed trousers. Sohn, in his departing thoughts, realized they may be local intelligence officers trying to identify him; their role to separate the peasants from the real defectors. Sohn recognized it was his only choice at that moment. He sensed his life ebbing away.

Sohn managed a frail whisper, in his best Mandarin.

"I am Sohn Tae Jae. Sohn Tae Jae," he started. The man closer to him leaned in to hear. Sohn continued, "I am a radiochemist at Yongbyon Nuclear Scientific Research Center. I was in convoy transporting..." Sohn stopped, the word for "nuclear weapon" eluded him, so he used a Korean term instead: "We drove six 'dark sun' to Kusong... One 'dark sun' missing. One 'dark sun' is missing. Sent to the water. You..."

Xue Kwan, the first intelligence officer, frowned as he heard these words, straining to understand him. He rose, his eyes working in calculation as he tried to interpret what Sohn had said. Kwan gave a questioning look to his superior who said nothing. Sohn's voice had been too weak; his boss hadn't heard a word from where he was standing. Kwan shouted outside the room for an orderly to come and take Sohn to a hospital.

Sohn faded. He lost consciousness for the last time. He could hear commotion as the darkness surrounded him. He had made it across the Yalu River, barely, and relayed his secret. Sohn died on the metal table.

Kwan helped the orderly cart away the body. His superior walked out of the interrogation room, only half turning to remind Kwan to "write it up" before heading back to his office. Kwan acknowledged and followed the wheeled body down the corridor. As they rolled, he felt Sohn's hands, the palms and the fingertips. He instructed the orderly to photograph Sohn before following the body disposal procedure.

Kwan stepped outside and lit a cigarette. Xue Kwan was a junior fifth-year intelligence officer for the PLA, stationed at the frontier where the North Korean defectors arrived en masse. There were entire communities of them living among the local Chinese towns along the Yalu. It was Kwan's job to find and interrogate as many of these escapees as he could, escalating any useful intelligence that he could extract.

As Kwan exhaled a jet of smoke, he thought about what he'd heard on the metal table. Most defectors he encountered were farmers or factory workers who had fled and made it across the river. They were peasants and worthless to him. Kwan could tell them immediately by their hands, like leather with thick calluses. They were also underfed and malnourished. But Sohn was not one of these. Sohn was frail but not indigent. And his hands were softer and less worn. He had a better life over the line, he was taken care of, important.

The sun was rising in white light over the western Yalu. As Kwan smoked, he reviewed in his mind the few brief last words spoken by Sohn. He was alarmed, too, by the specific statement, and how he had delivered it. Sohn's delicate appearance gave him credibility. He also believed what he claimed about his position to be true. Farmers and laborers would never even know to proclaim they were a radiochemist from Yongbyon. They'd have no idea about that, Kwan reasoned. Kwan also felt Sohn didn't think that he'd make it any farther. If you were trying to defect, and you were caught, you'd say anything to be let go, make up any story you could invent, Kwan thought. But if Sohn knew he was likely dying, he'd have no motive to invent anything; it was more like he was trying to relay a message.

Kwan's mother was Korean. His parents had met during the Korean conflict, his father a Chinese soldier. It was because Kwan grew up with a Korean mother and spoke good Korean that he was picked for this frontier role, which he despised. And because he spoke Korean, he knew exactly what Sohn meant by the term "dark sun," a Korean affectation for a nuclear bomb.

All these details made Kwan nervous. He finished his first cigarette and lit up another. What had happened? Had Sohn defected from Yongbyon with a secret? Or was this a ruse by the wily North Koreans, the latest gambit by leader Kim? Since the nuclear test last year, there had been several legitimate nuclear program defectors. Some of them came to China, while most went to South Korea. Many of the scientists involved in the nuclear program did not agree with Kim Jong Il's nuclear test, believing it would further isolate their country. These defectors were valuable to Kwan's superiors.

Kwan contemplated his other dilemma. How to report this, and to whom. Kwan had his official Chinese PLA chain of command, but he also regularly sold information to the Americans and to the South Koreans. They paid very well. Since the nuclear test, the Americans had become especially eager, understandably, for any North Korean nuclear program intelligence, and Kwan's CIA handler would pay a premium for this, he knew.

As Kwan doused his last cigarette, he decided: he would send his American handler a message, through the usual coded channel, but he would also write up his report for his PLA bosses—he would just delay sending that for a few days. That would cover him, he calculated. He could never be certain what his own Chinese intelligence service would do with something like this, and if Sohn weren't for real, he wouldn't be penalized for otherwise shouting "fire." But if

Sohn was, in fact, legitimate, it would be the Americans who had the assets to investigate this further, and the need to know, he thought. Kwan eyed the North Korean hills across the Yalu River as he pivoted on his heel and went back inside the station house...

Monday, September 17, 2007

Baku-Tbilisi-Ceyhan Oil Pipeline Near Erzurum, Turkey

The silvery pipeline glinted against a blue sky as it undulated with the grass covered Palondoken hills of eastern Turkey. Erzurum was an ancient Medieval Turkish city and the capital of its own district, a region that hosted the strategically important Baku-Tbilisi-Ceyhan (BTC) oil pipeline.

The single-barreled BTC pipeline originated four hundred miles to the east, in the Azeri-Chirag-Gunashli deep-water oil fields of the Caspian Sea. It pushed one million barrels of crude oil per day to the Mediterranean, where the crude was shipped to buyers across Europe and the Middle East.

To keep the BTC from freezing in the winter, the snaking pipeline was elevated about a meter off the ground by steel and concrete supports. And along this section of pipeline overlooking Erzurum, there was something affixed to four of those supports—demolition blocks of military-grade C-4 plastic explosive, about twenty kilograms on each column.

The explosives were lined up in vertical bars and joined together by duct tape, which also strapped the C-4 around the columns. Emerging from the ends of each block of C-4 was a thick, plastic-clad detonator wire that fed into an electronics control box attached just below.

A breeze blew across the hillside. There was not a soul anywhere. A softened ringing tone, like that from a cell phone, trilled inside the control boxes below the explosives. Silence followed. A second ring rattled moments later, followed by another silence. On the third ring, the C-4 exploded with a thunderous *ker-blam*!

The girders bearing the pipeline blew apart. Mangled shrapnel flew out over the hilltop. The pipeline buckled without its supports, and the explosion sent torn hunks of molten steel through the pipeline's skin, cracking it open in long, jagged gashes. Fissures ripped open the tube's sides and ignited high-pressure jets of the oil in fiery plumes.

The exposed, severed ends of the pipeline collapsed to the ground, and like the mouth of a hose, belched a continuous flow of burning crude oil onto the green hillsides, instantly turning them shiny and black as the oil coursed, aflame, down the slopes. The slick widened as more crude spurted out in gurgles. A column of dense black smoke rose from the hills into the blue sky above Erzurum...

Ritz-Carlton Residences, Lower Manhattan, United States

Yellow morning sunlight beamed across Manhattan, shining over the Upper Bay of the Hudson River and the coppery-green Statue of Liberty, gilding the skyline of Jersey City. The view from this penthouse apartment atop the thirty-eight-story Ritz-Carlton hotel and condo building was stunning. It commanded a panoramic scene of where the East River joined the Hudson, the Statue of Liberty, and the hilly grade of Staten Island in the distance. If the isle of Manhattan were a ship, this building, located exactly at its southernmost tip, would be its prow.

The penthouse bedroom was a mess. Blue and white oxford shirts were strewn about, as were halves of custom-tailored wool suits, and trousers splayed on the floor with pant legs inside out. On a corner end table stood an open bottle of $400 Macallan 25 scotch, half consumed, its cap nowhere to be found. An empty glass with scotch residue sat paired with the bottle. The drapes had not been closed the night before, and the sun now burned into the bedroom.

A cell phone on the nightstand beside the bed started to buzz. It vibrated incessantly before a hand groped for it and finally grabbed it to answer.

"Yeah?... Hang on, hang on—wait, what?... Ah, God! I'm sorry. I'll pick her up after school, then... Don't tell me when I can and can't see her—it's my day! I want to see her... Fine—" And the cell was hurled into a chair against the far wall.

Kyle Springer rose from his bed and swung his legs over the side and sat up with a wide yawn. Shirtless, in his boxers, he was a fit, athletic form for his thirty-six years. A decade of high school and collegiate lacrosse, followed by more years of gym workouts, had, at that point in his life, compensated for the many late nights and profuse drinking, a lifestyle that hadn't yet caught up with him.

He fumbled along the nightstand for his glasses, a pair of lightweight gold wire-rimmed frames, found them, and fit them on. He blinked and focused as the bright morning came into view. With his specs on and his cut form, he struck an almost Clark Kent–like appearance.

Kyle frowned after the tossed cell phone. His ex-wife, Amy, had interrupted his sleep and reminded him that it was his day to see their daughter and that he needed to pick her up from school. They'd been divorced for two years. He and Amy had one daughter, Jill, who was seven. And Kyle, who had been thrust back into his bachelor lifestyle years, was still adjusting to the schedules and to the rules of their joint custody arrangement.

He stood up, not in any particular rush, oddly, and wandered over to the chair to retrieve his phone. When he looked down at it, he caught the time, 7:45 a.m.—

"Shiiiit!" he cursed.

Kyle shot out of the Ritz-Carlton lobby and onto West Street. In one of his suits with a leather over-the-shoulder bag slung across his chest, his hand went up to hail a cab. His attention was on his cell as he scrolled through news and emails.

A New York City yellow cab bent around the block and skidded to a stop in front of Kyle, who jumped in and shut the door.

"Greenwich and Beach Street in Tribeca," Kyle directed, without looking up. The cabbie squinted into the rearview and accelerated into West Street traffic.

"It's a beautiful day. Why don't you walk?" the cabbie inquired. Kyle looked up from his news, annoyed.

"You don't want me to hire you and give you business?" Kyle impatiently challenged, and then added, "I'm late, just get me there," he made clear.

The cabbie remained facing ahead and didn't say anything more.

Kyle returned to his cell, scanning the news, which was invading with increasing frequency. He glowered into the screen. Frustrated by what he was reading, he cursed and dialed to make a call.

"Hey, Pete, it's me, not so good morning... Yes, now I'm late. Thank you for your support... Why is front month crude up two bucks?" Kyle listened to a rambling reply on the other end, and then replied himself, "You're useless. Of course, I don't see any news. Why do you think I'm calling?... Riiiight. Call around to some of the other desks, find out what they're hearing—or talk to some of our idiot brokers, rumors are usually the one thing they're good for... Yes, I know—Pete, don't—don't tell me the fucking number." Kyle lowered the phone from his ear, ignoring Pete as he spoke. Flushed, he raised the phone back. "I know it's in our face. We blew through four strikes already. How short are we here?... Then buy a couple hundred to stop the bleeding. I don't know, we'll figure out the rest when I get in. I'll be there in a few."

Kyle, frustrated, jabbed off the phone and punched the seat divider, jolting the cabbie, who shot him a fearful look in the rearview, but he kept driving. Kyle watched the Tribeca brownstones flash by as the cab accelerated through a green light. His temples pulsed. He pushed out a long, burdened exhale through his nose.

Kyle was an options trader for Fortnum Bank, on their Special Situations Derivatives Desk. It was his job to make money for the firm through a combination of proprietary options trading strategies, dubbed "prop" in industry lingo, and by accommodating large customer orders in options.

Options were financial derivatives that paid off when certain price ranges of their underlying asset were hit. Kyle mostly traded options on energy products, like crude oil and natural gas, as well as options on energy stocks, like Exxon Mobil and British Petroleum.

Trading options for a bank was really no different from making and selling a product at any other profit-driven company—the goal was to produce your product or service for less than you charged your customers for it. That difference was your profit. If a customer wanted to place a bet that crude oil was going higher in the next quarter, for example, they might buy a three-month call option on crude oil futures and pay $5 a contract for it. If Kyle could produce that option trade for, say, $4.50 a contract, Kyle and the bank would make money. If, on the other hand, it cost him $5.50 per contract to manufacture, the bank would lose money and Kyle's performance-driven bonus would suffer.

Options, and other derivatives, were always *based on* another thing. That "thing" could be a stock, or a future, or a commodity, or an index, like the S&P 500 stock index. The option's value at any one time depended on where its underlying "thing" was trading. Whenever the bank facilitated large options trades for customers, the traders needed to *hedge* the options with those underlying "things"—futures or stocks. That was part of the manufacturing process. And options were especially sensitive to the gyrations, or *volatility*, of their underlying products, that is, the speed at which they moved.

Earlier that morning, something had caused the price of crude oil to jump suddenly, and Kyle's current "book," or set of positions, was exposed, negatively, to this exact type of rapid move in the price.

Kyle had expected the price of crude oil to subside in the upcoming months, and that's what he had positioned for. The Iraq War was stabilizing. There was talk of bringing troops home. More Iraqi oil fields were coming back online, and supply disruptions were becoming less frequent. Additionally, the US economy had recently started to show signs of weakness, and markets were beginning to worry about cracks in the mortgage market that could possibly lead to a recession. All of that meant global demand for crude oil would be soft for the foreseeable future, as global supply was increasing, both of which meant lower prices.

But the price had now unexpectedly reversed. His position was losing millions of dollars. As Kyle's cab approached the Fortnum Bank office, he obsessed about the hole he was in—not good.

Fortnum Bank Building, 392 Greenwich Street, Lower Manhattan, United States

Kyle beat through the Fortnum Bank lobby. At 392 Greenwich Street was Fortnum Bank's main global trading house headquarters, although the merchant banking part of the business was run out of a separate office on Park Avenue, the Greenwich Street building in Tribeca was the bank's effective headquarters. The sales and trading and investment banking groups, which together controlled massive flows of capital across global financial markets in equities, fixed income, currencies, commodities, and private equity, operated from there.

The site itself was familiar to most New Yorkers. Twin forty-story buildings stood overlooking the Hudson River. The south tower was known as the Travelers Building, which housed Citibank. The famous Travelers red umbrella logo, which had adorned the office tower in bright neon, had only recently been removed, as had the red umbrella sculpture on the Greenwich Street promenade. The north tower was Fortnum Bank, Kyle's office, which hadn't changed much since its completion in 1988.

Kyle crossed the white marble-floored, three-story-high lobby and approached the elevator bank turnstile, when he heard his name.

"Springer?" reverberated in the echoey hall.

Kyle spun around, irritated at being delayed. He spotted Carl "Sully" Sullivan sitting atop the shoeshine console next to the magazine vendor.

Sully tapped the shoeshine guy on the back with a twenty-dollar bill and jumped down from the chair, jogging over to Kyle.

"You working a half day today?" Sully chided Kyle for his late arrival.

Kyle returned a humorless sneer as he pushed through the turnstile and smacked the elevator call button.

Sully was an options trader, too. He ran the Index Volatility Desk, a critical book and strategy responsible for managing the bank's dealing in equity index derivatives. Kyle and Sully had been friends since college. Both growing up on Long Island, they met playing in the off-season lacrosse leagues. Sully had gone to Harvard, and Kyle went to Colgate, which were in different collegiate divisions, but they had gotten to know each other through local summer competitions.

"I'm getting run over this morning. Who wants to play when you're losing?" Kyle complained.

"Crude—pipeline explosion," Sully concurred. But Kyle hadn't heard that yet.

"No shit, really? I saw the move, I didn't see any news on it..." Kyle nosed into his cell, searching for the report.

"Turkey, Azerbaijan, some shit place like that," Sully informed.

Kyle was reading, not looking up as the elevator doors opened.

"That's the BTC. Big line. Million barrels a day. Shit," Kyle chafed.

"If you say so. What's the butcher's bill?" Sully snooped, bringing up Kyle's profit and loss, or P&L, as he caught the elevator doors and nudged Kyle inside.

"I'm down thirty sticks now. I'm crushed," Kyle somberly replied as they rode up. A stick was trader jargon for $1 million, so thirty sticks was $30 million.

"You've been down worse."

"This is real, though, this is a pain trade. Fuck. I'm always two steps behind. I'm worried Garner's gonna flag me on this one," Kyle fretted, referring to their boss, Ted Garner, the global head of derivatives trading.

Garner wanted his traders to always make as much money as they could for the bank, but once a position or book started to exceed risk limits, he flipped out. He would be in their faces telling them to close their positions, a process that in itself could exacerbate losses. Garner was terrified of the firm's risk managers. And once anything got on their radars, he would go from Jekyll to Hyde in a blink.

The elevator doors drew open, and Kyle and Sully stepped into the vast, football-field-size trading floor. Sully head-bobbed, *see ya!* to Kyle, who waved as each made for their respective desks.

The fifth floor was the Equities and Special Derivatives Trading Division. It filled the entire footprint of the office tower, almost an acre. The trading floor was populated with over three hundred individual trading desks, arranged in long rows that vanished toward infinity when you gazed down the length of any one of them. Every ten desks, there was a break in the rows for an access aisle.

The two floors above equities, the sixth and seventh, were carbon copies of this trading floor. Fixed income occupied the sixth floor, and currencies and commodities occupied the seventh. These three trading floors were so similar, with the same layouts, same décor and desks, that it wasn't uncommon for a trader to absentmindedly get off on the wrong floor, walk the path to his or her trading station, and sit down at what he thought was his desk, only to notice a throng of unfamiliar faces.

Kyle wound through the rows toward his station, trying to ignore the battery of good-morning "hellos" and the obsequious sales traders already bashing him with "shows" before he'd even sat down. Kyle didn't respond. He was in no mood.

To the external eye, the trading floor was dizzying. It was difficult to tell one individual from another, as every desk had the same configuration. Each person sat in a black Aeron chair at a six-foot-wide station facing an arc of four flat-panel monitors. Despite the homogeneity of it all, there was a strict organization and hierarchy on the floor.

Closest to the entrance were the sales traders. Sales traders, despite the title, were effectively internal brokers. They were generalists, it was their job to support the bank's clients. They would take their client's calls, fulfill their orders, pitch new products and trading ideas, and wine and dine them after hours at high-end restaurants and events. Sales traders were incentivized by the business, or flow, they generated; the more and larger-sized trades they generated, the bigger their bonuses. A junior rep could make $250,000 per year, and some of the highly skilled rainmakers, who had deep and loyal clients, could pull in upwards of $5 or $6 million in a good year.

Beyond the rows of sales traders, the floor spread into separate desks, or strategies. The term "desk," not to be confused with the individual physical station where a person sat, was an organization of several traders according to a product or strategy. There was the Programs Desk, which traded large baskets of equities. There was the Cash Desk, organized by sector, like telecoms, or biotech/pharma. They traded the individual stocks of those sectors. Next to them was the Convertible Bonds group. The Derivatives or Volatility Desk was after that, which Sully was the de facto head of.

Lastly, Kyle's desk, which was the Special Situations Derivatives Desk. His was a much sought-after group as it traded a "prop" strategy. Prop, short for "proprietary," strategies had far greater latitude than the facilitation desks like cash or equity volatility. Prop desks could put on positions of their own choosing, and even though they also facilitated client business, they weren't limited to it, solely.

The balance of the seats on the floor was occupied by analysts, who supported all the trading desks; risk managers and compliance officers; and by technology people who kept the thousands of machines and monitors and specialized trading software running smoothly.

Kyle arrived at his station and, without a word, peered at Pete, who despondently returned his look. He removed his suit jacket and draped it over the back of his chair and set down his bag, but he didn't sit. Kyle visually swept the floor and each of the large-screen TVs mounted on the interspersed support columns blasting news and financial channels.

"What are you waiting for, a fart to come or something?" Pete mocked Kyle's drama. Kyle didn't respond to him, but he finally sat down with a frustrated exhale and began switching on his monitors.

"I bought us two hundred crude," Pete reported. He was referring to crude oil futures contracts they needed to buy to hedge their deteriorating option position.

Futures were contracts to buy or sell something, *in the future*, thus, their name. For the financial world, it was much easier to trade the futures that represented its physical version of something, rather than push around the actual commodity like thousands of barrels of crude oil, or a ton of gold bars, thousands of bushels of corn, or millions of shares of stocks. Instead, you just traded the financial contracts, the *futures*, that delivered those things.

"Ock's still climbing, up two-thirty now. We're right at strike, short gamma's killing us. What else you want me—"

"Yes, I got it, thank you," Kyle sharply cut him off with an intransigent tone, annoyed his junior trader was telling him the state of *his* book. Ock meant "October," the future for October delivery.

Pete Graff was the junior trader on Kyle's desk, his assistant who was responsible for helping Kyle do anything and everything. Pete answered phones, called and instant messaged the brokers, monitored their positions, executed trades, hedged their book, watched the news, dealt with the bank's sales traders, built spreadsheets to calculate the desk's risks, and even fetched coffee when ordered. Twenty-seven years old, also a lacrosse player, from Princeton, Pete had a broad face, roguish brown eyes, and thick eyebrows. He was essentially a double of The Who's Keith Moon, but fortunately with less of his temperament.

Kyle's monitors lit up, and he for the first time saw the damage in detail. He started driving—and playing defense.

"We need to put a fucking tourniquet on this thing," Kyle declared. Pete regarded him with a sardonic smile, as if they could do anything at that point.

"How short are we if we blow through another handle?"

Pete was half paying attention until Kyle shot him a harder, demanding look. He dialed up their risk slides in their market making system, called Scout. The risk slides calculated and graphed risk metrics at different price points. If they wanted to know how much they would make or lose if crude oil went up another two dollars, or even five, the risk slide would calculate and display those projections. At that moment, they were most concerned about what their gamma was doing.

"Crazy short at eighty, insanely short at eighty-one," Pete gave him a wise-ass answer after looking. Kyle didn't say anything.

Gamma was an option risk sensitivity. It effectively calculated the speed at which you needed to hedge an option position. As the underlying product, crude oil, approached an option strike price where they had concentrated positions, currently eighty dollars per barrel, this gamma sensitivity would increase substantially, meaning that they needed to hedge (trade the crude oil futures) faster and faster. It also meant the magnitude of losses accelerated.

Kyle studied his Scout risk display as it ticked with the market. The software calculated and tracked their P&L. Kyle scowled as he watched the red digits flash in a painful reminder: "-$34,746,000." Red font meant negative or down, and green was up or positive in the trading world.

Pete stared at Kyle, waiting for some instruction. He clutched one of his trader turret phone handsets against his chest, ready for Kyle's order, ready to do business. But Kyle was still in thought.

"I don't like how it's been trading," Kyle said, in part under his breath, but Pete caught it because he was so focused on him.

"I don't like it, either. What do you want me to do?" Pete replied. "Do we sell more futures here? We could be through another strike soon," Pete worried.

Kyle still didn't respond but kept eyeing his screens, mentally assessing.

"I'm more worried about Garner," Kyle finally said, somewhat changing the subject. Pete rapped the handset on his desk.

"He say anything to you?"

"Nary a peep. No IM, email, nothing. Makes me even more worried," Kyle responded as he eyed his emails. "He can shut us down, that's what scares me the most. We might be able to trade out of this loss, given some runway, but we're fucked if he makes us puke it," he added.

"Then I'm looking for another job," Pete replied, half joking, half serious.

"You may have to... Yeah, do another thousand here. And ladder it up, be aggressive on the other side of eighty. And let's see if we can spread some of these, play the term a bit. Hunt for cheaper vol further out the curve," Kyle conveyed to Pete.

Kyle was proposing they could find some risk-reducing trades using options that had longer-dated expirations than the options that were currently killing their book. Pete grinned, finally seeing some trader life in Kyle.

"Got it," Pete acknowledged and swiveled to his monitors to enter electronic orders for the futures and scan for decent time spreads. A time spread was an option strategy that played a nearer option against a more distant one.

"And I'm not pulling another Sunday-night bender," Kyle confessed.

Pete laughed.

"Yeah, solo Sunday-night drinking is *really* a cry for help."

Kyle chuckled, too.

"Scotch therapy," Kyle quipped, but his lightheartedness vanished, and he posed, "I want to figure out if this is a one-off."

"If what's a one-off?"

"This pipeline explosion. Let's think about it. What do you we know?"

"What do you mean? Smells like a terror attack to me. I haven't seen anyone claim credit yet, but that's what the wires are reporting," Pete answered.

"No, I mean, who pulled it off and why. Let's think like they did. What was their motivation?" Kyle posed, rhetorically, then continued. "There haven't been many of these attacks lately. Most of the infighting in Iraq is dying down. Prices have been up. The different Iraqi factions are getting paid."

"Ends up being a disruption," Pete added, following Kyle.

"Exactly. Less justification for damaging infrastructure to get a better negotiating position. Plus, this was in Turkey. They haven't really been in play, to date. Strange location to do an attack, and this probably gets repaired quickly, too," Kyle reasoned out loud.

"You thinking this is a sell here?" Pete arrived at Kyle's conclusion.

"I'm thinking maybe it is. Vols are richer. Easier to get off some good sales. Only problem is—"

"Shit, we're gonna bust through our risk limits if we add to this monster, Kyle. And *you*, *you're* the one worried about Garner."

"Garner can go to hell," Kyle spat.

"No, really...?"

"Really. I think I can make the case to keep the position."

"And if you can't?"

"Garner can go to hell," they both announced in unison.

"You're a gambling motherfucker. You have a problem," Pete chided him.

"I have a lot of problems... Stop working those time spreads. See if you can sell another million vega here, at least three months out," Kyle instructed him, ignoring Pete's reproach.

Vega was another option risk measure—the amount of actual dollars risked on an option position. One million vega meant Kyle wanted to dial it up even more.

Pete got to it, at once obedient and petrified. He knew if they were caught in another fast rally in oil, it would compound their already significant losses. They were doubling down. It was risk upon risk. But Pete was also consummately loyal to Kyle, who had handpicked him from the two-year rotational analyst program to be on his prop desk three years ago and then hired him directly after his analyst tenure ended. Kyle knew he could mold Pete into a sharp options trader on his desk. And for Pete's part, he had seen Kyle trade out of difficult jams before, bad positions, volatile swings, reverse huge losses—he was one of the best, and Pete trusted him. Still, although Pete picked up the phone dutifully and started calling brokers, he couldn't ignore the aching pit forming in his stomach.

Zhenzhu Residential District, on the Yalu River, China

Kwan paced in his twelfth-floor apartment living room as he half watched the evening Yalu River traffic out his window. He had just gotten home from his border station job, and it was a few minutes after eight p.m. His mind was busy reviewing the episode with the Yongbyon radiochemist, Sohn, from earlier that morning, and he was stressing over what he was going to relay to his American CIA handler.

Kwan snapped open a can of lime soda, lit a cigarette, and walked out onto his balcony overlooking the river. As he dragged, he tapped the ashes over the railing and gazed beyond the rows of wispy pine trees on the North Korean side of the Yalu. He took more sips of his soda and flicked his half-finished cigarette into the air in frustration. *What would I tell them?* he tested himself, over and over, and more importantly, *how would I relay the message?*

Kwan didn't know much about his CIA handler. He knew he was American Chinese, or a Hong Konger, given his accent when he spoke Mandarin. He had only met him in person twice; the rest of his interactions had been over chat or on the special communication phone they had given him for secure messages. He had also done two dead drops, but on dead drops, you never interacted with your handler; that was the whole point. And Kwan hated dead drops. All those did was risk your being tailed and outed by the Chinese counterspies.

Kwan's lips silently rehearsed different compositions of the message to send his handler. He realized the highlights of the event weren't extensive and so calculated he could fit it into a lengthy text message using his special handset. Relieved, he reentered his living room and glanced at the wall, imagining with a smile the glossy, flat-screened TV his bonus from this information was going to get him.

This was prime silver, the Americans were going to love this, he thought to himself, as his grin widened. He was increasingly certain this intel was legit and knew it would be very valuable to the Americans.

Kwan shut his balcony door and drew the curtains. He walked into his kitchen, and from an empty tin of turtle jelly soup mix, he removed the secret flip phone for communicating with the CIA. He switched it on. He entered his special two-digit code—that was his identifier to the Americans, and then he set the randomizer. Kwan didn't know what that was or how it worked, other than it helped to encrypt the communication. As a set of random characters displayed, he cross-referenced which ones to use for which character he needed for his message, and then he systematically entered the following text:

This morning, five a.m., NK defector was found on access road near PLA guard station. Had crossed Yalu been shot many times by NK. Was near death. Questioned him at station. Said he was high-up radiochemist at Yongbyon. Said his name was Sohn Tae Jae. Said he came from convoy transporting six "dark sun"— Korean nickname for nuclear bomb—and that one "dark sun" had gone missing and was sent "to the water." Sohn died after...could not verify story but believe truthful...

Kwan hit the send button. A moment later, the intel phone chimed with a "message received" acknowledgment. Kwan smiled, switched off the phone, and dropped it back into the turtle jelly soup tin. He grabbed another cigarette, and lighter, and walked back out onto his balcony.

US Consulate General, Shenyang, Liaoning Province, China

Albert Liu rubbed his eyes, strained from too much computer work. It was after eight p.m. and he was getting started on his second job. Albert was a consular and legal affairs officer at the US consulate, a dumpy, three-story drab brown building in the crowded diplomatic district of Shenyang.

The consulate covered the northern regional territory of China for US consular needs. Albert's days were filled with the drudge work of issuing visas, refereeing cross-border marriage disputes and child custody struggles, and helping the US business community navigate on the ground. That was his day job, his cover job. His second job, like some members of any foreign diplomatic mission, was collecting intelligence.

Albert was a CIA case officer. He had joined "the Company," as it was known internally, shortly after 9/11. Having grown up in both Hong Kong and San Francisco, Albert was a US born citizen but also raised by Chinese parents, his mother from Hong Kong, and his father a mainlander, from outside of Nanjing. He spoke both Mandarin and Cantonese fluently as well as what he viewed as his "native" American English.

After CST (Clandestine Service Training), Albert was assigned here to Shenyang. It was tough going being a spy recruiter in China, but he'd started to come into his own playing to his local strengths. He liked to spend his weekends traveling and exploring the northern reaches of China. He had a great cover as he had some relatives in the area, and because of his comfort in the mainland, he was able to slip his Chinese counterintelligence tails and freely explore the territory and develop relationships with its people.

Albert learned quickly that he was good at "flipping people"—convincing targets to start feeding him information. He had, over the last several years, built a portfolio of producing assets, ranging from Chinese military officers to defense industry executives to his most recent quarry, PLA border officers who developed into great sources of North Korean intel. He had impressed his superiors at Langley with his ability to rapidly engineer relationships that were "productive," intelligence speak for assets that offered valuable human intelligence (HUMINT).

Albert refocused on his computer screen and scrolled through his latest emails. He was about to get up and make himself some tea when one of his secure phones, one used for communicating with his assets, started to buzz. He opened his desk drawer and retrieved the rowdy device. He switched on the display and waited for the message to be decrypted. As he read the text, he swallowed:

This morning, five a.m, NK defector was found on access road near PLA guard station. Had crossed Yalu been shot many times by NK. Was near death. Questioned him at station. Said he was high-up radiochemist at Yongbyon. Said his name was Sohn Tae Jae. Said he came from convoy transporting six "dark sun"— Korean nickname for nuclear bomb—and that one "dark sun" had gone missing and was sent "to the water." Sohn died after...could not verify story but believe truthful...

Thoughts accelerated in Albert's mind. He couldn't keep track of them as they flew by. He reread the message, and then again, and then again. It was from a Yalu River border guard named Xue Kwan he had recruited about two years ago. Kwan was a good asset. He was credible and reliable. His intel typically dealt with defections, reporting on when there were surges or lulls, and communicating any descriptions of North Korea from the inside. Mostly, though, the insights Kwan provided were tiles of a mosaic, to be assembled into a larger picture by Langley. So, when Albert read this message, it struck him at once with a forceful weight. The message, if legit, was immediately actionable.

Albert parsed every sentence. He scrutinized each word for intent, for tricks, for any red flags that would hint this was a ruse, or a trap, or if Kwan had somehow been compromised. But Albert detected none of that; it all appeared fresh and sincere. Albert rocked back in his chair as he considered every angle.

The message had one key advantage, one that lent credence to it—the defector was named—Sohn Tae Jae. This man's existence, and his role at Yongbyon, was verifiable, Albert knew. His name and job functions were specific and unlikely to have been invented. Further, Albert reckoned, it was exceedingly unlikely his asset, Kwan, could have known of or researched this figure, which made it even more credible.

Albert rose from his chair. He grabbed the secure phone and hurried down the hallway. Arriving at his boss's door, he knocked.

"Yes?" answered a forceful male voice from behind it.

"Albert," he replied.

"Come on in," the voice granted.

Albert entered and waved to his boss, Colonel Mark Hebble, US Consul, and the CIA station chief for the Shenyang region. Colonel Hebble gnawed on a set of peeled carrots from a small white porcelain bowl sitting before him amid stacks of papers, documents, and reports. Hebble was a stocky five foot five, though that was difficult to see in his seated position. He was balding and had a thick black mustache that distracted from an otherwise slightly chubby face.

"I think you want to take a look at this." Albert gave no detail aloud, simply shut the door behind him and offered the colonel his encrypted phone.

Hebble wiped his hands on his seat cushion and grabbed the cell, taking a moment to read the message.

"When did this come in?" Hebble asked quickly, eyeing his watch.

"About twenty minutes ago."

"And supposedly happened this morning?" he asked rhetorically, not looking up from the phone. Hebble's eyes scanned it like it was a photograph.

"Supposedly."

"How long you been working with this asset?"

"About two years, sir."

"Confidence scale, in your opinion?"

Albert pondered for a moment, "At least an eight out of ten."

"What gets you to a ten out of ten...or to a zero?"

"The identity. Someone could verify," Albert replied, assuredly, pointing at the cell phone. Hebble re-scanned the message.

"Good eye…shit, very good."

The colonel finally raised his eyes to Albert. He handed his phone back. He studied Albert's face, and, without removing his eyes from him, commanded his next moves.

"Kate Harrison, you know who she is?" Hebble asked.

"Of course, but never worked with her. I'm sure some of what comes into me makes it up to her, so she knows who I am."

"She's got the Langley SMEs to run this by. She can do the bona fides on this," the colonel started, and then he lowered his head but kept his stare on Albert.

"We want to do it *now*, you understand?" Hebble instructed, as he referred to his watch again. "They're just getting in," he said, noting the twelve-hour time difference between them and Eastern Standard Time. Albert acknowledged as Hebble paused and then resumed.

"Transcribe this message, every fucking comma and space and letter, verbatim, and cable it to her," the colonel said as he leaned back in his chair and half swiveled, finally removing his eyes from Albert.

"And I'll make a few calls, including to her." Hebble glanced at Albert's phone, and ordered, "No contact until we know what we're dealing with."

Albert concurred and moved to the door. As he was about to leave, Hebble added, "Get some food. We're going to be here a while."

CIA Headquarters, McLean, Virginia, United States

Kate Harrison idled in her metallic-blue SUV at the intersection light of Dolley Madison Boulevard and Georgetown Pike, watching the trail of cars hook out from the Pike and onto 123, as the locals referred to Dolley Madison. Annoyed by the length of the light, Kate balked at the traffic, carping aloud.

"Enough already. It's *our* turn!"

Her light flicked green, and she accelerated down Dolley Madison and swung a left into her destination, the George Bush Center for Intelligence, otherwise known as the CIA, or simply Langley to its employees. As she drove through the security gates, her phone buzzed. She glanced next to her where her purse was with phone inside and, with one hand, swatted her daughter's soccer shin guards away to find it. Her phone kept buzzing.

"*Relax*—where the fuck are you?" she bickered with her elusive cell as she plumbed for it in her purse, keeping one eye ahead on the access lane. She finally recovered it and answered.

"Harrison… Oh, hi, Colonel, how are you? Late night as usual?… A cable? OK… I'm pulling in now. I'll be up in a few. Talk in a bit."

Kate flew into the parking lot, steering one-handed, and braked the car with a screech. Her face became stoic as she shut off the car and gathered her things.

Scanning through the entrance, Kate hustled upstairs and into her office, where she tossed her purse and coat onto an empty chair and booted up her PC. Her hand impatiently tapped the desk as she watched the apps fade in on her machine. She opened the secure cable application and tabbed through her messages, absently easing into her desk chair until she finally came to the one from Albert. She read, her lips mouthing the words of the message. As she read it a second time, she sank backward into her seat. Her gaze rose to the ceiling, and her eyes flitted about the room, reflecting the urgency of her thoughts.

In a second, she was up, and approached her bookshelf, tightly packed with rows of homogenous binders and other books on the Koreas. Her fingers drew along a second row of volumes, and she called out, "Right," as her hand grabbed a specific tall, blue notebook.

Kate plowed through the binder until she found the Yongbyon personnel section. There, she stopped. Her index finger traced over each profile finally tapping an older black-and-white photograph with the name Sohn Tae Jae, and the native equivalent in Hangul Korean characters next to it. A frail-looking, spectacled North Korean radiochemist stared up at her.

"Shit. We know this guy. This is real," Kate said softly but out loud. She compared the binder profile to the name in Albert's message just to verify it was, in fact, the same. There was no mistake, it was him.

"This may be high confidence, then," she whispered.

"And we need to escalate this." Kate's own words echoed in her head. She pursed her lips as she stared at the forlorn profile of Sohn Tae Jae on the page.

Kate was not a typical CIA officer. She wasn't what they called a CT, a career trainee. She had been with the Company for twelve years, having arrived there in the mid-nineties in a roundabout way. She was originally from the South, an unheard-of town outside of Natchez, Mississippi, but she was scrappy and ruthlessly intelligent. She had put herself through community college waiting tables and then had managed to transfer to Millsaps College in Jackson, a small but astute liberal arts school.

After she graduated, with a BA in Greek and Roman studies, she, on a whim, decided to go teach in Seoul, South Korea. She spent four years there and loved it. She became conversational in the language, and even dated a few Koreans. After that time, she returned to the US and did her master's in government. Between her Korean experience and the government degree, she was able to nab an entry-level analyst job at a DC-area think tank, where she worked for a number of years.

In the early nineties, the Clinton administration began demanding better intel on North Korea. In 1994, the North Koreans had restarted the Yongbyon reactor and began processing spent fuel with the aim of—what was externally expected to be—developing a weapons program. Intelligence shops increased their Korean desk budgets and competed for the best subject matter experts. Kate was brought into the CIA, initially as a consultant, to read and report on publicly available intelligence (open-source intel), but she was soon admitted full-time to the NE Asia desk. Since then, she'd risen to head the CIA's Asia Pacific Directorate, which covered China, North and South Korea, Japan, and Taiwan.

Kate drummed her fingers on the binder cover as she calculated. She read the message again. What did it mean? If the report was credible, then Sohn had indeed defected, and had been killed trying to do so, she deduced. Sohn was also ranked in the apparatus, which meant that his warning was reliable, Kate reasoned further. But what was his warning of, *specifically*? Had a weapon been diverted internally? Had a weapon disappeared? Was it all a mistake or a bluff operation? *Or*, the worst case, had a weapon been stolen or exported and was now making its way to some destination where it would be employed, to great disaster. Kate zeroed in on the line, "And was sent to the water…" She had to figure that out, she knew. The reasonable interpretation, she thought, was that it was being transported on a ship.

Another side of the message bothered her. The few nuclear weapons the North Korean state possessed were treated like religious artifacts. Kim Jong Il would never let one get stolen or, worse, exported or transferred. Kate concluded that Sohn must have witnessed precisely this act or discovered it, neither of which he could rationalize, which must have then triggered his flight.

Kate glanced up at the set of clocks on her wall, Eastern Standard Time, Greenwich Mean Time, Korea Standard Time. Korea was currently twelve hours ahead of EST. For Kate, in Northern Virginia, it was nine a.m. Monday morning. It was nine p.m. Monday evening for the Koreans. If the most dreadful interpretation of Sohn's message was, in fact, that a loose nuke was making its way somewhere now, it also meant that whoever had acquired it had at least a sixteen-hour head start.

Kate slapped her desk phone speed-dial to the head of the Directorate of Intelligence (DI). The speakerphone scratched on.

"Bob here."

"Bob, come over. Now."

Fishing Trawler, Yellow Sea, 37.44 N/124 E

Dusk faded into an encroaching night on the Yellow Sea as the Honggon-do fishing trawler rolled up and down with the churning waters. The boat's half a dozen crewmen huddled on the bow, having a smoke. The engines had been shut down, and the trawler was drifting with the currents. They were in a secluded area of the seas; the only vessels nearby were some tankers on the western horizon.

The tall Syrian joined the fishermen. He eyed them as he lit his cigarette and leaned against the trawler's short bulwark, blowing a stream of smoke as he fixed his eyes on one of the vessel silhouettes on the horizon. The stouter Syrian, standing a level above them on the wheelhouse guideway, motioned to his partner to join him.

Casting an annoyed glance at him, the tall Syrian flicked his cigarette into the seas and headed toward the wheelhouse. He climbed up to the deck where his shorter partner displayed an open fishing sack with two Norinco Type 85 Chinese-made submachine guns. Crouching to obscure what they were up to, the Syrians nimbly unfolded the weapon stocks and slide-cocked the firing action on each weapon. They both spied the fishermen to ensure they weren't being watched.

At once, they rose and unloaded on the crew. The shots cracked so furiously and suddenly the fishermen couldn't react. Dozens of bullets strafed them from the higher deck as they were each dropped in seconds, cigarettes still in their grasp.

A moment later, at the bow of the trawler, a pile of dead fishermen lay jumbled like so many tossed mannequins, limbs thrown about. Streams of their blood collected and pooled back and forth with the rocking of the boat.

The Syrians unclipped their guns, folded up the stocks and cinched the weapons back into the fishing sack. Approaching the bodies, they lashed them with wire, threading in steel weights, cleats, and other anchors with the windings. They lifted each body and pitched it over the side into the Yellow Sea.

And with factory-like efficiency, the Syrians moved from that task to belowdecks. There, they retrieved three heavy-duty carrying cases—thick polymer containers, waterproof, lined with molded foam, meant for transporting photographic equipment or fragile electronics. The Syrians transferred the bomb components, gingerly, from their wooden crates into the equipment containers, teetering with the shifting boat as they repacked each component, taking special care with the ultra-sensitive high-explosive lenses.

The shorter Syrian climbed back into the wheelhouse and started up the engines while his taller partner eyed a freighter on the horizon through a pair of binoculars. He called out to the shorter one.

"Steer to the west—my arm," he shouted, aiming at the freighter.

Pitching up and down with the seas, the trawler belched thick black smoke as it revolved toward the ship in the distance...

Fortnum Bank Equities Trading Floor

Kyle glanced at Pete, on two phones, one at each ear, shifting back and forth as he switched conversations.

"I hear you. We just need it done... Another five hundred here. Hit bids, as long we're below a one handle. Call me if you see any more," Pete relayed to the broker in his left-ear. He lowered both handsets and leaned over to Kyle.

"Sold another fifty K of vega," he reported.

Kyle slowly nodded in response. He watched their crude oil position growing in real time on Scout as the trades Pete was executing appeared in their accounts. The electronic trading happened instantaneously, although some trades went up on physical exchange floors, executed by human brokers and market makers. There were also trades called over-the-counter, or OTC, that were completely manual.

Kyle's P&L blinked at him. His loss was swelling, now at: "-$41,906,000."

"Keep 'em coming," Kyle called out to Pete, who relayed that to a different broker in his right ear.

"We're vol sellers, sellers here. Show us any decent bids you see... Yes, keep working those offers, too," Pete shouted into his phone and finally clicked off both lines and tossed the handsets onto his desk. "Dumb shit," he derided the last broker, and eyed Kyle, who was monitoring their progress.

"How we looking now?" Pete asked him.

"Almost there. We've doubled from where we came in." Kyle tallied their trades, moving his finger down the electronic blotter on his rightmost monitor.

"Bingeing," Pete joked. They both scrutinized the price of crude oil, which had stabilized in the last few minutes. They were relieved at the price when a shadow loomed over their desks from behind.

"Springer, let's talk about this."

They both half-swiveled to see Garner standing behind them. How long he'd been there, they couldn't tell. Kyle threw Pete a *goddamn it!* look.

"Come on," Garner beckoned as he made his way down the aisle of trading desks toward the perimeter glass offices.

"Piece of shit," Kyle commented under his breath as he rose from his chair and shoved it into his desk with a jolt.

"Don't—until I return," Kyle reminded Pete, who gave him a thumbs-up.

"I've got a bad feeling about this," Pete carped as Kyle followed Garner away.

Garner sat down behind his desk. Kyle entered, shut the door behind him, and sat facing Garner. The office was a twelve-by-twelve, glass-enclosed box facing the trading floor with a small window at the back that faced out to the north. The room was unencumbered with personal objects of any kind, either on the wooden desk or on the sparse wooden bookshelf against the side wall.

Ted Garner, a lean six three, with rimless glasses and an elongated head with male-pattern baldness, stared at Kyle through those lenses without saying a word. Kyle uncomfortably looked to each side, waiting for him to speak. Garner had been an option trader, too, before he'd been promoted to global head of equities. He even used to run the equity index book, the role Sully was in now. Garner had gotten his start at one of the premier derivatives shops on the street, the fabled UBS O'Connor & Associates, a group of ultrasmart options traders who had the power to "correct the market" whenever it was mispriced. The fact that Garner had a derivatives background had a good and bad to it—the good was, Kyle could explain things to him, and Garner could understand; the bad was, Kyle couldn't bullshit him.

"What the hell are you doing? You're gonna bring down the entire desk!" Garner fumed without even any foreplay.

Kyle inhaled but didn't immediately reply, as he wanted to choose his words—and not lunge over the desk to punch the guy.

"I'm a bit over the limits, but the edge is worth it here. This thing's reverting soon," Kyle responded, referring to his expectation that the price of crude oil risk, implied volatility, would reverse its recent run-up, along with the crude oil price itself. "Edge" was lingo for the anticipated profit an option trader could make.

"Maybe you misfired on this one," Garner retorted.

Kyle squinted and tried not to get upset as Garner continued.

"You sold vol on crude plumb into a big run-up—that went in your face— then you didn't reduce it when you knew it was a losing trade, and *then* you were under-hedged, leaning short, when some faction blew up BTC this morning. And now you're doubling down on this lump of excrement," Garner scolded.

"Why didn't you just say *turd*?" Kyle gave him a wiseass response.

"What?"

Kyle clenched his jaw, felt his anger rising, but he continued to keep his cool. He focused on making his case.

"Crude fundamentals for Q3 and Q4 haven't changed. This thing's gonna be stable and predictable. That means low vol. That means a sale. If I could keep selling it here, I would. Vol's trading too high. So's the price," Kyle explained.

"And what's your plan if it goes in your face again?"

Kyle was silent, now growing impatient. Garner went on before Kyle replied.

"Of all people, *you've* seen this movie before," Garner lectured. "You know what happens, you double down on a bad position, tip your hand to the street, and then you get fucking squeezed, and it gets worse and becomes a total disaster. It's *September* already." Garner paused and peered hard at Kyle through his specs, emphasizing what they both knew he meant—annual bonuses.

"The division's been having a great year. If this thing you're riding keeps going south, you're gonna bring down the entire group," Garner warned.

"You know you'd do exactly the same thing if you were wearing this. This is what you pay me to do, this is where the edge is," Kyle protested.

Kyle was right about that. Garner knew where the value was, he understood it. The problem was, in his head of trading role, his perspective and incentives had changed. He was much more worried about risk and compliance—and his own performance—than he ever was about where the edge was anymore.

Garner let out an impatient exhale. He didn't like it when they didn't obey.

"I don't want to come in tomorrow morning and have another thirty-million-dollar cup of coffee. *You get me?*" His voice rising as he pushed his fists down.

"Fine. I can stop building it here," Kyle offered.

"*Stop* here?" Garner thundered. "No, you're gonna trade out of the position."

Now Kyle wanted to lunge at him across the desk for real.

"That's the worst thing to do now—I'm gonna get killed even more, *and* lock in the loss!" Kyle yelled at him.

"Lose the fucking position. I want to see it zeroed out by the end of the day," Garner commanded.

Kyle stared at him but didn't say anything. It was a tense standoff for almost a minute. Finally, Kyle thrust his chair backward as he stood up and exited Garner's office without a word.

Kyle reappeared at his trading desk with an expectant Pete looking at him for any indication of the trip to the principal's office.

"Close the position," Kyle grumbled to Pete.

"What?"

"You heard me. I said the close the fucking position."

"But—? *The whole thing?*"

"Yes, the whole thing, because Garner's such a fucking moron he doesn't know when free money hits him in his goddamned face!"

Kyle slammed one of his handsets into the desk so hard it shattered plastic shrapnel into the air around them.

"Ohhhh!" cheered the nearby traders.

Kyle yanked off his tie and tossed it in a wastebasket and walked off the floor.

Pete watched him for a moment and then started calling brokers and click-trading his way out of their crude oil position. Garner coldly regarded Kyle as he stomped off the trading floor.

CIA Headquarters

In Kate's office were the head of the Directorate of Intelligence (DI), her boss, Bob Stalfort, and two analysts, Dr. Clare Ahn, a career North Korean weapons program expert, and Sarah Sussman, a two-year junior analyst in the APAC Directorate. They had a map of the Korean Peninsula spread out onto the table.

Sarah was walking the arms of a compass about the map, drawing concentric arcs emanating from different ports on the North Korean Yellow Sea coast.

"Assuming they're using a fishing vessel or teapot freighter, with an average pace of twelve knots, and without knowing wind speed, currents, or sea conditions, this is the farthest they could have gotten in sixteen to twenty hours," she announced, moving her hand to emphasize the outer arcs.

"Let's be as conservative as possible," Bob started. "We have to assume closer to twenty hours. The defector had to have a few hours' head start before he was found on the other side of the Yalu."

"At least," Kate stated. "And if he was on foot, that's another few hours to tack on," she added.

They looked to Bob. He knew what they were thinking without their asking.

"I can't call State, or Pentagon, not yet. And I can't issue a flash without something more. We need something more. If we get greater confidence in this assessment, I can get some hardware on this," Bob appealed their tacit lobbying.

Kate shot Bob a glare, *you can do better*, but he only shrugged his shoulders in response. They all searched the map in thought. Kate snapped her fingers, recalling something.

"Today's Monday. We should have—"

"Overheads, yup," Dr. Ahn finished her sentence. Kate was referring to satellite imagery, overheads, as they called them.

"If this did originate from Yongbyon, we might have some IMINT from the latest runs," Kate realized. "How long does it take Chantilly to process your weeklies?" she asked Dr. Ahn.

"Half a day, maybe."

"Call our joint collaboration cell. Tell them we have something actionable," Kate started. "I know we don't have a flash yet"—Kate shot Bob another glare— "so bullshit them. Tell them we need preprocessed, raw from the bird, anything."

Dr. Ahn huddled in the corner of Kate's office to make the call.

Chantilly was the headquarters of the NRO (National Reconnaissance Office). Since the start of the War on Terror and the 2003 invasion of Iraq, those two efforts dominated NRO's resource deployments, and Kate and her directorate were constantly fighting for more "eye in the sky" time. The situation had improved somewhat following North Korea's 2006 nuclear test, and it had become easier for Kate to request NRO flight time.

Dr. Ahn hung up.

"I think we have something—IMINT of a convoy leaving Yongbyon late Sunday night. They're sending the films now."

"Convoy?" Bob asked Dr. Ahn for clarification, who concurred with a raised eyebrow. He quizzed Kate, "What did that message say, again?"

Kate returned to her desk and slid on her reading glasses. She read aloud the part of Sohn's message.

"Let's see… said he came from *convoy* transporting six *dark sun…*" Kate read the excerpt.

"That's corroborated," Bob agreed, his expression souring.

Sarah lifted her eyes from the map.

"Those films will have time stamps. We can back up the defector to a more limited start window," she said.

"Did you get them?" Dr. Ahn asked Kate.

Kate tabbed through her incoming messages, searching.

"Here." She motioned to them and swiveled her monitor so the others could see it. "Get Chantilly on the phone," she requested as the images unfolded on her screen. They crowded around the monitor as Dr. Ahn dialed the NRO.

"Brown," a pointed female voice chimed in on the speakerphone. O-2 Samantha Brown was a first lieutenant in the United States Air Force and an analyst with the NRO, assigned to Kate's CIA joint collaboration cell.

"Sam, what are we looking at here?" Kate demanded.

"You definitely have a bogey. Looks like an in-motion target on the south end of the complex. Another run. This is probably the fourth in as many months," Brown replied and continued. "These are hyperspectrals of the reactor facility shortly after twenty-three hundred, local. You have an eight-vehicle convoy exiting out the south side tunnel."

"That's a standard-config weapons-transport. Probably headed to Kusong," Dr. Ahn assessed.

Sarah resumed her travel-time calculations as soon as she heard the time stamp. On Kate's monitor, they observed a still image of several buildings and vehicles from overhead. It resembled an x-ray of bones.

"The whiter equals warmer, the darker, cooler," Sam explained. "We love nights like this because the surrounding landscape cools off, gives a lot of contrast to anything living or any working machinery," she further detailed.

The images were sharp. It was clear there were eight vehicles, and the brighter, heat-densities of people and engines inside were identifiable as well.

"You can see the drivers and passengers in each vehicle. I'd say a couple of command or guard trucks here and here. Then you have a troop transport, third, about a dozen helmets. And then three cargo trucks in a row, two riders in each cab. Note, the heat profiles of the payloads," Sam paused.

"These are the bomb component trucks." Dr. Ahn pointed to the three middle vehicles, which displayed higher heat signatures in their rear transport bays.

"Correct," Sam confirmed. "Two humans in the cab, and the engine below them. And then there is a heat return here in the holds. We assess this to be from a radiological source," Sam explained. Kate and the others exchanged glances.

"If those are plutonium cores, can we discern how many each truck is transporting?" Dr. Ahn asked.

"Our resolution is limited, but our prelim analysis says, with medium confidence, that the heat profile signature is similar to those from previous runs out of Yongbyon. That means one to two warheads on each truck," Sam replied.

"Two on each, equals six. Exactly what the message stated... Keep going, Sam," Kate beckoned.

The image on Kate's monitor began to fast-forward through different time slices. The convoy accelerated along the road and then the image froze again.

"We follow the target for about twenty more minutes. It remains within the bird's aperture range. The convoy then takes a route through a wooded region, which makes it more difficult to render—the trees can emanate a heat profile that lowers our contrast—but with the hyperspectral, we can still follow the target for a bit longer." She paused again.

On Kate's monitor, the thermal film of the convoy was fast-forwarded again. The vehicles swam through the mountains like a water snake until Samantha froze the frame.

"So, here, something interesting. It appears the trucks halted. We have a three-minute roll in the clock. We need further analysis to perceive why. We also note, a number of personnel exited vehicles. The convoy then resumes—*except* one of the cargo trucks splits off from the rest. We can't track both targets, so we only see the main group, now seven vehicles long, continue through the mountains. The detached truck drives west and exits our aperture."

The group exchanged more ominous glances.

"Ever see this before—a split in one of their transports?" Kate polled Dr. Ahn.

"Never."

"Can we tell which vehicle it was?" Bob asked.

"It looks like it was the fourth overall, the first of the cargo trucks. Medium confidence on that," Samantha replied. That was also followed by a foreboding silence in the room.

"Sam? Put this on the front burner and send your deeper analysis the second you have it," Kate urged.

"Yes, ma'am, affirmative," Sam responded and hung up.

The four hurried back to the map on the table. They zeroed in on the path of the convoy. Sarah had already traced a thick, winding route with a red felt pen. She had also circled the spot where the vehicles had briefly stopped.

"Where did the radiochemist turn up?" Bob asked.

"Couple klicks south of Gulouzixiang, here." Sarah tapped the spot on the Chinese side of the Yalu River.

Their eyes all traced an imaginary dotted line connecting Yongbyon, and the path of the convoy, to the area where Sohn turned up.

"Work backward," Kate charged. "What time was he found?"

Dr. Ahn checked the message from Albert Liu.

"About five a.m., local."

"And when does our convoy split?"

"Why at the split point?"

"I'm thinking that's when he jumped ship, when he saw the truck break off," Kate theorized.

Dr. Ahn dialed the image reel to the moment the convoy halted.

"Eleven forty-five, local."

"Can we get from here to there in about five hours?" Kate asked, pointing to the two spots on the map, the convoy split, and where Sohn was found. "How long would this trek be, on foot?"

Sarah gazed at the floor in mental calculations and pointed to the hilly region approaching the Yalu.

"About five hours. This isn't easy terrain here," she pointed out. "This is about fifteen kilometers. You can walk a straight klick in about twenty minutes. Given the forests and hills, it would have to be at pace, but yeah, it is definitely possible," Sarah concluded.

"If he were running and under duress," Bob added.

"Sohn either learned of the plan to divert a weapon while at Yongbyon and left from there, or he escapes at the split point," Kate reiterated what she believed.

Bob nodded in agreement with the second theory.

"Confirms he *was* part of that convoy. He can't make it to Yalu from Yongbyon in five hours on foot. But he can from there. Makes sense, given the timing and message. I think when they left Yongbyon, all was in order. Everything unfolded as planned," Bob speculated.

"Message stated that, too. Where was this thing headed?" Kate asked.

Dr. Ahn tapped the Kusong facility with her index finger.

"Almost certainly the missile assembly lab at Kusong," she said.

"Kim is in hurry-up mode to mate as many missiles with warheads as possible in case we bomb him," Kate reminded Bob.

"And it would have been expected protocol for Sohn to accompany the warhead components to Kusong?"

Dr. Ahn initially indicated *yes*, but then her brow furled, somewhat perplexed.

"If one vehicle did break off from the main convoy, I don't think it was authorized," Dr. Ahn reemphasized. "That's not how Kim operates. Each of these runs is a big deal. They keep very tight controls over everything. That cargo truck left with no guard vehicles. This appears rogue," she added, with some concern.

"But if that changeup wasn't authorized, the troops would have moved. There would have been action," Kate rebutted.

"How do you accomplish that, then?" Bob posed.

"It must have been a ruse of some sort," Kate suggested.

"A staged breakdown, maybe?" Dr. Ahn proposed, and then added a more sinister possibility. "Points to an inside job, high up. This would have been planned, by someone in control."

There was a fretful silence, which Bob finally broke.

"Where are we going here?" he pondered aloud as he shuttled his index finger between the spot where the truck separated and its possible destinations.

Sarah drew an icon in red of a single truck. She highlighted, in different colors, the winding roads heading away from that point.

"If it separated here, there's only two choices. The vehicle heads back toward Yongbyon, or it can follow this spur, here." She indicated with the tip of a marker.

Sarah placed a ruler with its straight edge in the direction of the Yellow Sea shoreline and scored directional lines that could arrive at Yellow Sea ports.

"*To the water...*" Kate repeated the message Sohn delivered on his deathbed. The four eyed the path to the Yellow Sea.

"And if it is in fact seaborne now," Bob rhetorically commented as his finger traced that segment of coast on the map.

"That's thousands of vessels, one of the most densely trafficked maritime—" Dr. Ahn started.

"I know. I get it," Bob interrupted her.

Dr. Ahn glanced at Kate for rescue.

"Bob, we're going to need—" Kate started.

"I can't have the director issue a flash without—" Bob stopped himself, not wanting this to turn into a shouting match.

Kate addressed Dr. Ahn and Sarah. "Will you excuse us a moment?"

Sarah and Dr. Ahn exchanged glances and stepped outside.

"What do you want from me?" Bob defensively pled once they'd exited.

Kate didn't respond, just stared at him with her penetrating, icy look he couldn't combat until he broke away.

"You know the process. I can't escalate this without something else. Give me something *more*," Bob appealed.

"You *know* this is a flash. If this isn't critical, what is? I mean—we need DoD, navy help on this, big time," she insisted.

Bob gestured in agreement. Kate eyed the map, shaking her head in irritation.

"We need more NRO support, too. And, goddamn it, Bob, if this is a real broken arrow, we need to get NNSA involved *now*."

NNSA was the National Nuclear Security Administration. Created in 2000, it was the NNSA's responsibility to protect the nation's nuclear stockpile. But they were also involved with security to prevent adverse radiological or nuclear events. NNSA had specialized teams that could be deployed throughout the globe in hours to search for, locate, and secure radiological devices, weapons-grade materials, or even weapons themselves—broken arrows, or loose nukes, as they were called.

Bob found his pluck to face her again.

"Get them on the phone. They have a good relationship with the navy. They can get us some DoD muscle without us alerting all of DC," he started. "Tell them we may have a high-confidence broken arrow situation in the Yellow Sea, backed up with both HUMINT and IMINT. Tell them we need a spotter, visual confirm. See what they can do. See if they can request navy P-3s, something, anything, even if they're JMSDF or South Korean," Bob finished.

P-3s were the US Navy's workhorse anti-submarine warfare aircraft. They were outfitted with sensitive surveillance electronics that could detect many different types of anomalies in the ocean as well as on board visible oceangoing surface vessels. The JMSDF was the Japanese Maritime Self-Defense Force, the Japanese Navy, who, along with the South Korean navy, also operated P-3s.

Kate said nothing. She walked over to her desk and picked up her phone.

Bob moved to exit but commented.

"And I'll raise this with the director now. It won't be a critical, but I'll get you something," he said as he closed the door behind him.

Hudson River Esplanade, Lower Manhattan, United States

Kyle beat along the river, hands in pockets. He absently gazed across the surface of the Hudson, which was billowing in the late-morning light. He looked behind him at his office, the Fortnum Bank building. His jaw muscles clenched. He hadn't been this pissed off in years. He could almost see directly into Garner's office from where he stood. He wanted to kill him.

Kyle tried to calm himself by focusing on the water's rhythm. He rotated his predicament in his head, taking stock of it all. It would take Pete a few hours to trade out of their crude oil position, large as it was, which would then leave their book down $50 million, a significant hole. He thought about his year-end bonus and realized it would likely be zero at this point because there was no way he could recover from a $50 million dirt nap with only three months left in the year.

But a wry smile did form on his face. He thought about his outburst on the floor after his argument with Garner, and this brought him at least a tiny bit of satisfaction. He hadn't done something that unprofessional—get up and leave in a spectacle like that—in years, since the FBI, he reflected.

Kyle recalled from his stint at the FBI, where he'd had to go to great lengths, especially when he was working as an undercover narc, to suppress his quick temper. His supervisors had feared that about him and worried it was a weakness, especially in a role as a narc. He had many tells, he reminded himself, from his jaw muscles clenching to his temples bulging and the veins on his neck swelling. He remembered, with some amusement, all the cover stories he'd had to develop to explain away those tics if perps spotted them during a sting.

Kyle shuddered as he realized—he needed to pick up his daughter, Jill, from her school that afternoon—the only thing he was looking forward to. That returned him to reality and the thought of going back to the floor soured his mood again. Glancing at his watch, he shook it all off and moved to cross the West Side Highway to rejoin his world.

Fishing Trawler, Yellow Sea, 37 N/123.07 E

Amid pitch darkness, the taller Syrian downshifted the fishing trawler, slowing it to a drone. As the choppier waters hissed and dashed across the narrow deck, the shorter Syrian, gripping onto the bow for stability, motioned up to his partner to cruise alongside a freighter they were fast approaching.

The ship, a 190-meter bulk carrier named the *Alder*, was coursing fifty kilometers from the Chinese coast, following it southward at four knots. It was a giant megalith next to their miniature fishing boat and loomed like an imposing cliff as they neared it.

The tall Syrian angled their trawler alongside the freighter's stern. His shorter partner wildly hand-motioned to guide them but took care not to shout. The *Alder's* crew was unaware of this stalker quietly approaching its transom.

Several dangling ropes fell to their deck, dropped from the *Alder's* bulwark above. The silhouette of a figure, face indistinguishable in the darkness, waved down to the Syrians, who waved back. Snatching one of the rope ends, the shorter Syrian wound it around a cleat at the bow of the fishing vessel. He signaled to his partner, who cut the boat's engines, allowing the freighter to tow them.

Tethered to the larger ship, the Syrians worked quickly, threading hooks onto the ends of the dangling ropes and then securing the transport cases containing the bomb components onto them. They fought against the gap between the vessels widening and narrowing with the waves, frustrating their efforts. Above them, a second silhouette of a figure joined the first and beckoned for them to hurry.

The taller Syrian disappeared belowdecks into the trawler's bowels. He grabbed an axe from the utility store and stumbled into the rear galley, where he began to chop the wooden flooring. He chopped until it fractured, bubbling seawater inside. He tossed the axe into the rising water and scrambled above deck.

The Syrians hoisted themselves onto the ropes and scaled up the freighter's side, climbing toward the bulwark. The ship's rocking pushed and pulled them into a swing until they could finally grab onto the carrier's deck rails. The dark figures on board helped pull them over the top.

All four of them clambered to hoist the three bomb cases hooked on the ropes. They reeled up the boxes with choreographed heaves, finally lugging each case over the railing and onto the deck.

They slid the three cases flush with a nearby bulkhead, covering them with a tarp. One of the dark figures removed a long bowie knife from his belt holster. He approached the taut rope that was towing the waterlogged craft. He sawed through the rope with his knife until its remaining fibers couldn't bear the weight and snapped, releasing the fishing trawler behind them.

They watched as the abandoned boat fell away, subsiding into the seas. Job completed, they passed around cigarettes and rested against the railing as the freighter continued its progress south...

Kate Harrison's Office, CIA Headquarters

Kate banged the phone handset against her desk. She had made several attempts to reach a worthy analyst, someone, anyone, at NNSA, but to no avail. Accepting defeat, she dropped the handset back onto its cradle and sagged in her chair. In thought, her eyes roamed among the objects on her desk, over the heap of unevenly stacked papers and the photos of her daughters that were slightly askew in their brass frames. Something then occurred to her, and she rose and approached the map spread on the table. She projected with her finger along the trajectory lines Sarah had drawn, originating from the convoy locations and emanating out to the Yellow Sea coast.

"It can't be any farther than here, right now; if it is on a ship," Kate noted.

Dr. Ahn interrupted, entering Kate's office carrying a stack of photographs.

"Keyhole shots of the same area. Most recent, about a week ago," she said, passing Kate the footage.

Keyhole was a KH-11 spy satellite. They were older, traditional photographic spy satellites, so these were actual pictures, unlike the multispectral nighttime images from the Onyx they had reviewed earlier. All these films were taken during daytime, most of them from early morning.

"Let's have a look."

Kate reached for the top ones. Her focus zeroed in on the objects and features that ran along the upper North Korean coast. The photos showed, in acute detail, to an accuracy of a few meters, multiple small fishing settlements along the wetlands. Dozens of them populated the nooks and inlets along the muddy, jagged coastline. Clearly discernible were the hundreds of fishing craft lashed side by side at docks, bridges, and even to trees. Most were slim wooden skiffs, not much bigger than rowboats; only a few were larger, motor-powered trawlers of ten to thirty meters.

"What are these here?" Kate indicated the rows of boats.

"Skiffs or rafts, wooden. Pretty inferior," Dr. Ahn answered.

"These can't manage in deeper, open waters, can they?" Kate asked.

"Not a chance. Shore-range fishing, that's it."

"To get anywhere, you'd need a larger vessel, especially in the Yellow Sea?"

Kate's phone rang before Dr. Ahn responded.

"Harrison," she answered as she tapped on the speaker.

"Hi, is this Kate Harrison?" a voice inquired.

"Yes, go ahead."

"Hi, Brent Lowry, NNSA. I got a message about—" He was cut off.

"It's about time. Brent, what office do you work at?"

"NA-80, I'm undersecretary for counterterrorism and counterproliferation. I got a message marked critical from you?"

Kate wasted no time.

"Brent, we have good confidence a North Korean warhead, either fully assembled or in parts, may have been stolen or exported and could be on a ship in the Yellow Sea this moment, out of nation-state control." Kate stopped. Even stating the words out loud, she hardly believed it.

There was a long silence. "Brent?" Kate asked to ensure he was still there.

"I'm sorry—did I hear you right?"

"You unfortunately did, yes."

"Jesus...*good* confidence, you said? What intel do we have?"

"Brent, ordinarily, you realize I couldn't relay that, but we're behind the clock here—we have a verified defector, a radiochemist who worked at Yongbyon who reported the device missing, and we have IMINT confirming a convoy transporting devices with greater-than-background-heat returns. We believe one device was diverted from this convoy and was most likely placed on a boat or a ship, which now may be making its way south in the Yellow Sea," Kate rattled off.

"What are we talking about here? If this is a North Korean weapon, or components, do you believe it's a complete warhead, weapons-grade material?"

Dr. Ahn approached the speakerphone. "Hi, Brent, it's Clare Ahn—"

"Yeah, hi, Clare."

"We expect this to be a Fat Man–style NK type 1 plutonium warhead. If it is like the others being manufactured, they're designed to be mated with a medium-range ballistic missile. We don't know if this target's been modified or dismantled, or even if it is a working device, an IND, or only fissile material. But we have good confidence it is at least one of the above," Dr. Ahn assessed.

"And for risk management, let's assume the worst?"

"Range, a twenty- to forty-kiloton yield," Dr. Ahn answered.

"Right...have you guys issued a critical or immediate on this?"

"No, that's why I called. We need your help. We need to get the assessment to a higher confidence level. You know this chicken-egg game, Brent," Kate pleaded.

"I sure do. I'm thinking—we do have some assets on bases in South Korea. Air sniffers we put up after their tests, AMSs, we call them. Dr. Ahn knows about these. They measure air and ground radiological contamination. If there are exposed plutonium pits, their scanning could pick 'em up. If they've got 'em shielded, it'll be much tougher," Brent offered.

He continued, "If they were careless, they could be leaving a trail everywhere from the decaying plutonium. We know from samples from their testing their plutonium is not clean, full of different isotopes, it can leave a signature."

"Can we get a closer look at that shore? We can give you target coordinates."

"Possibly. This is hostile territory. We have limited side-scanning, which means medium confidence at best. And let me repeat, we're talking hostile sovereign territory here, we can't exactly be overhead," Brent emphasized.

Kate and Dr. Ahn exchanged glances. Kate understood what he feared.

"We have your back, you understand? Instrument malfunction, strayed off course if goes bad." Kate paused, waiting for Brent's acknowledgment.

Brent was looking for a line of political protection from her should the worst happen, like his AMS aircraft get shot down or if another potential international incident were to occur.

"Thank you," Brent replied, with some relief.

"What else can you get us? That's a lot of water. Can we get some navy P-3s up there?" Kate pressed.

"I think I can order one up on a specialized patrol, yeah. I'll need you guys to call the Pentagon liaison office, though. I can't just commandeer a flock of P-3s."

"Deal. I'll work on that. Can you get those AMSs going now, though?"

"We can, these are under direct NNSA control. Give me about an hour scramble time."

"Just get them up there."

"Yup—"

"And call me directly."

"Got it."

Fortnum Bank Equities Trading Floor

Kyle walked through the maze, returning to his desk. As he approached, he spotted Garner talking to Pete. Garner gave Kyle a stony look as he finished up with Pete and left before Kyle arrived at his desk. Kyle tried not to get agitated by it; he played it cool, ignoring him. He pulled out his chair and sat.

"Garner wanted a report." Pete anticipated Kyle's asking.

"I figured."

"You alright, dude?"

"I think you know the answer to that."

"Ten-four."

They both dialed up screens and monitored the markets. After a few minutes, Kyle posed to Pete. "That doesn't mean hold out on me. Where are we?"

"Sorry. I'm outta two-thirds of it. It's ugly. Street's got us. I'm paying up."

Kyle nodded sourly. He scrolled through Scout and stared at the bright-red number. His prediction was dead-on, the number blared a painful, "-$47,600,000."

Kyle averted his eyes.

"I'm ill, you know?" Pete confessed. "I'm only a third year. This is a fucking dirt nap. How we getting out of this?"

Kyle half smiled at him.

"You think *you're* ill? I coulda heaved a bucket into the Hudson out there."

Pete snickered. Kyle finished answering him. "I don't know... What sucks is Garner won't let us back into the crude markets for a while, at least in any size. That's our bread and butter. It'll take us a while to even get into anything that can dig us out," Kyle paused as Pete soberly raised his thick eyebrows. "Keep working out of it," Kyle added.

"Crude keeps climbing, though—maybe it's good we're getting out," Pete snidely commented.

"Shit, Pete, I'm teaching you nothing. This is where the edge is. This is where people start to do stupid stuff, pay stupid prices."

"Yeah, like us." Pete laughed at his own joke. Kyle chuckled.

"It is weird it keeps trading higher. EIA keeps printing builds," Kyle noted, referring to the US Energy Information Administration's weekly crude oil inventory reports. A "build" was an indication there was more supply than demand in the oil markets, usually a reason for the price of crude oil to fall, not go higher.

Pete was about to answer but did a double take when a dumpy sales trader, Sammy Bender, entered their row.

"Shit," Pete warned Kyle under his breath.

"Hey-hey, the options guys, the smart guys. How much you think I'd be trading if I had your guys' brains? I wouldn't!" He broke into a paunchy laughter. "I'd be on a Maui beach sipping mai tais and ordering virgins to serve me, ha-ha!"

Kyle and Pete exchanged irritated looks.

"Not a good time, Sammy," Pete urged him.

Undeterred, though, Sammy sidled up to Kyle.

"You deaf? Get out of here, Sammy," Kyle made it clearer.

"Crude going in your face?" Sammy shot back.

Kyle swiveled to face Sammy but stopped himself from beating this short, fat waste of a human being with his metal stapler.

"Sammy, puke it and get the fuck out of here," Pete shot.

"Nah, you guys don't want to miss this. I got something good. I think you guys can pick him off, too," Sammy started.

"Picking off" meant it was a customer who they could quote a high price to, who wasn't very sophisticated or price conscious. Kyle, already dubious, listened to the rest of Sammy's "show"—a pitch for a trade.

"I gotta hedge fund guy, OK? He's always taking shots on gold. He loves gold, always thinks the world's gonna come apart—"

"Sammy, how many times we gotta go over this? We trade options on crude oil, nat gas and energy stocks. Don't come to us with anything else."

"I know, I know, guys. Don't forget that oil punter I gave you. You made fucking bank on him. That's why I knew you'd want to see this—"

"Spit it out," Pete impatiently snapped.

Sammy shot Pete a look over Kyle's shoulder, but he got the point.

"He wants to buy a truckload of calls on gold. I mean a truckload. And get this, for *this* Friday."

"A one-week punt on gold? What's the strike?"

"Eight hundred," Sammy informed, chuckling.

Kyle and Pete exchanged *this guy's full of shit* looks.

"Fuck off, Sammy. You're wasting our time," Pete said to him after hearing the ridiculous strike price.

"Gold's at seven hundred dollars now. Did you even look? Is your guy even real, or you fishing as usual?" Kyle impatiently reproved.

"*I* know where gold is. No, this guy's real. He comes in a lot, no joke. And here's the kicker. Drumroll. He says he's size, I mean, *size*. He wants a market on fifty-million ounces, half a million options, *and* he'll put it up OTC, too."

Pete and Kyle eyed each other again and then Sammy.

"Sammy, you *have* to do a trade that size in gold options, OTC. You blow out the market, otherwise," Pete retorted.

In general, banks, and especially options traders at banks, liked to put trades up OTC, or over-the-counter. Trading OTC gave the banks increased edge because they could be in control of the contract specifications—the fine print, in other words. Traders also liked it because it was more discreet, it was easier to do large options trades, and get their respective hedges off. OTC trades didn't show up on a public exchange's tape for the world to see. They were private trades between client and dealer. Sammy was trying to pitch the OTC element as an advantage to doing this trade with his client.

Kyle looked Sammy up and down. He'd had enough.

"Get out of here."

"No, I'm serious. This guy's dumb money. You can pick him off. I think he'll pay a buck even."

"A *buck*? This guy wants to bet fifty million gold will be higher than eight hundred by this Friday?" Pete and Kyle eyed each other and laughed.

Kyle glanced at Sammy. "Sammy, you fat fuck, you know my day was going like crap, but I'm glad you brought a little sunshine to it," Kyle ribbed.

"Fuck you. This guy's for real. Come on, just give him an offer, work with me," Sammy begged.

"Beat it," Pete dismissed, without even looking at him.

He and Kyle swiveled their chairs to return to their own trading, turning their backs on Sammy. Sammy finally skulked off after getting the door closed on him. Pete shook his head, annoyed.

"He gets more unreasonable every time."

Kyle half paid attention as he dialed up a chart of gold on his machine.

"I don't think he'll be working here much longer. He's a hustler."

Pete angled to spy on Kyle's monitors to see what was draining his attention.

"What are you doing? You're not thinking of putting that trade on, are you?"

Kyle scoffed. "Hell no. I don't even think it's real."

Pete eyed him skeptically.

"They want a hundred-point move in gold in four days. Why would someone want to do that?" Kyle inquired out loud.

"It's gotta be a risk overlay or something," Pete surmised. "If it's even real."

A risk overlay was a large trade, usually done across many accounts or funds, meant to cover correlated risks across different positions if there was a major market fluctuation.

"Doesn't make sense. An overlay you usually want to do for a longer duration, you know, three months, six, not four days. This is a lottery ticket."

"Pricey fucking lottery ticket," Pete added.

"Fed's Wednesday, maybe it's an overlay for that."

"That makes *slightly* more sense, but not much."

Kyle didn't say anything. And then he stood.

"Where are you going?"

"Talk to an analyst," Kyle replied.

"Wait—*this gold trade*?"

Kyle removed his glasses, placed them on his desk, and walked down the aisle. Pete stared after him.

"Shhhhit…"

Osan Air Base, Joint US–South Korean Air Operations, South Korea

An arrow of landing lights converged into a point at the end of the primary runway. The zero-dark morning hours were pierced by the whine of readying jets on the tarmac. A narrow-body, gray-painted Cessna Citation V jet rotated from the taxiway and onto the runway threshold. It paused for a moment, and then cleared, accelerated down the strip.

The Cessna, with its drab paint job, appeared more like a corporate jet and out of place on an air force base—were it not for the two pods hanging underneath each wing. Inside each pod were sensitive detectors that could pick up tiny traces of different forms of radiation from several kilometers up. This Cessna was an Aerial Measuring System (AMS) sniffer plane, one of many around the world kept on twenty-four-hour standby to respond to nuclear or radiological events.

The jet coursed down the runway and smoothly rose into the night air, its wheels retracting into its body as it angled higher and disappeared. Inside the cramped cockpit, two pilots guided the plane up to three thousand meters. A pair of nuclear physicists sat behind them in the cabin, hunched over laptops. The sensors from the external wing pods fed real-time data into their machines.

The Cessna shot toward its target—the North Korean Yellow Sea coastline. They were searching for not only a needle in a haystack, but that needle in the haystack from several kilometers in the air. And not even the actual needle. They were looking for evidence that a needle had *recently been* in that haystack. It was radiation detection hell. Add to that, they had to do it skirting very hostile North Korean airspace.

"Leveling at three thousand meters," the pilot announced.

"Approaching theater," the navigator called over his shoulder to the physicists behind them.

"Got it. Starting sweep," replied the first physicist.

The physicists sent commands to the wing pods to start collecting data. They fixedly stared at their small screens as the returning digits began rendering radiation profiles of the black landscape below.

Fortnum Bank Equities Trading Floor

Kyle approached Shirin Abedi, a wicked-sharp quant analyst who supported the derivatives desks. Shirin, a twenty-eight-year-old MIT graduate with architectural-style green-rimmed glasses, wrote quantitative research on the options markets for the bank's customers. She, along with the other analysts, also served as subject-matter experts for the traders when they needed deeper analyses or had a quantitative problem requiring some mathematical "heavy lifting." As Kyle neared, Shirin didn't cease keyboarding but leaned her head toward him with mock disdain.

"Springer, what do you want?" she clipped, squinting at him skeptically through those green frames of hers.

"Need your help with something," Kyle returned confidently.

"What trouble am I going to have to bail you out of now?"

"Why do you always assume that?" Kyle replied with a half-smile.

"You only show up here when you're in dire straits, when your position's gone to hell, and you need some deity to pray to. I am that deity." She glared at him over the tops of her frames. "This wouldn't have anything to do with your storming out earlier, would it?"

"You saw that?"

"Kyle, the whole floor saw it. What happened?"

"Garner happened."

"Enough said. So, I repeat my question…?" And she gestured, *get on with it.*

"Since I know I can't lie to you…" Kyle started.

Shirin reminded him with a *no, you can't* headshake.

"I need your help on a gold option trade."

"Gold options? You don't trade gold."

"Not usually. This one's got me intrigued."

Shirin eyed Kyle skeptically over the horizontal rims of her glasses, again.

"This going to take me down the drain with you?"

"Probably." Kyle smirked.

She grabbed a small pad and let out a sigh.

"Give me the deets," she said, with pen tip on the paper, ready to scrawl.

Kyle pulled up an empty chair and sat so he could discuss it more discreetly.

"A paper customer—hedge fund probably—wants to buy a ton of eight-hundred dollar strike calls, expiring this Friday."

"Friday—*this* Friday?" she clarified, her brow furrowing with doubt.

Kyle affirmed with a short nod.

"Kind of like, short-short term?" she commented. Shirin banged in the four-letter symbol for gold on her keyboard, waited a moment for the chart to appear, and grimaced when she saw it.

"Gold's at seven hundred—seven oh five, to be exact; that's a—a thirteen and a half percent move in four days," she scoffed, as she impressively did the calculation in her head. "Pretty remote chance that happens," she pronounced.

"Exactly, you see it the same way, but that's why I need your help. Crude's second nature to me. I know every event, every number. I don't for gold. What could move gold in the next week? What is it sensitive to? Any flows you're seeing, central bank buying, that kind of thing. We've got the Fed on Wednesday. Is it a Fed play?" Kyle downloaded his shopping list.

Options were probability animals. An option's price essentially encoded the market's probability expectation for a particular outcome. Very similar in concept to the pocket bets on a roulette table. A bet on a specific number in American-style roulette had a one-in-thirty-eight chance of hitting, or about a 2.6 percent probability. The cost of this bet was $1, or whatever the table's minimum bet size might be. If a customer placed a $10,000 bet on a specific outcome, say twenty-three, if the table was fair, they would very likely lose that $10,000. In fact, there was a 97.4 percent chance they would lose it.

Options, similarly, priced probabilities of outcomes. Buyers and sellers of options were putting money on specific results of the underlying commodity or stock prices. The price of that asset that an option would pay off against was called the strike price. Call options paid off when the asset finished above the strike price, and put options paid off when the asset finished below. Whatever the outcome, it had to occur by a prespecified, fixed date, which was called an expiration. All options expired. Some were very short term, others lasted for years, but they all, at some point, expired.

When a customer called the desk wanting to place an option trade, knowing *their* beliefs helped option traders, like Kyle, significantly. Dealers could be more confident in making a market, risking the bank's capital, taking the other side of the customer's trade—and minimizing the chances they could get run over.

If a customer was just speculating, dealers would trade with them all day long—good edge, as it was referred to. But there was also a chance the customer had done their homework, or had better analysts, or worse, was in possession of prescient information. Putting up this type of trade could lead to significant losses. An analyst like Shirin could take upcoming events and perform what was called scenario analysis—and help the trader judge if it was a good trade or a total trap.

"The Fed. The Fed. The Fed," Shirin uttered, almost without hesitation. "Other than that, I don't think there's a lot upcoming, at least in the next few days, that could cause any significant move in gold," she added. "But let me do some more homework. When you need this by?"

Kyle glanced up at the wall clocks.

"Liquidity probably not great the rest of the day. Let's say, tomorrow morning? I'll stop by then. If the customer's still around and this isn't bullshit—and you think I won't get my head cut off, I'll put him up."

"If I thought you'd get run over, I'd tell you to do it, without hesitation, and I'd savor every minute of the disaster." Shirin winked at him.

"Shirin, you're the hottest analyst I know."

"HR, Kyle."

Kyle smirked at her and headed back to his desk.

Kate Harrison's Office, CIA Headquarters

Kate paced up and down. Bob, Sarah, and Dr. Ahn were back in her office. Brent Lowry from the NNSA was on the speakerphone.

"What I have is *not* the highest confidence. We had no background comps to start with, so we're only looking at relative outliers," Brent started.

He was referring to maps of background radiation of a target area the NNSA detection relied on. Radiation was ever present in the environment. Lots of things radiated naturally. Most rock had small bits of naturally occurring uranium, radon, or other radioactive elements. Without knowing a baseline of background radiation for a specific geography, it was more difficult to tell what actually stood out.

"There were some excess returns in one location, again with little statistical significance, but there was *some*," Brent continued.

"Give it to us, anyway," Kate coaxed.

"The aerial survey detected traces of alpha radiation, in an area of coastal islands, an archipelago of small size—the coordinates, let's see—thirty-nine, thirty-seven North, one-twenty-four, fifty-four East."

Sarah dropped to the map and quickly triangulated the location.

"Honggon-do island," she whispered, vigorously tapping the spot on the map.

Kate, Bob, and Dr. Ahn zoomed in to where Sarah had fixed.

"What was the signature?" Dr. Ahn asked what everyone was thinking.

"One possibility, the alpha radiation could be consistent with traces of decaying U-235/238. But what we *believe*, again, non-scientifically, is these are decay products themselves cast off plutonium-239," Brent answered and paused.

Dr. Ahn shot a look at Kate, who, in turn, glared at Bob. Brent continued.

"These signatures were detected on what appears to be a pier—if we're overlaying film overheads. There were no other excess returns in that area. And we can't tell how far inshore the trail goes, either. The aperture declines quickly."

Sarah, using the straight edge, drew a thick line to the surmised pier from where the convoy split, connecting the two locations. She made a racket tapping on it, drawing everyone's attention to the relationship.

Kate leaned toward the speakerphone and asked, "Brent, if a device were placed on a boat or a ship, could we see any radiation traces in the water?"

"No, it disappears quickly. We could detect a device or materials *on* a ship, but not in the water itself. Most of these isotopes are very heavy; they sink or get scattered quickly. We were lucky enough to realize these signatures because the backgrounds are very neutral," Brent explained.

"Thanks, Brent," Bob interjected. "And confidence is only medium?"

"Affirmative."

Kate glowered at Bob when he asked that. She knew what he was up to.

"Brent, thank you and the team for moving so fast," Kate submitted. "We're going to discuss this. Send us the underlying data right away. And we may need you again," she finished as she gave Bob a pugnacious sidelong look.

"You got it. We're on standby here." Brent signed off.

The three of them regarded Bob.

"You heard him. I can't go to the director with *medium* confidence. I'm sorry," he said, with insincere remorse.

"You know that's the scientists just being formal. We can't look at the data in a vacuum. You *know* that, Bob. That's all we do around here. Conditional probability. If this were isolated, I would probably agree with you, it's an anomaly. But *given* we have a credible report of a loose nuke, *given* this is a very likely direction the target was headed in—" Kate eyed Bob expectantly, but got nothing. She shook her head in frustration.

"*Given* the isotopes detected likely come from weapons-grade plutonium, which is the material in the North Korean fissile cores," Dr. Ahn boldly asserted. Kate followed with an emphatic nod.

"This has to be a critical cable, now! We need to get DoD—we need operational units in theatre, we need—" Kate stopped herself.

Bob was studying the map, in thought, and rose from it after getting familiar.

"I'm protecting you—us," Bob told them, to their disgruntled reactions. He explained himself, "Let's say you're right, everything you just said is correct— *good* intel—how long do you think we're going to be in the lead here? You know how it goes, as soon as I raise this to the director, this becomes a DO show. A *loose nuke*, are you kidding? CTC will exert all jurisdiction, and we'll be shoved aside, just like Nine Eleven." Bob paused, pressing them with lecturing eyes.

Sarah and Dr. Ahn exchanged uncomfortable smirks with the ugly weight of internal territoriality filling the room. Kate stared back at Bob, but her expression relaxed somewhat, appearing to give Bob's logic a moment of chance.

CIA divisional politics—Bob was a master at it—were gross, but someone had to do it. Bob, Kate and the team were the DI (Directorate of Intelligence). DI were the analysts, the processors, the assessors of all the intelligence that was gathered across the globe. They assembled the picture of what all the bad guys were up to. They reported those conclusions to the president in his daily brief, to the NSC (National Security Council), to the Pentagon, and to other agencies.

The DO (Directorate of Operations) was the gathering and action arm of the CIA. They ran the Clandestine Service, the spies, the SAD (Special Activities Division) with its paramilitary arm, and, importantly for this situation, the CTC (Counterterrorist Center). CTC was the CIA group that immediately took over the US response following the 9/11 attacks. They were the first ones on the ground in Afghanistan and laid the tracks for the military invasion. They were some of the most effective operators, but Bob wanted to ensure the DI maintained control of the situation, for as long as they could, especially on something as dangerous as this and valuable, intelligence-wise.

"We're going to need DO help anyway—and very soon, if this pans out." Kate was, in part, with his thinking, but played devil's advocate to test how far he'd calculated their gambit.

"True, true, but I may have an idea. Put this all together for me. Sell me on it," he beckoned as he pompously sat in a chair, testing the three of them as if he were expecting some sort of performance.

"You jackass. If we even had the time to spare, I'd roll my eyes at that," Kate scolded. Sarah and Dr. Ahn chuckled.

"I'm very serious. Help me write this memo, start from the beginning, let's see if it all fits," he said. Kate continued to play along, to see if there was a light at the end of the tunnel.

"Okay. Number one, we have the developing North Korean nuclear program. They have been extracting reactor plutonium for at least ten years. Last year, they detonated a small plutonium-based device—"

"How many devices and of what size and yield do we believe they have now?" Bob interrupted.

"Enough for at least twenty bombs, plus half a dozen more every year. Fat Man sized and design, twenty to forty kilotons. The Kim regime has had a deployment strategy of dispersing their nukes to missile assembly facilities across the country to limit their vulnerability to a US attack," Dr. Ahn rendered her expertise with Kate nodding at every point in affirmation.

Dr. Ahn continued, "Reinforced by *four* previous convoy runs to missile assemblies from Yongbyon. We have multispectral evidence each convoy transported radioactive materials. Sunday's convoy would be the fifth."

Kate further built on the evidence. "Two. We received high-confidence intelligence a radiochemist who worked at Yongbyon attempted to defect sometime Monday morning local. The defector's identity has been scrubbed. The defector, importantly, conveyed that a device had been diverted, quote, *to the water*, end quote, which we believe, was an island pier on the Yellow Sea coast."

Kate paused again. Bob had folded his arms, but Kate was undeterred by his bullshit body language.

"Three. It is our belief that either an assembled weapon, or the components of, were transferred to a ship currently in the Yellow Sea. An AMS aircraft detected isotopes consistent with the recent presence of plutonium on dock structures on a North Korean island in the north Yellow Sea."

"Four. If a working device, or fissile material, has fallen out of state control and been smuggled out of North Korea to waiting buyers, it has a twenty-hour head start on us. And five, we know al-Qaeda and other terrorist groups have been trying very hard to acquire nuclear weapons and materials," Kate finished.

Bob's eyes widened at the last two points. He didn't seem to like them but knew Kate had stuck them in there to test him.

Bob rose and reflected for a moment.

"We need to work on the motivation. What are our theories?"

"We agree, that part's not adding up. It's fundamentally inconsistent with the Kim regime's current posture, especially going into the six-way talks," Dr. Ahn started. Kate continued for her.

"Unless we consider something more radical like fractured elements of the Kim military hierarchy trying to sabotage the six-ways—which would be a very aggressive and risky move for them. We may have to seek a banal motivation," Kate registered, shaking her head, not wanting to consider the inevitable.

"What does that mean?"

"I don't know. A rogue general may have done this for the money, and outright sold one of these things," she conceded fatefully.

"Start working on that. That may play into what I'm thinking. Do the usual network audit, who could they reach out to, who they've interacted with, past communications…"

Kate's patience finally ended. "Bob, what *are* you thinking. We don't have much time here," she implored.

"We play the contraband angle to the director, which *may* or *may not* include nuclear materials. That will keep this op in our house for the time being, but also get the resources we might need, some DO help or Pentagon," Bob explained.

Kate finally smiled but erased her smile quickly so as not to give him any visible credit.

"We'll start with their diplomats. They're the holes in that sieve," she offered.

Kate then motioned to the clocks on her wall. The Eastern Standard clock read about three thirty p.m.

"How quickly can we get some action?"

Bob consulted the world clock array.

"I'm thinking fifteen to brief the director, another fifteen to half hour for the DNI, probably out by four thirty," Bob calculated. "Draft me the memo, on the angle we *discussed*," he told them.

"You'll give us air cover for more NNSA time?" Kate asked with a whisper.

Bob thought for a brief second.

"Get them back up there. They might spot something," he said with a nod.

Rockefeller Park, Lower Manhattan, United States

Kyle walked along the Hudson River esplanade with his daughter, Jill. She was a cute seven-year-old with long blonde hair and chubby cheeks but wore a serious scowl that was almost adult. Kyle toted her little backpack, along with a kids-size lacrosse stick and helmet as they walked toward the park, with Jill always dashing a few feet ahead of Kyle.

"See, that's where your dad works." Kyle pointed to the Fortnum Bank building, farther down the esplanade.

"I know where you work. You tell me every time we walk here," Jill chided her father.

"Right." Kyle chuckled.

"And that's where Amy works, at the FBI waffle building," Jill presented, pointing to the white Federal Plaza building farther in the distance.

"Your dad used to work there, too. Why are you calling your mom *Amy*?"

"That's her name, *Kyle*," she said triumphantly.

He laughed. "I can't argue with you."

"Where's your tie? You always have a tie at work," Jill asked, skeptically inspecting him.

"Observant little thing, aren't you? You see, there was kind of an accident..." Kyle trailed off.

"Like a car accident?"

Kyle smiled at her.

They arrived at a wide, grassy field on the edge of the river, ringed by the esplanade. The park was full of people enjoying the remaining warmish days of early fall. Couples were lying on blankets spread on the grass, teens were playing touch football, and kids were running around chasing dogs.

"Jill, here's a good spot," Kyle decided, and dropped Jill's pack.

Kyle removed his suit jacket and set it with their other stuff. Rolling up his sleeves, he grabbed her lacrosse helmet.

"Here, fit this on," he said to Jill, passing her the helmet.

But she had already bolted after a long-haired golden retriever that was bounding about with other kids playing in the field. Kyle watched her for a few minutes. He got lost in her happy, carefree frolic, chasing the dog and frisking him as the retriever entertained a bevy of children. It made him feel more relaxed watching her, and for a moment he forgot about his loss and the stress of the trading desk. In a blink, Jill came tearing back over to him.

Kyle handed her the helmet, and she fit it on, responsibly tightening the chin strap. Kyle stooped to help her, trying to fasten it properly.

"No, that's too tight... I can do it. Let me..."

She wriggled away from him and finished clipping it together herself. She tilted her head up, looking at him for approval through the mask cage.

He gave her a love tap on her helmeted head and then another.

"Stop, Kyle," she rebuked.

He passed her the lacrosse stick.

"You want your gloves, too?"

"No gloves," Jill protested.

"How will you protect your hands?"

"I won't miss catching it."

Kyle laughed at her.

"Head over to about there." Kyle pointed.

Jill charged off to a spot directly in line with Kyle forty feet away. Kyle bowled a grounder at her. The ball dribbled down to her feet, and she deftly swept it up with a curl of her stick. She cradled the ball in the pocket, twisting it several times, and hurled it back at Kyle.

Kyle caught it with both hands, impressed by the edge on it.

"Nice pass." And he tossed it back to her.

She caught it in one swift hook. Kyle clapped. This time, she beamed it back at him. It made a resounding *smack* that stung his palms.

"That had a little juice on it," he proudly praised her.

She suddenly stopped and came running back over to him.

"What's wrong?"

"My finger got squished. I don't want to play anymore," she whined.

"Come on, play hurt. You're doing good. You see what your last throw did?" He displayed his reddened palms. "That was great."

But her attention wandered to the retriever. He nudged her back to him.

"Fine." She sighed and returned to her spot in the grass.

Kyle managed a few more tosses with her until she discovered she could throw the lacrosse ball to the golden retriever, who went rifling after it and obediently returned the ball to her. That was a lot more fun. Kyle lost that competition and settled for watching her play catch with the dog.

"Looks like good lacrosse practice she's getting," Amy announced sarcastically as Jill went back and forth with the retriever.

Kyle turned to see his ex-wife, Amy, appear next to him.

"He was a better wing than I was."

Amy was a strong brunette, with dark eyes, a bright complexion, high cheekbones, with an athlete's build. She was a bit shorter than Kyle, at about five seven. She wore a work suit, jacket and knee-length skirt, her nine-millimeter Glock holster was visible with her jacket parted.

They watched Jill race around with the dog, trading small talk.

"How's the terrorism business?"

"You know, usual crap. Following leads and tailing targets who end up turning out to be halal food vendors," she replied cynically. "How's your work? How many people did you rob today to make another million?"

Kyle threw her an unsmiling glance.

"Strike a nerve, did I?" she baited.

"Had a shitty day. Thanks for bringing attention to it," Kyle told her, sourly.

"I'm sure you'll figure it out and then tomorrow it'll go the other way," she retorted with false sympathy.

"*Jill?* Your mom's here," Kyle shouted to Jill, desperate for a subject change. Amy didn't say anything.

"Let me take her this weekend," Kyle dropped.

Amy winced but didn't reply. Kyle persisted. "I'm serious. I want to spend more time with her. She's growing up quick."

"You going to teach her to drink scotch?"

"Come on…"

Amy shifted to call out to Jill.

"Jill? Come on, Mommy's here…"

She pivoted back to respond to Kyle.

"I don't think so. You know how things go—"

"Don't piss me off. She's my daughter—"

Jill appeared before them in an instant and detected the tension.

"No fighting!" she scolded them.

Kyle grabbed Jill, hoisted her up, and kissed her on the lacrosse helmet and put her back down.

"Bye, Kyle!" she shouted as Amy took her pack and led Jill away. Jill peeked over her shoulder and waved goodbye to Kyle, who smiled and waved back.

Operation 912 Task Force Center, CIA Headquarters

Kate stood clenching a phone handset with both hands like a baseball bat as she impatiently minded a CIA technician who was hurriedly connecting her new phone. The tech gave her a polite grin as he joined the plugs. The phone light stuttered as it finally came online, bound to the primary network.

"How am I supposed to make—" she started to complain to the technician, who motioned to the illuminating base station.

"Enter your ID and you're good to go," he instructed as he grabbed his gear and left the new, larger control-center they had just moved into.

Bob had successfully persuaded the director into issuing an immediate cable—based on the dangerous materials contraband premise. While not the highest alert in the intelligence community, it was enough to get some resources but not too loud that it would cause other power centers to swoop in.

"Do we have our navy liaison?" Kate called out to several analysts working at half-assembled desks.

The hastily convened task force center—number 912—as it would be officially called, was on the fourth floor, and stretched fifty by fifty. There were about a dozen analysts, desk officers and liaisons who were presently arriving. Space-wise, they had gotten lucky, as some of the CTC division had recently relocated to an expansion office complex off Lewinsville Road, a few minutes away, still in the McLean area. The Office of the Director of National Intelligence (ODNI) was also on that campus.

"Here—me, Lieutenant Junior Grade, Graham," a shortish redheaded naval officer called out to Kate with an accompanying wave of his hand.

Still holding the handset in her hands, Kate half shouted over to him.

"P-3s? What can we get?" she anxiously blared at him.

"Working on it," LTJG Graham replied, holding his own handset in the air for her to see.

"Yokosuka. Don't we have a carrier stationed there?" Kate pressed.

The redhead shook his head emphatically, *no.*

"The *Reagan* returned to North Island back in April. I'm working on helicopter carriers, naval air bases. I'll get you something, give me a few," he relayed as he resumed his conversation on his phone.

"Come on, we need some eyes up there," Kate grumbled to herself.

She checked her watch. It was just after six p.m. Kate shuddered at all the tension between the CIA and the military, but she really needed DoD help.

Dr. Ahn and Sarah entered the new task force center and sat at desks surrounding Kate's. Bob arrived shortly after and joined the three of them.

"Anything?" he asked.

"No carrier. They're trying to find us something—somewhere," Kate reported and motioned toward the redheaded naval officer.

Bob sat down next to Kate.

"Director bought some of it, fortunately. I had to push the clear radiological signatures of this thing—materials, not weapons. He still thought it was a mistake or something else explainable." Bob paused and then added, "And he did ask the AQ question, so we may not have a lot of time if his antenna's already up."

Kate chuckled. "The irony being, this *could* be al-Qaeda, for all we know. If they've gotten their hands on a loose nuke, I'll be the first to punt to CTC," she sardonically added.

Bob smiled. "I did a great job of playing up the UN export ban angle. But he'll keep asking about it. We'll need to show something or else hand it off."

Kate, in part, ignored him, and leaned to Dr. Ahn, lowering her voice, "Speaking of AQ, anything?"

Dr. Ahn raised her arms in the air as a technician placed a PC monitor on the desk in front of her and ran cables to set it up.

"Too early. We're just starting to look at wires from some of the accounts we track—the ones we know for sure are NK dips or party members. Maybe someone took a payoff. CB's on it," she replied, referring to the CIA's Covert Banking group that worked with the US Treasury Department to locate and track illicit money flows around the globe. Kate was satisfied that was being pursued, but she remained frustrated by the resource inaction and angled again to see the DoD desk.

"Hello?" Kate scolded, leaning out to make eye contact with the navy liaison.

"I think we got a couple of responses. The USS *Essex*; she's currently in the East China Sea on maneuvers. She's got a complement of Seahawks. They think they can deploy two. Their range is more limited, but they can at least cover the southern edge of the Yellow Sea," the officer finally replied.

"That's still not enough. What about land based?" Kate persisted.

"I got a couple P-3s being prepped this moment at Osan. NNSA giving them op briefing on instrument returns of what to look for. Also, I think we can get an Arleigh Burke over there in a hurry. The USS *Mustin*," he announced proudly.

The USS *Mustin* was an Arleigh Burke–class destroyer, the US Navy's workhorse ship. Fast and lethal, the US Navy had dozens of them deployed around the world, including a number stationed at the Yokosuka, Japan, naval base.

Kate signaled back to the liaison officer, *good!*

He returned a grin, pleased with himself that he was able to keep up with her, at least for now.

"Now we're only twenty-two hours behind," she commented to Bob dourly.

Osan Air Base, Joint US-South Korean Air Operations

Dawn cast a pink light across the main Osan airstrip as two hefty US Navy aircraft taxied to the base of the runway. These were Lockheed EP-3s—four-prop airplanes outfitted with a bulging underbelly of scanners and detection equipment and an internal cabin packed with electronics and specialists operating them. The aircraft were nicknamed ARIES, which stood for "Airborne Reconnaissance Integrated Electronics System." They could image theaters, expose hostile radar installations, jam communications, and identify bumps in the oceans that could betray a hidden submarine.

The EP-3s wheeled to line up with the airstrip and barreled down the runway, climbing into the air and leveling off. They shortly split, and each vectored toward a separate quadrant of the western Yellow Sea. In an hour, they would be over their target ranges of coastline, deploying a sensitive electronic dragnet to detect any speck of radioactive particles being cast off by a suspicious cargo.

USS *Essex*, Helicopter Carrier, East China Sea

An active East China Sea pelted the hull of the USS *Essex* as it steamed northward toward the South Korean island of Jeju. The *Essex* was a helicopter carrier, a smaller type of aircraft carrier in the US Navy's fleet. These ships carried dozens of fighter aircraft and helicopters, in addition to a detachment of almost two thousand US Marines.

Flight crews on her deck prepped two SH-60 Seahawk helicopters. The Seahawks were ubiquitous navy helos that were adapted to everything from close-in air support to rescue operations to special forces deployment.

The blades of the two Seahawks whirred into a loud drone. A yellow-jerseyed plane director—the on-deck officer responsible for the movement of all aircraft on the flight deck—hand-signaled to the first to lift off. The helicopter elevated into the air with a loud rush and then tilted forward and throttled out over the open sea. The plane director then beckoned the second, and it followed aloft, being sucked straight up into the air, the morning light striking it as it raced after its partner.

Kyle's Apartment, Ritz-Carlton Residences

Kyle, Pete, and Sully joked and drank scotch as they played poker, seated around a square glass table in Kyle's apartment. A wall-mounted flat-screen TV on mute behind them strobed the financial channel, its blue-and-white ticker crawling across the screen, recapping the day's stock and commodity prices. Towers of poker chips of varying heights were arrayed before them, along with a pile in the center pot.

"Why do we let you talk us into poker on a glass table every time?" Pete complained as he awkwardly eyed his hand, holding it flat against his stomach.

"Called nibbling. Wears you down until you get sloppy and forget that it's glass and you forfeit your edge to me," Kyle joked.

"Graff, man, you can use it to *your* advantage, too, you know?" Sully winked at Pete and motioned to him to lay down just one or two cards on the glass.

"Amy gave it to me in the divorce. She didn't like this table, so now I have to justify using it," Kyle replied as he bent one card to glimpse his hand.

"Didn't you just end up writing her a big check?"

"Pretty much. Wrote her a big check. I write her another honking one every month. She's the richest agent in the New York field office. I don't know why she even still does it."

"I thought you said she quit."

"She doesn't trust him," Pete reminded Sully. "She's gonna keep working, squirreling away everything she gets. Remember, she's the smarter one." He peeked at his hand again. "I'm in for four, I see it," he finished, pushing a short stack of chips into the pot.

"I told her about my crude oil loss, too. She was flip. Uncaring. She should care. She has a vested interest in my performance. You'd think she'd be rooting for me... I see the four. I call." Kyle extended his chips.

"I'm out," Sully started, laying his cards down. "You told her about crude?"

"I call you," Pete interjected.

"Not the details. I told her I had a big loss. She didn't give a shit... Here." Kyle laid down his hand. "Three ladies," he said, overturning three queens.

"Straight." Pete spread out his cards faceup, and with a wide grin, scooped up the stacks of chips. He gathered everyone's cards and shuffled the next round.

Sully took several gulps of his scotch.

"What the hell's going on in crude, anyway?"

Kyle shook his head, *not sure*, as he watched the cards come to him.

"It ain't trading right. Feels like there's a big buyer in there, I don't know. Doesn't make sense. There's an ocean of supply, too, but it just keeps going up."

"Something else besides the pipeline attack?" Sully posed as he reviewed the new cards dealt him. They anted up. Pete finished dealing and exposed the first faceup card. In unison, they eyed the new card and checked their own hands.

"Headline risk. Crude should have sold off after the initial pop from that news. It's a big line, but they can repair it quickly. We sold a ton of vol into that," Kyle commented with a frustrated air.

"And then Garner crushed you."

Kyle eyed him with bitter agreement.

"And then he crushed me. I should have tossed him through his glass windows today."

"You should have called me over. I would have helped you do it. He still owes me for screwing me on last year's bonus," Sully started with a tinge of resentment. He continued his diatribe. "I'm convinced as soon as you leave the desk for management, you drop twenty IQ points. Probably the dumbest thing he could make you do. He used to know better. Remember, I used to work for him when he ran the index desk. He woulda never done something like that when he managed a book. He hurt the entire division today, not just you guys, all the desks are affected by that, too, you know?" Sully complained spitefully, and then added, "Ten in," and pushed a handful of chips into the pot.

"Small-dick syndrome or something." Kyle chuckled.

"We're in a fucking hole now, too, I'm praying we get some decent October vol this year," Sully added.

"Shit. Am I gonna see *any* of my bonus this year?" Pete whined. "In for ten."

"Me too... Shut up, Graff, you'll get what I pay you and like it. And you'll learn your place," Kyle added sarcastically.

"I need fuck-you money. When am I getting fuck-you money?" Pete cried.

"When you stop calling it that."

Pete dealt the next upturned card. The three of them checked it and consulted their hands.

"You tell him about the gold trade?" Pete threw in.

"Sammy showed you that gold trade, too?" Sully asked them.

"Yeah, how'd you know about it?"

"He fucking shopped it to every vol trader in the building. Even called upstairs to the FX guys. Like the thoroughbred each Derby everyone talks up, but nobody bets on," Sully snickered.

Kyle laughed. "Did he really?"

"What do you think his sales credit'll be on that thing? The fat-ass was licking his chapped lips."

They laughed at Sully's rendering.

"But nobody would touch it," Sully finished.

"Springer might," Pete betrayed.

Kyle shot him an irritated, *you dick!* look.

"Ha, you serious? You're not thinking of actually doing that trade, are you?"

Kyle pursed his lips, unhappy about being outed. "The thought had crossed my mind. Plus, you can't beat that edge. It's fifty sticks. I'm down about fifty sticks. See how that math works out?" Kyle smiled at him.

"Them's rookie words. It ain't about the edge. I'd put up the trade, too, if it was only about the edge. It's the risk flag. Nobody wants that, not even Barlow on the metals desk, and he *trades* the product. How you gonna get around the risk limits? If Garner sees it, you're out the door, shredded silk tie and zero bonus," Sully stumped.

"I might have a plan," Kyle revealed, taking a quick drink of the scotch.

Pete rolled his eyes and looked to Sully for help.

"We just blanked out our entire book. I got the bullets. Plus, the thing's OTC. I'm thinking I put it up, wait a day or two, and *then* enter it into Scout. By then, it's Thursday, and before Garner spots it, it's Friday, the thing'll expire, and I'll ring the fifty mil."

"You got it all worked out, don't you?"

"Wait, wait, wait, wait, wait!" Pete shot Kyle a look of shock. *"You kidding me?* We're gonna stuff a trade in the drawer? They send you to jail for that shit," Pete protested.

"They send you to jail when you do that for several months to hide your losses. We *have to* enter it, it has to clear, otherwise we're not gonna see the fifty when it expires. We're not hiding anything. We're just really busy, and we forgot to enter it into the risk system for a day or so—in the chaos that is our trading day. We're just *delaying* a bit," Kyle emphasized.

"Shit," Pete muttered. He glanced at Sully again, thinking he had an ally. "Help us out here."

"Might work," Sully confided.

Pete shot them both an incredulous look.

"Oh, fuck you guys." Pete turned to Sully again. "And what about you? Two minutes ago, you were all, *oh, who'd put on a crazy trade like this.* You sure changed your tune real quick," Pete called him out.

Sully smirked. "I liked Springer's thinking on it."

"We need to get out of this hole. I can't play size in the crude markets for a while. This could be a good trade," Kyle casually but logically explained to Pete.

"Man! Who'd do a trade like this anyway? Who'd spend fifty million to bet gold will make a superman leap in four days?" Pete skeptically posed.

"Gotta be Fed positioning. Only thing that makes sense," Kyle answered.

"Fed's Wednesday," Sully added.

"What are we expecting?"

"A quarter."

"Yes, a quarter-point. And that's on top of the fifty they did in August."

"Gotta be hedging an adverse Fed move. Either that or punting."

"Still doesn't make sense. How much does the dollar move on a Fed lower? How much does gold move? Not *that* much," Pete disputed.

"Who the fuck knows. Some are worried the subprime stuff'll get worse. Maybe it's got something to do with that. They're doing an overlay, they've got big risk, I don't know, or else they're punting. Or maybe they just like buying crash," Kyle speculated.

Crash was trader talk for "crash protection"—buying insurance options that rarely pay off but protect against very extreme events.

"Protection, Pete. We get guys like that in the S all the time. They buy downside insurance. Pretty much all I do is sell crash. You guys know this game. You sell that shit, too," Sully commented.

The S was a nickname for the S&P 500, the main equities index product that Sully was in charge of trading.

Pete dealt the next faceup card. The three leaned to look at it.

"We see those in crude, yeah, but the protection guys are always going for longer time, ya know? Three months, six months, a year. A four-day shot's not unheard of, but it's pretty rare," Pete challenged.

"So what? Even if there's an adverse move, gold pops, it's not getting to *eight hundred*. I'd do this trade all day." Kyle became more convicted as they spoke about it.

"In for five more." Kyle pushed in some chips.

"Prob right. Now you're making me jealous I shoulda done the trade," Sully said. "I'm good for five. And I'll raise it ten," he offered with a gleam in his eye.

"I have an analyst on it. We'll see what she says tomorrow. I'll decide then."

"Oh shit, that cute quant in derivatives—what's her name?" Sully grinned.

"Yes, her—her name's Shirin, you horny bastard."

"*Shirin*, that's the one."

Sully leaned to Pete. "Graff, you should ask her out."

"She's cute, but…isn't she a bit too hairy?"

Kyle flicked Pete on his forehead with a loud *snap*.

"Dang!" Pete recoiled from it.

"*You're* too hairy," Kyle scolded him.

"I'm just saying."

"You guys would make a good couple, then."

"What are you going to do about those eyebrows of yours?" Kyle ribbed.

"Couple of caterpillars crawling around your forehead," Sully piled on.

"You could get 'em waxed."

"Shave 'em, you know, a razor?"

Pete covered his forehead. "I got it. I'll play nice," he relented.

"She'll put some actual brains on it," Kyle continued, then regarded Pete with a smile. "Then you can take her to Cancún, show her your gratitude."

"Who says I won't do that anyway," Pete retorted, taking a swig of scotch. "But putting her aside for a moment, I keep thinking—what was that saying?—if a guy wants to bet you a hundred bucks he can pull a silver dollar from behind your ear, you take the bet, but if he bets you a hundred thousand? He knows something," Pete cautioned. "I'll see your fifteen, and, raise you another ten." He pushed in more ducats.

Kyle slapped down his cards. "Skunked. I'm out of this one."

Sully spied his own cards, and then the faceup cards again.

"Here's ten…and another…thirty." Sully dragged the new stacks into the pot.

Kyle surveyed the table.

"He's bluffing. You got this, play him." Kyle winked at Pete with confidence.

Pete shrank back. He peeked at his hand again, scanned all the chips that were stacked up, eyed Sully, then Kyle.

"I call you. What you got?" Pete moved thirty thousand into the pile.

Sully revealed a full house. Pete had a flush and buried his face in his hands.

"Ohhhh!" they all shouted.

"Shit, that was close," Sully admitted and swept all the chips toward himself.

"Graff, margin call. Or do you just want to toss my salad and call it even?"

Pete's eyes widened.

"Now we *have* to do the gold trade. I'm *Bud Fox*, I'm tapped out."

EP-3 ARIES, South Yellow Sea, Fifty Nautical Miles East of Jiangsu Coast, China

The four-engine EP-3 banked in a predefined pattern at 180 knots, its patrol speed. Flying at a few thousand feet, it dipped below a low-lying cloud bank to maximize visibility of the water below. At this altitude, ships were discernible by type—freighter or tanker, junker or trawler. The plane's electronic sweepers also worked optimally under these conditions.

The pilots held the discipline of scouring in a strict grid. Like coloring a segment of a drawing, they dithered this quadrant of the Jiangsu coast, vectoring up and down. They were also careful to hold at least twenty nautical miles beyond the Chinese coastline. Since arriving in theater, they had already been shadowed by a Chinese J-11 fighter jet. The navy pilots were also crafty to ensure that, to the Chinese, their flight pattern and behavior appeared like a routine snooping patrol.

Inside the central fuselage was the EWMC (electronic warfare mission commander), directing a wing of EWOs (electronic warfare operators), who monitored detection returns from scanners mounted on the underbelly of the aircraft. Detecting radiation was not the primary mission of these aircraft. But they had also cross-trained, and each ARIES plane had taken off with an NNSA technician on board who could assist the EWOs with interpreting signals.

The pilots dropped the left wing as they banked to the next zig in their pattern. As they did, the plane crossed over a freighter that was sailing south, following the Jiangsu coastline, about forty NMs out. The cockpit marked the ship visually, but thought nothing of it, as there were so many bulk freighters like that one.

Behind the flight deck, the EWOs stared at the array of screens, digital oscilloscopes, and other signal detectors. Their vision of this ship was quite different when it rendered electronically. Right away an EWO noticed a spike in what was called the activation effect on one of his monitors.

Certain types of radioactive materials, especially plutonium, were constantly ejecting high-speed neutrons. Sensitive equipment could detect these fast neutrons directly, but another good way to detect them was to watch for the effect the bombarding neutrons had on surrounding materials. Through this activation effect, other stable elements, such as iron, which these ships were constructed from, produced radionuclides when they were struck by fast neutrons. Detectors looked for those resulting particles.

"Hey, are we over a target?" the EWO called out to the EWMC.

"Affirmative," replied the commander.

"Freighter. Medium sized, about two hundred meters," another EWO added.

"Can we make a repeat pass?" the first EWO requested, and then he motioned to the NNSA officer. "Take a look at this."

The pilots banked the aircraft again and then leveled it out for a second sweep. They flew over in an intersecting path with the freighter, several times, to ensure a reliable reading. Inside, the NNSA technician stood over the console with the EWO and closely watched the returns as they crisscrossed the ship.

"These are high radionuclide levels, very high beta emitters," the NNSA technician noted to the operator, and tapped the screen several times to make sure it was working right. He called out to the EWMC. "Captain, I think we have a hit."

Alder Freighter, South Yellow Sea, Eighty Kilometers East of Jiangsu Coast, China

The shorter Syrian joked with one of the crewmen who had helped hoist the bomb boxes the previous night as they leaned against the stern guardrails. The early-morning sun was hazy, causing them to squint in the humid light. The second crewman who helped them arrived balancing cups of coffee from the galley.

The three kept chatting and drinking their coffee when they heard a buzzing noise overhead. The droning was patterned and repetitive, persisting for about ten minutes. At first, they didn't pay much attention. Occasionally, one of them would look up, but because of the haze, they never spotted anything. They just kept drinking their coffee.

The taller Syrian interrupted them, bounding up the ladder from the lower deck where he'd been.

"Hey...*hey?*" He tried to get their attention without shouting.

They watched him, puzzled, as he rushed to them, pointing in the air. They all squinted into the hazy sky. An aircraft, difficult to identify from where they stood, was passing at a low and sharp angle over the freighter. They followed it for several turns. The plane would fly in a straight line and then bank and fly in another straight line.

"Binoculars," the shorter Syrian barked to one of the crewmen who retrieved a pair. He looked through them at the aircraft, focusing for a moment, and then called out to the group. "Americans!"

He threw down the binoculars, and the four of them rushed to the bomb containers secured to the deck. They snapped away the tarp rigging and then cautiously, but quickly, hauled the cases up two deck levels, awkwardly relaying the boxes in a bucket-brigade-like manner.

The taller Syrian climbed up to a lifeboat and cut away its safety harness. He banged open the crew portal, and the four worked to transfer all three cases to the craft. They tightly lashed the containers together and secured them to the interior seats. The Syrians then shook hands with the crewmen, and they boarded the lifeboat, sealing the hatch behind them.

The rogue crewmen winched the craft down from its davits, lowering it to the waterline. They cut the ropes, and the boat splashed into the water, where it bobbed with the waves, taking a few moments to stabilize.

Inside the vessel, the Syrians, with their bomb cases and their personal packs, started up the craft's motors and steered it westward, separating from the freighter. The covered boat pitched and rocked up and down as it gained speed and shifted its heading toward the Chinese coastline...

Basement of a West Village Brownstone, Manhattan, United States

A man struggled, bound to a chair in the center of a basement faintly lit by a single light bulb hanging from the ceiling. His hands were secured behind his back and his ankles were tied to the chair's front legs with wire.

Sweat and blood soiled his ripped oxford shirt. He still had on his polished wingtip dress shoes. Blood seeped from his mouth and from wounds on his arms and dripped onto the cement floor. His head sagged from the pain.

A gaunt figure with a swarthy complexion, narrow face, and a nose hooked like a hawk's loomed over him. He waved a long bowie knife in front of his victim's face. The victim raised his eyes and stared at the blade and shook his head in desperation.

"Please...?" he begged. "I—I gave you those passwords... Please, I'll give you money... I have a wife... Go... Take whatever you want..." he trailed off.

The Hawk-Nosed Man didn't respond. His face remained stoic. The victim's labored, pain-filled panting was the loudest noise in the room. He finally lifted his head back up and faced his evil torturer, and he started to weep.

The Hawk-Nosed Man visually searched the room. He scanned the walls, and he especially eyed a small ceiling-level basement window. It was dark outside, so no light was coming in through the lone opening. He angled around to find the sole source of light—the ceiling bulb behind them.

He stepped over to it and reached above him and unscrewed the bulb. The room faded into blackness.

"No, please! What do you want? What do you *want*?" the victim shouted in horror, enveloped in the darkness.

The Hawk-Nosed Man slipped behind him and raised the knife.

"Noooo—!" was cut off by gurgling and gasping sounds.

The Hawk-Nosed Man kicked him and the chair to the floor. The victim struggled in his final moments, his arms and legs straining and jerking in their bound paralysis as blood coursed onto the cement floor around him...

Kyle's Apartment, Ritz-Carlton Residences

Kyle and Sully laughed loudly as they reclined on loungers, sipping scotch on Kyle's high-floor balcony. The sun had set, and it was now dark outside. They gazed out over the Hudson and Statue of Liberty on the clear New York fall evening as they chatted.

"Don't sweat it. You'll get out of this hole, man." Sully offered, becoming more earnest.

"Don't know if I'm feelin' it anymore, ya know?" Kyle confided.

"What does that mean? You're the best vol trader on the street. Except for that MIT kid, what's his name, over at Bear—?"

"Dixon," Kyle filled in.

"Billy Dixon, but that kid's such a freak, he doesn't count. You're the best *normal guy* vol trader on the street."

They chuckled.

"No, I meant I might be done, *done* done, with trading," Kyle dropped.

"Wait, what? What do you mean, like, *done with trading*? Like, leaving the bank, quitting?"

"Quitting trading, yeah," Kyle revealed, and continued. "I was with Jill this afternoon. Sucks, I never get to see her. When she was a baby, I didn't really think about it. Plus, Amy and I didn't want to have anything to do with each other back then. But now, it's like, she's getting big. She's growing up, she's figuring stuff out. I'm not getting any of it. I see her a few hours a week and some more in summer. I'm not liking it," Kyle explained.

"That's custody shit, that's not your career."

"I know, but I feel like, Amy thinks the bank is the reason we split up. She hates it. I don't know, I'm figuring, maybe she changes her tune if I left, got a new career, something."

Sully took a drink of scotch, and then blurted out almost with a sarcastic laugh, "You're not thinking of going back to the FBI, are you?"

"Shit, no. Nothing like that. But something else, I don't know. Maybe I'm just thinking out loud."

"Do I need to remind you *why* you left the FBI?" Sully raised. "Getting you out of there was the best thing I ever did. You were making fifty K a year, getting shot at, playing dress-up on drug busts, fearing for your life every day, while all your friends, me among them, were making five hundred and not looking down gun barrels when we went to work. You did have the badge and the gun, I'll give you that, best hookup chum ever. But that one bonus of working as a fed, you didn't even cash in. You met Amy and got married and had a kid. And then you *left* the FBI. Best move you ever made," Sully declaimed, and then added, "Trading's in your blood."

Kyle searched the glittering Jersey City skyline as the building lights were coming on.

"Maybe…"

"If you did leave, when would you do it?"

"I was thinking I'd trade out of this debacle, get *something* of a bonus this year, sell this pad, and then move into, I don't know, a more family-oriented place, ya know?"

"Not the Springer I know."

Sully's tone became more disappointed sounding. He took another gulp of scotch. Kyle felt his displeasure and filled the void.

"Maybe you're right. Maybe I get through this loss, and I'll feel different."

"Now, see, that's a more sensible attitude. Forget this family shit. Move on," Sully said darkly.

Kyle responded with a, "*Ha*, you're a cold motherfucker, sometimes."

"You gotta think about things more *numerically*," Sully stressed.

Pete walked out onto the balcony to join them. He was jokingly wearing an apron and carrying a steaming pizza box. He looked at both of them and sensed the dour seriousness.

"What'd the condom break? Why you guys so grim?"

Operation 912 Task Force Center

Kate was trying to ponder over several key details of the operation but kept getting distracted by all the new people being added to the center. The larger space was now almost full. Two technicians noisily banged away at the front of the room to hang a large projection screen on the wall. The monitor would display live feeds, maps, and operation status. But Kate couldn't care less about the monitor; she just wanted some quiet. She was about to return to her office when Bob entered.

"It's after eight. You need to go home?"

"You're joking, right?" She laughed at him.

"I'm just checking—"

They were interrupted by a commotion from the DoD desk. LTJG Graham was yelling into his phone. He stood up and twisted toward Kate and Bob.

"I think we have something—the Seahawks came up empty, but one of the EP-3s in the East China Sea—" He raised his handset back to his ear. Kate and Bob exchanged hopeful glances and approached Graham's desk.

"High-confidence return, on a freighter sailing south in the East China Sea, about forty miles off the mainland coast," Graham relayed.

"Who are you on with?" Bob demanded.

"A Captain Martin, US Navy, Naval Security Group—"

"Give me that." Bob grabbed the phone from him.

"Captain?... Yes, sir. Let's arrange a conference call at"—Bob consulted the wall clock—"fifteen after. And we need multiple eyes on that freighter... Yes, sir, thank you." Bob handed the phone back, and told the redhead, "Get the details of that ship—where it's flagged, destination, everything—you got it?"

Graham dutifully nodded and got back on the phone.

"We're going to need to interdict," Kate told Bob with a stern sidelong look as they walked back to her desk.

His brow furrowed as he heard her. He knew exactly what that meant.

"An interdiction is a big deal, you know that. We have to involve State, cover all the bases. This thing's growing larger, fast," Bob fussed.

"Bob, this was *your* plan. Whatever you have to figure out, do it, *fast*. Anything that could take time—time we don't have—what if it heads into Chinese waters? Our shot is *now*." Kate's eyes widened emphatically.

Bob did agree with her, but his bureaucratic brain was taking hold of him. He was momentarily saved when the navy liaison motioned to them.

"Conference call starting," Graham eagerly shouted.

Bob and Kate both picked up headsets and joined in.

"Hi, Brent Lowery, NNSA," Brent announced, followed by, "Rear Admiral Mike Choe, US Navy..." The intros on the call paraded on.

There were about twenty people conferenced, including Bob and Kate, reps from the navy, NNSA, US Department of State, NRO, and several others. Brent from the NNSA gave the immediate debrief.

"Approximately zero seven hundred hours, local time, a US Navy EP-3 electronic warfare aircraft, code-named ARIES, on a sweep mission for Operation nine-one-two, identified a target, a Marshall Island–flagged freighter sailing southward in the East China Sea, approximately forty miles from the Chinese mainland coast. The target registered with excess activation effect returns." Brent paused after the initial description, and then continued.

"Now what does that mean in English? The EP-3 aircraft do not have the equipment with the same sensitivities as the specialized AMS aircraft, however, there are some identifying signatures they can pick up. One of them is called an activation effect. This occurs when fast neutrons that are thrown off in the radioactive decay process from a material, such as plutonium, impact other surrounding materials. Those surrounding materials are reciprocally affected such that they react in detectable ways. This is an event we can identify with the instruments on the ARIES. I'll pause here." Brent stopped.

Kate unmuted herself and asked, "Brent, Kate Harrison, CIA, thank you for that. What's your confidence level this is a plutonium source?"

"A plutonium-based source is our most likely candidate—good confidence. We're not up close and personal, but not many other elements can produce this specific signature," Brent replied to her and continued. "Also, these returns only appear in a very limited section of the target ship's stern, something consistent with an illicit cargo hidden in one isolated compartment of a ship."

Kate narrowed her eyes at Bob on hearing that. Brent then finished up.

"Our conclusion, and, based on the other evidence collected so far in this operation, is that we are tracking some radioactive contraband material in violation of UN Resolution 1718," Brent finished.

There was a brief silence on the line, and then the admiral spoke up.

"Bob, ball is in your court. I've ordered the USS *Mustin*, she's an Arleigh Burke, and the USS *Essex*, a helicopter carrier, to turn west toward the freighter," the admiral informed.

Bob responded. "We have three options. One, send the thing to the bottom of the East China Sea, two, destroy the materials in situ, which would likely cripple the ship, or three, an interdiction. Any of these will require POTUS sign-off—"

Kate tapped the desk in front of him to get his attention. Bob covered the receiver to hear her, and she whispered to him, "We *want the device*. That's first choice. We need to confirm what it is, and the political capital of having this—"

Bob raised his hand for her to stop. Kate was shrewd as hell. She knew the Washington game and what was really valuable. He resumed his response.

"Our first choice would be an interdiction. I'm preparing a brief for the DCI so he can get POTUS approval. We should have a formal directive by twenty-three hundred at the latest—"

Kate motioned to a map to remind Bob about the Chinese territory issue.

"Admiral, we need to keep your assets beyond immediate visibility. If we scare them into Chinese territorial waters, we lose all options, clear?"

"Clear. I'll order standoff distance, but track," the admiral concurred.

The conference call ended, and they all hung up. A few moments later, the redheaded Graham came over to them. He had a bunch of notes on a pad and started reading them to Kate and Bob.

"The freighter is called the *Alder*. It's in our databases. It's Marshall Island flagged, a 190-meter bulk cargo ship—bags of cement, steel rebar, barrels of slag, anything. It left the Chinese Yalu River port of Dandong two days ago. Our sources are reporting a shipment of rebar and—"

"Destination?"

"Oh, uh—Singapore," he answered.

"Dandong? Pull that up on the monitor," Kate yelled out to the media operator, who keyed into his PC until a map of North Korea, Northern China, and the Yalu River appeared on the newly hung wall monitor. The map zoomed in on the city of Dandong, which was on the Chinese side of the Yalu River, and on the Yellow Sea.

Kate asked Sarah, "You have that map from earlier?"

Sarah nodded and unrolled her map across their table. She pointed to Dandong and traced an imaginary line with her finger that traversed the north Yellow Sea and then hugged the Chinese coast southward. She then shuttled her finger between the freighter's position and the Honggon-do fishing pier in North Korea where they believed the bomb was transferred.

"Looks like we might have had a ship-to-ship," Sarah said the obvious.

Kate faced Lieutenant Junior Grade Graham with a satisfied grin.

"You did good."

Kate and Bob relocated to Bob's office to prep for the ODNI and POTUS brief.

"This is a pickle," Bob initiated.

"We need to be prepared for a take-out, too," Kate insisted. "If we see that ship turn—I mean, we can't let that fall into Chinese hands," she fretted.

"It is a sign they don't know yet, the Chinese, I mean. They would have interdicted the freighter themselves by now if they knew," Bob added. Kate was more skeptical.

"It won't be long before they find out and that thing disappears. You're right, if they knew, it'd be gone. This is a ticking clock. We need to get our hands on it. I mean, the intel value—"

"It would be a trump card in the six-ways. It gets buried quick if it disappears, I get it," Bob finished her sentence.

"If that ship tacks west, we have to hit the thing immediately," she repeated.

"Means we need to develop a backstory. The Chinese'll wonder—if they don't catch us in the act—why the hell a freighter sank near their coast in a mysterious explosion. It'll stink. POTUS and State will need to be prepped for that. I need to get the director's thoughts on that part of it, too," Bob considered.

Kate observed her watch and exhaled anxiously.

"We want eyes on this. In fact, we may want to be in charge," she stated.

"You know—"

"I *know* what that means—time to involve DO, and SAD," Kate admitted. "I know some senior people we can trust. We can do it without alerting CTC to this mess," she calculated.

SAD was the Special Activities Division, a key unit in the DO. SAD was the CIA's own special forces group that operated in the most secretive and dangerous missions—ones the US government could invoke plausible deniability if any were ever compromised.

Within SAD, it was the SOG (Special Operations Group) that ran the force of operatives. SOG was one of the most elite units in the world, recruiting from the military's SPECFOR teams, like Delta Force, the Navy SEALs, Army Rangers, and so on, and layering CIA training on top of that. The SOG ops, PMOOs (paramilitary operations officers) or SSOs (specialized skill officers), as they were called, could operate solo or as part of larger commands, joining or leading Delta Force soldiers or Navy SEALs or even detachments of foreign armies.

"We may have more air cover than you think. They're really not looking this way yet. The director was curious, but they have a hundred other ops they're juggling." Bob sat on the sofa, and his eyes scanned the floor in thought. "And you're right, we need someone from SAD we can trust. I think I might know a guy, a good operator. I'll talk to him before I raise it with the director, tell him we need to keep this quiet. He'll get it," he said.

Kate forcefully added, "That freighter's going to enter the Taiwan Strait in a few hours. Once it's there, we lose it. We can't pull off anything there, which means we have a very limited window—three hours to put an interdiction team together," Kate pressed Bob, who remained seated in thought. He didn't immediately address her statement, he just kept thinking aloud.

"And the director will want to hear motive. We have no motive yet—Dr. Ahn got anything?" he asked Kate as he lifted his eyes back to her.

Kate shook her head *no*.

"I can bullshit him on that part of it, say we have some leads. Let's go with the corrupt members of the military with profit motive. I'll keep the *T* word out of it for as long as I can. It'll be enough to get POTUS, DNI, and NSC attention on it for op approval—I can say that's our working theory, which it is, and that we're networking to verify it but don't have anything hard yet," Bob meandered.

"Stop worrying about the motivation. We have to focus on getting this thing—these materials—out of circulation. Press 'em on that. They can't wriggle out of that," she plainly reminded him.

"Right, you're right." Bob paused and looked at Kate, who was looking back at him, still awaiting a response from two questions back.

"The interdiction team. When I speak to Admiral Choe, I'll request a SEAL team. There's one in Yokosuka at the ready," Bob said.

"*After*, you speak to SAD," Kate impatiently prompted, jabbing the chair with her knuckles for emphasis.

Bob grinned at her and snapped his fingers.

"I know—Terry Scanlon—he's a senior officer, runs a full deployment group over there. He's good, knows the best people."

"I know Terry. He'd be perfect for this," Kate agreed.

Bob nodded. "Call him. And tell him we want someone good to lead a SEAL team. Someone who won't fuck things up," Bob said.

Kate smiled at Bob's response, the one she wanted to hear. She left to go make the calls.

Commander Fleet Activities Yokosuka, Yokosuka, Japan

Inside a naval aviation unit briefing room, a platoon of sixteen US Navy SEALs filled the chairs downloading orders from their CMC (Command Master Chief).

The platoon he was briefing was from SBT-12 (special boat team). These were SEALs profiled for MIOs (Maritime Interception Operations), precisely the job Kate and her team needed. The SEALs, veteran warriors, steely-faced and serious, ingested each word from their CMC as he went over the action.

"VBSS, this is *your* profile," the CMC started.

A VBSS was a visit, board, search and seizure operation, one of the profiles SBTs specialized in.

"There is a one-hundred-ninety-meter freighter currently bearing south in the Yellow Sea. We're looking at a FRIES assault from a Seahawk HAF off a destroyer," the CMC went on, pointing to a still photograph of the freighter displayed on a wall-mounted screen. FRIES stood for "fast rope insertion and extraction" from a HAF, or "helicopter assault force."

The CMC eyed his briefing doc, clicking his pen several times before continuing with the instruction.

"That's about all that's *standard* with this assault." The command master chief looked up and paused, his gaze inspecting his SEALs before he revealed, with strict professionalism, their true objective.

"We have a broken arrow that is being transported aft on that target freighter. This is a violation of United Nations resolution seventeen eighteen. On the main deck of the freighter are four derrick masts. They are a hazard. Be alert on insertion. As such, the helos will drop you from a greater height—fifty yards, to be safe. This means harder landing. The derricks can also swing out and interfere with the ropes." He paused again and adjusted his stance, lowered his gaze to his clipboard, clicked his pen a few more times, and then looked back up at the SEALs as he continued.

"We estimate two dozen crew. We do not know the level of hostility. Expect CQB, expect anything. You're going in hot. You are enforcing a United Nations resolution; full deadly force authorization." The CMC paused once more and then continued, "Your op will be led by an OGA PMOO, and you will also be responsible for two NNSA specialists. They will scan the ship and verify any radiological source. Once insertion is complete and the ship has been secured, you will escort the Nuclear Emergency Support Team throughout the vessel to locate and neutralize the materials or device."

The SEAL command master chief then emphatically raised his voice.

"Objective one, disable the device or secure the materials and take possession of whatever you can and return it to your staging craft. If that is not possible, your goal will be to permanently neutralize the device and materials, leaving the Alder otherwise intact. If neither of those is possible, you will deliver a system-level failure to the entire vessel." The CMC turned his back to the team.

"This is a nuclear or radiological device, an IND. There is the possibility for radiation release. There is the possibility of a fissile event, either deliberate or accidental. Obey your SOG op and the NEST techs at all times. Understood?"

As cold as ice, they nodded, a few replying, "Aye, *sir*."

The CMC turned back to face them, and finally, with a barely detectable half smirk, finished his brief.

"Your insertion is Yokosuka to the USS *Mustin* currently in the East China Sea. You know her and Captain Penha. Captain Penha's expecting you. You'll meet your SOG mission commander when you arrive on board. Good luck."

Noriko's Noodle House, Toshima City, Tokyo, Japan

Commander Ken Kelso sat hunched over on a barstool, slurping noodles with chopsticks, squeezed amid three others doing the same in the tiny shop. His broad-shouldered frame barely fit in between the two much slighter Japanese patrons on either side of him, so much so that Kelso even respectfully kept his left arm awkwardly at his side so it wouldn't consume any of his neighbor's space as they all politely slurped from their bowls.

Kelso was enjoying his latest quaff when his cell phone buzzed. With a deft twist, he extracted himself from the counter, leaving his bowl, and stepped outside.

"Yeah?" He answered in a whisper. And listened closely for several moments.

"When?" he asked of the speaker on the other end. "I understand." He tilted his wrist and eyed his watch.

"I will see them shortly," Kelso said in a calm, unemotional voice.

He hung up and, in a reverse of his stealthy evacuation from his seat the moment before, reinserted himself onto his stool. He stared down into his bowl and glanced at his watch again. Better finish and not insult the staff at Noriko's, rather than obey the emergency order he had just been given. He calculated he could slurp his remaining noodles in moments and still make the C-17 that was now awaiting him at Yokota Air Base.

Kelso was an operative in the CIA's Special Operations Group. SOGs lived in a deeply shadowed world, being tapped only for the most secretive and sensitive operations. They were ununiformed agents that could be brought into the highest-stakes gambits like assassinations, *or* to secure lost or stolen nuclear weapons.

Originally a Navy SEAL from DEVGRU (Development Group), Kelso lived with his Japanese wife in Tokyo and covered the Northeast Asian sector for the CIA. His job was to be a fucking ghost for the US government, unseen and unheard—get in, do the job, and get out. He was on call around the clock. He could be eating noodles one minute and parachuting in behind enemy lines the next hour. There were fewer than two hundred CIA SOG operators in existence.

Kelso eyed his watch again. He inhaled his last round of noodles and then swilled the remaining broth from the bottom of the bowl. He gave a short head bow to the server behind the bar and edged out of the tight array of patrons. He exited Noriko's and hailed a cab...

Operation 912 Task Force Center

It was close to midnight. The assault force was assembled, briefed, and staged on the USS *Mustin* in the South China Sea, awaiting their go order. Kate's speakerphone chimed on. It was the director.

"We have sign-off. This thing's gotta go down quietly, you understand? We don't want to alert the Chinese. Or anybody else, for that matter."

"Got it." Kate depressed the Off button.

They were back at 912 in moments. Several new individuals were now present, including a senior SAD officer, Terry Scanlon, who was responsible for the SOG operations. He greeted Bob and Kate with a bated look as they entered.

Bob sat down at his seat and uttered a single word to Terry: "Approved."

And Terry picked up his phone.

"Nine-one-two, operation magnet, go. Repeat, go. Copy?" Scanlon relayed.

A muffled and slightly delayed, "Copy, sir," responded.

Terry put down his phone and uttered, "We're underway."

DDG-89, USS *Mustin*, Arleigh Burke–Class Destroyer, South China Sea

Inside the helicopter bay, Commander Kelso, armored in gray fatigues with a black tactical combat vest and helmet, clipped his HK MP5 submachine gun onto his belt, tugging it twice to ensure it was secured. The SBT platoon earlier briefed at Yokosuka were in the hangar as well, now all similarly kitted up. Two NEST field techs, lugging radiation detection gear, lined up with the squad.

Kelso approached and inspected the NEST techs' rigging. He rattled their instruments several times to test they wouldn't drop or get damaged during the fast-rope insertion process. They both looked at Kelso for reassurance.

"Stay close to me," Kelso ordered them.

He about-faced to the SEAL platoon and saluted the platoon chief. Kelso, being a former SEAL himself, was confident taking SEAL teams into any op.

The nineteen of them trotted out of the hangars onto the edge of the aft helo pad. The first of two SH-60s was readying, its blades whipping around in an accelerating spin. Ten SEALs boarded the first helo. The Seahawk's rotors flung to full speed, and it elevated off the pad straight into the air.

The second SH-60 was wheeled out of its bay and its blades were unfolded. The pilots fired up the Seahawk's engines, and Kelso, the two NEST techs, and rest of the SEALs boarded. They lifted off and joined the first helo hovering over the water. The two Seahawks shot off like bullets, sprinting toward their quarry, the *Alder* freighter.

Kelso watched the USS *Mustin* shrink to a dot below and vanish behind him. He squeezed a quick-attach-detach suppressor onto the barrel of his MP5. His focus shifted out the open bay and toward their target, which was now coming into view.

The *Alder* freighter was coursing along in the open water at an even twelve knots. Both Seahawks approached from starboard, and abruptly rose into the air and braked, hovering almost motionless above the freighter. The first SH-60 positioned over midships, and the second Seahawk hovered over the bow.

Inside the cockpit of the first Seahawk, an EWO engaged signal-jamming that sprayed the ship with anti-cellular and anti-satellite communication static. The radio noise impaired the *Alder's* navigation systems, blinding its bearings and stopping signal transmissions.

Half a dozen ropes unraveled from the side bays of the hovering helos, bombing the deck of the *Alder*. The ropes were threaded through harnesses on the SEAL's utility vests. Two at a time, the SEALs plumbed down the lines and impacted the *Alder's* deck. Kelso hitched up the two NEST techs and shoved them out the bay and then zipped down after the last of them.

All nineteen dropped onto the freighter in seconds. The *Alder's* captain, alarmed at what was happening, had cut off the ship's engines, and the freighter was now drifting with the sea's currents.

Four SEALs fanned out along the foredeck, MP5s leveled. They secured the forepart of the ship, yelling out, "All clear, forward." Others covered midships and the main deck, herding the crewmen against the superstructure bulkhead. Kelso and three more SEALs raced up ladders toward the bridge.

Guns leading, they burst into the pilothouse. The captain, the navigator, and two crewmen threw up their hands, terrified at the sudden assault. Two of the SEALs took control of the freighter's bridge and its navigation. SBTs were trained to know how to pilot virtually any waterborne craft, from small motorboats to large VLCC tankers and everything in between.

Kelso pushed the captain and the other three crewmen against the rear bulkhead of the bridge.

"Filipino?" Kelso shouted at the captain.

The captain nodded tightly. Kelso addressed him in broken Tagalog.

"Manifest? Where's the ship's manifest?"

The captain motioned to a metal box affixed to the side bulkhead. Kelso gestured to one of the SEALs, who pulled it open and revealed a thick clipboard inside. The SEAL flipped through its sheets, consuming their details.

"Official lading, looks like a bunch of steel and cement bound for Singapore. Origin was a factory in Dandong, China," the SEAL read off the clipboard.

The third SEAL bound the captain's and the three other crewmen's hands behind their backs with plastic zip ties. Kelso signaled to the SEALs, *secure*, and he moved out of the bridge and jumped down the ladder to the quarterdeck where the two NNSA technicians were assembling their detection equipment.

"We're set," one tech announced. Kelso motioned for two other SEALs to escort them as they scanned the ship.

They started scanning amidships first, but it wasn't long before one of their detectors picked up a hotter spot toward the stern. The team crept in formation toward the concentrated readings. Kelso and the guard SEALs followed the techs, to a location aft port side near the bridge island bulkhead.

They arrived to see a deflated tarp that appeared like it had been ripped off something and left like a dropped bedsheet. One of the techs waved his Geiger counter up and down and side to side. He zoned in on the tarp. He kicked part of it away and hovered the Geiger counter over the deck steel. Kelso impatiently watched him.

"Commander, something was here," he finally reported to Kelso.

"What do you mean, *was*?" Kelso demanded.

"Activation effect. The detection returns we're getting are consistent with the decay of radioactive material into the surrounding area, but not the material itself," the NNSA technician explained.

Kelso didn't like the sound of that. He had to confront that they might have arrived too late to the party and that their quarry was one step ahead of them.

"You certain?"

The other tech agreed with his colleague. He scraped a few chips of rusted metal from the bulkhead and the deck into a leaded vial.

"Scan the rest of the ship, see if whatever was here was stashed elsewhere," Kelso ordered the techs.

Kelso himself moved to the quarterdeck of the freighter and peered over the transom railing. He eyed the sea slapping against the lower stern of the vessel. His gaze lifted, and he scanned the horizons. He pulled a small pair of binoculars from his vest and searched the sea in a sweeping, edge-to-edge turn.

Not seeing what he wanted, he stepped to the port side, leaned over the rail, and examined the ship's superstructure, searching. All appeared in order there, so he repeated this on the starboard side. There—he spotted it.

On the superstructure, two levels above the main deck, Kelso eyed a pair of davits, swinging unfastened from their berth. He leaned farther out over the side, almost risking his pitching into the water to confirm his suspicion.

Those davits and winches were for lowering the ship's lifeboats. Kelso counted; the ship should have had two on each side. But there was only one on the starboard side.

Kelso bounded back up to the bridge and flew into the pilothouse. The two SEALs were helming the freighter, maintaining its vitals and headings. He bent down to the captain who was seated on the floor, arms still bound. Kelso yanked him to his feet.

"Where's the ship's event log?"

The captain stared back at him with a puzzled look. Kelso repeated himself.

"Event log? Was there a rescue event?"

The two SEALs eyed Kelso, unclear of what he was doing. One of them grabbed the manifest clipboard and showed it to Kelso.

"Straight voyage. Loaded. Departed. Clear weather. No crew events," the SEAL recapped the log. "Commander, what are you looking for?"

Kelso didn't look at the SEAL. His eyes bored into the captain. In a second, Kelso flung out his Pup knife, a five-inch gleaming, partially serrated steel blade, and raised it to the captain's face. The SBTs exchanged worried glances. They both gripped their MP5s to be ready. These SOG guys could be crazy, they knew.

The captain's eyes widened in fear, and he cried out as Kelso rotated him, and with a single, swift cut with his knife, severed the plastic ties that bound his hands.

"Come with me," Kelso ordered, pushing the captain out of the bridge.

"Down," Kelso directed, and the captain climbed down the ladder and jumped to the next level. They wound down one more deck, and Kelso prodded him starboard, where they had a clear view of the lifeboats.

Kelso grabbed the captain by the back of the collar and thrust him, head and torso over the railing.

"No!" the captain screamed, feeling Kelso was going to toss him overboard until his eyes caught the two swinging davit skids and the empty berth. His expression slackened to one of surprise. Kelso eyed these changes closely, clear lie detectors, he could tell the captain wasn't aware of this development. He was genuinely alarmed himself at the missing lifeboat. Kelso pulled the captain back onto the deck. The captain, now getting it, shook his head.

"I—I don't know. Two boats, each side," the captain pleaded to Kelso.

"You confirm you left with four, total?" Kelso demanded. The captain nodded tightly with wide eyes and even peered over the side again to check his disbelief.

"Which crewmen know how to operate these davits?" Kelso led the captain toward the crew on the main deck.

As they arrived, the captain pointed at two crewmen—the two who'd assisted the Syrians—who were smoking under guard of the SEALs. The two crewmen shot each other a look when the captain made them.

Kelso pulled the cigarettes from their mouths and ordered them both toward the lifeboat berths. They walked reluctantly, with Kelso jabbing them several times to keep them moving.

As they approached the ladder to ascend to the upper deck, the first crewman spun around and pulled a knife from his belt. He lunged at Kelso as the second crewman tried to grab Kelso's weapon in a simultaneous ambush.

Kelso dodged the knife thrust with a blinding switch, pulled his MP5 from over his head, and pumped three rounds into the knife-wielding attacker. The shot crewman careened backward, arms flailing, and dropped to the metal deck into a motionless pile. The second crewman barely had time to react before the muffled report of a burst of rounds punched through his neck, jaw, and chest. He fell face-forward like a log.

"Fuck!" Kelso cursed under breath. He reversed to see if any on deck had witnessed the skirmish, but they were not in line of sight. Kelso studied both the dead crewmen. He eyed what they were wearing, and he went through their pockets. He searched their faces for any clue as to where they'd come from. Kelso pushed the bodies aside to ensure they were out of sight.

A few moments later, Kelso was back on the main deck. He gave instructions to the sentinel SEALs to get everyone onto the bridge. He also ordered two other SEALs to get some body bags, told them where to locate the bodies and that they were to be returned to the *Mustin* to be autopsied and scrutinized for clues as to their identities.

The NEST techs reappeared on deck and approached Kelso.

"Commander, there's nothing here. We scanned the entire ship," the first tech announced, to which Kelso plainly responded, "Follow me."

Kelso brought the two techs to the empty lifeboat berth and asked them to scan it. They hurriedly ran their detectors up and down over the access gangway. They glanced at each other after reviewing the readings and quickly did the math.

"They took it," one tech confirmed out loud.

"I'm thinking this was a temporary stop and they're gonna keep it moving. All the crew are accounted for, and I think there were two aboard who were helping the mules. They came and went, and so did the target," Kelso theorized. Both techs concurred with nods.

"Whatever was here wasn't here that long ago. Few hours, tops," one said.

"*What*, what was here?"

"Weapons-grade plutonium, my best guess," one of them answered.

The other added, "Based on the radionuclides, it may be either just a core, or a working weapon disassembled. It's not well shielded, which is why we're able to track its decay products," he said.

Kelso eyed them with some angst. They moved to the next berth where the SEAL platoon chief and an additional SEAL joined them.

"Action phase, over," Kelso declared when they arrived. He turned to the platoon chief. "Get the techs back to the *Mustin* so they can do a proper OPSIT. Take the two vics with you, get some forensics to figure out who they were," he continued.

"Copy that, Commander," the SEAL platoon chief responded.

"High confidence broken arrow or IND on an escaped lifeboat"—he turned to the other SEAL— "what's the speed of one of these things?" An IND was an "improvised nuclear device."

"Eight to twelve knots, sir," the SBT SEAL judged.

"And how far are we from the Chinese coast?"

"About thirty nauticals, give or take."

Kelso turned back to the platoon chief. "The mules are most likely within Chinese territorial waters now. Tell them we need imagery." He paused and then looked at one of the NEST techs.

"What's your best equipment for spotting this thing at a distance?"

The first technician grabbed a device that resembled a professional movie film camera that sat on a shoulder with an eyepiece.

"This," he answered. "It's called a neutron sniffer. It picks up fast neutron densities that are being ejected by plutonium. Works up to about five hundred meters. Just aim it at your target," he finished.

Kelso grabbed the neutron sniffer and cranked open the hatch to the lifeboat. He tossed in his pack, his gun, and the neutron sniffer and then stepped in after.

"Commander, what are you doing?" the platoon chief begged.

"Relay I'm in now theater," he started. "Close me in and lower me down," he ordered the special boat SEAL. "After I'm away, get this ship back on its course. Tell the captain we had to arrest the two crewmen."

The SEAL tightly shut the hatch, sealing Kelso inside. The others helped with the davit winches, and they lowered the craft onto the water and detached its mooring ropes where it bounced and teetered with the swelling seas below.

The lifeboat started up its motor and pulled away from the freighter, rocking in a jagged line with the waves in the direction of the Chinese coast...

Kyle's Apartment, Ritz-Carlton Residences

Kyle lounged on his living room sofa, watching TV in his boxers, glass of scotch in hand. The TV was tuned to the financial channel and was replaying the day's earlier segment recaps.

"Equities closed lower today, the S&P 500 sold off as sentiment about the slowing economy and weakness in the previously hot subprime mortgage sector worried markets ahead of Wednesday's Federal Reserve Open Market Committee meeting. The sell-off was also exacerbated by a terrorist attack on an oil pipeline in Turkey, which sent the price of crude oil higher by more than two dollars..." the business channel newscaster read.

Kyle glanced at his watch. It was almost one a.m. Pete and Sully had since left, and Kyle thought he should probably be getting to bed. But something bothered him, and he dwelled on it as he watched the market recaps. He stared at the crawler drag across the bottom of the television screen. He visually zoomed in on gold and crude oil prices. *Something doesn't make sense,* he thought.

Usually, Kyle liked it when the markets were ambivalent. Ambivalence meant that assets that usually traded together weren't, that they couldn't agree. Often, this was an opportunity because one or more of those assets was over- or undervalued relative to the other and would soon snap back into line.

He was still upset about the huge crude oil position he had built and been forced to bury. He scowled as he rehashed the day's frustrating events in his mind. He took another swill of scotch, his eyes lingering on the gold and oil prices as they scrolled by.

"A fucking puzzle," he bleated aloud.

Kyle was convinced that his current worldview was the right one. The economy *was* softening, he thought, and reiterated to himself the fundamental truth that crude oil was a product in demand by a *growing* economy, not a slowing one. So, then, why was crude oil trading higher?

"Shouldn't be going up," he answered the television commentator out loud, like a crazy person.

"In other commodities, gold saw a second-day price rise as positioning ahead of Wednesday's Federal Reserve meeting drove buying in the precious metal..." the TV went on.

Kyle sat there, sipping his scotch. He grimaced when the TV reminded him of the gold trade that Sammy the sales trader pitched him earlier. And that just made him more depressed because he thought about his P&L and his family situation.

Still, he couldn't ignore the gold trade. What was that trade about? Everyone expected the Fed would lower interest rates twenty-five basis points. If that happened, Kyle thought, gold was fairly priced where it currently was, at $705. Even if the Fed lowered by fifty basis points, or even seventy-five, which would never occur, gold still wouldn't move by *that* much.

Kyle mockingly shook his head at that idea. Someone betting $50 million gold would make a $100 move in a week was ludicrous. Part of him wanted to ring the cash register and grab the easy money to erase his loss. The other part of him was paranoid as hell about the trade. It stunk. It shot up all sorts of red flags.

His mind drifted back to his FBI days. He smiled, recalling right after 9/11 how he became a paranoid agent, suspecting anyone, and would hassle his superiors to get this or that warrant because he *was convinced* a target was planning some terrorist attack. Ironically, paranoia was his special ability in trading. It gave Kyle a sixth sense and forced him to think about outlier risks and so-called black swan events, which happened far more often in reality than financial probability models predicted.

Kyle fell into a haze. He thought about his daughter, Jill, and he thought about getting his family back together. He also remembered the fights he used to have with Amy over his drinking. That only upset him more thinking about it.

He eyed his almost-empty tumbler and took his final gulp for the night.

Operation 912 Task Force Center

The center had thinned. It was late, but intelligence and covert ops were a twenty-four-hour business. Bob and Kate, both looking drained and dehydrated, huddled over a speakerphone with their analysts and officers. JSOC (Joint Special Operations Command) was on the phone debriefing the task force on the interdiction op.

"No device was located, repeat, no target recovered. However, NNSA reports with high confidence that either a fissile plutonium core, disassembled weapon, or

IND had been stowed on an aft location of the vessel, hours prior to the interdiction." The rep paused. Kate looked at Bob and shook her head, *not good.* The JSOC rep continued.

"There was also evidence that two rogue crew members had accompanied the package on board and had escaped with the contraband. A shipboard lifeboat was found to be missing—"

"Christ!" Kate exclaimed. Even though the JSOC rep wasn't finished with the debrief, Kate pulled Sarah over to their original map on the table behind them.

"Draw. Where?" was all Kate could utter, but Sarah understood and began penciling out what had apparently occurred. Kate helicoptered over Sarah, studying her every pencil mark on the map.

"This is—this is what happened," Sarah described, gesturing fiercely at it. Kate motioned for Bob to come over and inspect.

On the map, Sarah had sketched a jagged line that paralleled the Chinese coast showing the track of the freighter. She had highlighted a zone on that path representing when the mules most likely escaped—with the IND on board.

"Those things probably move ten knots, max, and would be subject to whatever currents there are," Sarah said and then indicated a widening arc toward the Chinese coast with her hand.

"They could be anywhere in this zone about now. Sometime in the next hour or two they land on the Chinese coast, along here."

Kate squinted at it, skeptically assessing the motivations of the mules.

"This doesn't make any sense," she complained to them. "Why would they bring it *into* the Chinese mainland?"

"We have to inform State. And they'll need to cable China straightaway."

"Bob—?" Kate stopped herself, being in front of the junior analysts.

"The director's going to love this," Bob whined. "And just wait 'til POTUS hears it. How could we fuck this up?"

Kate stepped back and pondered.

"I don't think we did. I think the escape was planned—but I can't surmise why. Why would you risk entering Chinese territory?" Kate posed again.

"We can't get at it," Sarah cleverly noted.

"Right. We can't get at it there," Kate agreed.

They were interrupted when Terry Scanlon, the SAD officer, pulled them aside, away from others and out of earshot of the analysts.

"There's another detail: The SOG op who led the interdiction grabbed a lifeboat off that freighter. He's now headed to the Chinese coast to track the target," he whispered.

Kate and Bob exchanged shocked looks. But then a slight hint of satisfaction appeared on Kate's face.

"This thing's getting out of control!" Bob raged. "I need to get some air."

He stormed out of the op center. Kate inclined her head to Terry, trying to hide her contentment.

Terry implored Kate, "We need eyes, overheads, anything. We need to figure out where this lifeboat lands. We can't direct our man without it."

"We're on it," Kate happily replied, and was already beckoning over the NRO rep. She regarded Scanlon with her sidelong look. "This guy good?" she asked.

"One of our best," he replied with an affirming smile.

Coastal Marsh, Rudong County, China

The two Syrians, inside their lifeboat, testily kicked the floor as they glared outside the front portal. They were about a thousand meters from the coastline, and the craft had become stuck, running aground in the muddy tidal zone.

"We're done. Tide's out," the taller one admitted.

The shorter one had already concluded that and was forcing open the side hatch. His partner joined him, and together they bashed it open, each of them squeezing outside and sinking knee deep into the muddy Chinese coastal marshes.

Hoisting himself back inside the craft, the shorter one removed a hammer from the boat's survival kit and serially smashed each rivet that fastened the top cover to the hull. The two braced against the floor and strained to break the top half free from the shell. As it separated, they maneuvered the cover above their heads and gave it a strong heave, casting the boat top into the marsh. It flooded with muddy water and subsided into the muck, out of sight.

They slogged to the stern and, with whatever leverage they could produce in the mud, shouldered the craft forward. Reluctantly, it released, and they began to make progress toward the shore ahead.

Dusk was settling in, which also helped them to remain unseen. The Syrians spied a low screen of trees on the shoreline. With a hundred meters to go, their footing at last became more solid, but the lifeboat stubbornly lodged in for good.

They pulled their packs and hoisted the heavy bomb cases out of the vessel and finally abandoned it altogether, concealing the hull as much as they could with water and marsh grasses.

The Syrians dragged the bomb boxes up the bank and burrowed into the copse of trees to hide. It had become almost completely dark. The shorter one switched on a flashlight, the beam loudly brightening the grove around them.

"Off, off! Turn it off!" the taller one scolded him, after which they were blanketed in darkness again.

Inside the brush, the two Syrians removed their clothes. Stripping down completely naked, they cleaned themselves with water bottles and rags. The short one fumbled in their packs and extracted two dry-cleaned business suits, still wrapped in the dry cleaner's plastic. They fitted on clean underwear and socks, and then dressed in their business suits, even threading their neckties through their collared shirts, and helping each other tie the knots in the darkness. Lastly, they each stepped into a pair of spit-polished wingtip dress shoes.

After fifteen minutes, two respectable-looking Syrian businessmen emerged from the shoreline woods, business backpacks over their shoulders, pulling three large roll-aboard carrying cases behind them. They could be business travelers at any international airport.

In the dead of night with little visibility, they hauled themselves and their "luggage" across acres of flat farmland. In the distance, along a nearby country road, they spotted the halo of lights from a local shore town. The two glanced at each other with some relief and made their way toward the glow, keeping to the edge of the farmland road.

East China Sea, Coastal Waters North of Nantong, China

Commander Kelso urged the small lifeboat forward at its maximum speed as it bounced and bobbed in the seas off the Chinese coast. He squinted out the narrow front portal through his set of binoculars, searching.

In the nighttime darkness, he was able to identify a segment of shoreline, in between two bands of faintly glowing regions he knew were towns or settlements. With one eye on his handheld GPS, he calculated where he could make landfall.

The waters were becoming thicker as he entered the sticky coastal marshes, slowing the boat in the increasing density. Kelso forced the craft deeper into the boggy wetlands until it finally ran aground. He revved the motor several times but knew from its clogging sounds, it was finished. He killed the engine and sat still for a few moments, appraising his position.

He opened the emergency kit and fished through it, grabbing anything that was both light and useful, stuffing the items into his SEAL pack. He wrapped the neutron sniffer inside two plastic bags and cinched them with zip ties.

Kelso struck open the hatch and exited the lifeboat, carrying his pack, MP5, and the neutron sniffer over his shoulder. He splashed down into the knee-deep mud and gripped the portal edges of the craft, rocking it up and down several times; finally getting enough momentum, he rolled the thing onto its top, reducing its profile and making it more difficult to spot. Kelso turned and waded through the marshes toward the shore…

Tuesday, September 18, 2007

Kyle's Apartment, Ritz-Carlton Residences

A hazy gray early-morning light crowded into Kyle's bedroom. His alarm blared and his hand smacked it off. Six a.m. Kyle lay there, his eyes still closed, his mind foggy, hungover, craving more sleep. He rolled over, sat up, and looked around the room. Gradually, he stood, and as he rose, images of the depressing events from the previous day reappeared. Kyle soured and flicked on the TV.

Financial channel droning in the background, he brushed his teeth, half listening to the morning report. "…the S&P 500 futures are plunging this morning, down over thirty points as fears of a slowing economy grow. Markets might be sending a signal to the Federal Reserve, which meets tomorrow. Traders expect a quarter-point rate cut to offset those risks… In commodities, crude oil continues to climb this morning, up almost a dollar to eighty-two dollars per barrel, following continued stability jitters after a terrorist attack crippled a major crude oil pipeline in eastern Turkey yesterday. Overnight, US Central Command in Iraq and OPEC oil ministers made separate statements that they couldn't rule out further attacks. Pentagon sources also indicated that the level of chatter on more oil field and infrastructure targets has been increasing, although they were quick to caution that nothing specific had been identified and that this was typical after an attack, as other groups boasted in sympathy. A DHS spokesperson said the terror threat level in the United States remains unchanged, at yellow, or elevated…"

"That's bullshit," Kyle muttered at the TV as he finished getting ready.

Fortnum Bank Equities Trading Floor

Kyle strode onto the trading floor and made his way to his desk to find Pete waiting for him with his coffee.

"What. Up?" Pete greeted.

"Hey, the Spoo, what we thinking?" Kyle questioned, grabbing his coffee.

Spoo was the trader nickname for the front-month S&P 500 futures contract, currently for September, with the *U* expiration code. The *SPU* shorthand had, over time, become the nickname for the active S&P 500 futures contract.

"Seems rattled, doesn't it? I didn't see any news. Sully said it was the market trying to get more out of the Fed tomorrow," Pete told him.

"Thanks, I need this," Kyle commented, referring to the coffee. "Probably right," he added, replying to what Sully had told Pete as he set his jacket on the back of his chair and sat, switching on his monitors.

Kyle slumped in his seat, drinking his coffee. He scanned across his array of screens, eyeing charts of the many different markets, all tiled across his monitors.

He shortly zeroed in on the blinking chart of gold, which was green (up), moving higher from the overnight session, up $2.50 per ounce to $707.50. Kyle then sneered at his P&L, locked in the ugly, "-$47,650,000," in painful red.

"Gold's up a couple," Kyle noted out loud.

"First thing you checked, huh? How much tossing and turning you do about the trade last night?" Pete pegged him on it.

"Why you think I need the joe so bad?" He paused. "I'm still on the fence. I like the trade. I don't like the sketchiness of it."

"Either way, we gotta start trading out of this shit," Pete urged, with a little angst in his voice, his bonus not too far from top of mind.

"You comin' around now?"

"Maybe. I'm coming around on doing something to get our bonuses up. I'm not like you, I can't carry a year or two yet."

"Relax. We do this gold trade, or we trade the shit out of something else."

"Said the guy who came to work still half drunk," Pete admonished, his frustration intended.

Kyle gave him a slower, earnest nod, *yes!*

"Where's gold vol now anyway?"

Pete punched it up.

"Looks like the front-month ATMs are about twelve," he referenced. ATM stood for "at the money," which referred to the options with strike prices near to where gold was currently. So, with the price of gold at $707.50, the ATM options would be puts and calls with strikes of $705 or $710 (option strike prices were usually in $1, $5, or $10 increments, depending on the price range of the product). Pete had just quoted Kyle where the October $705 and $710 strike options were trading, at 12 percent implied volatility.

An implied volatility was basically a one-year standard deviation for that asset—or, effectively, what the market believed its future price range would be. The mathematical models that priced options all used what was called a Gaussian, or standard bell curve, distribution to estimate the probabilities of anything—stock prices, or crude oil, or gold, being at a specific price by a specific date. An implied volatility of twelve, or 12 percent, meant the market believed gold's range, in a year, two-thirds of the time, would be up or down 12 percent. So, there was a 67 percent probability that gold would land somewhere between $622 and $792 within a year—or so said the market.

"That where it's been lately?" Kyle asked, referring to where gold's implied volatility had been historically.

"No, it's a bit high, usually trades like eight or maybe ten," Pete reported, meaning 8 percent to 10 percent implied volatility was normal.

"That does seem high. Fed priced in, probably," Kyle replied.

After the markets had opened, Sully dropped by their desk.

"How they let you escape?" Pete chided.

"Can't stay long. I'm getting run over. So much fucking paper flow ahead of Fed," Sully complained.

"Springer, you doing this gold trade or what?" Sully probed, turning to Kyle.

"Why, you want it now, too?"

"Where is Sammy anyway? I shoulda thought he'd camp here overnight. Oh wait, I forgot, he's gotta have his breakfast and take a shit, first. He'll waddle over here at about eleven."

They laughed at Pete's description. Kyle finally answered Sully.

"I don't know. Still mulling it… What's going on with equities this morning? What'd you do?" Kyle changed the subject to the sell-off in stocks.

"I don't know. Hoping it's the Fed. S&P is in free fall. Vols are bid. It's in my face already. I'm always short a ton of gamma going into a Fed meeting, every time. Paper never sells," Sully complained again.

He was referring to the market's dynamic of customers predominantly buying options—protection—ahead of a Federal Reserve meeting, anticipating a sharp move or hedging their books. Since Sully was the dealer, he had to sell those options to the customers, which meant he was short volatility and getting shorter. It was an inventory game. A good flow trader would build up supply ahead of an event like a Fed meeting so they could then work that off as the customers came in. Sully hadn't, or hadn't enough, and was now feeling pain because of it.

"You go through this every FOMC, like us ahead of any OPEC meeting. You'd think you'd learn."

"Gotta get back to the abuse," Sully bid and hopped to his desk.

And no sooner had Sully jogged away, Sammy duckwalked up to Kyle.

"Springer?"

Kyle did a double take. Both he and Pete, at once, yelped, "Ah shit."

"You doing this or what?"

Kyle shook his head. "I don't think so, Sammy."

"Wha—*why not*? This is a layup. I thought you guys had balls?"

Both Kyle and Pete shot Sammy a look of disgust, not at the body-part reference, more at the insult that it was coming from a tool like Sammy.

"Whoa, I didn't mean no offense. I know you guys got 'em, that's why I'm sayin'. Ya know, I can't even see mine anymore," Sammy parried.

"Shit, man, didn't need the fucking picture painted. If I wanted balls, I woulda looked down in the shower this morning," Pete muttered. Kyle grinned, and then switched to Sammy, erasing any friendliness.

"Sammy, who is this guy, anyway?"

"I told you yesterday. Some hedge fund trader. Likes to take shots, big shots," Sammy replied, his hand running nervously along the edge of Kyle's desk.

"You know him?"

"I don't *know* him personally. He comes at me through another broker. I do stuff for him here and there, ya know? Show him stuff, too. But this one, he keeps calling me on. It's a big trade. He knows he's not getting it done any other place. That's why I think you should put him up." Sammy paused, inspecting Kyle, whose poker face revealed nothing. "Shit or get off the pot, man," Sammy insisted.

Kyle bristled. "Fuck off, Sammy. And tell your guy to fuck off, too."

"Aw, come on. *You serious?*"

"We need a big fucking flyswatter for you. Big," Pete stated with his arms outstretched, sizing a giant flyswatter.

"Assholes," Sammy snapped at the both of them and wandered off.

Kyle and Pete exchanged grins. It was a trader's bluff. They were still interested in the gold trade, but they had made Sammy believe they weren't to see how desperate his buyer would become. After the brief entertainment, they both rolled back to their machines and resumed trading.

"I got other first-world problems," Kyle said after a few moments.

"What are you talking about?"

"I'm asking Amy if she wants to grab lunch today. See if she wants to discuss getting back together."

Pete fully rotated toward him with a look of horror for dramatic effect.

"Shit. You kidding? How much scotch *did* you drink last night? I think I need to get Sully back over here, stage an intervention."

"Maybe you're right, it's a big fucking mistake. But I feel like I gotta try, ya know?" Kyle looked at Pete, who was still perplexed. "I know you don't. You'll understand when you get a kid."

"Who says I don't already got one?" Pete added with an impish grin.

Kate Harrison's Office, CIA Headquarters

Kate dozed on her sofa. An occasional snore emitted from her as she managed to get in some winks. A door knock ended that. She stumbled to a weak stand, patting down her clothes and hair, as if she would actually pass for having had a full night's sleep.

"Come in."

Sarah entered.

"You get any sleep?" she asked Kate, to which Kate shrugged her shoulders. "You?"

"A few scraps."

"What do you have?"

"SOG op report. He's convinced they're taking a vehicular route south. Wants us to set up a fence."

Kate perked up at this, shaking her head to loosen the cobwebs.

"Bob in yet?"

Sarah shook her head *no*. "So, we still have a little time."

"Overheads?"

"We identified where they ditched the lifeboat," Sarah replied, nodding.

"Good, let's go check it out, because we have maybe an hour, two tops, before Bob arrives and starts screaming POTUS," Kate said as they exited her office. "You get us—"

"Breakfast?" Sarah anticipated, smiling. "It's there, yes."

They entered the task force room. The large projection screen displayed a coastline map of China, and zoomed insets of the marshes. Captain Carly Bolling, the NRO rep, greeted them.

"Morning, so we think this is the ditched lifeboat," Carly said, lassoing the spot on the map with a laser pointer. The inset displayed an aerial image of the coastal grassland and a pinkish overturned boat top with the outline of what appeared to be the hull lying next to it in the salt marsh.

"These imprints were not present in the reference image from two days ago." She pointed out the film.

"Given the estimated point and time of separation from the *Alder*, and the currents, this is a viable location for them to have landed. Also appears they got stuck, which may have slowed their progress."

Kate stared at the films, quickly waking up. She didn't miss a beat.

"Great eyes. Who the hell found this?" Kate rhetorically complimented them.

"So, if they landed here…" Kate followed, as she approached the projected image, waving her hand over the map. Sarah continued Kate's line of thinking, filling in the specifics.

"This is outside Rudong County. Here's the closest city," Sarah said, tapping that spot on the large screen.

"And where did our SSO land?"

The tech scrolled the map and moused over Kelso's location.

"He hit coast here and reported in from outside of the city of Nantong, here," Sarah informed as Carly zapped the locations with the laser pointer.

"And if they are continuing south, which I would agree with given their maritime path, *and* given they're driving, which are the most likely routes?"

They all peered at the map, and one of the other NRO analysts jumped up and pointed. "It could be this," he said, tracing a snaking yellow line with his finger. "I know that area well," he offered. "This one, China National Highway, number fifteen, or just G15. It's the main route. Follows the coast, all the way down. Goes through Nantong, crosses the Yangtze, ends up in Shanghai," he finished.

"Would they be that crazy?" Kate wondered aloud. "Assuming they're in a hurry and they're calculating that traveling on more populated roads will make them less conspicuous?" she pondered but didn't want to immediately commit to that theory. She padded back and forth by the projection screen as she thought.

"These are all large, urban areas," Sarah stressed.

"It's a big assumption, but let's go with it until we're proven otherwise. Tell the op we want direct surveillance along G15. Eyes on this target. A bridge would be perfect—if they are moving south, here." Kate pointed to the bridge over the Yangtze on G15. "Bridges are choke points. Set up the fence on the other side," Kate instructed, eyeing Scanlon, who was already two steps ahead of her and on his headset with the Beijing station.

Shortly after, Bob was just arriving at his office when Kate barged in. He was initially startled, probably thinking it was going to be a normal day.

"No, it's not a normal day," Kate reminded him.

"What is around here?"

Kate got right to it.

"Bob, we can't inform the Chinese yet."

As he was hanging his coat, he shot her an intransigent look.

"You must be fucking crazy. We can't risk any sort of international catastrophe if we *knew, knew*—that means having prior knowledge, which we do—that there was a broken arrow, or an IND, or whatever fucking radioactive thing, on Chinese sovereign territory and we didn't inform them," Bob fumed.

"They'll find out on their own sooner or later. Think of the reverse. Do you believe they would inform *us* on the timeliest basis? They would want to confirm it first, do their own intel. We're doing the same. Besides, we can be almost certain China is not the destination. It's just a transit point," Kate fired back.

"How the fuck can we be certain of that? No, no, I want to offload responsibility for this thing ASAP. It's China's problem now."

"Bob, you're not thinking of *our* interests. You're thinking of *theirs*, and your own, like the bureaucratic lizard that you are," Kate rebuked. "We move from a position of control to one of being beholden."

"The fuck we do. We're hardly in control now. We're still searching for a thing we don't even know what it is, who's pulling the strings, where it's going." Bob paused, scratching his chin, eyeing Kate's red hair. "And besides, I am thinking of my own interests, yours, too, if you would stop to think for a fucking minute—what if they do find it? Or worse, what if there's an accident? And they found out we knew beforehand?" He gave a slow warning nod for dramatic effect. "Do you have any idea how many investigations? How many congressional inquiries, grand juries? Shit. I don't even want to contemplate," he finished and finally came away from his office closet and sat down at his meeting table.

But Kate was unmoved, steadfast in her plan. "The nanosecond we inform them, they have a dragnet and this thing vanishes. We lose everything—who's behind it, where it's headed, plus the technical intel if we're able to get ahold of it; leverage over the NKs in the six-ways, everything." Kate halted and regarded Bob, who was dwelling somewhat on her imploring, then he posed, "Are you sure your opinion of the CCP isn't coloring your thinking?"

"Of *course*, it is. They funded the North Korean nuclear weapons effort in the first place, goaded the Kims into creating a bomb program, pushed the NKs in between them and us—to use as a cutout in their own strategy of never having to confront us directly." Kate broke off and looked Bob smack in the eyes. "Yes, my assessment of the lying, totalitarian Communist Party of China that has nothing but our own destruction as their aim *is* coloring my thinking on the matter, Bob," Kate asserted, becoming intransigent herself.

Bob echoed with an admitting nod. He did agree to some extent with her strategic assessment of the CCP. Kate had been pushing her superiors, the NSC, the Pentagon, the administration on the dangers of the CCP for some time. She ran the NE APAC sector for the DI; it was her job, expressly her job, to know. She'd seen the intel of what the CCP did to their own people. No rights, no recourse, a human life was worthless to the CCP. They essentially ran a modern-day industrialized slavery operation on a gargantuan scale. Kate had seen the translated intercepts of their multi-decade plan—undermine the social structure in the United States, create internal chaos and divisions, sow dissent among our overseas alliances, achieve technological parity by stealing our intellectual property, build up their military, expand overseas, weaken the US dollar.

The CCP was our number-one intelligence concern as far as she was concerned. The Wars on Terror and Iraq and Afghanistan were *huge* distractions. And the CCP knew that. It was their goal to keep us mired in both wars, spread out across the globe, not investing in military innovation, depleting blood and treasure and *not watching them*. It irked Kate to no end. And she viewed this current broken arrow situation in the context of that larger strategic positioning.

Kate sat at the table across from Bob. "And besides, even if we inform them, who's to say they *will* find it? What if it slips through their net, too? Now we've just ceded all intel as well as tracking and monitoring. It's a double negative for us," she argued.

Bob rubbed his forehead with the back of his hand. He knew he couldn't combat her on pure logic of argument. His only way out was CIA bureaucracy. He played that card.

"This should have been DO from the start. We never should have gotten involved. I don't know how I let you talk me into that." He regarded Kate testily, but then couldn't keep eye contact as he bluffed her. "But it's really that policy is above our paygrade, you *know* that. This is not our call," Bob leveled.

Kate quickly returned a *bullshit* squint. And she wasn't giving up.

"Give us a few more hours, until overnight, local?" she proposed.

Bob looked around, up to the ceiling and outside his window at the accumulating cars in the vast West Parking Lot glinting in the morning sunlight. After his contemplation, he finally returned to her.

"Let's agree we were working on conjecture and wanted some corroborating intel before we informed the Chinese. Got it?"

She acknowledged with a grudging nod and left his office.

Sutong Yangtze River Bridge, Bixi Residential District, China

Kelso and a local CIA operations officer, Jeff Tse, from the Beijing station, who'd been tapped to come assist Kelso, positioned themselves by the base of a bridge pylon. From their vantage, they had both cover under the shadowed bridge recesses, as well as an unobstructed view of the bridge traffic above them.

Kelso eyed the flow of late-evening vehicles through binoculars as he whispered his assessments to Jeff.

"We only need to scan coming this way, toward us," Kelso judged, his eyes pinned to the binocular eyepieces as he dialed the focusing wheel.

"And we don't know for sure if they'll take this route?" Jeff checked.

"What do you want from me? Put yourself in their shoes, how would you go?" Kelso impatiently replied. "Anyway, it'll be a while. I figure there's probably a five-hour watch window, if they do show."

Jeff didn't reply but listened dutifully. Kelso passed him the binoculars, and Jeff peered through the lenses at the coursing traffic above them.

"If I get a hit with this," Kelso started, tapping the neutron sniffer, "I'll describe the vehicle. You need to call it in to your control officer to relay. We need to shadow the thing on the spot, got it?"

The kid nodded, still looking through the spyglasses.

The Sutong Yangtze River Bridge was an elevated viaduct on a string of pillars, ten to thirty meters high, raising the auto traffic high above the Yangtze River and allowing barges and freighters to pass underneath.

"You have our cloak set?" Kelso asked Jeff as he balanced the neutron sniffer on his shoulder. It resembled a professional movie camera, and was also deliberately part of their cover, or cloak, which referred to their cover story.

Jeff held up a pair of badges on neck straps that appeared like commercial video personnel IDs. Kelso grabbed his badge with his free hand and fit it over his head. They were "Canadian filmmakers," shooting a documentary, all approved by the Chinese government. Usually, any filming required a government escort, but that was the genius of Jeff's setup. Jeff was a Canadian documentary filmmaker and ran a small production company in downtown Beijing—and was small enough to avoid their scrutiny.

The neutron sniffer itself had a round, protruding lens in the front; a bulky, box-shaped body behind that; a cylindrical viewfinder with an eyepiece; and a battery compartment at the back. Where it differed—significantly—from an ordinary movie camera was what you saw when peering through the viewfinder. The "camera" still displayed a magnified, lensed view of the world that it was "filming," with the key exception that it registered any fast neutrons from the downfield object the sniffer focused on. There was a red-bar display in the viewfinder that ranged from one bar to ten depending on the density of fast neutrons present around any "filmed" object. Ordinary background readings kept the number of bars at zero or one.

Kelso uncomfortably adjusted the neutron sniffer on his shoulder, pointing it upward at the traffic, and pressing his eye into the eyepiece.

"That thing heavy?"

"Shut up and pay attention," Kelso dictated.

"Sorry." The junior officer obeyed and tilted his head up to focus on the vehicles through the binoculars.

Fortnum Bank Equities Trading Floor

Kyle approached Shirin at her desk.

"Good morning," he blurted with a smile.

She spun toward him, startled, "Kyle? Sorry, I was just looking at something," she commented, turning back to her monitor. "Hey, I've got some stuff to show you," she added vaguely.

"Was hoping you'd say that."

"Let's go to a conference room," she motioned, grabbing her notebook.

They strode into one of the glass-walled conference rooms that surrounded the trading floor. They sat down, and Shirin opened her notebook, her index finger zigzagging down the page searching for the highlights.

"So, um, the only real event you have this week—that could move gold—is, *duh*, the Fed meeting tomorrow. Thursday and Friday, no economic releases that could affect gold. A couple of international numbers, but nothing of consequence, nothing that would impact gold, *at all*, really," she started.

"OK. So, what's the average move in gold when the Fed lowers?"

"Relax, I'm getting to that."

"I heart you," Kyle teased.

She eyed him skeptically over the tops of her rectangular frames.

"Average move in gold on a Fed quarter-point lower, two and a half percent."

"Two and a half percent? So that gets us to—"

"Seven twenty-five," she did in her head, shooting him a resentful look.

"Right, seven oh seven now, Fed lowers, it jumps to seven twenty-five. This guy's betting gold will shoot past eight hundred. So, where's the other seventy-five dollars come from? You plugged in a fifty-basis point move?"

"I did. An emergency meeting or a fifty-basis-point reduction gets you a four percent jump in gold."

"That's…"

"Seven…*thirty*-five," she beat him again, disappointed at the no contest.

"Statistically, if this guy's really playing the Fed, there's no way gold's getting past eight hundred from a cut," Kyle summarized her obvious conclusions.

"Even if there's price follow-through the next couple days after. I looked that up, too—a day, two days, three days after—on average, there's only an additional half percentage point. So, maybe you're talking seven forty by the end of the week if the Fed drops fifty bips and something like, they make a comment the economy's in the tank. I think that's, like, the only path to get there," she added.

Kyle stood up and meandered for a few paces around the end of the table. Shirin watched him with some impatience.

"So, these are the *known* events. What about *unknown* events?" Kyle raised.

Shirin flipped a few pages in her notebook.

"So, for *unknown* events…earthquakes. But only a seven magnitude or higher near a major G7 city gets you a two percent pop."

"Earthquakes, good. And unless this guy's fucking Zeus or something, there's no way he could know of an upcoming earthquake. Wha—"

"Poseidon. Poseidon was the Greek god of earthquakes," she chided.

Kyle cracked a smile. "What else?"

"Anything dollar-cheapening or inflationary. A massive drop in the dollar, there's a reciprocal jump in gold, like, um, large fiscal outlays, deficit spending…"

"Dollar, good, but that, too, equals Fed. Plus the dollar's been kind of strong lately. Doesn't seem dollar related, then. What else?"

"Strikes or closures at major gold mines."

Kyle stopped his pacing and turned to her with raised eyes.

"*That's* interesting," Kyle said, nodding, his expression lighting up. He sat down again. "How much of a move on average for those?"

"No more than two to three percent, *if that*. You'd need like a country-wide strike in South Africa or something."

"Damn, any labor negotiations going bad at any mines right now?"

"Not that I could find." She shook her head.

"I still like this one, though. Could be a mining exec front-running unrest, knows something," Kyle speculated.

"Could be, but unlikely, IMO."

"Anything else?"

"Terrorist attack—" Shirin started, but Kyle quickly interrupted her.

"Terrorist attack?"

"Yes. Gold jumps on these. Three percent, on average, sometimes more. The larger the attack, the larger the jump in the price of gold," she explained.

"The larger the attack, the bigger the pop. How big a move on Nine Eleven?"

"About a ten percent jump. So, applied to gold now, that gets you to about seven eighty," she said, already answering what he was going to ask next.

Kyle stared at her, thinking.

"This fund is playing for a greater than thirteen percent jump. Thirteen percent gets you past eight hundred dollars," Kyle framed. Shirin concurred.

"Using your scale, statistically, would be an attack *larger* than Nine Eleven."

"*If* that's what they're betting on at all," Shirin said. "Remember, this is a remote probability to begin with."

"Yeah, but this hedgie's *betting* on a remote probability."

Kyle let out a tense exhale. He didn't want to contemplate that; 9/11 was terrible and a difficult time for him, personally, not to mention the entire country. Kyle had been an FBI agent during 9/11, which had turned the agency and his life upside down. Shirin sensed a chill in his demeanor and reminded him again of the remoteness of something like that happening.

"But those probabilities are *so* low," she repeated.

Kyle initially regarded her, satisfied, but then her attempt at calming him backfired and he drilled down into the possibility.

"What are the probabilities your models are implying?" Kyle asked.

Shirin looked askance, not wanting to delve into it, but then relented.

"If you look at a normal Gaussian distribution, the historical average probability for a move this size happening in four days is a tiny, tiny fraction of a percent, like, so many zeros after the decimal, it doesn't even register. This trader is prepared to pay the equivalent of a *fifteen to twenty percent* implied probability," she stated emphatically.

The traders and quants at the bank had specialized software that could calculate the probability distributions that option models relied on. The software could also be tweaked to reverse this distribution calculation—and reveal the probabilities different option prices were *implying*.

Returning to the roulette example from before, if a *fair* roulette wheel hit any given number one out of thirty-eight times, or 2.6 percent, that was its probability distribution—every number having the same probability. Options on traded assets, like stocks and oil and gold, were priced using a different distribution, called the normal distribution or Gaussian distribution, which estimated that prices closer to where the asset was trading today were much more likely than extreme prices. This probability distribution was shaped like a bell, thus the "bell-shaped curve" it was so often referred to as. So, overlaying this shape on the current price of gold, showed there was a much greater chance of gold going to $712 from $707 in a few days than there was of the price ever reaching $800.

And with the casino analogy, if a casino player suddenly began betting repeatedly on a single number, you'd consider them either stupid or superstitious, or perhaps, like in the movie, *Casablanca*, you might consider the table to be rigged: "I'm shocked, shocked!" But if that casino player had better information about a particular number they were betting on, its implied probability would be much higher. On a rigged roulette table, that might translate to a specific range of numbers, like thirteen to twenty-four, each instead having a 5 percent probability of hitting, twice their fair probability of 2.6 percent.

Shirin eyed him back and restated the extreme figure.

"The implied probability, based on what you told me this guy was willing to pay, is around *twenty percent*, which is spectacularly high," Shirin reemphasized.

"What's the baseline probability, on a normal distribution?"

"Like I said, it's tiny, infinitesimally small, like a ten-thousandth of a percent. This option should have no value at all. None, zero. He wants to pay a dollar for something that should be utterly worthless."

"No jokes here," Kyle chided. Shirin rolled her eyes and put it more bluntly.

"Someone is betting, what do you guys say—a rabbit pops out of the hat?"

He half acknowledged her, tugging on his thinning hair in thought.

"It's gotta be the Fed, only thing that makes sense," Kyle absently concluded.

"If they are betting on the Fed, then this is an easy sale. Even I'd do this trade," she started. "If they're betting something *else*, I don't know what that could be, you should stay away," she finished ominously.

Kyle, still in thought, half absorbed that. "Yeah," he muttered.

He rose and moved to the conference room door.

"Thank you. Let me know if you think of anything else."

"Happy to help, and—" But Kyle was already out the door.

Townshend's Steakhouse, Tribeca, Lower Manhattan, United States

Kyle sat alone at a white-linen table in a crowded lunchtime steakhouse across the street from the Fortnum Bank building. A busboy brought him waters and set the table as Kyle perused a menu.

A flustered Amy appeared with the help of the hostess and made her way over to Kyle's table, squeezing by patrons and wearing an annoyed expression. She sat, uncomfortably, in the seat adjacent to Kyle and gave him a peeved smack.

"I can't have a *steak lunch* now—I've got a ton of shit to do," she launched.

"Order a fucking salad. You think *I'm* not busy?" he shot back.

"Busy robbing people," she sniped, grabbing her menu. She twisted to set her purse over her chair and turned back to scan what to order. They both hid in their menus, unable to face one another yet, but continued bickering.

"You still don't understand what I do. And I love how you judge me given this is what pays for your Gramercy apartment and feeds our daughter."

"Excuse me, Kyle, I—" She stopped herself, shaking her head. "I'm not going to get into one of these traps with you," she asserted, and then raised her eyes to him, sighed, and reset the conversation. "What did you want to talk to me about?" she asked him, more businesslike, pulling her jacket lapels together, self-conscious her nine-millimeter Glock was visible.

"Can we order first? It's not an easy thing," Kyle responded.

She frowned at him, half puzzled, half worried at what he was going to bring up. Then she jounced, remembering something, and lowered her menu and leaned in toward Kyle.

"Oh, hey—you know this guy—Stephen Brooks?" she asked him, wiping her mouth on her napkin.

"Stephen Brooks? Yeah, of course. He's our chief risk officer. How do you know about him?" Kyle's attention was piqued.

"Uh...*risk*, exactly," Amy concurred, and then she raised her menu and used it as a kind of shield so others couldn't quite hear what she was saying to Kyle, and she leaned toward him again.

"Wife reported him missing. We have an agent looking at it," she revealed.

"What are you talking about? I saw him yesterday at the office."

"I don't know the details. I guess he disappeared or didn't come home or something like that. Hit our new case files this morning," Amy divulged.

"But that's a missing persons, NYPD. Why you guys looking at it?"

"You forgotten everything since you left?"

"Pretty much."

"You know how it goes, these high-profile execs of big banks come directly to us, cops don't even get involved. One of these chief-whatevers gets a shoe stolen, it's our jurisdiction."

"I guess that's true." Kyle chuckled "High profile, yeah right."

"I don't know. He probably went on a bender with an escort and his wife knows he's cheating. She's teaching him a lesson." Amy chuckled dismissively.

"Ha—Brooks? I don't think so."

"What do you mean?"

"The guy's like a chess moron, or something, he's the quietest guy. Well, maybe that's it, maybe he did flip out. I guess you never know if someone's got a fetish or something. What do I know?" Kyle talked himself out of it.

"Yeah. He'll probably show up tomorrow or the next day back home. You know how it goes."

"It is strange, though," Kyle puzzled, and looked off into space for a moment.

They gave the waiter their orders, and then Amy switched to him again.

"So...? What's so important you had to pull me off three different cases?"

Kyle came back to the present but delayed as he searched for his words. He removed his glasses and folded them and laid them on the table next to his water.

"I...want to talk about...us getting back together," Kyle began, awkwardly.

Amy laughed out loud, thinking it was a joke. But Kyle didn't laugh with her.

"Seriously, Kyle, why are you wasting my time?" Amy asked again, annoyed now. Kyle didn't reply; he merely looked at her with an earnest expression on his face. After a tense silence, she gulped her water to gain some composure.

"You're serious? Are you serious?" Off his stern expression, her eyes shot around the room as she tensed. "You're a real son of a bitch, you know that?" Her voice rose.

"No—no, Amy, listen to me for a moment, will you *listen*?"

Amy felt the urge to get up and leave, but something compelled her to at least stay for his pitch.

"Just hear me out," Kyle pled.

Amy folded her arms, and stonily replied, "I'm listening."

Kyle took a deep breath, scanned the noisy restaurant, a blur of white linens, and looked down at his water.

"I'm thinking of leaving the bank. I'm not saying just leave the bank, I mean *leaving, leaving*, quitting trading for good. Doing something else."

Her eyes widened. Now he had her attention, or at least for a little bit longer. "I got to thinking, I was playing with Jill yesterday, I loved it. I really miss her. She's getting older, figuring stuff out. I don't get to see her that much. She needs a dad, ya know?" Kyle went on. Amy settled down a bit and listened more.

"I don't want to *not* be there for her. It sucks, you know? I know I'm responsible for—I don't want to get into that—I'm just saying, I'm offering, I don't want Jill to grow up with a split family and only see her dad a fraction of the time. I want to be there for her. I want to be there for you, *us*—" Kyle stopped.

Amy couldn't believe her ears, and then responded when there was silence. She shook her head, trying to contain her rage.

"Where was all this? Where was all this four years ago, when you fucking left us? When you were out with different girls every night, drinking, pretending to be a hotshot Wall Street asshole? *Huh?*" She paused only to catch her breath.

"You abandoned us. Do you recall *that*? Like, does that register with you? I had to deal with a little kid, *and* my job at the FBI, while you fucking went out and cheated on me and, and—you didn't care about Jill then, did you?—and now—"

"I know, I know. I ruined us—"

"You're goddamned right you *ruined* us, you—"

"Listen. Just listen, will you?"

Amy turned her head away in disgust. Everything came flooding back to her. She stared across the room, shaking her head, being pulled back into a painful era.

"I'm sorry, *OK*? I am, I really am. I wasn't there for you guys. I wasn't a husband or a father."

Amy gave a cynical laugh. "You're a real piece of shit, you know that?"

Kyle didn't respond, and then Amy changed the subject. "So, what are you going to do? What do you think you're going to do now? Come back to the FBI?"

Kyle looked down at his water again.

"I don't know—no—I don't think so. I don't know yet. I was planning to trade through year end, get my bonus in February, and then resign. I'll probably sell the apartment. That'll give me enough money and time to figure things out."

She eyed him scornfully as he went on.

"Maybe...*maybe*, we could try living together again, after I leave the bank." Kyle studied her for her reaction.

Amy shrugged her shoulders, looking up at the ceiling for rescue.

"I don't know what to say to that. I mean, I really don't. I hated you for so long, and then I got over the hate, and I stopped hating you, and I disposed of all that. And *you*. I got over you—you just became Jill's dad, like, some other person, ya know? I concentrated on Jill and my work, and I just moved on." Then she stung Kyle with a sinister look in her eyes. "And now you want me to put all that aside, and pretend everything didn't happen and just...*go back*?"

"That's not what I'm asking," Kyle replied calmly.

Amy fell back against her chair and cocked her head. She thought for a moment and then leaned forward again.

"And what about mommy and daddy?" she posed, emphatically raising her eyebrows. "Say we move back in together, are we going to pretend? Live a life of actors in front of Jill, just for her sake?"

"I think we still love each other," Kyle answered with surprising confidence.

Amy didn't expect that. She lowered her eyes to the table and said nothing.

Kyle then reached over and put his hand underneath her chin and leaned in and kissed her. For a moment, she did nothing. And then she came to her senses and shoved him back.

"What. The hell. Are you doing?"

She didn't wait for a response. She stood up, grabbed her purse, and started to leave, but not before discharging, "You're an asshole, you know that?"

Amy pushed her way through the lunch crowds and fled the restaurant.

Kyle sat there, upset with himself. Maybe he'd overplayed that, he thought. He called the waiter over.

"Can you make it to go, and get me the check?"

Sutong Yangtze River Bridge

A beat-up, partially rusted white passenger van idled in nighttime traffic on the Yangtze bridge. Inside, the two Syrians, dressed in their suits, sat in the second rear seat, the only passengers. The driver, a local Chinese man, smoked away while he impatiently edged the van forward, braking suddenly whenever the vehicle in front of them abruptly stopped.

The bomb cases, stacked in the luggage bay behind the Syrians, rattled and shifted as the van lurched and halted. The taller Syrian leaned backward to examine them, concerned as they jostled around.

"Hey, could you stop that?" he barked at the driver in broken Mandarin as he slid from another halt.

The driver eyed him in the rearview and exhaled a stream of smoke.

"Almost across the Yangtze. Faster driving after," the driver finally uttered.

The Syrians exchanged annoyed glances as they jerked forward again. The short one checked his watch.

Pitched against one of the bridge pillars, Kelso and Jeff monitored each vehicle above them as it crested the bridge on-ramp and rode onto the shoreside expressway. Kelso kept the neutron sniffer aimed at the traffic while Jeff spotted with binoculars.

"Looks like there's a backup somewhere," Jeff noted.

"That's good and bad for us. It'll slow us down, but if our target is on the highway, gives us more time for a better reading," Kelso responded, without removing his focus from the eyepiece.

Jeff didn't acknowledge but kept his binoculars angled at the vehicles proceeding along the bridge.

The traffic edged slowly ahead with each row of cars, vans, and trucks advancing at a time, halting and then accelerating off the bridge. That rhythm repeated itself every few minutes.

"What time is it?" Kelso asked Jeff.

Jeff lowered his binoculars, rubbed his eyes, and checked his cell phone.

"About twelve fifteen."

"This slowdown will probably add an hour to our little exercise here."

Kelso was fixed on a row of four vehicles—two cars, a van, and a truck—that were now at the head of the traffic column. The number of illuminated red bars in the viewfinder suddenly jogged and widened. The display grew from zero to four and then to five, increasing in strength. Kelso looked away and blinked his eyes and stared back into the viewfinder, scrunching his face to loosen his muscles.

"What do you see, what do you see right now?" he pressed Jeff, a new urgency in his voice.

Jeff dialed the focus wheel.

"Looks like two cars, drivers, couple passengers; a van, a driver, I think some passengers in the rear, a truck, one driver," Jeff counted.

"I think I'm getting a hit, but I can't tell which vehicle," Kelso revealed.

"Really?" Jeff twisted the focus wheel to zoom in as much as he could.

"Looks like they'll stop and then start again in a moment," Jeff said.

"Don't take your fucking eyes off that group. Tell me *exactly* when each vehicle moves ahead," Kelso ordered.

"Car number one…" Jeff started.

Within the neutron sniffer viewfinder, the blueish car cruised across, and the five red bars died away to zero.

"Not the blue two-door," Kelso affirmed.

"Light covered truck now," Jeff continued.

The viewfinder bars again didn't budge as the truck rolled past.

"Not the truck."

"White or gray passenger van coming up next."

Kelso focused in on the viewfinder. Through the eyepiece, he watched the passenger van cross his field of view. The van appeared white or yellow in the nighttime sepia rays cast on it by the bridge's road lights. Kelso altered his grip. In the scope, the bars flung out to seven as the van drove through.

"It's the van, the van, the white van!" Kelso cut sharply, and then, for the avoidance of doubt, "They've got it in that van."

Jeff angled the binoculars onto the target.

"I got it, I got it. One driver, two—two passengers in the rear," Jeff verified.

Kelso followed the van through the viewfinder until it disappeared within traffic and accelerated onto the south bank highway.

"Call it in, now, now," Kelso demanded.

Jeff got on his cell phone.

"We have a mark—a passenger van, we think white or yellow, four wheels. Looks like one driver, two passengers in the back seat. Just ramped onto G15."

Jeff hung up.

"They'll call as soon as they acquire it and get into position," he relayed.

"Get the full fence ready." Kelso glanced at his watch. "Where does this route lead?" Kelso finally lowered the neutron sniffer off his shoulder.

"G15? Goes down to Shanghai, but they can switch to any of the other highways from there, and then keep going south or turn west."

Kelso pondered for a second.

"My gut is they'll keep going south, but to where, I don't know, so we have to stay glued to them."

Jeff's cell phone rang.

"Yeah?… Got it, thank you… We need at least three forwards… Right, thanks." He turned to Kelso.

"We're on 'em," Jeff confirmed.

Kelso picked up his satellite phone.

Operation 912 Task Force Center

Analysts swirled around their desks exchanging updates. Kate sat at her laptop, staring at a map of China. Scanlon, the SAD officer, interrupted, waving her over.

"We got it, we have it," he shouted to her.

Kate approached him and he continued.

"There's a white passenger van, looks like a hired transport, with two targets and some cargo in the rear that lit up the neutron sniffer, high-confidence return."

"Show me. Where is it now?"

Scanlon loaded a map of coastal China onto the projection screen. He pointed to a blinking red icon representing the van traveling southward on a freeway.

"Right there, real time," he replied.

"Fuck," Kate cursed under her breath.

Kate motioned to Captain Bolling to join them and rattled off instructions.

"We need overheads on that target, whatever you got, you understand? We've got on-ground pacers, but we can't let this thing out of our sight."

"Affirmative." Captain Bolling was barely up before she was back at her desk making the calls.

Kate leaned over to Terry.

"Keep him on the mark," she instructed. "And let's ID those passengers," she whispered to him with emphatic eyes.

A few minutes later, Kate and Bob were in the director's office.

"We have a fucking stolen nuclear weapon, or IND, or whatever, making its way through Shanghai *right now in a car?*" the director shouted at them.

"Actually, it's a van," Kate snidely observed.

The director shot her a *don't fuck with me* look.

"I can't let this go any longer," he inveighed, literally pulling his hair.

"We've been over this—you *know* the Chinese. Target vanishes in a cover up the moment State cables them," Bob parried, suddenly taking Kate's position.

The director looked at Bob and then Kate with his set of stony brown eyes and sat down. He removed his thick 1970s-style black-rimmed eyeglasses. He wiped them against his sleeve.

"Fuck the Chinese," he finally broke his silence, muttering in an aside. "This is more about North Korea. And it's about ensuring we stop this thing and that more bombs don't come from them. You're right, I agree with you, this is the most valuable intel for the six-party talks. The capital of this thing to the administration is *huge.*" The director paused, returning his glasses to his face. "But I'm so far out on a fucking limb here. I bought you guys time—enough time—and now, we don't play this right, it comes back to all of us," he said grimly, and then changed his intonation a bit.

"Do we have anything more on who could have financed this or organized it? And are we *certain* this thing is disassembled?"

Kate and Bob nodded simultaneously.

"It's gotta be disassembled if it's even a fully functioning warhead at all. We know it was siphoned off a deployment run. They only transport components, so it's almost impossible it was traveling fully baked. Plus, a full-sized warhead has a much larger profile," Kate explained.

Bob addressed the first part of the director's question.

"CB's looking at it. Nothing yet. If it was a rogue general or intel officer, we don't see anything in the offshore accounts we monitor. No transfers, no sudden large balances, not a whiff yet," he said.

"Keep 'em looking at that," the director snapped at Bob, adjusting his glasses higher. "Nothing like this happens by accident. There's a money trail somewhere, digital fingerprints, transfers. You know that," he griped.

"We may know more about the mules shortly," Kate said, with Bob nodding.

"Go on," the director granted.

"The passengers in the van look like the same ops who were on the freighter and stole the lifeboat," Kate started. "The visual description we got on them was longer faces, more angular features. European, Eastern European, or Middle Eastern and not Asian. Very unusual you'd have a nonlocal transporting this thing *unless* they're the original couriers," Kate finished.

"Implies it's a small team, and that China is not the destination, just a pass-through, meant to lose us—more confident in that now," Bob added.

The director eyed both of them dubiously but appeared to agree with the last point. He lay down on his sofa without removing his eyes from the two of them.

"You may be right. This is China's fault; blowback. They've been funding and covering for Kim's nuclear ambitions for over a decade now. Practicing, what do you call it—?" The director spied Kate.

"Avoiding *direct conflict*, straight out of Sun Tzu—the Chinese get a cutout, and the North Koreans, who are ultimately expendable, get to be the snarling pit bull, keep us distracted and preparing for war with them. It wears us down and keeps China from having to fight us directly. Part of their grand multi-decade plan," Kate filled in.

"Exactly. So, part of me wants to fuck the Chinese, let a loose nuke ricochet around their cities, like a goddamned pinball machine, see how they like it. Another part of me wants this off our hands, just have State cable the Chinese straightaway and be done with it, not our problem anymore. And another part of me wants us to get this thing," the director went on. "Which is it going to be?"

"You gotta buy us more time," Bob enjoined.

"I bet it's not in mainland China more than a day," Kate added.

The director's eyes fixated on the tips of his shoes sticking up on the opposite armrest as he thought.

"And this is smelling more and more like UBL and al-Qaeda. They've been quiet lately. I don't like it. Haven't pulled anything nasty since London. UBL trail's gone cold. We're distracted with the War in Iraq. Perfect calculus for them, perfect time. Purchase a nuke or an IND, God…"

"We've tapped the AQ teams; they're not picking up any links to this. We're taking a fusion approach here," Bob deftly gave him a palliative and submitted skepticism to the director's al-Qaeda worry.

The director tilted his head back on the armrest of the sofa and sought the ceiling of his office. He thought for a moment and then yelled in frustration.

"Well, then where *the fuck* is it going?"

Neither of them replied to that. After a few moments of staring at the ceiling, the director rose from the sofa. And he got in their faces.

"This thing has to be out of Shanghai proper in the better part of an hour, you understand?" He left a dramatic pause and then went on.

"And have a plan for a rendition. If we can get the package somehow—quietly—let's do it. If it lingers in the city, I *have* to inform POTUS, the NSC, and then it's going to State, and they'll make the calls, *you understand?*"

Kate and Bob exchanged edgy looks. They knew this was a fifty-fifty shot. They only had a theory about where the thing was headed, but they both answered the director with solemn nods.

On their way out, he added, "Get me the second you've made those mules."

Fortnum Bank Equities Trading Floor

Kyle was back at the bank following his debacle of a lunch with Amy, his jaw locked in a bitter clench. He stomped through the entrance hallway, unfortunately encountering Sammy in the midst of a coffee run.

"Hey, Springer? What the fuck, man?"

Kyle angled toward the voice, not in the mood to deal with anyone. Realizing it was Sammy, Kyle ignored him, and continued through to the trading floor.

But inside, Kyle halted. He reflected for a second, and he reversed and went back to the reception area. Sammy was still there waiting for an elevator. He wheeled when he saw Kyle fast approaching. Kyle glanced around to see if anyone else was present and, satisfied they were alone, seized Sammy by the collar.

"Hey? What gives, man—what are you doing?" Sammy pleaded, alarmed by Kyle grabbing him, and no match for the taller, more athletic Kyle. Sammy grasped at Kyle's hands to pry them off.

"This guy better be for real. No tricks, Sammy, I don't want to get run over," Kyle launched. Sammy looked up at him, realized he was talking about the gold trade, and stopped clawing at his hands. He obsequiously reassured him.

"You won't—you won't. You can ring this one up, I promise. So, you'll do it?" Sammy eagerly asked.

"I'll sell him at a buck twenty-five," Kyle offered.

"A buck and a quarter? He's bid—" Sammy paused, recognizing this was his window. "You're up. How many?" Sammy replied with a copious grin.

Kyle let him go.

"The whole thing."

"*The whole thing?* I fucking love you, man!"

"And that had better have been your top," Kyle insisted, referring to the price at which he just sold the options, $1.25 per contract—the top would be the highest the customer would have paid. Kyle was ensuring he'd squeezed Sammy.

"It was, it was. You rang the bell. You're done, filled. Fifty million ounces, the whole thing, right?"

"The whole fucking thing, Sammy, all five hundred thousand contracts worth, fifty million ounces. Send me the deal confirm when you get back to your desk," Kyle instructed. One gold option contract represented one hundred troy ounces.

Sammy thought he was about to get away, and then Kyle grabbed him again.

"One more thing." Kyle stared into Sammy, deadly serious. Sammy watched him anxiously, unsure what he was going to say or do. "Do *not* enter the trade into the risk system, got it? I'll take care of that. Repeat what I said," Kyle demanded, gripping him.

Sammy nodded tightly at first, and then Kyle shook him.

"OK! *You'll* enter the trade into risk—I—I got it."

Kyle let him go and watched as Sammy slunk back onto the trading floor.

Kyle returned to his desk. Pete was there and gave him an update and fill reports on their latest trading activity, in between mouthfuls of a meatball sub.

"Equities still dropping but slowing. Crude's still bid," Pete reported.

"Strange. The crude part," Kyle said, and then revealed, "I did the gold trade."

Pete almost spit out his food.

"You did it? All of it? We're short *five hundred thousand* gold options now?"

"Got a buck twenty-five, too. Where's gold trading?"

"It's up, seven ten. A buck twenty-five, nice, nice! Sixty-two and a laugh, brother. That gets us out of the abyss," Pete rejoiced with a grin, already ringing the register. The sixty-two and a half was the $62.5 million they would make if those call options they just sold expired worthless by week's end (if gold finished below $800). It was now early Tuesday afternoon. Pete's excitement vanished as quickly when the reality hit him of having a trade this large on their books.

"How the hell are we going to hedge this?" he asked with dismay.

"Start with a straight futures hedge. Figure out the implied delta, double it, then buy the futures. We can get fancier after that," Kyle instructed.

The delta was the hedge ratio of the underlying future to an option. The delta calculated how many futures you needed to hedge an option trade at any one time. Options with strike prices that were close to where the underlying asset was currently trading were about .50 delta, or "fifty delta," in trader speak. A .50 delta meant that a single option behaved like half of a future. If the future moved up by $1, the option would move up or down $0.50.

The $800 strike call options on gold that Kyle had just sold, however, had a very, very small delta—because they were so far away from where gold was trading. In fact, given that gold was currently trading near $710, an $800 option had such a tiny delta it wasn't even 0.01. But Kyle wanted to *over* hedge, so whatever the option models told him the correct delta was, Kyle had wanted to err on the safe side, increasing their hedge, to be more protected.

The "get fancier" instruction meant hedging the trade with options. Traders often hedged OTC option trades with listed (exchange-traded) options, sometimes even the very same option, if it existed.

"We're too far out on the curve, I don't think we can use listed options to hedge," Kyle said.

"There's gotta be something. We can't just do futures and pray."

"We'd blow out the vol surface if we even hedged part of it with options. Let's bide our time," Kyle replied. "We're wearing it now," he added balefully. He then faced Pete and, with a lowered voice, told him, "One other thing: Don't enter it into risk yet. Just book it into Scout as a paper trade so we can at least monitor."

"Wait, what?"

"If the trade hits the risk system—"

"Garner will see it, got it," Pete realized. "So, this is your plan. But we have to enter it sometime, otherwise it's not a real trade. And what about Sammy's side? What about clearing?"

"I told Sammy not to enter it into risk. Clearing will see it, he'll enter it there, but because it's OTC, they won't raise a stink about it for a couple days. We'll plug it into risk on Thursday. Friday will come, and it will expire before Garner even notices it."

"What could possibly go wrong."

Pete calculated a delta for the gold options, and then bought ten thousand gold futures to hedge.

"Done. Only two bucks of slippage, seven twelve now," Pete commented, faux-proudly.

Slippage was the effect of moving the market's price when you were working into or out of a position. If the liquidity wasn't immediately there, you had to pay more to attract sellers, and so on.

"I kissed Amy," Kyle announced, suddenly changing the subject.

Pete laughed out loud. Then regarded Kyle when he didn't hear him joining.

"Shit. You for real?"

"It was a mess. Lunch didn't go so good."

"So, then how'd you pilfer a kiss?"

"I don't know, I misread it; sucks," Kyle lamented.

Before Pete could comment, their attention turned to crude oil, which was surging higher. The charts notched a straight line up, to $84, from $83 only moments before, and it wasn't stopping.

They checked positions and scanned reactions in adjacent markets and hunted for any news. Equities resumed a leg down, with the S&P 500 chart dropping like a stone, and gold had started to lurch in unison with crude, rising above $712 and then $713, from where Pete had just pushed it.

"You got that hedge off?" Kyle double-checked with Pete.

"I did. What do you think's going on?" Pete inquired as he searched markets and news sources.

"Here, look at this." Pete found a news post, "US Department of Defense official expects more attacks on Middle Eastern oil infrastructure."

They both watched crude as it rose before their eyes.

"I'd still be a seller here," Kyle commented.

"Of course," Pete acknowledged, dryly. "Weird, though, more of this?"

"It is—shit, I forgot—you want weird? Amy gave me a little inside dirt on the Fort," Kyle started.

"What do you mean?"

"She said Brooks's wife reported him missing this morning. Feds are looking into it," Kyle divulged.

"Brooks—Chief Risk Officer Brooks?" Off Kyle's nod, Pete reacted, "Shit, you serious? Like he's missing? Like kidnapped or ran away with a tart?" Pete laughed at his own description.

Kyle shrugged his shoulders.

"Any and all of the above."

Pete couldn't help himself and kept going.

"Or face down in an alley off a meth bender? That guy's such a tool. How does he even have a wife to report him missing in the first place?"

Kyle laughed.

"That's probably why. He's probably in the closet and finally decided he's done with her." They both chuckled.

A moment later, Sammy appeared, a big grin on his face.

"Springer?"

"Ah shit," Pete groaned when he saw him.

"Thanks again, man. My guy's really happy. Nobody else would do that trade. He needed to get that thing on to hedge his book," Sammy started.

"Are you thanking us on behalf of your customer, or for the monster sales credit we just gave you?" Pete called him out.

"Hey, man, what are we here for? I owe you guys a beer. This was great! And

I got this guy's trust now. He'll come back to us, not other dealers, you know what I'm saying? It's great," Sammy rattled on.

Kyle and Pete mostly ignored him.

"Cool," Kyle offered with half sincerity, trying to get him to go away.

"Can't you see we're busy? Don't you see what's going on in crude?" Pete scoffed at him.

"I know, crude, stocks, everything. We gotta prep for Fed tomorrow—hey, what do you think's gonna happen? Twenty-five or fifty? I'm thinking fifty..." Sammy droned on.

There was no reply from Pete or Kyle. They were in full-on ignore mode.

"Oh yeah, I entered the gold trade into the sales system, so it should be all taken care of," Sammy added and was about to step away.

Kyle and Pete shot him a look of fury.

"What?" Kyle almost shouted as Pete and Kyle exchanged panicked glances.

"I thought that's what you wanted me to do? Don't enter it into risk, just clearing." Sammy played innocent.

"Sammy, you dumb shit, your sales system books *into risk*, automatically, you know that!"

"How am I supposed to get my sales credit, then?" Sammy whined.

"You son of a bitch. I told you to bring me the confirm ticket and that *we'd* take care of it. You'd get your sales credit two days later. Are you fucking *deaf?*"

"Wha—?" Sammy pleaded.

"How long ago did you do that?" Kyle pressed, frantic.

"Right after we talked. After you did the trade with me."

"Fuck," Kyle and Pete both cursed at once.

Pete punched up Scout and scrolled through the trade blotter.

"There it is, there—*motherfucker*," Pete spat again as he confirmed it. He half stood in his seat looking over to Garner's office to see if he was upset, or for any sign that Garner had noticed the trade.

"Sammy, get out of here, *now*," Kyle warned.

"Is there a problem?" Sammy asked dumbly.

"Yes, there's a *fucking problem.*" Kyle rose from his chair and towered over Sammy, like he was actually going to hit him. A few traders angled to see what was going on. Sammy's face drained of color when he saw Kyle lording over him again, and he finally scurried away. Kyle sat and glanced at Pete.

"We're fucked. We're done as soon as Garner sees that thing," Kyle agonized.

Pete half stood again and peered into Garner's office.

"He's on the phone. Better not be about us. Shit, I can't breathe."

"He look pissed?"

"No, he looks like his normal pain-in-the-ass self."

"That's even worse. We need a plan." Kyle thought for a moment. "This is an *error*, OK? It's a real trade, but Sammy entered too many digits, *fat-fingered* it. It was noticed and it's being corrected. It'll be corrected by tomorrow. Ya got it?" Kyle prepared Pete.

Pete then asked, "What if he checks with Sammy?"

"We tell him Sammy doesn't know what the fuck he's talking about."

"He hates Sammy, too. He'd believe us over him," Pete agreed.

"I think we can kite him to Friday. Besides, with the Fed and the swollen size of the equities and interest rate books right now, it may not even be a blip on their radars," Kyle rationalized.

Pete half stood for a third time and observed Garner.

"He doesn't look like he's seen it yet," he reported again.

"Stop doing that, will you?"

Kyle stood up and scooted his chair into his desk.

"Where are you going?"

"Upstairs to risk to cover our ass, see if they can reverse out the entry for now," Kyle planned out loud.

"But I thought you said we're going to tell Garner it's an error if he asks?"

"If that were true, we *would have* talked to risk to get them to correct the trade, understand?"

"And if they adjust it, it'll show up as a trade break from clearing. And we'll have to readjust it later anyway. And Sammy could notice, too," Pete complained, poking many holes in Kyle's plan.

"All true, but we need to hide it from Garner first and foremost. That's what's most important now. We can deal with the others as they happen."

"Oh, what a tangled fucking web we weave," Pete sighed.

"Relax, it'll be fine. We just need to deal with this immediate fuckup. I hate Sammy, useless piece of shit. I gave him crystal-fucking-clear instructions, too— bring us the confirm, nothing else. The little bitch."

Pete smiled in agreement. Kyle stepped away but then turned back to Pete.

"If Garner does come, just tell him the fat-finger part and I'm upstairs at risk getting it corrected."

Shaoxing Rural Roadway, Shaoxing, Zhejiang Province, China

The white passenger van throttled down the rural turnpike, doing a hundred kph. They had passed through the city of Shanghai and had continued south on a two-lane rural route. The road wasn't in great shape, which caused the driver to frequently slow down, irritating the Syrians. It was late and dark outside as they zoomed through farmland country.

Inside the van, the driver continued to smoke as both the Syrians took turns napping and smoking as well. The partner who wasn't asleep kept watch out the windows and paid special attention to any car or truck that came alongside them and lingered. Every so often, one of the Syrians would twist around to check on their bomb cases and to peer out the rear window for any vehicles that might be tailing them.

An older blue Toyota four-door coursed along the route. Its driver, a local deliveryman on his way to a nearby farm, approached the white passenger van from behind and pulled out into the opposing lane to pass it. The deliveryman paid no mind to the van or its passengers as he drove by it, his eyes remaining fixed on the road ahead of him vaguely illuminated by their sapped headlights.

Behind the deliveryman, in the back seat, under a blanket, was a CIA op readying a high-speed camera with a telephoto lens protruding a sliver out of the cover. As they passed the van, the CIA op aimed the lens at the two Syrians in the back seat, slightly obscured by the cigarette smoke adrift in the van's interior. The camera made a series of rapid shutter stops taking as many photos as possible.

Inside the van, the taller Syrian scrutinized the blue Toyota passing them. He peered inside the car. From his higher vantage, he eyed the older driver and then glanced into the back seat but saw no other passengers and so resumed his smoking, looking absently at the darkened landscape. The Toyota accelerated and overtook them and shortly disappeared from view down that rural road.

And about five hundred meters behind the van, back just far enough, Jeff and Kelso trailed them in their Chinese-made subcompact. Jeff drove with Kelso in the front passenger seat and the neutron sniffer on this lap. Kelso also had a blanket at the ready if he needed to quickly lower his seat back and conceal himself underneath the wrap.

"If you can, always keep another vehicle between us. We won't lose them, the van's height is easy to make," Kelso reminded Jeff. Kelso eyed the one or two vehicles behind them visible in the side mirror and added, "And don't forget to let me know if we have a passer; I'll need to duck down, because, you know…"

Jeff blushed and displayed an uncomfortable grin.

"Where's the next big city?" Kelso asked.

"Uh, Taizhou, on the coast, and then Wenzhou, also on the coast, prob half hour each. This Shaoxing road goes through both of them," Jeff answered.

Operation 912 Task Force Center

A profiling analyst approached Kate and her team. A profiling analyst worked to identify individuals, putting a name to a face, or vice versa. They scoured photo catalogues, internet social networks, and DNA databases, looking for clues that could help identify a mug.

The profiling analyst presented some photographs of two faces from the smoke-filled van, taken by the hidden CIA op from the passing blue car. The multiple photos were good but not great. But that was intelligence. You never got a Hollywood headshot.

"Egyptian, Eastern Mediterranean," Kate muttered straightaway.

The profiling analyst had the same thought.

"That's my immediate conclusion, with a wider definition, I'm thinking, Eastern European, or Levant Middle Eastern, or a mix thereof. Syrian, possibly," the analyst informed.

"This thing's going to get complicated if these guys are from a known terrorist group," Kate added.

"What about the two dead from the freighter?" Dr. Ahn asked.

The profiling analyst shuffled her stack of photos and slid out two shots.

"These," she replied, pointing to the photos of the two helpers from the *Alder*.

"We don't know much about them, unfortunately. May never know anything," she noted realistically.

Dr. Ahn realized something, putting the pieces together as Kate did the same.

"Syrian?—Outside the Box!" they both said, snapping their fingers at once.

Operation Outside the Box was an Israeli bombardment of a clandestine Syrian nuclear reactor. It had occurred merely days before, on September 6, and was broadly quieted by much of the Western media. The CIA and the Pentagon had provided air support to the Israeli lance of F-15s and F-16s. The operation had been a success, as it leveled the entire Syrian site, rendering it totally inoperable.

What was more, and suddenly apparent in a possible connection to this current broken arrow situation, was that North Korea had been working with the Syrians, providing reactor fuel and technical expertise. The relationship had been ongoing since at least 2001, and the US and Jordanian intelligence agencies, as well as Israel's Mossad, had been monitoring this growing connection.

"I can't believe we didn't consider that," Kate chided herself.

Dr. Ahn's eyes were wide with excitement on the new lead. Kate stepped away, pacing as she began to put things together.

"This could be a part of that effort, but now *after* the Outside the Box operation, they've adapted and gone underground," Dr. Ahn speculated. "Could be an attempt to still deliver nuclear fuel," she added.

"This is good, very good. I'll tell Bob about this line of exploration." Kate then prodded the profiling analyst, "That means you start with Syrians, got it? Go to your—whoever you work with on Syria, in the MED. Start there. After that, the Israelis. We can get you Mossad help if you need it. I bet we hit pay dirt quickly," Kate said, eagerly, and then shooed her away. "Go, go, what are you waiting for?"

The analyst smiled and hustled back to her desk.

"I can't believe we didn't think of this, it makes perfect sense, well, could make sense," Kate stated, "and this is fresh, a few weeks ago."

"And we know who's involved, too—Chon Chibu, and his group," Dr. Ahn reminded Kate.

Chon Chibu was a nuclear physicist who worked at the Yongbyon Nuclear Scientific Research Center. The previous year, in 2006, Chon had been photographed meeting with Ibrahim Othman, Syria's atomic energy agency head. That interaction betrayed there was a nuclear program relationship between them.

Kate and her team, providing their North Korean expertise, especially Dr. Ahn's meticulous personnel tracking of the Yongbyon organization, had been indispensable to the CIA and Mossad who had been monitoring the developments.

Kate's team had also been involved in the post Outside the Box intel processing, helping to validate soil samples taken by the Mossad from the area near the al-Kibar site, where the Syrian reactor was located. Dr. Ahn, working with NNSA and Sandia National Laboratories, had validated that the soil taken from the al-Kibar grounds contained radioactive decay isotopes, clear traces of nuclear activity in the immediate vicinity. More telling, the isotopes had matched those from the North Korean Yongbyon facility, which Dr. Ahn's team had a database of—meaning their reactor fuel was from the same origin and had the same level of enrichment to start.

"We're still deriving intel from that op, too; this may indeed have been a part of that entire effort, especially if we rewind the planning cycle. See what you guys can learn—everything, talk to our friends at Mossad, the CB guys. Have them scour transactions from the list of participants," Kate rattled off and then bolted from the task force center.

Fortnum Bank Risk Department

Kyle arrived on the risk management floor. The risk department's function was to calculate and aggregate all the risks from all the books, desks, and trading strategies across the entire bank. Kyle's book was just one of hundreds in the enterprise, granted, one of the larger risk books, but still, it was only one of many in the dealing operations the bank had.

Kyle spoke to the receptionist and asked her to phone a woman named Tara, who was a risk manager for Kyle's group. The receptionist motioned for Kyle to enter the offices and buzzed him in.

The risk department was much quieter than the trading floors, and arranged like a normal office space with cubicles and physical office rooms. Kyle circled the floor and finally found Tara's cubicle.

"You're hard to find," he said to the young, curly-haired blonde. She looked up at him with gleaming green eyes.

"What are *you* doing here?" she asked, a bit surprised—the traders typically weren't allowed on the risk floor for compliance and conflict-of-interest reasons.

"A sales trader fat-fingered a trade into our book. It's a hundred times the size it should be, so I want to get it corrected," he started.

"I can do that. You came up here in person for this?" she coyly asked.

Kyle smiled at her.

"I wanted to make sure this was done right," he said, chuckling.

"I can fix it, and then it'll be reconciled when it clears. Is this listed or OTC?"

"OTC, which was why the mistake."

"Yeah, almost all of the error trades are OTC. That's why the push to make everything electronic. One sec..." she said as she typed into her systems.

Since OTC trades were basically agreements between two parties, e.g., a bank and a hedge fund, and not traded and cleared electronically on an exchange, everything about them was manual. You get a busy clerk or distracted sales trader in the heat of battle, and fat-finger mistakes happened all the time with OTC trades. It was not unusual in the least—and a believable ruse for Kyle and Pete. Clearing was the event when cash was exchanged between accounts at the banks of those individuals or companies doing the trading.

"Let me add your accounts," Tara started. "What's the trade?" She watched him, awaiting the details.

"It's a gold options trade, done earlier today, five hundred thousand contracts were entered, should be five thousand," Kyle invented.

"That *is* a fat-finger error," Tara commented jokingly as she clicked around her software.

"I don't see any—you did this in your main prop account?"

"Yes, 515. It should be in there."

"Are you sure, today? It wasn't a different account—wait—I can look at your others, let's see..." She clicked some more. Kyle frowned, a bit puzzled, as he closely followed her expressions.

After a few more moments, Tara shook her head. "I don't see any gold option trades. I see some gold *futures* traded. Would that have been your hedge?"

Kyle acknowledged that but was becoming flustered.

"I don't see it, Kyle. Maybe the sales trader didn't enter it yet? Or booked the wrong account?" she suggested.

"Do you have, like, a blotter? Can you see the entries themselves?"

"Yeah, hang on…" She keyed in another command and peered at it. "No gold options trades," she said.

"So, according to your systems, no gold option trades exist in our accounts or have been traded by us today?" Kyle reconfirmed.

Tara shook her head again. "Nothing risk can see, at least," she said.

Kyle was now confused.

"How long does it take to hit your systems?"

"As soon as someone enters it into Scout or the sales trading system. It's instantaneous. Maybe they didn't enter it yet?" she said, giving him an out.

"Maybe." Kyle took it.

"But how did you know it was fat-fingered if it hadn't been entered yet?" she skeptically inquired.

Kyle flushed as he interpreted the question as suspicion. He grew defensive and quickly covered.

"I don't know, maybe *I* made the mistake. Let me go talk to Pete. Maybe he booked a paper trade, and I mistook it," Kyle said, making up a quick lie.

"Come back when you do, I can help you sort it out," she offered.

Kyle didn't even say a proper thank you. He rushed off to get back downstairs.

Fortnum Bank Equities Trading Floor

Kyle startled Pete when he appeared behind him, frantically ordering, "Let me see our book in Scout."

Pete awkwardly twisted around to give Kyle a perplexed look and then back to face his monitors. He mouse-clicked to bring their Scout app to the forefront.

"Where's the gold trade?"

Pete frustratingly swiveled again to show Kyle his irritation.

"You don't see that? The largest thing on the screen," Pete proclaimed as he tapped the row on the monitor, displaying a "-500,000 OXAU Sep 21, 2007 $800 call," which rendered their position perfectly, the minus sign meaning they were short the options, and the "OXAU" was the system's symbol for gold options.

"Did *you* enter that?" Kyle accused.

"What—are you serious? We both heard Sammy tell us *he* entered it. I didn't enter it, you *know* that. You told me not to, remember, like ten minutes ago?" Pete flushed, disconcerted and wondering where the questioning was leading.

Kyle squinted his eyes at Pete's screen. He sat in his seat and pulled the same risk view up on his own monitor. Pete reached over and pointed to the gold option entry. There it was, the very same "-500,000 OXAU Sep 21, 2007 $800 call."

"Something really weird's going on. Did Garner come by?"

Pete shook his head *no*.

"And that's *not* your paper trade entry?"

Pete again shook his head *no*.

"*Twilight Zone* shit. Sammy put this thing in, like, a few hours ago. Garner's been in there the whole time. He would have had to see it by now. I've been sitting here sweating with the fucking sword of Damocles over me—you know how hard it is to trade like that?"

"What did risk say?"

"That's what's messed up. They can't see the trade."

"What do you mean, *they can't see it*? How could they not see it?"

"No record. Whatsoever. They see our futures hedge, but no option trade."

"WTF, man?"

Kyle shook his head and shrugged his shoulders.

"I don't know. I thought *I* was crazy, but I asked Tara like five times; she didn't see *any* gold option trades hit any of our accounts. She didn't even see any trade blotter entries. I mean, this is the same risk system we're all using, right?" Kyle looked at Pete for reassurance.

"Yeah—as far as I know. A trade gets entered in one place, everyone can see it," Pete assured, with Kyle studying him closely to check he heard right.

"Scout is connected to the main enterprise risk system. It's the same system on the back end—we see it, they see it?" Kyle reconfirmed with Pete.

"Affirmative. How could it work otherwise?"

Kyle took a deep breath.

"Something's not making sense. Maybe they'll see it tomorrow?"

"Kyle, if it's not showing up, I mean, we better get paid, don't tell me this thing's a phantom trade. I knew it was too good to be true," Pete worried.

"No, this is risk. It's not the clearing and settlement system. That's a different system altogether," Kyle explained. "Trust me, we're *gonna* get paid, but this is a mind fuck."

"I don't get it. I mean, you see it right here. *Here* it is." Pete tapped the trade entry on his screens again.

"And Garner hasn't said a word?"

"How many times you gonna ask? Not even a fucking glance over here. I've kept an eye on him since you left, too. BAU, man, just prepping for the Fed."

"He must not be able to see it, either, only explanation," Kyle surmised.

"Impossible, like an elephant in high heels. He has the same Scout system we do. Why you think he's always in our face—he sees everything. But you're right. A trade this size, he woulda been here faster than Carl Lewis," Pete attested.

"You couldn't have said Michael Johnson?"

"I always liked Carl Lewis," Pete quipped. "So, what do we do now?"

"I don't know—maybe you're right and there's a system bug or something, and we wait until tomorrow—maybe it shows up then and we deal with it?" Kyle proposed. "I just don't like this. It's not a good feeling."

"And if it doesn't show up?"

Kyle shook his head, *I don't know.*

"We keep trading it. It'll hit clearing and risk and clearing rec every few days, so it *has* to go in eventually. It'll show up as a trade break, otherwise."

"What about Sammy? Maybe he fucked something up on his side?"

Kyle chuckled.

"That's a given. He emailed you the confirm?"

"A while ago."

"Everything look good?"

"To a fucking T," Pete answered.

A confirm was the formal, legal trade agreement between the two parties for OTC trades—in this case, Fortnum Bank and the hedge fund Sammy was representing. The confirm had all the trade details clearly spelled out, like which options were being traded, the quantity, the dollar amounts, and trade price.

"Yeah, let's see what the system says tomorrow, *and* if we're still employed," he added cynically, half standing to check on Garner again.

Pete didn't like that last part and shot him an angry glance. Kyle sat and dwelled on it, inwardly. Something wasn't adding up. Paranoid thoughts started to race through his mind.

"Meanwhile, crude keeps trading higher, gold, too," Pete stated out loud the obvious of what they were watching.

Oil was approaching $86 per barrel and gold had tipped $715 per ounce.

"Equities, continuing sell-off, too," Kyle added. "Let's hope the Fed resets all of this tomorrow," he finished.

There was a beat of silence between them. The equities markets closed shortly and so trading was accelerating into a louder buzz going into the close.

"Hey, on our way to Ox Bar tonight, I gotta stop by the West Village for a few," Kyle told him.

"How long will it take?"

"Hopefully not long, but I want to do it while it's still light," Kyle said.

"While it's still light, what does that mean? That's like, we have to go before six or seven."

"We should have time," Kyle said.

Pete only regarded him and tentatively agreed with a quiet but suspicious nod. "OK…"

Operation 912 Task Force Center

Kate and Bob entered the director's office. Kate shut the door and revealed two dossiers—the Syrians.

"Amir al-Khonari and Farouk al-Khonari. Syrian brothers. We're positive on Amir, near positive on Farouk, his shorter brother," Kate announced.

The director came out from behind his desk and looked at both Kate and Bob and lifted his glasses to inspect the dossiers.

"We're confident they picked up the package directly from the North Koreans and have been escorting it the entire way," Bob added.

"That's the good news," Kate interjected.

"And the bad?" the director lowered his glasses, passing back the papers.

"They're freelancers. We've got a lot on them, but they don't have an affiliation. They've worked for al-Qaeda but aren't part of their organization. They've worked for both Iranian and Syrian intelligence but aren't agents. They've smuggled for the Europeans when it suited them. They've run drugs for the Russians when it suited them," Kate started.

"These guys are floaters?" the director asked rhetorically.

"Which means they could be subcontracted by anyone. They do dirty work, outsourced stuff. Cutouts. We've seen them mostly doing courier-type work, like this, right up their alley. We don't see them in actual attacks, but we can't rule that out, either. They may have participated in bombings and assassinations," Kate further explained.

"This does narrow the field, gives us something," the director responded.

"Something, yes," Bob partially agreed, "but it also means this could pan out in a number of ways, some state-actor based, others not."

"So, this *could* be al-Qaeda and UBL. It *could* be related to Outside the Box. Or it could be something—someone—entirely unrelated and new," Kate said.

The director acknowledged with a deliberate nod.

"I do like the Syrian connection, though. We should pursue that one more. It fits, and it's completely unacceptable if the NKs are outright selling warheads to Assad, now," he said, and then added, lowering his glasses, glaring at them, "and, that line of investigation keeps CTC at bay a little longer."

Kate ignored the politics trap—better Bob should deal with that.

"That may have been part of the deal, you know, insurance, in case something like Outside the Box happened, they'd be compensated," Kate conjectured.

"Would be a termination of the *understanding* we have with Beijing and Moscow that Kim wouldn't resort to directly selling his weapons," the director implied with some disdain.

"The package might still be the fissile material only and not an entire warhead," Bob added.

"*And*, we do have to consider this could be an entirely unrelated one-off. I do like the Syrian connection, but it might be a misdirection," Kate said, deflated.

"Could be, yes. God, I hate this," the director lodged as he paced. "What are we thinking now? We still have the China problem." He started taking inventory. "With *this* intel, what does that say about where this package might be headed?"

"I think that's the one area this intel does help—I mean—these guys are not the final takers, they're the mules, which most definitely means this thing is *not* in China long. Probably a part of their original plan, to wash it inside China, lose tails, and emerge with a cleaner origination," Kate explained as the director listened intently. She continued.

"Which also means, we can narrow its exits from China. We think the most likely is it gets loaded onto another freighter, with it currently heading south following China's coast. They get past the Taiwan Strait—there's too much naval activity in there, they would want to steer clear of that—so they find a southern port, Guangzhou, maybe even Hong Kong, and go from there," she finished.

"If it gets put on another boat, we can tackle it—"

"Provided the thing doesn't slip us again."

"If you're right, how long do we have before they get into that southern area?"

"I'd say two to four hours at their current rate."

The director eyed both of them and sauntered back behind his desk.

"I have something in mind, risky as shit, but may be warranted," he started.

Kate and Bob exchanged concerned looks, and the director continued.

"I'm thinking we move on this thing while it's *still* in China. Either we destroy it in situ, or it's a rendition. Or the Chinese figure us out and shut it down. Regardless of the outcome, I think we at least thwart the plan, whoever's it is. Do you see my thinking?" the director proposed.

Kate looked at Bob and then at the director. She disagreed with him.

"I don't think so."

The director shot her a surprised glance with a chuckle.

"Tell me," he prompted.

"I'm not sure we have the time—to pull off an op like that. We have half a dozen officers on this and one SSO. I mean, I've been the one insisting our best play is a capture for the intel value, but I don't think *in China proper* is the best loc for a bag job. I mean, think it through, just to get everything tight in only a few hours lowers our success probabilities." she insisted.

The director scrutinized Bob.

"Maybe she's right. We need to figure out something, though, fucking ASAP. I mean, I can't deal with this. I can't have this hanging on me any longer. I have to go to POTUS and the NSC in a few hours. I'm still buying time on the interdiction miss. NSC asking questions already." The director shook his head uncomfortably.

Bob thought and then offered.

"What about a best-efforts audible?"

An audible, like in football, had a similar meaning in the intelligence op game. It meant you gave the control officer on the ground the choice of whether or not to initiate the operation based on what they saw.

"I can live with that," Kate accepted.

West Tenth Street, Greenwich Village, Manhattan, United States

Kyle and Pete hopped out of a yellow cab on the corner of Hudson and West Tenth, a charming residential street lined with contiguous three-story brownstones in the pricey West Village neighborhood. The homes were impeccably manicured with polished window trim and waist-high wrought-iron fences that enclosed the half story of steps ascending to a front door.

"You gonna tell me what it is we're doing here?" Pete asked as he paid the cabbie and shut the door.

Kyle scrolled through his cell phone, looking for something.

"Here on the left, nineteen twenty-one," Kyle said, heading down the street toward the brownstone.

"And who's at that address?"

"Not somebody who should be," Kyle replied neatly.

They approached a fine-looking dark-red brick façade with black-trimmed windows and the preserved original, sandstone-style foundation level. It was unclear if there were any lights on inside, as the window curtains were drawn shut.

"Nice place. Ah, I get it. This is part of your new family plan. You gonna make on offer on it?"

"Ha," Kyle chuckled. "May be coming on the market soon, who knows. This is Stephen Brooks's place," Kyle revealed as he sized up the abode.

"Our risk manager, Stephen Brooks? The guy *missing*, Stephen Brooks?" Pete reacted, disconcertedly. "Shit." Pete eyed the brownstone and then Kyle. "I'll ask you again, *Kyle*, what are we doing here?"

But Kyle was now only half paying attention to Pete. He commented out loud as he scoped the place.

"There's no police tape. That means they're only doing background on him. They haven't even swept the house yet."

Kyle rose to his tiptoes, trying to see inside the first-floor windows, which were a half story above street level. Pete continued to monitor him, unsure of what he was up to, but it wasn't headed in a good direction.

"You want to ring the bell, talk to his wife? Ask her if she's seen her husband lately?" Pete facetiously asked him.

Kyle finally came off his toes and called to Pete.

"Don't you think it's a strange set of coincidences that we put on a super-large trade, one that should have triggered risk alerts, on the *same day* our global head of risk goes missing and the very risk system he governs starts behaving oddly?"

"Shit." Pete rolled his eyes. "You know you *left* the FBI years ago?"

"Maybe it's nothing. I just wanted to check it out," Kyle assuaged, only to crane onto his tiptoes again.

"You satisfied? Can we go now?" Pete urged, nervously eyeing passersby.

"Not quite," Kyle responded as he started walking down the street, beyond the Brooks brownstone, and then past the one after that. Kyle angled to eye any alleyways or spaces in between the townhomes.

"I can't easily get around back, can I?" Kyle contemplated.

Pete followed him, trailing two steps behind.

"They all have little yards and patios. You know what they look like. They're all *private houses*," Pete half shouted.

"Come on. I know how to get in there."

Kyle hurried to the end of the street, where he turned right. Pete hustled after him. Kyle strode quickly over to the next block and made another right. They were one street over, on Eleventh. Eleventh resembled West Tenth, lined with brownstones, but at the corner of this block, there was an old hotel, a fifteen-story plain gray masonry building, with an adjacent alleyway.

Kyle approached the alleyway, on the left side of the hotel building and peered straight into it. Pete chased him down again, watching Kyle like a train wreck in slow motion.

"The hotel uses this for trash removal, but I think it can also access the back of Brooks's brownstone," Kyle speculated, spying the end of the alley.

"Springer, are you kidding me? Trespassing? *Dude!* You can get arrested."

Kyle removed his suit jacket and handed it to Pete.

"Here, keep an eye out. Yell if you see staff, maintenance guys, whatever."

"Oh, lovely."

Pete stood there holding the wad of Kyle's suit jacket as he stared at Kyle creep into the alley.

Kyle skulked about twenty yards in but encountered a locked steel gate. He scanned the surrounding walls and was satisfied there were no windows from which people could see him. He stretched his arms up and grabbed the bar forming the top of the gate and, hoisting himself to waist level with the bar, anchored his foot against the wall, vaulted over the top, and dropped down on the other side.

Pete, back at the mouth of the alley, half watched Kyle mount the gate, then coughed in angst, turning away, unable to watch his mad boss.

On the other side of the gate, Kyle listened to see if anyone saw or heard him. The noise of the hotel's HVAC blowers drowned anything else out. He kept moving. He continued behind the hotel where he spotted a narrow path that ran in between the rear yard walls of the brownstones—exactly what he was looking for.

Each brownstone had a little yard or patio extending about twenty feet behind. Some of these were beautifully rich and tended gardens with full two- and three-story trees; others were merely empty concrete slabs with a couple deck chairs.

Kyle counted to the third brownstone down the row—the Brooks residence. He squeezed as far as he could through the narrow path, which was no real path at all, just an errant space in between the backs of each townhouse's yard.

The Brooks' "backyard" was a plain rectangle of grass with no trees or shrubs, just a thin lawn that met a narrow rear porch. Kyle prowled across the yard, right up close to the back wall of the Brooks home.

The light outside was fading, and it was getting harder to see. Kyle stood again on his tiptoes to try to see inside the back windows. There were no lights on. Everything appeared dark inside.

He was about to turn and head back when he did a double take, catching the ground-level basement window. It wasn't much higher than a foot and maybe two feet wide. Kyle crept up to it. No light was on in there, either. He crouched to peer inside for a better look. From what he could make out, he saw an empty room with an unfinished cement floor and a naked lightbulb with a string switch.

Kyle squinted to see more clearly. As his eyes adjusted, he saw a chair against the side wall, and it was difficult to tell, but he also spotted what appeared to be some string tied around one of the front chair legs. Kyle peeked over his shoulder behind him to check if anyone was watching. He peered back into the basement window, this time pressing his forehead against the pane, cupping his face with his hands to minimize any outside glare.

He still couldn't see much more than he already had, but then he noticed a long, dark blotch near the center of the floor. He focused in on that stain—what was that? Kyle pulled out his cell phone. He pressed the view screen against the windowpane and maxed out its brightness to employ as a flashlight. A dull blue-white glow spread throughout the darkened basement.

Kyle focused on the blotch. The cell phone light revealed one characteristic of the substance—a soft sheen—a property recently dried or drying blood has. The stain appeared dark purplish, which was also consistent with drying blood, especially on a surface like cement that was porous and absorbent. He tilted the phone back and forth a few times to illuminate the reflection in the stain and confirm his suspicion.

Kyle rose back to his feet. He brushed the dirt off his pant legs and fit his cell back into his pocket. He paused for a moment in thought, processing what he'd just seen. A look of uneasiness drew across his face as he headed to rejoin Pete.

Route G324, South of Xiamen, Fujian Province, China

Jeff struggled to keep his eyes open as they pursued the van, now driving on Route G324, part of China's new National Highway System. Jeff was aspirating, with deliberate, rapid inhale-exhales—something they taught him in CIA training to help stay awake. He tightened his grip on the wheel and widened his eyes to keep them open and stay on their quarry.

Kelso glanced at Jeff, seeing he was in some distress. He pulled an energy bar from his pack and handed it to him.

"Thanks." Jeff took it with one hand and tore off the wrapper with his teeth and bit into it.

"It's tough, I know," Kelso offered. "I've been there, many times. Hell Week in SEAL BUD/S was the worst, up five days and nights straight. I don't think I ever did an op since then that I was up that long. Not in DEVGRU, not for the Company. If I did that, you can do this."

Jeff helplessly regarded him as Kelso further handed him a vitamin B12 pill.

"This, too."

Jeff swallowed it.

"What time is it?"

"Don't worry about the time. We have another hour or two before light," Kelso told him.

Jeff yawned. Kelso observed him again. He realized he needed to get his partner in the game if they were going to stay focused.

"Here, keep driving," Kelso started, and then leaned down to where Jeff's feet were, by the car's pedals. Kelso untied Jeff's shoes and retied them, pulling the laces so tight, they squeezed Jeff's ankle flesh above the cuffs of the shoes.

"Ow, son of a bitch!" Jeff hollered.

"Shut up and keep driving," Kelso uttered from down in the footwell as he wrenched the other foot and then rose back up.

"Freakin' hurts, man," Jeff cried.

"Good. You won't fall asleep now."

"Does everything you guys do involve pain?" was all Jeff could say, but indeed, he was more alert now, focused on the road.

"You know the game plan? We'll be coming up on it in a few minutes," Kelso tested him.

"We're gonna stop the van. Our guys will be dressed as local province police. We play along and hang back, stop with any other cars," Jeff rehearsed.

"I'll dismount and find a spot up-range. You stay at the wheel and follow my lead. Be ready to pull around and chase the van if it doesn't look good, got it?"

Jeff nodded.

"They'll be four of ours. Two will stop the van, the other two will move to the package," Kelso stated.

Jeff nodded again, somewhat nervous.

Inside the white passenger van, the driver kept on with his smoking as the two Syrians dozed off in the rear seat row, the taller one with his face against the glass window, the shorter one, his head flung straight back in a noisy snore. They were passing through a more wooded and hilly section of the country, no longer the flat, open farmlands.

The driver shuddered when he spotted two provincial police cars, parked at angles, blocking the highway, their roof lights roving in warning. The police were stopping and inspecting vehicles. A sedan and a light truck ahead of them were already slowing into the checkpoint.

The van's driver braked as he flicked his cigarette out the window. He reached behind him and tapped the taller Syrian, who awoke, initially upset at being disturbed, but he quickly fathomed the scene and shook his partner.

The shorter Syrian came to and grabbed his pack. He unzipped it and removed a snub-nosed pistol, concealing it inside his jacket. He head-motioned to the driver, who was awaiting their instruction.

"Stop, but don't cut the engine," the shorter one said.

The driver braked and idled a length behind the sedan.

Jeff slowed their subcompact into the traffic stop. Two other vehicles came to a halt between them and the passenger van. Kelso removed his HK MP5, fitted on its suppressor, and snapped a night-vision scope onto the gun's rail.

"Keep it running," Kelso reminded Jeff.

Kelso slipped out, silently shutting the door behind him. He leapt to the side of the road, unseen, into the darkness. Kelso ascended to a treed ridge, about ten meters off the road's shoulder. It was a good vantage with a slight elevation and clear downrange view of the van.

Kelso monitored the setup through his night scope. Four CIA officers dressed as local police were "inspecting" vehicles as they approached and clearing them to drive on. He spied the two Syrians in the rear of the van. He watched them sit up and position themselves. He knew they could be unpredictable. But he didn't know if they were armed or how aggressive they could be, or how well trained they were for these types of situations. He had to be keyed up for anything. Kelso also had a dozen civilians on the ground to watch out for.

The "officers" spoke with the drivers of the two vehicles in front of the Syrians' van. They had a few words and then waved them through the barricade. The sedan accelerated around the angled "police cars" and continued down the inter-province road. The light truck followed shortly after.

The white van edged toward the checkpoint as one of the "police" signaled for them to stop. Two of the "officers" approached the van's driver. The other two walked toward the rear of the van.

The Syrians anxiously watched as the four officers split up, not liking the two who deployed behind them. The shorter Syrian readied his pistol and half twisted around to observe the two at the back.

The driver rolled down his window as the police instructed him to exit. The taller Syrian whispered to him to keep the keys in the ignition with the van on.

"Shut off your vehicle," the first police officer ordered the driver.

The driver pretended to not hear and left the keys in the ignition with the motor running and opened the door.

"Turn off the van and give us your keys," the second officer repeated loudly. But the driver simply stepped outside, leaving the keys engaged. The first officer yanked the driver clear of the van.

Kelso noticed, through his night-vision lens, the lighter-gray plume from the van's exhaust, which meant the vehicle had not been shut off as instructed.

"Damn," he hissed. He trained his sights on the driver. He then guided his kill box to the back of the van, observing the other two officers "inspecting" the rear doors. He could see the two Syrians inside the van shifting uneasily.

He knew the bomb components were in the luggage bay, behind the Syrians' seat. If he had to shoot, he had to be very careful, as a bullet could strike and set off any high explosive they might be carrying. That would be a disaster and posed a huge risk. Kelso sighted the driver again, who was now arguing with the other two officers.

In his car, Jeff raised his head to see what was going on. There were two other vehicles in between the van and him, and the van was probably about thirty meters ahead. He glanced over to where he thought Kelso was in the darkened roadside tree cover but couldn't see him.

Jeff turned back to the van. He could see the "officers" through the windows of the vehicles in between them. It wasn't a clear view, especially in the dark—the only illumination was from the vehicle lights. He held his breath as he watched.

The shorter Syrian eyed the two police behind the van, who were now peering inside the rear windows. He could hear them discussing something. One of the officers tried to open the rear van door, pulling its handle, but it was locked. He tried two or three more times. The shorter Syrian started at this, anxious. His hand gripped his pistol, and he drew it from its hiding place but kept it concealed below the flap of his jacket. In a blur, he spun around and fired right at the forehead of the first police officer.

A loud *cap-cap-cap* erupted from inside the van. The rear window shattered in an outward burst. The first officer was struck in the right temple and collapsed, dropping onto his knees, and then succumbing backward onto the road. The second officer ducked below the window level, using the back of the van as cover.

The taller Syrian leapt into the van's driver seat as the two officers upfront lunged to stop him. He slammed the door in their faces and kicked the accelerator pedal, wrapping the wheel sharply left, and banking the van straight into the officers and the driver.

The front officer dove to the street as the van flew by him, barely missing his head. The van nailed the second officer, his head slamming into the short hood. He was flung off as the van swerved and sped around the two parked police cars.

The van's grill plowed into its own driver, striking him squarely in the chest. He fell backward onto the pavement and into the path of the van, which barreled over him. Unbelievably, the undercarriage was high enough that it didn't injure him as it rode right over him. The Chinese driver popped up and fled on foot down the street in the opposite direction.

Kelso reacted. He pumped two automatic bursts into the van, vaporizing all three of its right-side windows as it swerved. His shots missed the Syrians, piercing the side of the van as it pulled away. Kelso was then faced with the back of the van and held his fire to not endanger hitting any bomb components.

"Shit!" he yelled, stopping himself from letting off another volley of rounds.

He sprang down from the hill and sprinted toward the fallen and injured officers and after the accelerating van.

The driver of the car behind the van, alarmed at witnessing the provincial police officer shot, laid into his accelerator, his car lurching forward.

Two cars back, Jeff, seeing the CIA officer shot in the face, pulled out his car and accelerated into the fray. He didn't see the intermediate driver spook, and suddenly swerve. Jeff slammed into the rear of that car, ramming into its trunk and coming to a sudden halt. Jeff's head struck the steering wheel and dash and then whipped backward, knocking him unconscious. The frightened driver that he plowed into kept revving his car, jamming his accelerator, until his car freed from Jeff's. He veered around the two police vehicles and sped down the highway in a puff of dust, not looking back.

The other waiting car went into reverse, almost hitting Jeff as he crashed into the first fleeing car. The car in reverse shot past all of them, fishtailed in a 180 to a forward position, and then screeched down the highway, escaping the chaos.

Kelso bounded onto the road, sprinting after the accelerating van. He came to within five meters of it before it caught speed and surged away. Kelso kept after it in a full-tilt dash. In mid stride, he ripped off the MP5 suppressor and reached over his head, pulling an arrow-like projectile from his pack and inserting it down the barrel of his HK, an archer nocking an arrow.

Kelso dropped to his knees and into a prone position. He fixed the fleeing van through his night scope and squeezed his trigger for a single shot. There was a *pop* sound and the arrow-shaped projectile launched out of the HK barrel, zipped down the road and stuck into the rear bumper of the van where it lodged in with a *thunk*. Four short antennae popped out of the affixed shell.

Inside the van, the shorter Syrian ducked as he saw Kelso coming after them, expecting incoming fire. He aimed at Kelso, ready to shoot, but they were gaining speed and distance, so he lowered his pistol. Neither of the Syrians noticed the specialized projectile that impacted and wedged into their rear bumper.

"Faster, faster!" he yelled at his brother, who was also ducking but keeping his eyes on the road, driving as best he could with half its windows shattered.

Kelso watched the van disappear down the highway.

"Fuck!" he shouted in fury at their escape.

He jumped up and ran back toward the mess. He helped up the one officer who had escaped the white van as it plowed into them. He was alright, he just had scrapes and bruises. The other forward officer was unconscious on the flat of the roadway. They both carried him into one of the "police vehicles." The second officer got inside the driver's seat and started it up.

Kelso then ran over to the officer who got shot. The third officer was on his knees administering CPR. Kelso felt the downed officer's pulse. He was gone.

"I'm sorry. We gotta get out of here," he ordered his teammate.

The officer looked up to him with tears in his eyes as he pumped the fallen CIA officer's chest, not wanting to give up.

Kelso left them and ran to Jeff, who was slowly coming to in his crashed car. He tried forcing open the driver's side door to extract Jeff, but the surrounding metal had been crushed shut by the impact.

Wrenching open the passenger-side door, Kelso grabbed the dazed Jeff and his pack and neutron sniffer with his other hand and pulled the half-conscious kid out along with the equipment. Kelso staggered toward the CIA car with the waiting and wounded officers. He fit the woozy Jeff into the back seat with the other unconscious CIA officer and stuffed his gear onto the floor below them.

Kelso went to the first "police cruiser" and got into the driver's seat. He shifted into neutral and wheeled to face the side of the road and then rolled it off the edge and jumped out, letting the car trundle down the embankment, falling into the brush and trees, out of sight from the highway.

The road surface was a mess. Shattered glass, bullet casings and blood were spread across thirty meters. Kelso searched the street with his flashlight. One by one, he collected the shell casings, sliding the handful into his pocket.

The third CIA officer was still administering CPR to their shot teammate. Kelso physically pulled the officer off the body.

"Come on. Let's get him out of here," Kelso repeated.

They grabbed the fallen officer's shoulders and lugged him to the remaining "police car." They opened the trunk and fit the body inside and shut it after him.

They had to hurry. Kelso urged the CIA officers to come help him. The three of them coaxed Jeff's damaged vehicle, pushing it from behind, off the street and over the edge of the embankment as well.

There was an oblong bloodstain on the roadway where the killed CIA officer had bled out. Kelso poured water over the blood, diluting it and washing much of it away. Finally, Kelso pointed to the many bits of glass everywhere. Using their feet, they swept the shards off the road.

The group returned to the sole remaining "police car" and piled inside. As another car approached, they shot away, leaving the failure and covered-up mess behind them.

Operation 912 Task Force Center

"What a fucking setback!" Bob cursed.

"One dead. Three more wounded," Kate echoed with dismay.

A somber hush filled the task force center after word of the failed operation and a downed CIA officer came across. Kate stared resolutely at the large monitor displaying the map of southern China.

She took a deep breath and collected herself. Fixated on the map, Kate didn't forget about their mission and the outstanding risk. She huddled with her team. Terry Scanlon joined them a few moments later. He and Kate exchanged despondent looks that also conveyed an understanding. There was one certainty in the CIA—whenever they lost one of their own, they doubled down, and became more determined than ever. Kate raised her head and looked out at each of them.

"We need to stay on that van. Do we understand?"

"How does that tracker work?" she asked Scanlon, referring to the specialized projectile that Kelso had shot into the rear bumper of the van.

"It's GPS, so we have real-time pinpointing. But we lose 'em if they go into a parking garage or a tunnel. We also need to watch for a vehicle switch, especially after that firefight," he warned.

"They shot out three windows," Sarah noted.

"No way that van stays on the road very long," Bob agreed.

"They could lose us," Kate summarized the immediate threat.

"Get the SSO back on them with line of sight," Bob directed, and then soberly added, "And I'll go update the director now."

Before Bob exited, Kate coaxed his attention to the map of southern China. The van was nearing the mega ports of Guangzhou and Hong Kong.

"Bob, one more thing. They're only about fifty klicks away now," Kate pointed out. "There's half a dozen major ports in here." She swept her hand along the southern Chinese coast.

"Navy," Bob saw where Kate was going.

They called over LTJG Graham who conferred with them by the map.

"We need a fucking blockade along the southern coast," Kate put forward.

The navy lieutenant assessed the geography.

"Looks like there's about, what—a hundred nautical mile zone to cover?"

"Air *and* sea, you understand?"

"What kind of political cover are we going to have? China considers all this their territorial waters." The lieutenant motioned with his hand from Hainan Island all the way over to the Philippines.

"We'll figure that out. Do the best you can, routine transits, exercises, whatever you need to do. We just want coverage assets over there ASAP. They could be seaborne again in—I'm thinking within an hour or two."

Graham gave an abrupt, "Yes, ma'am," and hurried back to his desk.

Ox Bar, Ninth and Gansevoort, Meatpacking District, Manhattan, United States

Kyle, Pete, and Sully ogled short skirts as they ate oysters and downed vodka shots at the noisy bar of a jam-packed meat-market restaurant.

"Springer, I don't get it. What do you think you saw?" Sully chastised him about his earlier snooping adventure.

"I *know* what I saw. I was in the FBI, remember? I know what dried blood looks like. Something happened in that basement," Kyle returned with all gravity.

"You *actually* did this?" Sully incredulously repeated his questioning of Kyle, and then turned to Pete and gave him a mock shove. "How could you let him do this. I pay you to keep a leash on him."

Pete laughed.

"I was hoping he'd get pinched. Mugshot woulda been glorious. Use it for my computer wallpaper."

Kyle downed a vodka shot, not amused.

"Something happened to him," he insisted.

"And that's why the risk system didn't trigger when your gold options were booked?" Sully ribbed him more, winking at Pete.

Kyle downed another shot.

"It sounds something ludicrous when it's put that way…"

"No, sounds perfectly reasonable," Sully retorted, with dry sarcasm.

Pete and Sully kept exchanging grins, egging him on as he continued.

"Let's look at this *my* way for a second… I get this lunatic show—from fat-ass Sammy—who's repping a sketchy hedge fund guy who's probably front-running the Fed and has inside info, and who has the coin to make a sixty-million-dollar bet, two days after I almost get canned for a monster loss. Garner's now on me like a fucking fly on shit, and I put up this crazy trade in gold options, which I don't usually trade—think about all this from a risk management perspective—it's like red flag after red flag, but all of the sudden, it's crickets from Garner. I mean, if he wanted me out, all he needs to do is look at my sheets. But then Garner can't *see* my risk sheets because the global risk system, which only this guy, *Brooks*, mister bloodstain on his basement floor, has the password to, and the risk system starts acting funny the day the FBI opens a case because he went missing."

Kyle finished his rant and gave Pete and Sully a triumphant sideways look as he gulped down another vodka shot.

"His wife, it's gotta be his wife," Sully jokingly proposed, deliberately ignoring Kyle's speech. "She called it in, right? She probably got sick of him, ya know? He's been pulling in, what—what do those guys make?"

"Prob the-orders, base, plus another four or five, takedown," Kyle filled in.

The-orders was a trader nickname for "three-quarters," which referred to three-quarters of a million dollars a year in base salary plus another four to five million in bonus and stock.

"No, head of risk, globally, Fortnum Bank? My market's one at one-five on the base," Sully rebutted. "Anyway, he's been making decent ducats for two decades, easy gig. He's got a great pad in the village, prob eight sticks that thing, easy, she figures, ya know, I'm tired of this dreadful log. My husband's worth twenty mil, but maybe there's a bulletproof prenup, in which case, she's like, fuck this guy, realizes it's easier to kill him than divorce him—"

"Hits him on the back of the head," Pete joined in, illustrating with a whack for effect.

"Yeah, tricks him into the basement, hits him on the back of the head, *voilà*, the blood," Sully finished.

Kyle laughed. "Yeah, maybe. The guy is a dead end."

"Stop being so paranoid about everything," Sully appealed.

"Thank you!" Pete gave an emphatic nod.

"Then I really shouldn't be drinking," Kyle joked.

"At least you finally put up the gold trade," Sully told him.

"No thanks to Sammy," Pete added.

"It cleared, though, yes?" Sully asked.

Both Pete and Kyle confirmed. "It hit," Kyle said. "Sammy booked it directly into risk instead of just giving us the confirm, like he was supposed to. If there *was* something wrong with the risk system and it gets resolved by tomorrow morning, Garner will call me in. I'm still exposed here, guys."

"What are you going to say to him?"

"It was a fat-finger mistake that's being corrected. By the time he learns it's real, it'll be expiration Friday and the options will be worthless, our book will be up sixty mil, and the whole thing will be over. And Garner can go fuck himself."

"That's not bad, buys you time," Sully agreed.

"And if it takes longer to fix the risk system, then OK by us, too, even better."

"But what if your conspiracy theory is true?" Pete posed Kyle, tauntingly.

Sully smacked him. "Why you gotta bring him back to that?"

Kyle laughed, seemingly off his rant now.

"If the risk guy was for-real tortured and killed for the passwords to the risk system, then I think we're all fucked, and something very bad is going on," Kyle morbidly joked.

"Amy say anything more about it?"

Kyle shook his head. "No, she only knew about it in the first place because they have a system that shows all the newly filed cases each day. She's not even working it, different group. And I don't think they're taking it that seriously from what I saw at the house. Didn't look like anyone had even been over there yet. Probably be a week before they get around to it."

"You gonna tell Amy about your little detective story?" Pete tested.

"Fuck no. I already scared her away today. Screwed that up, big time. I'd just make it worse if I told her I broke the law snooping around the place. She'd arrest me." Kyle laughed with wide eyes.

Sully smiled and downed a vodka shot with some satisfaction.

"I don't know why you keep bothering with her. Anyhoo, the Fed'll lower rates tomorrow, all this crazy market positioning will subside, things will reset," Sully reassured, offering a refreshingly rational picture. Kyle and Pete each took another shot.

"You're right. Gold will probably jump, but not that much, and we'll ride sixty million into Friday, and I'll be out of this P&L hole," Kyle cockily endorsed.

"Ka-ching!" Pete toasted them as they all knocked down another round.

"Now if we can only get crude to stop rallying, then everything will be as it should," Kyle added.

"I saw that. Still bid, huh?"

"Makes no sense. And, what's fucked up, if I didn't have Garner on my back, I'd be selling more of it here, selling vol, selling gamma, back-end vega, every mother fuckin' thing. The whole product's a piece of shit at this level."

"Them's fightin' words," Pete cracked.

"I say crude resets, too, after Fed tomorrow," Sully added.

"And if it doesn't?" Kyle peered at him through his specs.

Sully shrugged his shoulders.

"I trade index vol. What the fuck do I know? You're the energy guy."

Sammy Bender Residence, Tribeca, Lower Manhattan, United States

Sammy lazed in his leather recliner, footrest extended, watching a sitcom. He had a bottle of lager on a side table, the remote in his hand, and an open bag of chips in his lap. Sammy rippled with laughter as he watched the show.

Sammy's apartment was a third-floor loft with a wide living room, ten-foot-high ceilings and two grand arched windows overlooking Duane Street below.

Sammy shoved his hand into the bag of chips, grabbing another wad as the sitcom laugh track rolled on in the background. A shadow appeared and loomed across the living room and then receded. Sammy did a double take, puzzled as to what it was.

He glanced at his windows. Sometimes cars passing below could cast funny lighting effects into the apartment, but his drapes were closed. Not seeing anything, he took another sip of his lager and got back into his show, chuckling with the jokes. But the shadow reappeared and stretched across the room again, halting for a few seconds on the ceiling only to vanish as quickly a moment later. Annoyed, Sammy put his beer down and retracted the footrest so he could stand and probe what the hell was doing that.

He peered around the room, but still couldn't surmise the source of the shadow. He shook his head, *weird*, and turned back to the TV to sit again.

The shadow surged back and filled the expanse above him. Sammy didn't have time to react—two gloved hands clutching a garrote came down around his neck and yanked back with a vicious heave.

Sammy squawked a muffled cry and retched. He was hoisted off his feet from the strong pull, almost hanging. His alligator arms desperately grasped behind him, swiping in the air. He clawed at the wire strangling his neck, scratching at it, trying to pull it away. His legs kicked out in a distraught fight, a battle for breath.

He kicked over the side table, sending the beer bottle cartwheeling through the air, where it shattered with a wet *pop* on his wall. His arms battled everything, swinging wildly, searching for something, anything.

Sammy's limbs weakened, losing their strength, and limply sagged by his sides as he went unconscious from lack of oxygen. The garrote was pulled tighter. Sammy's head drooped over his neck as life exhausted him. His full, hefty body slumped. His attacker loosened the wire and let the body crumble to the floor into a pile. He coldly regarded the lifeless Sammy at his feet.

It was the Hawk-Nosed Man from the Brooks basement. He hoisted up Sammy's body and dragged it closer to the recliner and shoved Sammy onto it. The Hawk-Nosed Man briefly left but returned a moment later with a long body-sized sack.

He grabbed the remote, switched off the TV and unzipped the large duffle.

DCI's Office, CIA Headquarters

Angered by the latest events, the director glared at Kate and Bob.

"We've reacquired the van. Definitely appears headed into the Hong Kong area. They're still on route G324, driving west. They'll be able to exit onto roads leading to Hong Kong in about twenty minutes. If they don't, it'll be Guangzhou," Kate informed.

"Navy's assembling a blockade, they'll—" Bob started.

"Blockade? We can't have—"

"They know to make it appear like routine patrols," Bob reassured.

"The Chinese think those are *their* waters," the director complained.

"We know that. They'll play it right."

"What do you mean, *play it right*? How the fuck have you guys played it *right* so far? We've already lost an officer, three wounded, *and* we have a goddamned loose nuke headed for Hong Kong—what if *that's* the target?" the director screamed. "We're talking about a major international financial center, on a very densely populated hillside, that could be in ruins in a second—did you think of that?" he bleated.

"We're almost certain that's not the destination," Kate asserted.

"Oh, almost certain?" the director mockingly shot back.

He was breathing heavily. He went and sat on his sofa, tormented, rubbing the back of his neck, and mechanically removing and cleaning his glasses, hardly even aware he was doing it.

"What makes you so sure?" he questioned.

"If you wanted to take out Hong Kong, you wouldn't hire a couple of Syrians who don't know anything about that region. These guys have hardly been out of the Middle East. They don't operate well outside of there. They wouldn't have killed what they thought was a Chinese highway cop otherwise. You hire these guys because you have a target or destination *in* the Middle East. The way they've been traveling, not stopping or resting, it's like they're on a schedule. They want to get through China as fast as they can," Kate reasoned.

The director replaced his glasses on his face and stared at her through his lenses for a seemingly silent two minutes, processing her logic.

"What kind of radiation detection do the Chinese have at their ports? Any chance they could pick this up?" the director asked, his anger subsiding.

"Random checks with handhelds. It's possible but unlikely they'd find it. These are busy ports. Plus, I'm thinking it's likely the brothers thought of this and are planning to thwart it somehow," Kate responded.

"And what about the fuckup in Fujian? Chinese on to that yet?"

"No sign. We're keeping an eye on it. It'll probably be covered up as a bandit robbery that went bad. Our guys cleaned it up pretty good," Bob explained.

"Locals see anything?"

"Some witnesses, yes. They'll likely keep their mouths shut and pretend they didn't see anything. It was confusing from their perspective anyway," Kate added.

"And we lost an officer," the director lamented.

"We did," Bob commiserated.

"One more for the wall," he said somberly.

There was an uncomfortable silence. Then the director resumed his inquiry.

"Do we have ground visual on that van?"

"Not yet. We're moving as fast as we can because we expect them to ditch it, if they haven't already."

The director flattened his eyes at them.

"Shit get on that. We miss that, we miss everything."

"As soon as they turn, we'll have teams in place," Kate covered.

"Damn it, we'd better." The director let out a loud sigh, and then pressed, "And what about Assad, and the North Korean nuclear program connection?"

"ME sections at it, and Mossad's pulling stuff for us. They're still jammed after Outside the Box, but we got them piqued, given this could be part of the same op," Bob told him.

The director nodded with some satisfaction.

"Be transparent. I'll even call Moshe myself," the director insisted.

Moshe Dayan was the most senior Israeli spymaster. Their relationship was a good one, especially when US and Israeli interests aligned, like they did here.

"You should call him anyway, for courtesy's sake. If the lower officers think this has anything to do with the Assad-NK railroad, it'll bubble up fast. You know how they are. And we need any nugget they might have. It'll help us," Bob further persuaded the director.

He looked at Bob directly through his specs and grinned.

"We're bringing them in early, even before our own administration. They love that," the director added coyly. "Speaking of which, get me a draft for tomorrow's pudder. This has to stay in front of POTUS and the NSC now."

Kate and Bob were back in the center. There was a rush as a US naval intelligence contingent had joined them. They worked feverishly with all the CIA analysts to move navy assets into place for the dragnet. Kate was about to log into her machine for an update when a liaison approached her.

"You guys must of have greased the wheels with Mossad because they're suddenly giving us a ton of fresh," the liaison opened a folder with a wealth of new data to show Kate. "They know these Syrian brothers but confirmed they're more freelancers. Assad's agents use them here and there for courier stuff, never sensitive operations and almost never state-level business. They're cutouts, and not al-Qaeda," he explained.

"They're not?"

"They said only that there could be a looser affiliation, but they weren't really inside the network, you know, Shia-Sunni thing," he continued.

"Interesting. What about Iran, Hezbollah?"

"Closer, but still loose. They've done one-offs for them, too. They'd rather work with them than al-Qaeda, but—"

"But what?" Kate pressed him.

"We've also got some NSA hits from a keyword scrub. There's increased traffic involving these guys and some other nodes in the Middle East—a poorly masked code word for Ras Tanura shows up more and more," he reported.

"Ras Tanura?"

"Largest oil loading terminal in the world. Saudi's crude gets loaded onto tankers," he informed.

Kate shifted, becoming much more interested and unsettled.

"And this is brought up as a possible *target* in this traffic?"

"We think so, yes."

Kate logged onto her machine, punched up Ras Tanura, and zoomed into the profile. A map displayed a spur in the western Persian Gulf where the facility was located. Included in the CIA's internal wiki were photographs showing a sprawling sea terminal with scores of immense crude oil storage tanks, a vast array of sea derricks, and a long queue of fat oil tankers lined up to be filled with crude.

"How much of the world's oil supply flows through here?" she asked.

"Uh…" He flipped through his notes. "This is all of Saudi Arabia's output, so, twelve million barrels a day, about ten to fifteen percent of the world's supply."

"Christ," Kate uttered.

Ox Bar, Ninth & Gansevoort

The boys emerged from the bar, drunker than when they'd entered hours earlier. They each hailed a separate taxi. As the cabs converged, they waved to each other.

"Good night."

"Later."

"See ya'z tomorrows," Pete lobbed as his cab pulled away.

Kyle got into his and shut the door.

"Hi, Battery Park City, downtown—oh, but, hey? Can you drive through West Tenth street off Hudson on the way?"

The cabbie eyed him questioningly in the rearview mirror. "West Tenth, West Village?" he clarified.

"Yes," Kyle impatiently retorted.

Some minutes after, they approached the corner of West Tenth and Hudson.

"Here, make a right. And go slow," Kyle instructed.

The cabbie eyed him in the rearview again with a bit more skepticism but complied. They rolled down the quiet brownstone street Kyle and Pete had scoped out earlier. It was now about ten p.m. The street was dark and deserted except for an occasional dog walker striding down a sidewalk.

Most of the houses' lights were on inside, and some had the blue TV glow strobing rooms and windowpanes. Many also had their windows opened to let in the cool fall evening air.

"Slow, slow," Kyle insisted. He scooted over to the side of the Brooks house. Kyle eyed it closely as they drifted past. All the windows were dark. No sign of any life or activity. He paid closer attention to the upstairs windows. Unlike the other brownstones on the street, their windows were shut tight. Strange, given the nice fall evening.

"Thank you. We can go now," Kyle told him as he eased back in the seat.

The cabbie regarded him impatiently and then floored it and they accelerated through West Tenth and swung onto Hudson and continued downtown.

Later, Kyle was in his home office, scrolling through his emails on his PC. The TV was on, tuned to ESPN. His attention bounced between the TV and his inbox. Bored of tabbing through his email, Kyle brought up his quotes terminal, eyeing the current price of crude oil futures. The futures were trading higher, $87.10, up $1.10 from the earlier day session. He loaded the oil price chart, notching it to display in a daily frequency. The recent price path of crude oil showed a near-continuous, steady rise from about two weeks earlier.

Kyle, still partially drunk, vexed over it. He grabbed the remote and tuned the TV to the financial channel.

"...expectations for the Federal Reserve meeting tomorrow, all analysts surveyed anticipate, *at least*, a twenty-five basis point cut, if not a full half-point... In other markets, in the Asian overnight session, equities are recovering, up almost ten points. Gold also continues to rise ahead of the Fed meeting, up about two fifty nearing seven eighteen..." the announcer went on.

Kyle loaded up a chart of gold. He used the charting software to overlay the price history of gold with that of crude oil. They were wildly different until about two weeks ago when both started their recent upward push. Kyle noted the correlation between them, but he dismissed it as coincidence, or both being related to the Fed or reacting similarly to the recent attacks.

"...and crude oil, also trading higher in overnight action, up over a point. Elsewhere, the Nikkei..."

Kyle lowered the TV volume. He resumed tabbing through his work emails. He arrived at a summary note Shirin had sent him toward the end of that day, recapping everything they had discussed earlier from her research on the gold option trade.

His eyes skimmed over the summary, and he stopped at the bottom which read, "Top drivers of gold moving higher, 1) dollar weakness/inflation, 2) general uncertainty, 3) geopolitical events, 4) terrorist attacks."

He fixated on the terrorist attack reference. His focus bounced from Shirin's email up to the crawler on the financial channel and back to the charting software.

Kyle eyed the prices of crude oil and gold again. He dwelled on terrorist events in the context of both gold and crude oil rising recently in tandem. He moused over to the search engine on his browser and typed in: "largest terrorist attacks since 2000," and scanned through the results:

USS Cole, *Yemen, 2000; September 11 attacks, New York, 2001; anthrax, United States, 2001; Passover massacre, 2002; US consulate Karachi bombing, 2002; Bali nightclub bombings, 2002; Moscow theater hostage crisis, 2002; Riyadh compound bombings, 2003; Quetta mosque bombing, 2003; Imam Ali mosque bombing, 2003; Moscow Metro bombing, 2004;* SuperFerry *bombing, Philippines, 2004; Madrid train bombings, 2004; Basra bombings, 2004; Khobar Towers bombing, 2004; Beslan school siege, 2004; London subway and transit bombings, 2005; Baghdad bombings, 2005; Delhi bombings, 2005; Amman bombings, 2005; Mumbai train bombings, 2006; Sadr City Iraq bombings, 2006; Baghdad bombings, 2007; Yazidi bombings, 2007...*

There were also scores of other incidents. Kyle reviewed those attacks that involved high-profile Western targets, or oil infrastructure. He inspected the dates of those events and then cross-referenced with his historical price charts of crude oil and gold. Intriguingly, with some of the attacks, he noticed price run-ups in the days before leading up to the attack.

Kyle knew, because he made a living off it, that options were the vehicle of choice when someone knew of something in advance. If you had prior knowledge of an event, of a piece of good or bad news on a publicly traded company or asset, it was easiest to bet on it through options, rather than the underlying asset itself.

Kyle, Sully, and Pete, and all option traders, constantly dealt with players who had better information than they did. Sometimes it was easy to spot. Sometimes it wasn't. That was the art of it. Option traders referred to the business of trading options, especially *selling* options, as pinching nickels in front of an oncoming steamroller. It was a numbers game. The best options traders were adept at staying ahead of that steamroller and not getting clipped by it.

Insider trading, or front-running, as was the trading-desk parlance for it, with terrorist attacks was not new. Option traders had long suspected this had been going on. From the money perspective, it wasn't difficult to see that terrorism was becoming a business, effectively. There were financiers behind the terrorists—moneyed interests funding and donating to these terrorist groups. It didn't take long for these terrorist financiers to figure out there was a market reaction to an attack. Bomb an oil facility, and the price of crude oil would jump, and so forth.

Much of Wall Street recalled the scores of highly unusual trades ahead of the 9/11 attacks. The most notorious, to option traders especially, were, of course, the large put option trades on UAL (United Airlines) and AMR (American Airlines) merely days ahead of the attacks. Put options paid off when the stocks of UAL and AMR dropped, which they did, as those were the airlines that flew the planes that were hijacked on 9/11. The 9/11 Commission Report did make a mention of these options trades, and the investigation of them which determined the trades had innocuous explanations, but many on Wall Street remained skeptical.

Kyle toggled through different time-frame charts of gold. He got to 2001 and September 11. He saw the large jump in the price of gold as a result of the attacks. Shirin was right, price reactions in gold did appear to correlate with the intensity of the attack or with the financial importance of the target.

His half-drunken, blurry gaze wandered the room in thought. Kyle didn't like any of what he saw—paranoia or not, things felt a bit eerie. What to do about it, if anything, was the question.

Kyle knew one thing, though. The informational value in options was quite good. Those who were front-running events or earnings or takeovers in stocks or whatever and used options as their vehicle for illicit gains never understood how much information they were giving away to the marketplace. The choice of which options they traded, which strike prices, which expirations, betrayed so much. In the case of terrorism, that all conveyed *what* they thought would be impacted, and by how much, through which strike prices they traded, which also implied how far they believed the underlying asset price would move, which informed the expected *intensity* of the attack. Most importantly, the specific option expiration they chose would reveal *when* they thought an attack would happen.

Kyle added all this up in his drunken head. It also hurt his stomach. Or maybe that was the vodka and oysters. It was still difficult to convince himself. Was he being paranoid? Were all these just coincidences? He thought about Stephen Brooks. How strange it was he had simply vanished in what now appeared to Kyle like a foul-play situation. And the risk system Brooks controlled—a critical risk-management system for one of the largest money center banks in the world—was now behaving strangely. It made him even more uneasy.

It was midnight. Kyle grabbed his cell phone. He scrolled to Amy's number and selected it. His thumb hovered over the green Dial button for a few seconds. But he shrank and closed the clamshell and threw it across the room.

"Fuck!" he yelled in frustration.

Kyle switched off his PC and the TV and left the room to go to sleep.

Route 9, Hong Kong, New Territories, Hong Kong

Kelso sat in the front passenger seat of a parked SUV, peering through a pair of binoculars. A CIA driver sat next to him, and in the back seat, another CIA officer from Shenzhen also surveilled their target.

It was late morning, and they were on the shoulder of a single-lane dirt road in a developing residential district, monitoring a vacant lot amid a collection of three-story condos.

Kelso lowered the binoculars.

"That's our van. The right side and rear windows are shot out. And I have one target, and…" Kelso squinted with his own naked eyes across the unfinished lot and then raised the binoculars again.

He watched the tall Syrian bring the damaged white van to a stop in an alley between apartments. There was a blue Nissan parked a few meters behind it. The Syrian shut off the van and exited, still wearing his business suit. Eyeing his surroundings, he walked to the Nissan and opened its trunk.

Kelso observed the Syrian transfer a large case from the back of the van to the

Nissan's trunk. Giving the damaged van a final once-over, the Syrian removed his pack from the van, returned to the Nissan, got inside, and started it up.

"We got a problem," Kelso announced, lowering the binoculars, "I only see one target. Where's the second dude?"

The Nissan reversed out of the alleyway, curved onto the single-lane street and accelerated away. Kelso tapped the CIA driver to start up their SUV.

"Drive slowly past the van and then get on his tail," Kelso instructed.

As they approached, Kelso raised the neutron sniffer to the emptied husk of the abandoned van. No returns when trained on the empty rear bay.

"Yeah, he moved it to the Nissan," Kelso proposed.

The CIA team accelerated past the van and caught up to their quarry. They were directly behind the Syrian but kept their distance, deftly pacing him.

Kelso fixed the sniffer at the trunk of the Nissan. The readings blazed to max.

"This one's still hot. But they may have split up," Kelso confirmed the data. He looked down the road ahead of them. "Where's this going?"

The CIA officer in the back replied, "If he keeps on here, it'll lead into the Lung Shan Tunnel and then to Route 9, which goes into Hong Kong city proper."

"Where are the main ports, in relation to this route?"

"Nine leads right to Kwai Chung Terminal, largest port here," he replied.

"Stay on him. That's probably where he ends up."

Kelso got on his sat phone and dialed.

Operation 912 Task Force Center

The team huddled over a speakerphone as Kelso reported.

"...we're back on the target. Confirmed he's lit. Problem is, we lost one of them, and possibly cargo with him. We're latched on to the taller of the two, with just a single box. No sign of the shorter one. They must have siphoned off somewhere between Xiamen and Shenzhen. You better scour whatever overheads to figure out what happened. We're missing part of the picture now."

Kelso hung up. Kate cursed. She looked at Carly, who'd already anticipated her next ask. "Yup, calling over now."

Kate kept the group huddled together.

"We need to find this Farouk, the shorter one. Get all regional stations on that. He can't have gotten very far in a few hours. Mark any of the break-off points along this route—324—and we might have a worse problem if they're splitting up bomb components. We might assume, *might*, that Amir has the fissile core, and Farouk has the high explosives, which is going to make it ten times harder to find and detect him because he's not hot," Kate lectured her team.

"Sarah and I will scrub the overheads as soon as Captain Bolling has them. There must be something, a second vehicle somewhere," Dr. Ahn reasoned.

Kate offered a rare smile, which then vanished quickly. "And if both of them have lit cargo, then we're really fucked. So, find him, fast."

Dr. Ahn and Sarah beelined for Carly's desk.

Route 9, Hong Kong

The SUV kept on the blue Nissan. The Syrian was accelerating down the four-lane highway and weaving in and out of traffic. The CIA driver was now swerving in parallel to keep up.

"Just stay on him, don't be too cute," Kelso warned.

"He's crossing over to the exit side. That's strange. He should stay on Route Nine," the driver said.

"Look, he's getting off Route Nine," the officer in the back agreed, pointing. "Don't lose him."

"He's heading onto the Tsing Yi North Bridge. That's not going to the freighter terminals," the driver updated, indicating the Nissan was now deviating from the expected course.

"Is there another way to get to the terminals from the bridge?" Kelso asked.

"No, there isn't," he answered.

"He might have made us, so he could be trying to shake us now," Kelso speculated. "Where does the bridge go?"

The officer in the back was now sitting up in between them and more concerned with this development.

"It leads to the airport expressway," he revealed.

"What do you mean, the airport expressway—Hong Kong International?" Kelso probed, incredulous.

Both CIA officers gave a confident, "Yes."

The blue Nissan flew onto the bridge with the SUV staying in chase, only a few vehicles behind.

"Any shot he gets off before the airport?"

"There are some ports on the southern side of the island, smaller ones, mostly used for crude oil tankers. He could be going there if he turns south. But, if he gets on the Tsing Ma Bridge, he's going to the airport."

The CIA driver then swerved after the Nissan right onto the bridge.

"Airport," he confirmed.

"Shit. Who do we have over there?" Kelso demanded, referring to available officers at HKI.

"Only two ops on rotation. And a couple agents, but you know, we can't really pull them in," the officer in the back seat responded.

Kelso thought for a moment.

"Get on with station ASAP. We need resources to cover the terminals. You guys know this airport?"

The driver affirmed, "I do, yes."

"Get me at least one ticket so I can access each major terminal."

Operation 912 Task Force Center

The speakerphone chimed on again with Kelso. Kate and others gathered around.

"We have another change-up. Target is headed to Hong Kong International. They're gonna fly this thing out of here."

Kate shot a wide-eyed look at Bob.

"We'll get you a tail ID on the aircraft it gets loaded on, but we'll need to get assets in place to track the thing once it's airborne. I bet they drop it off at a cargo terminal, and it gets shipped, air freight, along with hundreds of other parcels."

Kelso hung up.

"This keeps getting worse," Kate voiced.

"I have another headache. I have to go think," Bob complained and left.

"Anything on Farouk?" Kate called out.

"Working on it," Sarah shouted back to her.

Airport Road, Hong Kong International Airport, Hong Kong

The Nissan decelerated with the rest of the traffic onto the terminal access loop and coursed around the passenger terminal. The Syrian kept driving, past the parking lots, but remained on the Airport Road, accelerating through the wide bend ringing the air freight terminals.

"These are the air freight hangars here," the officer in the back pointed out.

"He could turn into any one of these," Kelso alerted.

But he didn't. The Syrian kept moving along the South Perimeter Road. He finally slowed approaching a plain gray two-story terminal building with tall, vertical windows and the letters, "Hong Kong Business Aviation Center."

"Shit. He's moving it on a corporate jet. Any of our people in there?"

"Only the passenger terminals. We have to go through our liaison."

"Get me a ticket, access, whatever you can. Do it quick."

The officer started making the calls.

The CIA driver tailed the Nissan into the business aviation parking lot. The Syrian found an empty spot and drove in and stopped with a sudden jerk. Emerging from his car, the Syrian retrieved his suit jacket and fit it on. He combed his hair and patted down his temples. In a few moments, he appeared just like a professional, ready for corporate jet travel. The SUV trolled by, keeping a low profile, and then swung around, idling at the end of the lot.

The tall Syrian slung his pack over his shoulder and walked to the rear of the car and opened the trunk. Gently hoisting the large bomb case from the boot, he extended its handle and strode into the terminal, wheeling the bomb case behind him just like a large roll-aboard piece of luggage.

Kelso leapt out of the SUV with the neutron sniffer in hand.

"We can't arrange tickets in time. Grab your jacket and follow me," he directed the CIA officer in the back, and told the driver, "Keep it running."

The two of them jogged after the Syrian. Kelso halted a few paces before the terminal entrance. He peered through the glass doors. Inside, he could see about two dozen travelers being processed and exiting out the rear side of the terminal to the tarmac where the awaiting corporate jets were.

"Go inside without me. Get the tail number of the jet he boards," Kelso requested, and added, "I'll be by that gate around the side. I can scan through the slats. When you get the tail number, call me so we can verify if the package gets put on board." The officer gave a nod, and Kelso finished, "Can we stop a plane from taking off? We won't have much time. These things fly when they're ready."

"Very tricky. Some of the HKI authorities are still more British aligned. We could rely on good relationships, but the Chinese may spot it quick, especially when we detain an aircraft, but may be the lesser of two evils if that thing gets airborne. Who knows where it goes after?" he commented.

Kelso eyed him at that last part. "Head in now."

The CIA officer straightened his jacket, smoothed his hair, and entered the terminal. Kelso hurried to the side of the building where the slatted metal fences were, through which there was a view to the tarmac and line of sight to the jets.

Inside the terminal, the CIA officer was confronted by a terminal agent.

"Hi, which is your flight number, please?"

The officer craned around to locate the Syrian and spied him moving through security. He kept one eye on his target and addressed the attendant, inventing a quick distraction.

"Apologies, give me some minutes, please, just waiting for my luggage to arrive," he artfully replied.

"Yes, of course. You can wait over there, and security is through there," she informed him, pointing first to a short bank of a dozen leather seats and then to an in-terminal conveyor and x-ray machine.

The CIA officer gave a "Thank you" and stepped to the bank of leather seats, not removing his eyes from the Syrian.

The terminal doors behind security led to the tarmac. The whine of readying jets wafted inside whenever the doors opened and travelers exited to their aircraft.

The officer edged closer to the windows to gain line of sight to both Amir moving through security and to as many of the waiting jets as he could. From this vantage, he scoped the Syrian as he advanced to the metal detector.

A piece of plutonium, shaped however it was, would appear like any other metal object on an x-ray device. Unless security had specialized equipment, or training, to identify a radioactive source, the contents would not appear unusual. Sometimes the radiation could interfere with the x-rays themselves, creating a sort of cloudiness on the monitor.

The CIA officer fixed on the x-ray machine operator, closely observing his expression as the bomb case rolled through the x-ray cabinet. He also kept an eye on the Syrian, who was himself staring at the x-ray operator.

The operator suddenly stopped the conveyor belt. The luggage line slid to an abrupt halt. The Syrian, on edge, approached the man. A guard stepped to the Syrian. The CIA officer stared as this was developing. He couldn't intervene if there was action.

The x-ray tech squinted to see what was on his monitor. He slapped the top of the display several times, as if trying to get interference to clear. He pressed his eyes up to the screen as he banged on it again.

The now nervous-looking Amir scrutinized everyone close to him. He panned the terminal, and the guards, his eyes ricocheting among all the security cameras. He broke a sweat, wiping his brow with the back of his hand as he swiveled around trying to identify anyone who might be observing him.

And then, as if something instantly cleared up for the x-ray operator, he lost interest and sank back in his chair and resumed the conveyor. The bomb case rolled through onto the metal retrieval table.

The terminal continued to circulate as normal. Edgy and suspicious, the Syrian finally gripped the bomb case handle and hauled it off the x-ray table and stepped toward the tarmac doors.

The CIA officer repositioned himself to watch the Syrian exit the terminal. The officer counted each aircraft, mentally recording key details: its size, shape, number of windows, engines, and other features.

Amir emerged outside on the tarmac. The officer watched the Syrian pivot a few times, searching. Amir spotted his aircraft and beelined for a midsize beige corporate jet about fifty meters out. The officer saw at once which aircraft the Syrian was heading to. He dialed Kelso.

"Medium-size Beechcraft or Gulfstream, white or beige, seven passenger windows along the body, two rear-mounted engines, and, hang on..."

The officer retrieved a small set of spyglasses and subtly pulled them to his eyes. He mouthed the tail number as he committed it to memory, and just as fast, slid the spyglasses back in his pocket.

"And tail number: Tango-seven-one-two-Foxtrot."

He hung up and kept his eyes glued to the Syrian, who was dragging the bomb case toward the awaiting jet. He watched a flight attendant motion to the open luggage bay on the underside of the plane. The Syrian reluctantly released the bomb case to the attendant but then helped him hoist the case and position it snugly inside the compartment.

Outside the terminal, by the slat fence, Kelso stooped to one knee, positioning the neutron sniffer "lens" through the gate bars. Its nose barely fit in between slats, but there was enough play to aim the sniffer at the Syrian's jet.

Kelso squinted through the eyepiece. Its reading bars blazed to near full strength again as he aimed it with laser straightness at the rear side of the Syrian's aircraft. The gadget was indeed on that plane. Kelso put down the neutron sniffer and removed a small camera from his jacket, pushed the zoom lens out to max, and snapped a dozen photos of that jet.

Operation 912 Task Force Center

Two a.m., Kate was in everyone's face, shouting orders.

"Can we stop this? Can we stop this plane from taking off?"

"We're trying," shouted a liaison officer. "We're on with Hong Kong station chief. We're on with MI6. They're on with Hong Kong airport security. It may be too late."

Scanlon also reported, "We have the tail number; looking at registries now."

"Captain, we need to get tracking in place," Kate, with fourth coffee cup in hand, yelled over to Carly.

"We're piecing together coverage as soon as we can ascertain heading and flight plan," she hollered back.

"Hurry up, if this thing takes off, it's out of Hong Kong airspace fast and back into China's, and who knows where else it goes."

One of the liaison officers on with the Hong Kong station chief started to relay the conversation.

"We're losing it. It'll be airborne shortly. Tail number, Tango-seven-one-two-Foxtrot. Shit, flight plan says destination is Mandalay, Myanmar—Burma. Will land in about three hours."

"Damn it!" Kate exclaimed. "Get on with any Burma assets we have, now."

Kate calculated quickly, looking up at the large map of southern China. "Burma can't possibly be final destination, either. Just another flip station," she thought aloud. "And figure out who owns this jet. Let's get the manifest, leasing data, anything we can."

Airport Road, Hong Kong International Airport

Kelso tracked the plane as it taxied for takeoff, but the sniffer's readings became less and less reliable until the jet was out of range entirely.

The CIA officer who was inside the terminal found him, and they watched the plane zip down the runway and soar into the air.

Kelso pulled out his sat phone, dialed.

"We couldn't stop it?... Yeah, got it." He hung up.

"It's headed west. Come on, we're done here," Kelso resolved.

Kelso looked skyward in the direction of that ascending corporate jet. No longer visible, it had disappeared into the clouds. He squinted at it in the distance, as if he could still see the aircraft.

"Fuck."

He got into the SUV and slammed the door shut.

Wednesday, September 19, 2007

Kyle's Apartment, Ritz-Carlton Residences

Kyle rolled back and forth in his bed, unable to sleep. His eyes opened in the darkness. He blinked a few times and sat up. Reaching for his cell, he flicked on the light. The time displayed: 3:23 a.m.

"Always a three handle," he grumbled as he rose and shuffled into the kitchen where he poured a glass of orange juice and walked into his home office.

Kyle turned on his PC and the TV, which was covering the Asian and European markets. Absently sipping his juice, he loaded up his trading software and surveyed the current prices.

Oil was trading flat after its run-up the previous day, hovering near $87. Equity futures were also sideways. But gold was actively higher, up over $2, crossing $720. Kyle flinched when he saw it.

He scanned the news sites but didn't find any rationale for the move. Kyle leaned back in his chair and drank more of his juice as he tried to deal with insomnia and all the thoughts racing through his head. Something more therapeutic he knew was football. He loaded his fantasy football page and started reviewing his matchup for the upcoming weekend.

"Motherfucker. LaDainian, I should have played you last weekend. Won't make that mistake again. You're starting Sunday," Kyle whispered. He was about to click on his other players when he noticed a blinking on his quote terminal.

Crude oil futures were up $1.90 to $89 in a second.

"What the fuck?" Kyle looked up at the TV. But there was no news or other indication of the sudden jump. Kyle stared at the real-time trades plotting on the chart as they happened.

"Something's going on." He glanced around his office, a bit frustrated that he didn't have access to all his trading systems that he had at work.

Kyle gulped down the rest of his juice and hurried into his bedroom. He brushed his hair and got dressed.

Abqaiq Crude Oil Processing Center, Saudi Arabia

Gas burned and billowed into the crystal-blue air from the mouths of dozens of refinery stacks that poked above acres of interwoven metal pipes shining in the hot desert sun. Abqaiq crude oil processing center was a sprawling refinery, one of the largest in the Kingdom. The center distilled millions of barrels of raw crude oil into other products such as heating oil, gasoline, and jet fuel.

On an extended approaching road, a single sedan slowed and veered into the heavily guarded entrance gate. It was an ultra-high-security facility. Abqaiq had been the site of an attempted al-Qaeda attack in February of the previous year, 2006. Several bomb-laden cars had made it through the first layer of security but were stopped at the second, detonating early or exploding from the Saudi security force's gunfire.

Inside the approaching sedan, Abdel, a distillates chemist in his forties, dabbed sweat from his forehead with a cloth as his car crept to a stop at the outer gate. Guards emerged and surrounded his vehicle. He lowered his window and presented his facility ID.

Upon validation, several guards retreated, as he was an employee. One guard checked underneath the vehicle with a mirror, and a second approached the driver's side window. He motioned for Abdel to pop the trunk, which he did. The guard with the mirror scanned the empty trunk, closed it, and waved approval.

At the inner gate, Abdel again presented his ID. The second group inspected the sedan's interior and then advanced him on as well.

Abdel drove into the main complex and wound up a spiraling access ramp of a raised four-level parking deck. He reached the roof and found an empty slot and braked the vehicle, but he didn't shut it off yet.

He switched on his car radio and settled into the music, relaxing for the moment, dabbing his sweaty forehead again. He reached inside his shirt pocket and removed a photograph. It was an old, sepia-tone of a pretty woman, probably taken decades before. He smiled at the faded face and stuck the photograph back in his pocket. He lowered the volume on the radio.

Abdel peeked at his watch and then looked out through the windshield at the empty lot ahead of him. There was a low retainer wall ringing the top deck, and he dwelled on the refinery stacks sticking up beyond it. He inhaled deeply and floored it.

The car screeched off its blocks and barreled toward the retaining wall. He accelerated straight into it. The section of the wall exploded outward as the car burst through the barrier and, from four stories in the air, flew off the top of the parking deck and arced above the refinery, nosing down and drilling into the great briar of fuel lines.

The car impacted in the complex grid of pipes, thick and thin, rupturing and breaking them apart and igniting a massive explosion that surged into a smoldering black spire, rising, and spreading out into the air above the refinery. Dozens of secondary explosions blew apart adjacent sections of the network as shrapnel and flaming oil products erupted in a chain-reaction catastrophe. A reverberating boom accompanied a widening shock wave, blowing out windows and rocking the entire plant.

Fortnum Bank Equities Trading Floor

The trading floor was near empty when Kyle entered. The global trading clocks on the walls showed four a.m., local. Systems people bandied about the floor doing maintenance. There were a few traders and sales traders who covered the EMEA region scattered about the floor, but otherwise, it was deserted, still hours before even the early crowd arrived.

Kyle switched on his monitors and booted up his machine, his screens shining brightly amid the darkened setting. He grabbed a handset and was about to make a call when the wall television above him flashed a red "Breaking News" banner. The television's audio could be piped to the trading desk phone turrets, so Kyle dialed up the volume on his receiver.

"...a breaking-news alert, an explosion was reported at a Saudi oil refinery outside the city of Abqaiq. The initial damage assessment is reportedly extensive, but details are limited and we're still learning more. Our local correspondent..."

Kyle lowered the volume. The television broadcast a sky-high column of twisting black smoke.

"Two attacks in two days. What the hell's going on out there?" Kyle said out loud as if Pete were there next to him. He even glanced over expecting a reply.

Kyle scoured the markets. He had tiled charts of crude oil, gold, S&P, and ten-year treasuries in a two-by-two array so he could watch them simultaneously. Crude futures were shooting higher, up $2.82 to $91.82 and gold was up another $5 to $725. Equities were down, though not terribly, a few S&P points, and the ten-year treasury was up small.

Something didn't sit right. Kyle scrutinized the time stamps of exactly when the price moves in oil had occurred. He rewound the chart to when he was drinking juice in his apartment. Crude was trading flatly, little changed on light volume, but then started to trade higher, also on thin volume, at about three thirty a.m. his time. Kyle triangulated the time zones, referencing Abqaiq, Saudi Arabia, which was seven hours ahead, he lined up the equivalent at ten thirty a.m. local.

He searched news outlets to see if he could resolve the attack moment. He navigated to dozens of local Middle Eastern sites, discovering several that reported the incident as shortly before eleven a.m. local time, which, if accurate, meant there were buyers of crude oil futures at least a half hour before the attack.

Couldn't be another one, Kyle thought, shaking his head as he examined their options analytics software. He wanted to look at crude oil options volume from the previous day.

Kyle saw there was some higher-than-expected front-month call buying yesterday. It wasn't huge, but there was some. It could have just as easily been normal activity, but it did appear suspect as there were several conspicuous trades in higher, away-from-the-money call strikes.

Insider trading volume patterns in options were often easy to spot, if you knew what to look for. Typically, volumes of put and call options with strike prices close to where the underlying was currently trading would have the most volume. And logically, volumes of options with more distant strike prices would taper the farther away you got. But, if insider trading was happening, this pattern reversed. The volumes of farther out of the money calls or puts (depending on which way they were betting) would be greater than the volumes of contracts close to the current stock or futures price.

Kyle observed exactly this reversed stacking pattern in the volumes of crude oil options from the previous day. It was noticeable. He grew angry looking at the trades, banging his phone against his desktop as he made the realization. This wasn't an accident, he knew.

He wondered again if the huge gold option trade might be related to these recent attacks. That made him think about the trade details—was there anything he could extract to gain more insight, especially about the customer behind the trade? Sammy, of course wasn't in yet, but there were other sales traders on the floor, and they had access to the sales systems.

Kyle stood up and located a sales trader a few rows over.

"Courtney?" he cast a strong whisper. She swiveled to the approaching Kyle.

"Springer? What are you doing here so early? You pull an all-nighter and decide to not even go home?" she joked.

"I wish. I couldn't sleep. Insomnia, killing me," Kyle lamented.

"I'm sorry, that sucks. I've been there. Personal, or Fed stuff?" she asked as Kyle sat in the empty desk seat next to her.

"Both, I guess... Hey, I have a favor to ask," he started.

"What's up?"

"You can look up customer details on your sales systems?"

"We can, yeah. Who you want?"

"It's a hedge fund I did an OTC trade with yesterday. But they're a bit murky, so I want some more data," Kyle explained.

"Oh, OTC and ISDAs. You're gonna like what I got to show you. Come here." She beckoned him closer to watch over her shoulder.

An ISDA agreement was the International Swaps and Derivatives Association master agreement. This was the key to being able to engage in over-the-counter dealing with banks. An entity, such as a hedge fund, would work out an ISDA agreement before any trades were put up between the two counterparties. This master agreement was a lengthy legal document that demanded everything from bank records to addresses and credit histories of the principals behind the entities—like LLCs, or other structures. Basically, it was a gigantic legal bastion to ensure the banks got paid and that, if they didn't, know who they could sue.

"You're gonna like this," Courtney repeated with a smirk on her face. "I know a way to access the original ISDA master. There's a bug in the software. I figured it out by accident one time, hee-hee," she delighted, looking at him after her facetious laugh, but then gave him a ruthless look. "You tell anyone about my little secret, I'll fucking kill you. I don't care if you were a fed, I'll kick your ass." She was half serious.

"That's great. I love you. What do you use it for?" Kyle laughed with her but was inwardly pleased.

Courtney checked around her to see if anyone was within earshot.

"It's great. I can tell who's behind certain trades and who's fronting for what entity. It's given me superman powers to sniff out fast-money fuck heads, and call 'em out. I've probably saved the bank millions and millions, but I'll never get credit. It also tells me who the real players are who pretend to be minnows. I know I can show them size. I've done some big trades for the Fort, and I'll never be rewarded for that, either." She sighed, and then got back on it. "Who's the entity? I'll show you my x-ray vision."

Kyle had it written on a small Post-it and read from it.

"Victoria Cross Capital, LLC," he said.

"Victoria Cross? Sounds British. Let's see here." Courtney entered the name.

The sales trader system was designed to provide business intelligence and other analytics on their customers' activity, so the sales traders could squeeze more trading out of them.

"Here's what we got. Now this is what the normal system shows," she started, doing air quotes around the word "normal."

"Looks like they're based out of Cayman Islands—*quelle surprise*—already a red flag"—she winked at Kyle—"and they last reported their AUM at one-point-two billion, so kind of medium sized," she read out.

"Good, at least they can pay," Kyle remarked.

AUM stood for "assets under management," basically how much money the entity managed.

"Yeah. That's important." She smiled. "Now here's the cool part, this isn't supposed to work. I think it's connected to a clearing system that only clearing people should have access to, but the programmers don't know about this little hack. You see here, if you click this, it takes you to the part of the ISDA that everyone can see, which is basically only the header file that shows there is an ISDA agreement...but *voilà*." She appended an extension in the URL, and then an electronic version of the complete ISDA agreement appeared.

Kyle's eyes widened when he saw it.

"You should be a programmer. That's huge. Scroll down, let's see who the principals are," Kyle eagerly demanded.

"Yeah, fuck this trading shit," she said as she dialed down the page.

They arrived at the "Principals and Signatories" section. "Geez," she declared when she read it.

"What?"

"The principals are more LLCs. Look, this one, Isle of Man, this one, Guernsey, this one, Luxembourg," she read off. "If you wanted to hide something or were into shady shit..."

"That's the way to do it," Kyle finished her sentence. "So, no names at all?"

"Uh-uh, nothing." She gave him an exaggerated headshake. "And I bet if you could somehow get access to the registries in those jurisdictions, they'd be layered as well. This is designed to wash money and hide whoever's behind this," she said.

Kyle struck a disappointed look.

"I guess we tried. Thank you, Courtney, we almost had it."

Kyle had already backed into the aisle when she stopped him.

"Hey, wait a sec. Stop. The. Presses. I recognize *this name*. I've seen this before," she proclaimed with the satisfaction of catching a thief.

"What? Which?" Kyle wheeled back beside her.

"This LLC, here. You know how before I came to the Fort, I worked at Lehman? I worked in, guess what—client onboarding. I basically owned this process for the heinies," she explained.

A heinie, usually a butt, was an industry nickname for HNWs, or high-net-worth individuals, who were the monied, sought-after whales of the asset management world. Courtney continued explaining.

"Yeah, Middle Eastern guy, or the name is, at least. Who the fuck knows, he could live anywhere, but I remember his signature. Hang on," Courtney busily scrolled through other apps and electronic documents.

"You mean this one—New Carolina Patriot Fund, LLC?" Kyle pressed.

"I remember because I figured it out—who was behind it, I mean. A couple of derbies ago, there was a gelding named Carolina Patriot. He wasn't very good. But I bet every year, ya know?"

"Nice, you bet the Derby?"

"I bet four times a year. I bet the Gold Cup and the Triple Crown. And I remembered that horse—but it was his owner, this Arab guy, I figured out he had to be the guy behind this LLC. Here, the name couldn't have been a coincidence, *Carolina Patriot*."

She pulled up a website and searched for the horse's name.

"This guy, yeah, that's him," she said, tapping a footnoted listing of horse owners on the web page. "No photos, but in some registries of the horse stable and owner, he showed up, *Fadhil al-Hammadi*. I remember, and I remember seeing his signature on the ISDA master for New Carolina Patriot Fund. It was hard to read, but it looked like what that name should look like," she recalled.

"We don't have an ISDA with New Carolina, do we?"

She shook her head. "No. Here's the full list, alphabetical. Not here. Which is prob why it's behind the scenes. They want to loiter in the shadows, ya know?"

"I take that back. You shoulda been at the FBI, with me," Kyle said with an even bigger grin as he scrawled the name down on one of her napkins.

"I'd love that. Get a gun," she said, dramatically firing an air pistol.

Kyle stood up. "You're the best thing that's happened to me all week," he told her, with all seriousness and gratitude.

"Thank me by getting some of your big-energy players to give me their flow. I'll take good care of you." She winked at him.

Operation 912 Task Force Center

Kate dozed on the sofa in her office, her head on the armrest and her left arm thrown across her forehead. Her eyes suddenly flew open, and she shook off her cobwebs, standing up in a single move.

She hit a speed-dial key on her phone. "Come into my office," she said.

A few moments later, Dr. Ahn and Sarah both stood before her, reddened eyes, looking quite tired themselves. Carly, also looking beat, joined, too.

"The second brother splitting from the van, do we have anything yet?"

"We're combing through everything. Most of our imaging tracks the van on an uninterrupted path until we pick it up again with the brother missing. Just from time stamp and velocity calculations, it doesn't look like there was a stop or a break," Carly answered.

"Keep looking, and meticulously, too. You only need minutes to pull a switch like that. He didn't just *vanish*. Unless they shoved him in the bomb case itself."

They all chuckled at the morbid joke.

"Calculate any changes in that van's velocity. Even if you guestimate. I understand there's slowdowns and traffic stops and all that, but do your best. There's gotta be something," Kate insisted. She continued, changing gears, "And what about the jet? Where is that right now?"

Dr. Ahn replied, reading off her notes, "It refueled in Burma and took off bearing west again. It's over Tibet. Could be headed to one of the northern Stans. We have very good, continuous coverage there," she added, looking to Carly, who nodded in confirmation. The northern Stans were Kyrgyzstan and Tajikistan.

"All the Chinese telemetry tests are conducted there. We keep a good eye on those," Carly agreed, referring to the Chinese missile development and nuclear tests conducted in the Tibet and Xinjiang regions.

"Nice work. Now get out. Bob and I have to update the director. What time is it?" Kate asked, mostly to herself.

"About five thirty," Sarah responded as they left her.

A few minutes later, Kate and Bob discussed with the director.

"Moshe keeps calling me, woke me up a few hours ago. I'd gone home to get some shut-eye, but he called my cell. They're putting more resources on this. They don't like it one bit. They don't like there is a loose nuke that is steadily making its way toward the Middle East. And I don't either," the director delivered.

"Do they have anything more on the Syrian angle?" Bob asked.

The director shook his head. "They *don't* think it's related. Just a coincidence. That may be true, which is good and bad. Makes it more difficult, you know?"

Kate's forehead wrinkled in doubt. "If it's independents, how did they get the connections to do this? There had to be some established networks or relationships to pull this off," she argued.

"Kate's right. A group of ideological nighttime raiders couldn't just dial up a North Korean general and ask him for a nuke," Bob concurred. "The corporate jet, the hops. There's dough behind this, well planned and funded. You don't just climb onto a waiting private jet in the Hong Kong corporate airport with a nuke on a roll-aboard," he made his point.

"We're running network and traffic analysis on the brothers. There have to be leads further up the chain," Kate added.

The director sighed. "No disagreement from me. But you know how these things evolve. Fear starts to take over. Moshe's going to start pulling his PM strings, who'll call POTUS. They'll pressure us for action, a takeout, wherever it is," the director told them.

"At this point, I'm not against that," Kate responded. "Probably the best thing. We had our shot."

"And what about the other brother? Where is he? Where'd he go?"

"We're still looking. He vanished. There had to be a changeup somewhere."

"I don't like it," Bob interjected.

"Nobody likes it. We can't figure out where or how he split off. We think he might have shadowed his brother—in case anything happened, he could continue the job," Kate added.

"He take anything with him?"

"Possibly. They may have split up the high explosive and the core. Easier to transport that way."

"I'm not buying that, thank you. Increases their risk. And limits the buyer if one of them gets tagged. I like the shadow theory better." The director paused for a moment and rocked in his seat. "Let's fucking find him. He wasn't wounded in the firefight, was he?"

"Don't think so but can't rule it out. If there were a bleeding Syrian with a gunshot wound somewhere along the Chinese coast, I think we would have located him by now."

The director chuckled.

"I'm with POTUS in an hour. Get me *any* new developments before then."

Fortnum Bank Equities Trading Floor

It was after six a.m. Traders and sales traders were arriving earlier than usual for the Fed. There would be a ton of market action ahead of the announcement.

Pete appeared and removed his jacket, hung it on the back of his chair. He glanced over at Kyle and noticed his already on and lit-up machines.

"You look like shit. How long you been here?"

"Couldn't sleep. I don't know, four maybe?"

"The refinery attack?"

"Yes. And I saw the futures run up ahead of it, too."

"For real? Like, front-running?"

"Something not sitting right, Pete. Not. Sitting. Right."

Pete smiled and sat and flicked on his monitors. "It's terrorists versus the Fed," he joked. "I'm hoping for the Fed."

Kyle laughed. "Me, too."

"Gold's up more now. We doing OK?" Pete asked him, referring to their risk.

"I'm figuring, yes. Where is it—seven twenty-five now? I'm figuring we might want to hedge more. Come to think of it, why don't you do that? Buy some futures, will you?" Kyle directed him. "If we get a big move off the Fed, we can trade around it. But I'm still thinking most of the Fed move is already priced in. There'll be a pop and probably a sell-off after the announcement," he added.

"What about options?" Pete asked him, bringing back up the possibility they could hedge with exchange-traded options. But Kyle shook his head.

"Vols are still too high pre-Fed. We can take a look after, hopefully vols will deflate, but if we play our cards right and everything sells off, we probably won't need to," Kyle detailed.

This was a common pattern in asset moves and events—there was even a saying for it, "buy the rumor or expectation, and sell the fact." If that played out, the expectations for the Federal Reserve lowering the discount rate were already incorporated into the price of gold, and so when the announcement finally came, gold wouldn't have any further to go. Those traders or hedgers who bought in anticipation would take their profits and sell gold, driving the price back down. It was a self-fulfilling dynamic, really.

"I'm thinking we wait for the pop and then start selling again. I figure it drops ten, maybe twenty, points after," Kyle ventured.

"Got it."

Kyle half stood and observed where the quants sat.

"Good, she just got in," Kyle observed.

"Who?"

"Shirin. Need more from her," Kyle mumbled and headed to Shirin's desk.

"Kyle, already? Can't I even get my coffee?" She saw Kyle coming a mile away.

"I'll get you your coffee."

"Aww, that's sweet. You better hurry up. I'm not a pleasant morning person. So, what'd you want?"

"Yes. I need something, and I need it quick."

"Quick?" she probed, eyeing him above her rims and checking her watch.

"Like, this morning."

She frowned at him but didn't refuse. "I'm *waiting*."

"I need you to look at terrorist attacks over the last, I don't know, since, like, ninety-eight. Show me option volumes in affected assets leading up to the attacks." Kyle watched her expectantly.

"*This* morning? Like, today morning?"

"I really need to see something."

She appeared annoyed, glanced at her watch again and back at Kyle. "This had better be a great fucking coffee," she demanded. "And then you owe me after, too. Like a Mafia favor."

"Done. I'll go get your coffee." And Kyle bolted.

Outside, Kyle crossed the street toward the coffeehouse and encountered Sully, who was pacing up and down the curb half a block north. Sully noticed Kyle and waved to him.

"Hey, coffee run. Come with me," Kyle hollered over to Sully.

Sully appeared distracted, preoccupied, but joined him anyway.

At the coffeehouse, they talked as they waited in line.

"I suppose you already know about the attack?" Sully started.

"I've been here since four."

"You get the irony?"

"I could go a lot of ways with that."

"If Garner hadn't made you close your position, you'd be getting killed here," Sully said.

Kyle laughed. "It's true. I'd be down probably twice, hundred mil or so. I still think it's a sell here."

"Of course, you do."

"It traded up again, you know, ahead of the attack? I couldn't sleep. I saw it when it happened."

"Shut. Up. You gotta stop, Kyle. Stop. Focus on the Fed today and bringing the gold trade home," Sully rebuked.

"Maybe the no sleep is adding to my paranoia. There's a lot, you know?"

"I know there's a lot, you ran through everything *over and over* with us last night, remember? You ever consider Garner's in on it, too? He got you out of that huge oil short just in time," Sully sarcastically made his point.

Kyle chuckled and then turned to Sully. "You alright, by the way? You seem a bit elsewhere. And I'm the one on no sleep."

Sully replied with an absentminded nod.

"I got a monster position in the S. I want this Fed meeting over with more than anyone," he admitted.

"No shit," Kyle commiserated.

They grabbed their coffees and headed back to the bank.

Operation 912 Task Force Center

Kate patrolled the center as different analysts and officers approached her with bits of new data. Paul Kazemi, a desk officer from the Middle East Directorate who'd just been assigned to the 912 Task Force, came by with his report.

"We've got a decent network built around the brothers now. Different operations over the last ten years, jobs they did, who they did them for, as much as we could pack in," he told her.

"How many names are we talking about?"

"Reliably? Probably about two dozen, give or take."

Kate studied him for a moment, thinking. She liked Paul. He was serious and thorough. She'd worked with him on a few prior joint ops with the MED (Middle East Directorate), including the recent Operation Outside the Box. He'd been stationed in Cyprus for a number of years and had built a track record as a great case officer, developing quite a few productive contacts in that challenging spy haven. Kate trusted him and so asked Bob to "work his magic" and get Kazemi on the team—almost impossible given the entire MED was focused on Iraq, Iran, al-Qaeda, or the UBL hunt—nobody could be spared. What favor the worm, Bob, had called in, she didn't know, but was grateful.

"Broaden that to the second tier. That's usually where the gold is, you know?"

Kazemi agreed, "We can do that. Probably gets us up to sixty or so."

"Get those lists out to DIA, NSA, FBI, even DEA. Put 'em on that system— what do we call it?"

"Sweeper."

"Sweeper, right. I can't keep track of all these new databases. Get the names into Sweeper as soon as you got 'em," Kate requested.

Sweeper was an interagency platform that broadcasted "people of interest." Implemented post-9/11, replacing the ineffective Intelink, Sweeper was accessible by the nearly twenty intelligence agencies across the federal government. A team at one agency tracking a target could enter the names into Sweeper, which would then expose the aliases to the full intelligence community if the names were also an investigative target for someone else.

Sarah approached Kate after she finished talking to Kazemi and drew her attention to the overhead monitor, which was now displaying a map of the Arabian Sea, surrounded by India on the east, Pakistan and Iran on the northern side, and Oman on the western side. There was a blinking red icon on the map over the Pakistani city of Karachi.

"Our jet headed south an hour ago and flew the length of Pakistan. Appears to be landing in Jinnah International Airport now," Sarah reported.

"We have people down there?"

"A few. Entire station's on other ops. We're third in line, but we are getting someone," Sarah answered.

"That means rookies," Kate said cynically. "Karachi is a big crossroads. They could load it onto a truck at the airport, onto a ship at the port, or refuel and take off again. Whichever, we need eyes on the ground."

Sarah informed her, "There's one officer at the airport now and two en route."

"Where's Terry? What about our SSO?"

"Terry's got him forward-positioned at Bagram. And he's prepping JSOC for more tier ones if we need them. He'll move as soon as we have destination."

"They're going west. We need to keep him moving west," Kate told her, and then raked her hand across the map. "Now, where the hell *are* they going?"

Sarah examined the map, too.

"Where can you go from Karachi? If you keep edging west?"

Kate drew lines with her finger on the map.

"Easy access to Iran. That's why Moshe is so worried. He's justified. Put it on a ship, and it can head into the Gulf of Aden, or the Persian Gulf. We could stop it there. Yemen, the Horn of Africa. This sucks, they could go anywhere. Get him on the phone as soon as you can."

Sarah obliged, searching around for Terry.

Fortnum Bank Equities Trading Floor

Kyle, nose to screens, watched the opening market moves flash before of him. Gold continued to trade up, crossing $726 an ounce. Crude oil was stabilizing after the pop following the refinery attack, down small to $91.30.

Kyle got an IM alert. He saw it was Shirin calling him over.

"On my way," Kyle typed the reply as he rose to head to her desk. He tapped Pete's monitor displaying a full-screen chart of gold.

"If it breaks, you come get me," Kyle told him and walked over by Shirin.

Shirin and Kyle entered one of the glass conference rooms. Shirin shook her head in astonishment as she spread out some data before them on the table.

"This is amazing. Scary shit, really."

"What do you mean?"

"The analysis you asked me to do."

"Shit, you did that already—that's what we're looking at?"

"Well, not *every* attack, I only focused on the larger ones, but, yeah, we have a new historical option database that makes this kind of thing easier—I probably shouldn't have told you that. I could have had you believing I did this all by hand in record time," she commented.

"I wouldn't have known the difference." Kyle smiled.

"Anyhoo. There's front-running going on ahead of a lot of these. The face of evil. Let's start with USS *Cole* in 2000. There are buys of gold call options and S&P puts. Next, Nine Eleven, I'll come back to that because that's the biggest, no doubt. And there's a lot there. Note, the anthrax attacks later that year, there is no advance trading, none that I can see, at least. Tells us the anthrax thing was definitely domestic and not these terrorist financiers behind it." Shirin paused.

"Interesting. We thought that way at the time, right?"

"We did, but good additional data points corroborate that premise," she agreed, and then continued, "Bali nightclub bombings, 2002, they buy gold options and buy puts on the Jakarta stock index and also bought puts on the rupiah versus the dollar and versus the JPY," she continued. The rupiah was Indonesia's currency, and JPY was the ticker symbol for the Japanese yen.

"Next, the Riyadh compound bombings in 2003. Here, again we have gold call options, and this time, crude oil calls. 2004, the Moscow metro bombing, gold calls and they sold Russian debt. Madrid train bombings, also 2004, calls on gold and bought puts on the IBEX, the Spanish stock index." She paused again.

Kyle stood up, listening intently to her summaries.

"2004, Khobar Towers massacre, bought calls on crude oil and calls on gold.

2005, London subway and bus bombings, bought calls on gold, purchased puts on the FTSE 100 and puts on the British pound. 2005, Baghdad bombings, calls on crude oil, calls on gold. 2005, Delhi bombings, calls on gold and puts on the Bombay stock index." She stopped.

"Jesus," Kyle declared.

"You get the idea. But, coming back to Nine Eleven, the big one. There are a lot of trades. US treasuries and treasury options. S&P puts, tons of them. Calls on gold, a lot of them. Puts on airline stocks, American and United Airlines; puts on other travel stocks like cruise lines; puts on reinsurers, Swiss Re and Munich Re, both of which insured the World Trade Center; puts on US banks; puts on Morgan Stanley, which had a large office in one of the towers; calls on crude oil; and—"

"*Calls* on crude oil?"

"That's what I have. This was an interesting one, because it was one of their trades that didn't work out," Shirin noted.

"If there's any business slowdown, which there was after Nine Eleven, crude oil will actually trade *lower*, less demand for it. Sorry, keep going," Kyle said.

"Uh, let's see, puts on three dozen US companies, at least. Other airlines and travel companies, too, Delta, Continental, US Airways, Carnival and Royal Caribbean Cruise lines, uh, Boeing and Lockheed Martin, among others." Shirin stopped again.

She looked up at Kyle, who was in thought, listening, looking through the glass wall at the activity on the trading floor. He finally sensed she had stopped talking, and he reversed to her.

"How many of these trades made money?"

"Most of them. There's usually some kind of pop, and then they take profits. But they do miss sometimes. Those calls on crude oil on Nine Eleven I was mentioning, were a big miss. They miscalculated that one. They must have thought, terrorism equals a rise in crude oil. Gold is one of their big go-tos. It usually pops on a terrorist attack—geopolitical uncertainty, ya know? Gold did jump about ten percent on Nine Eleven. The front-running was never as big after Nine Eleven, though."

"There was a lot of heat from investigators. I was at the FBI back then, and I remember some of the agents working with the SEC investigating a number of those trades."

"It also seemed like there were a lot *more* people front-running that attack," she pointed out.

"What do you mean?"

"So, the attacks post–Nine Eleven, I can tell there were fewer entities doing it, maybe even only one or two, but more professional-like. They trade closer to the actual attack date, they pinpoint what will be affected, and there are usually several large trades in fewer assets, more concentrated. It's like a lot of people knew ahead of Nine Eleven, and the front-running was a grab bag. It was sloppy, people had a good idea of which markets and stocks could move, but weren't experts, you can tell that," she said.

"Got it."

"There are also a couple of events—attacks—that may have been thwarted. I saw evidence of this general pattern, calls on crude oil and calls on gold and puts on a stock market, depending on the country being attacked. There were large out-

148

of-the-money option trades, but then there's no attack. They either traded out at a loss or just let the options expire."

"Interesting…"

"And the other thing is we can tell what intensity of attack they think it's going to be, from a combination of the bet size and how far out of the money the put or call strikes are," Shirin described.

Kyle solemnly concurred, "An eight-hundred-dollar strike in gold implies a big move. You gave me that analysis. What kind of attack—what size of attack would that be? And we're seeing large call buyers in crude all week, two attacks already," Kyle wondered.

"Maybe that's what the gold option trade was for, if it's not for the Fed? Maybe it's these same guys betting on *those* attacks?"

"No, they knew those attacks—if it is someone front-running the past couple days—they knew they were smaller scale. *If* this gold option trade is, in fact, someone front-running an attack, then whatever's coming will be much, much larger," Kyle said ominously.

"You're scaring me, Kyle. What are you saying? A big attack is coming?"

"I don't know. But I don't like what all this is pointing to."

"What are you going to do about the gold option trade? You have the position now, don't you?"

"I do. I can't really do anything at this point. Either all this is bullshit and I'm up sixty mil at the end of the week, or it portends a big attack, and I'll lose my shirt. Pretty binary, huh?" Kyle explained as he eyed her and laughed.

"Ha—I'm glad you can be so flip about it. I'm going to make sure I'm drinking tonight," she morosely replied.

"Don't get alarmed about it. I'm sure it will come and go," he reassured her, turning to look out at the trading floor again. Peering over his shoulder at her, he said, "This helps. Thanks again for doing all this."

"Thanks for the cap." She smiled back at him. "Remember you have to, like, tire iron somebody for me now," she said, eyeing Kyle with a smirk.

"No problem there. That's a growing list."

Operation 912 Task Force Center

A CIA officer on the ground monitoring Jinnah International Airport was on a speakerphone updating the team.

"Target jet lifted off. Nobody exited the aircraft while it was on the ground. Door remained shut tight. Refueling didn't take long either, so our guess is it's not going that far, probably has a destination radius of a thousand klicks at most, that's maybe two hours of flight time," he reported.

Kate walked to the map projected onto the large screen. She surveyed it, leaning left and right, trying to eye different possible destinations.

"A thousand kilometers, can we confirm their heading?" she hollered over to one of the analysts, who relayed into his headset, "What's their heading?"

"Definitely looks west," he shouted back to Kate.

They hung up the officer in Karachi. Kate summoned Carly.

"Captain?"

"Finally, we're on home turf now," Carly said to Kate with a thin smile, referring to the Middle East. The NGA analytic manager who worked with Carly nodded in agreement.

"We've got every millimeter of this region covered with multiple overlaps. We can also switch to close-up seaborne, if we need to," she added as she looked at the redheaded liaison.

Sensing the pressure on him, LTJG Graham turned to them.

"Ms. Harrison, we might be able to get an F-18 up there, depending on how close they get to the gulf. We can track the target with seaborne Aegis radar. I'm contacting ships now, checking what we have in the Gulf of Oman," he informed.

Kate consulted the map again. She drew her hand across the western parallels from Karachi.

"They can remain in Pakistani airspace for a while, and even enter Iranian, if they have a legit destination there—maybe that's a final stop, who knows. Would definitely lose our tail." She chuckled, but then said, more seriously, "Or they can continue on to UAE or Dubai," she exhaled in frustration. "I need some coffee."

Kate walked over to the coffee machine and poured herself a cup. Not even a moment's peace before another voice called her name.

"Kate, come over here. You need to see this," Kazemi shouted out to her, with Dr. Ahn and Sarah waving her over as well. Kate hustled to them, coffee in hand.

"This just came in from one of the Mossad liaisons. Obtained off a captured laptop from a suspected terror cell safe house near Markadah. Looks like a planning animation of some kind. Here," Kazemi offered and swiveled his laptop toward Kate and pressed play.

The thirty-second animation showed a small, light aircraft like a prop plane, or maybe even a drone, flying low and then popping up above what appeared to be a sprawling crude oil ship loading terminal. The aircraft circled the crude oil storage tanks and exploded in a vast white pulse, vaporizing the terminal and raining glowing embers down over the remnants. The debris was animated with strobing effects, which faded into blinking radioactivity icons when the bits landed on the site. Then the animation ended.

"That's supposed to be Ras Tanura," Kazemi said with a hard exhale.

"Ras Tanura," Kate repeated knowingly.

"There isn't a substitute, I mean, that's it. There's no alternative in the crude oil markets. This video shows the entire place being vaporized and irradiated, by something—an airburst detonation above the facility—which would destroy much of it and then spread radiation over the rest. An attack like that would render Ras Tanura inoperable for years—decades, even," Kazemi explained.

"How legit is this video? I mean, is it fantasy, you know, AQ recruiting material, or is this actual operational planning collateral? And how old—three years, two weeks? We need to know this." Kate looked at the three of them, who didn't have answers for her yet. "Let's find that out ASAP."

Roger's Coffeehouse, Greenwich Street, Manhattan, United States

Inside the packed coffeehouse across from the Fortnum Bank building, Kyle waited in line and gathered his second order that morning. Holding his two cups, he moved toward the window with a row of stools and sat down.

Amy entered a few moments later with an annoyed look on her face. She rotated left and right, looking around, and then locked on to Kyle with a foul expression. She emphasized her irritation by looking at her watch in those few seconds it took her to shoulder through the crowd toward him.

"I gotta be at work in a few minutes. What the hell was so important we couldn't talk on a call?" she demanded.

Kyle handed her a cup of coffee with a pathetic smile.

"Good morning, nice to see you, too," he chided her. "I noticed you suggested a much more crowded place," he added.

She grabbed her coffee and pried off the lid, taking a sip. "Yeah, I figured you wouldn't try to kiss me again with so many witnesses." She lowered her cup and gave him a wry smile.

"Sooo?" she demanded again.

Kyle checked side to side to ensure no one was paying attention to them. He leaned in toward her.

"I've got a problem at work," he started. "There's something going on, like Nine-Eleven-type shit."

She frowned at that and dismissively shut her eyes, not liking where this was heading. He continued.

"I did this trade in gold options yesterday. It's not something I usually trade, but I did it because the edge was so good—"

"Just—"

"Sorry, it looked like a good trade to do, but the type of bet the customer is making is really weird, like, they're betting on a huge event, like a Nine Eleven attack or bigger—"

"Kyle—"

"No, hang on, listen to me." He clutched her wrist emphatically. "I shouldn't have put this trade on, either, like, it was too big from a risk standpoint. It shouldn't have been allowed. But the risk system that would have rejected it *didn't work* when I booked the trade. And do you know who runs that system? Who has the *keys* to it? One of the only people in the bank who can override the risk on a trade like that?" He paused to see her expression, which remained stoic, impatient.

"You're not making *any* sense," Amy said testily, and wheeled to leave.

"The guy who went missing. The one you told me about—"

Amy stopped and reversed.

"Wait, the guy from your bank I told you about the other day? I told you—"

"Yes, *that* guy. He's the only one who could override the risk system to allow me to put this trade on," Kyle said, still unconvincingly to her.

"Isn't that a coincidence? Did he return to work, by the way?"

"No. And get this, I was on the way to Ox Bar last night, and we drove by his brownstone in the Village. I kind of peeked into his basement window—"

"You did *what*? Are you nuts? I told you that in total confi—and you went by his *house*? How do you even know where he lives?"

"All the traders at the bank know where he lives. Anyway, yes, I snooped around. Can we not make that the point? But what I saw in his basement looked like blood—"

Amy rolled her eyes at him.

"I knew I shouldn't have come to see you. This was a fucking waste of time," Amy spat and moved to leave. Kyle grabbed her arm again.

"Wait—you *know* I know what bloodstains at a crime scene look like—you *know* I do," Kyle reminded her. She reluctantly remained, listening.

"Yeah? I also know your paranoia, your craziness, your drinking. Your entire group at the Bureau remembers that. Even now, Kyle, six years later, they still joke about it," she scolded.

"I get it, thank you, now let me finish. There was a big splotch, like an elongated stain—a what do you call it, a drain—"

"Drainage stain, yeah, when they're on the floor, bleeding out, and it pools and expands."

"That, and I did see the characteristic sheen, which would imply—"

"That it was recent, yes. So, let me see if I can put this all together. You think someone tortured and killed this risk guy to get the codes to this risk system so you could put on this—this gold trade and you wouldn't be flagged for it? This is utterly ridiculous, and you get this makes *you* look like a suspect?" She stared at him incredulously.

"I hadn't considered the torturing part, but—"

Amy shook her head in total disbelief and moved to leave yet again only to be grabbed once more by Kyle. She spun back around with a furious face. "You want me to shoot you?"

"That's why I suggested Roger's—public place." Kyle grinned, but she wasn't having any of it. Her patience had ended, but he persisted. "Not me, the other side of the trade—the buyer of these gold options. If the risk system hadn't overridden the flag, I wouldn't have been able to trade it. Nobody could have. No bank would have taken the other side of that trade—it's too big, too much risk."

"But what happens—I mean, how does this trade win? How on earth do you know what they are betting on?"

"That gold makes a colossal jump by Friday—*this* Friday, and the only way that's happening is with a big event, like a Nine Eleven," he stressed.

"*Again*, how do you know this guy's not just speculating, you know, taking a shot—or what do you call it—hedging?"

"Amy, this is a sixty-million-dollar bet. Not many people lay down sixty million that will vanish in days if they're wrong—unless they know something, or at least are very, very confident."

Amy paused at that. The numbers did put it into some perspective that seemed unrealistic. She exhaled impatiently.

"This is so stupid, what do you want *me* to do about it? And I do need to go, by the way," she insisted, checking her watch.

Kyle dug out the napkin he'd scrawled the name Fadhil al-Hammadi on, the guy behind the New Carolina Patriot Fund. He handed it to her. She read it.

"It is an Arabic name."

"That's the guy behind the trade, maybe, or somehow associated with the fund that bought those gold options from me."

Amy wasn't convinced and eyed him suspiciously.

"Where did you get this? Is this from some other sketchy snooping? I can't—"

"No, this was from an internal system, honest." Kyle gave her a bit of a white lie, not explaining the hack Courtney had used to access the name.

Half trusting him, she folded up the napkin and stuck it inside her purse.

"Are you authorized to see these names?"

Kyle gave her a sheepish grin. She clenched her jaw, seeing through him. "I'm not doing this."

"No, I'm serious, we pieced this together from publicly available sources—the documents I saw don't list his name. Can you just see if he's on any lists?"

She looked at him and neither agreed nor disagreed. She threw down the last swallow of her coffee and tossed the cup.

"Thanks for not kissing me," she said bluntly and walked out.

Bagram Airfield-BAF, Afghanistan

On a vast, darkening airfield amid the snow-capped Hindu Kush mountains, Commander Kelso and an Air Force loadmaster directed the bundling of gear for an assault force into the bowels of a waiting C-17 Globemaster transport plane.

Bagram Air Base and its sprawling runway, rows of compounds, hangars, and scores of aircraft revetments had become the main base and staging point in Operation Enduring Freedom, or more familiarly, the War in Afghanistan. Nicknamed the Bowl by some of the pilots because of its position amid the mountains, it was home to some three thousand US armed forces personnel. More importantly, for Kelso, it was also home to the regional Special Operations Command with officers from MacDill Air Force Base in Florida and housed several US Navy SEAL teams, operators from the Unit (Delta Force), as well as soldiers from the US Army's elite 82nd Airborne Division.

Kelso, and Terry Scanlon back at HQS, had been on with JSOC (Joint Special Operations Command) for the last several hours, arguing, negotiating, and securing an elite assault force for an on-ground kill/capture raid. They didn't know where the corporate jet transporting the contraband was headed, but they needed to have a strike team ready wherever it came down, if they weren't able to take the thing out in the air first.

The SEAL teams were unfortunately all spoken for. The only tier-one SOF (special operations forces) squad that was available for immediate deployment was a detachment of twelve operators from the Unit. These were Delta Force guys, and for Kelso, this was optimal. Not to denigrate his own kind, being a former SEAL himself, but the guys from the Unit were the best ones for this job. SEALs were great, the best, at executing on fixed missions, "profiles," as they were called, and outstanding at operating as a team.

But this mission was different. Kelso didn't *know* the battlefield environment they were heading into—it could be anything from urban to desert to CQB. He didn't know the type of bad guy they'd be facing, if any at all, or how well trained or armed they'd be. He didn't know if they'd all be vaporized in a nuclear detonation if something went wrong. So, for this objective, he needed aggressive, plug-and-play guys who could potentially be out there for days or weeks before an exfil. The operators from the Unit were perfect.

"Commander? Go for vehicle onboarding and inspection," the loadmaster announced to Kelso.

One by one, four Humvees were backed up the loading ramp and into the bay where Air Force loading crews secured them to tie down points. The loadmaster supervised the operation, which went quickly, given they were on the clock. He knelt and personally verified all chain bridles securing the Humvees and signaled, thumbs up, to Kelso, who beckoned the Delta Force team to board.

Carrying their bundles and outfitted in tactical arid-style fatigues and jump gear, the Delta Force operators boarded in single file. Each saluted Kelso, who returned their salute as they divided into two lines and sat in the rows of jump seats along the sides of the cargo compartment.

Kelso's assault team was fifteen strong. From the Unit, he had two scout snipers, a combat medic, two SAW (squad automatic weapon) gunners, a couple of breachers, a comms guy, and four combat drivers. The two NEST techs and Kelso, himself, made fifteen.

Kelso stood on the tarmac staring out at the Hindu Kush peaks, pink in the twilight, as he awaited the Delta Force operations chief with the *go* call. He had to admit to himself, he felt proud of the compliment just paid to him by the dozen Delta Force ops all saluting him. There were different levels of "elite" in the nation's SpecFor world. The Delta Force were among the highest in the American pantheon; even the SEALs aspired to join the Unit. But those soldiers had just bowed to him with respect. To them, Kelso was another tier, altogether, an OGA (other government agency) paramilitary officer, and *they* aspired to be that.

For Kelso, who was born and raised in the West End neighborhood of Atlanta, this was outstanding. He spent his youth dodging gangs and their bullets. Took him a decade busting his ass to exfil himself from that life to become one of the nation's most select warriors. There were maybe two hundred people who did what he did. The US was the only nation on earth you could be born in the mud and become a player. Thinking about that made Kelso even more determined in their objective now. He would find this broken arrow and neutralize it, and then he would find whoever was behind this and take care of them, too.

The Delta Force chief appeared and conferred with Kelso. They were greenlit.

"Godspeed, bro," the chief said to him as they shook hands. Kelso thanked him and turned and walked up the C-17 loading ramp and strapped himself in.

The C-17's engines ignited in a thunder as the rear bay ramp steadily rose and finally shut with a sealing hiss. The aircraft backed out of its revetment and wheeled around to taxi toward the main, three-thousand-meter-long airstrip. It rolled into position at the runway's base, and the Globemaster's four powerful engines screamed to a full throttle as it roared to the horizon and elevated into the evening sky...

Operation 912 Task Force Center

The center was crowded. All posts were engaged. Kate, Bob, and even the director, who had stopped in for a status, stood watching developments on the main projection screen. A liaison rose and reported, "Target heading directly west, over the southern Pakistani coastline," he updated.

"Can we put it up?" Kate requested.

The NGA analytic manager answered her. "We have operational coverage there, yes. Hang on..."

The main screen image projected a mostly dark background except for a narrow chalky-white pill-shaped object with a long, ghostly trail dragging behind it. The object was the infrared profile of the private jet tracked in real time by an overhead satellite. The sheer diffusion behind it was its ionization trail—heated air from the plane's jets which registered in the infrared spectrum.

Kate, Bob and the director conversed in low voices as the projection screen tracked their target.

"POTUS gave authorization to take out the package but not with collateral damage," the director told them. "What confirm do we have the jet is civilian?"

"All we know is the aircraft leasing company is private. Those could be regular businessmen on board."

"How many we talking about?"

"Two pilots, two crew, and seven passengers, including our man."

The director winced and toggled his glasses, eyeing them with arms folded.

"Let me discuss with NSC," he said after a few moments and then abruptly walked out of the center.

"Who do we have off their coast?" Bob asked without turning. There wasn't a response. He made it clearer. "Navy? Who's off their coast? Who's in theater?"

Lieutenant Junior Grade Graham lowered his headset and stood up. "USS *Bainbridge*, an Arleigh Burke on escort command, Gulf of Oman, sir. We can get her into range along the coast in about half an hour."

"Where is she now—on the map?" Kate asked him.

A few seconds later, the image on the large screen displayed the region of south Pakistan, southern Iran, and eastern Arabian Peninsula with the Omani crescent and the Gulf of Oman all in view. Two moving markers flashed on the map: the private jet, tracking west at a good clip, and a blue marker in the Gulf of Oman, the USS *Bainbridge*, which was equidistant between Iran and Oman.

"Lock it as soon as it's in range," Kate told him.

LTJG Graham gave a thumbs-up and relayed the orders on his headset.

USS *Bainbridge*, Arleigh Burke–Class Destroyer, Gulf of Oman

The USS *Bainbridge* sliced through the windless gulf waters at a full pursuit speed of twenty-eight knots. Locked on to the corporate jet target, her specialized ACS (Aegis Combat System) radars had an unchecked hold on the plane.

Inside the pilothouse, the ship's captain, Commander Nonas, eyed her quartermaster standing over the chart table, managing the *Bainbridge*'s course. The quartermaster was following the directions from the spy techs in the CIC (Combat Information Center) belowdecks who were tracking the jet on the Aegis phased array radar. They relayed through the RM (radioman) on the bridge.

"Two-six-one, two-six-one," the RM relayed to the quartermaster, who as sharply relayed to the helmsman, the sailor who physically steered the destroyer. "Changing course, two-six-one, two-six-one," the quartermaster called out.

The helmsman verified. "Two-six-one, very well," she replied as she adjusted the control. The heading "two-six-one," or "261," was close to the true west heading of 270. Commander Nonas followed the disciplined choreography as their ship hunted its quarry through the night seas.

The RM, a lieutenant junior grade, and responsible for all communications to and from the bridge, sat next to Commander Nonas and was on the radio with LTJG Graham at the CIA.

"Captain, task force nine-one-two requesting radar visibility of target aircraft," he called over to Commander Nonas.

"Positive radar tracking, and let's get fire control visibility," Commander Nonas requested as she looked to her RM. The RM, managing multiple conversations, affirmed and called down to the CIC.

"Fire Controlman, request fire control status of the target?" He waited a few seconds, heard the positive reply, and relayed to both the commander and the CIA. "Affirmative, VLS status green, repeat, affirmative."

The forward VLS, which stood for "vertical launch system," was a thirty-two-cell missile battery on the forward deck of the ship that could launch different kinds of weapons such as a Tomahawk cruise missile or SM2s or SM6s, which were surface-to-air missiles with different ranges.

Commander Nonas swiveled in her captain's chair, ordering the fire control officer, "Update any course change."

"Aye, Captain."

Operation 912 Task Force Center

LTJG Graham reported, "The *Bainbridge* has the target jet on radar and fire control tracking. They're awaiting further authorization."

Kate raised her hand to acknowledge as they watched the ghostly white pill on the dark map streak into Iranian airspace.

"They're over Iran now," Kate commented to Bob with some concern, unsure of what that meant, if it was final destination or another head fake.

"It's a black hole if they land there. Smart, no way we find it," Bob worried.

Kate spun around, searching the desks for Kazemi.

"Where's this Ras Tanura?" she shouted when she spotted him.

Kazemi approached the large monitor. He tapped out a spot in the Persian Gulf a few kilometers off the Saudi coast, north of Bahrain.

"Mark that, will somebody?" Bob called out to the NGA manager who could add the flag on the map. A moment later, a yellow icon appeared where Ras Tanura was located.

"They can't make it to Ras Tanura from here, can they?"

Kazemi hand-measured across the large-screen monitor.

"It looks like they're about seven hundred klicks away. If they refueled at Jinnah, that's well within range," he said.

"They can't use this aircraft—gadget's in the cargo hold." Bob commented.

Behind them, a commotion among the analysts. Graham and Carly rose. "Heading change. They're turning due south," they both reported.

The team watched on the monitor. The track was curving south, crossing out of Iranian airspace into the Gulf of Oman.

"Target aircraft dropping altitude," Graham followed.

"Toward Oman. Where the hell are they going?" Kate shuddered.

Bob ran to the navy desk, yelling at the lieutenant, "*Bainbridge!*"

USS *Bainbridge*

Captain Nonas pressed, "Confirm target and fire control lock."

The RM reverified with the tactical action officer (TAO) in the CIC, "Aye, fire control lock, Captain."

"TAO, gunner's mate, ready the forward VLS," Nonas instructed. "What are nine-one-two's orders?" she demanded.

"Ready fire, Captain. They're getting POTUS authorization," he relayed after checking with CIA.

"Gunner's mate, ready fire," the captain shouted to the bridge at large. She eyed the RM. "Sound General Quarters."

The RM grabbed the 1MC mic, "General Quarters, General Quarters. All hands man your battle stations."

Belowdecks, in the blue-light CIC, nicknamed Thunderdome by the crew, the TAO stood over the seated Aegis fire controlman tracking the corporate jet and monitoring the VLS weapon system. The ship's klaxons blared, and the General Quarters dispatch squawked over the 1MC.

"VLS status," the TAO requested from the fire controlman, who pushed a VLS Status button on her console. Her weapons system register selected a missile.

"Ready VLS, cell sixteen, missile four-eight-one-eight, Sierra-Mike two. Tracking a deadlock," she confirmed, priming a surface-to-air (SM2) missile. Then she added, "TAO, diminishing range, copy?"

He peered down at her Aegis console and realized—they had precious time before the target jet was out of range.

Back on the bridge, the captain shot an anxious look at the RM, who begged a response from CIA.

"What are orders? Target will shortly be out of range," he appealed. The RM pressed Graham at the CIA for a response. Nothing came back.

"No response yet, Captain. We *do not* have authorization," he repeated.

Over the comms, the fire controlman shouted to the RM, "We have another two minutes before target leaves reliable radius for four-eight-one-eight."

Captain Nonas shouted back at the RM again, "Two-minute window!"

The RM relayed and got back from Graham, "Still no authorization."

The fire controlman updated the RM, who shouted over to the captain, "Captain, about thirty seconds remaining, including SM2 flight time."

Breaking protocol, Nonas grabbed the headset from the RM. "Nine-one-two, we need authorization now, we only have a few seconds left. Do we have authorization?" she demanded into the headset.

They waited, and then heard over the line, "You have go-ahead."

Captain Nonas tossed the headset back to the RM and yelled, "Gunner's mate, engage. Repeat, engage," she shouted.

In the CIC, the fire controlman and TAO nodded to each other. The fire controlman depressed the VLS launch button.

"Four-eight-one-eight, launch. Bird's away," she confirmed.

On the fo'c'sle of the USS *Bainbridge*, a hatch on the thirty-two-cell launch array flung open. A loud hiss and an explosive charge erupted from the cell, and a surface-to-air missile lofted into the night sky with a blazing afterburner and arcing smoke column growing in its wake.

The SM2 raced toward the jet, locking on to its image with its nose radar, the missile's tail cone burning with a fury.

The corporate jet crew and passengers continued on their course, with no idea that a lethal missile was speeding to kill them.

The SM2, flying at a torrid Mach 3.5, closed the distance fast to the jet, which flew at six hundred knots, a snail's pace compared to the bullet coming at them.

On the bridge, they watched on the fire control radar screen as one white blip pursued another. The SM2 gained on the jet, approaching airburst proximity.

The missile flew a laser-straight line to within half a mile of the jet's tail and then started to wobble. Its engine sputtered. The missile suddenly nose-dived, its engine blacked out.

In the CIC, they watched on the radar as the SM2 ceased with only a half-second left to impact.

"We burned out. We burned out!" the fire controlman yelled as they all saw the missile's radar blip disappear as it ran out of fuel and tumbled to the ocean.

"Negative kill on four-eight-one-eight, repeat, negative," she shouted to the RM. She heard the response from the bridge.

"Confound it!" Nonas cursed.

Operation 912 Task Force Center

"Damn!" Bob yelled.

Graham looked at them, abashed.

"We were seconds too late. The missile fizzled out," he informed.

"Shit," Bob doubly repeated.

Kate was less emotional about the miss. She studied the image before them on the large monitor.

"They've descended to twenty thousand feet," Carly updated, referring to the jet's altitude.

"Are they headed to Dubai? Perfect place to hide a corporate jet and slip away," Kate said as she puzzled over the jet's vector.

"No, flight path matches as if they were going to land in Muscat, Oman," Kazemi stated.

"Muscat?"

"You can get outside of Muscat quick, and there's empty desert all over here. They could disappear into the sand to hide the thing until the next step. Open borders with Yemen, fly to SA," Kazemi detailed.

Kate had to agree with his logic. She searched for Scanlon.

"Terry, how far along is our team?"

"They're just out of Pakistani airspace now, flying into Gulf of Oman, probably an hour behind the target," Terry estimated.

"Can they do an airdrop?" Kate asked.

"They're rigged for it, yes," he affirmed.

"Radio, drop zone into Oman."

Bob referred to the map, eyeing the possible routes an operation like that would involve.

"If Ras Tanura is their target, it's much easier access from deep within the Omani desert. Only five hundred klicks, you could put the bomb on a light prop plane, skip above the sand dunes, below anybody's radar. Steer around US bases," Bob concurred.

"It's a straight shot. This is all desert." Kate repeated, as they both put it together. She was about to add to that when Carly called out.

"We have them descending. Approaching Muscat," she informed.

"Thank you."

Kazemi added, "We've got an asset there. He's on his way to Muscat International now. He'll be eyes on the ground."

The three of them scrutinized the map. Bob summarized their thoughts.

"We need them deep enough into the desert for the assault team to take 'em out." Bob turned to Scanlon. "Get one of our drones up there, too."

Fortnum Bank Equities Trading Floor

The trading floor was crammed by late morning ahead of the Fed meeting. Kyle and Pete were on and off their phones, fielding incoming customer flow positioning for the two thirty p.m. announcement.

Kyle hung up one call, annoyed. "These are all fucking time wasters," he complained, referring to the queues of customers plaguing them. Usually, the sales traders handled those calls, but for big and important clients, the sales traders liked to push them over to the heads of desks like Kyle, especially for something like the Fed. And the customers couldn't get enough of it. They would barrage the desk with inane questions just so they could brag to their own colleagues, "Well, I was on with the Fortnum Bank trading desk this morning, and they thought…"

Pete, who was still on a call himself and trying to trade at the same time, glanced over at Kyle and raised his eyebrows in accord.

Kyle took the interlude to check his charts. Gold was continuing to trade higher, now close to $730, up another $4. Crude oil was still trading sideways after the big leap from the earlier terrorist attack on the Saudi refinery, hovering close to $91. Equities were also treading water, swinging back and forth in a tight range, anticipating the Fed move in a few hours.

"Gold keeps climbing." Kyle looked at Pete and leaned over to him. "Let's enter some sell stops. I'm thinking it runs up to seven thirty-five, forty, tops."

Pete pulled his handset away from his ear so he could hear Kyle while his customer droned on.

Kyle continued, "Let's get those stops in at seven thirty-four and seven thirty-nine." Pete gave him a *you're filled* signal and started to punch in the orders on his keyboard, cradling the phone against his shoulder.

A stop order was effectively a trigger order. A sell stop, at $734, would trigger an order to sell if, and when the gold price hit $734, or subsequently, if it got up to

$739, the second stop. Kyle and Pete were betting the price of gold would keep rising until the Fed announcement, at which point it would top out and reverse. They were angling to scalp some of this movement.

"Oh—I think I learned who the customer behind the gold trade is," Kyle changed the subject. Pete cupped his phone and scooted closer to Kyle.

"You serious? How'd you find this out?" Pete whispered.

"Courtney, you know, hot sales trader Courtney? She has this trick—long story—she figured out the name of the fund, and then, get this, she remembered it from when she worked at Lehman, and the guy behind it from a horse he entered in the Derby years ago, no joke—and guess what? Arab name," Kyle declared.

"No shit?" Pete said, eyeing Kyle and juggling his phone. "Maybe your theory's on point after all. What about the fund? Hedge fund? You heard of 'em?"

"Never heard of them. New Carolina fund, some shit like that. Caymans, fishy as hell. The guy was into racehorses, ya know, Kentucky Derby, Preakness?"

"Gambler. I think we got the right guy," Pete grinned.

No argument from Kyle, who then abruptly said, "I gotta go talk to Sammy. I've been trying to IM him, but he looks offline."

"Hey, wait? Don't go scaring him. He may fuck with the trade—it's a good trade," Pete agitated.

"Oh, now you *like* the trade? Dick."

Pete smirked. Kyle stood up. "Don't worry, I'm just gonna feel him out."

Kyle found Sammy's desk empty. His screens were dark, and there was no sign of his personal stuff, no jacket over the back of his chair, bag or backpack, nothing.

"Hey, Allison? Allie?" he called to one of the sales traders who sat on Sammy's left. She tilted to him, not having a second to deal with him, her eyes demanding, *what?*

"You seen Sammy?"

She lowered her headset mouthpiece. "He didn't come in," she answered and resumed her call, turning away from Kyle.

One of the other sales traders who sat behind Sammy swiveled his chair to Kyle. "Springer, we haven't seen him. No call, no email. Never showed up. I been taking his flow all day. We got bets on him either hitting the lottery or having a heart attack. Which you in for?"

"I won't even ask what the heart attack spread is," Kyle dryly commented.

The sales traders in the vicinity laughed and then resumed their flurry of calls and customer orders. Kyle headed back to his desk.

He arrived as Pete was finishing with a broker.

"You give him, like, a Darth Vader choke hold?"

"He didn't show today," Kyle told him with a perplexed look on his face.

"Huh? What kind of miserable-worm broker doesn't show on a Fed day?"

"Exactly."

Pete grabbed his phone handset again for another call but pinned the receiver against his chest as he dialed. He leaned toward Kyle. "Probably a heart attack. That guy's one walkin' triple bypass," Pete morbidly joked and went on dialing.

Kyle didn't laugh. He just stared at his markets and didn't say anything.

FBI New York Field Office, 26 Federal Plaza

Amy spooned yogurt into her mouth as she sat in her cubicle in front of her PC, deflecting her emails. She finished the cup and tossed it into the wastebasket, and seeing no napkin on her desk, dug into her purse to find one. She grabbed what she felt was a tissue, and out came Kyle's napkin with the "al-Hammadi" name written on it. She almost wiped her mouth with it but did a double take when she spotted the ink. She impatiently sighed and unfolded it.

Amy stared at the name and at Kyle's handwriting. She smiled for a moment because it made her remember his wont to hand-scrawl any important thing on the most insignificant media, like a bar napkin or paper towel.

"Fadhil al-Hammadi," she whispered to herself slowly, sounding out the name several times before wiping her mouth with the back of her hand. She pulled her keyboard toward her and located the internal FBI application that lodged names and aliases against the many tracking lists they kept.

Amy methodically keyed in the name, checked and rechecked that she had entered it correctly. It was a running joke at the FBI that the mostly Anglo-oriented agents had so much trouble entering Arabic and Middle Eastern names. Too many civilians, people with names a letter or two off, had been inadvertently entered into tracking databases since 9/11. Amy hit enter, and the database processed with a spinning wheel...

A moment later, a result set dropped down on her screen. The top hit displayed, "Al-Hammadi, Fadhil," followed by an enumeration of alternated spellings and aliases, and then in blaring red, displayed a dialog box that read, "Sweeper Notification: Please contact interagency liaison officer immediately."

Amy threw her head against her headrest in dismay. "Oh, are you for real? Springer, what did you just do to me?" she scolded under her breath.

An agent was walking by her cubicle at that moment. She beckoned him over.

"Hey, Jim? Jimmy? Get over here." She gave him a frantic wave.

"Hey, Amy, what's going on?"

"You know what this is—this *Sweeper* thing?"

"*Sweeper?* I know it. Why, did you get a hit from one of your cases?"

"Not really," she responded, tilting her monitor toward him.

"Wow, that's a real hit. You know who to call—what's his name, Gabe?"

"Do I have to report this?"

"You do—well, you sort of already did. I think it sends an alert to someone that you got a hit."

"Shit. You gotta be kidding me."

"No joke. Why, you didn't mean for that to happen?"

Amy shook her head *no.*

"You looked up someone for a friend?"

"An *ex*-husband..."

He laughed. "Now, that's funny. This target's not from any of your cases?"

Amy again shook her head tightly.

Jim responded more logically, "But there's no way your ex could randomly pick a name out of a hat that's on a US intelligence alert list. I mean, there's not many tags in this thing at a time. Where did he get this name? Who is it to him?"

Amy dropped her head onto her arms and rolled her head back and forth in quasi-distress for a moment. She rose again. "I need to stop doing this for people."

"Hey, now, hang on. If you got a hit on Sweeper, that's a big deal. You'll be a hero," he told her.

"Really?"

"Heroine, sorry. So, what's the story? How does your ex know of this target?"

"He doesn't, really. Well, I guess he's being suspicious that he might be up to some—money laundering or something. I think he runs a fund, you know, like an investment fund, who's a customer of the bank he works at, said he thinks he's financing terrorist attacks, or something like that." She looked up to Jim with a plea in her eyes not to accuse her of craziness.

"Are you serious?"

"I mean, I'm sure there's more to it, but that's sort of how I understood his explanation, yeah."

"Could be the real deal. Nine times out of ten, it isn't—you know that. We get these mistaken *al*'s all the time—but the fact that it's in Sweeper in the first place, assuming it is the right guy, and the spelling is correct, it means someone else at another agency is looking for him. Could be NSA, DIA, CIA, Treasury, any of those. Go see Gabe. He's upstairs. Tell him what you just told me."

Amy watched him for some reassurance. Jimmy responded with a sober nod.

"I think that it's your ex makes it seem *less* credible." He smiled at her.

She thought for a moment. "You've got a point. Thanks, Jimmy," she said, more confident.

"They'll probably want to interview him," he added, now having some fun.

"Shut up," Amy shot back with a *ha ha* sneer at him.

She rose and exited her cubicle and beat to the elevator bank.

Operation 912 Task Force Center

Kate followed the images on the projector screen. They strobed a low-altitude live nighttime infrared feed of the hilly, arid landscape outside of Muscat International Airport. The real-time overwatch imaged a jeep or pickup truck that was escaping into the open Omani desert.

"What do we have up there?" Bob asked, referring to the type of drone.

"It's a predator, an RQ-1," Scanlon replied.

"Hot?"

"Not this config but can be. This is ours so we can get Hellfires on it," Terry continued. "Ours," meaning it was the CIA's drone, not the Pentagon's, so they could do with it what they needed. The CIA operated an airfield in western Oman they used to run operations into Yemen from.

"No, keep it up there. We can't afford to lose sight of the target now. We can arm it when the SOG team acquires visual," Kate interjected.

"Understood," Scanlon closed.

As Kazemi was approaching Kate, she confirmed with Scanlon, "*When* are we on the ground, by the way?"

"Half hour. They're over Oman now. Shouldn't be long," he assured her.

Kate wheeled to face the charging Kazemi.

"What do you got—why do you look so excited?" she wincingly asked, taking a step back. Kazemi had a shit-eating grin on his face.

"Sweeper returned a hit on our brothers." He could barely contain himself.

Now he had Kate's complete attention. She had the tall-eyed expression, almost expanding beyond her lenses. Bob overheard as well and knocked over an analyst rushing to hear more.

"What?" they both demanded he spill it.

"Came out of New York FBI field office," he blurted out.

Bob and Kate exchanged surprised glances.

"New York?" they both skeptically questioned, almost disappointed.

"Yeah, a special agent, who has an ex-husband who works at a New York bank, passed her the name, *Fadhil al-Hammadi*, as suspected money laundering or something, it was unclear what the actual intake complaint was," Kazemi started.

"What's the relationship to the brothers in the network? We know this guy?"

"We've been watching him for years. Saudi Intelligence and Mossad, too. Terrorist financier. CB's got a long rap sheet on him, and so does Treasury. The brothers often work for him. I guess they *do his bidding*," Kazemi described.

"What does that mean?"

"You know, they run around for him. Gopher work, logistics and operations. They get shit done for him. And he pays them well," he went on.

Bob and Kate listened intently.

"When did this hit come in?" Kate asked.

"This is fresh, like, this morning, not even scrubbed yet," he answered her.

"So, this could still be a mistake or unrelated?"

Kazemi chuckled. *"Possible*, but highly unlikely given all the circumstantial coincidences," he replied with confidence.

Kate and Bob exchanged looks again.

"Why, why did this show up now?" Bob pressed.

"That's what we have to figure out. The fed entered it this morning, but we don't know if it's stale."

"What's the FBI doing about this? And can we get in on it?"

"They'll interview the ex-husband from the bank. But they might not be giving it the priority we need," Kazemi said, looking to the both of them.

Kate rolled her eyes and looked at Bob. *"OK*. Let's bring them in now—but on two conditions—they push this to the top of the queue at the FBI *and* I'm personally involved," Kate demanded of Bob. "Them" was the CIA's CTC (Counterterrorist Center), which Kate and Bob had been holding off thus far.

"And we stay the lead agency," she piled on before Bob could respond.

"With this info, CTC has to be involved now. I'll massage it with the director, make certain you're on this," he wove delicately. "And, yes, no way in hell we're not the lead agency on this," he asserted.

"As if I wasn't going to be involved *anyway*," she patently reminded him.

USAF C-17 Globemaster, Sky above Oman

The C-17 coursed over the Omani desert at twenty-five thousand feet. Inside, the Unit jumpmaster was prepping Kelso and the assault force. Shouting over the roaring noise inside the aircraft, both Kelso and the jumpmaster personally inspected the NEST guys to ensure they were properly harnessed. They also readied the four Humvees to roll out of the cargo bay and drop into the desert. They were fucked if the Humvees didn't hit the drop zone.

The jumpmaster flashed the signal, and Kelso, the two NESTs, and the dozen Delta Force ops all lined up on either side of the bay at the jump doors. Kelso signaled the jumpmaster to lower the drawbridge. The rear cargo ramp opened with a blast of air that rushed inside.

The jumpmaster flashed the airspeed with his hands, *five, five, five*—meaning fifteen miles per hour, as five fingers equaled five miles per hour. He chopped his hand like a gate coming down, and a green "go" light blinked above them. The first Humvee slid out the back of the bay, followed by the second and the third and finally the fourth in precise sequence. Their gigantic chutes bloomed in the cold night as they drifted away from the aircraft.

The jump light turned red. Two seconds passed, it flashed green again. The jumpmaster gave his signal. Kelso, twelve Delta Force ops, and two NEST techs leapt out of the jump doors and plummeted soundlessly into the darkness below…

Fortnum Bank Equities Trading Floor

Kyle watched their positions like an eagle. The markets were swinging more as they approached the Fed announcement. His phone trilled.

"Springer," he picked up. "This is Kyle… Oh, yeah, hi… I can, like, early evening?… I remember where it is. Thanks." Kyle hung up. He turned to Pete.

"FBI wants to interview me," he announced with a pleased grin.

"Wait, *what*? You for real? The Arab guy? The gold trade?" Pete asked in disbelief. Kyle simply smiled at him.

"You got it."

"What. The. Fuck, man. Somebody wants to listen to your bullshit?"

Kyle laughed. "I don't think they know anything about the gold trade. The guy probably showed up on some lists. They want to figure it out," Kyle told him.

"Don't tell 'em about the gold trade. Come on, Kyle, we're almost there. The book will be back to flat by Friday," Pete begged.

"I'm gonna *have* to tell them about the gold trade. But, don't worry. They're not going to do anything about that."

"Fucking better not. I checked with settlements. It's fully cleared now. Money is in the bank. Somewhere, just not in our wallets yet," Pete informed.

"Good, Sammy disappearing worried me. Can't DK us now," Kyle said.

DK meant "didn't know," trading and clearing lingo for when one side of a trade, invariably the losing side, claimed they didn't know the trade, so they could back out of it. It was more a thing of the past and manual, exchange floor trading, now much harder to pull off with electronic trading, but it did sometimes happen in OTC dealing.

"Still not sure if they can see it in global risk, though," Kyle puzzled.

He half rose and peered across the trading floor into Garner's office.

"Garner still hasn't said anything about it?" Kyle checked with Pete as he sat back down. "He hasn't come over asking about it, has he?"

Pete shook his head, *uh-uh*.

"If you have to tell the FBI, Garner could find out," Pete worried.

"I thought about that. We have to take our chances, but I'll be delicate."

Kyle shifted back to his screens. Gold was up $2 to $732, and oil was climbing again, up $0.70 to $91.70. Equities were higher in the S&P 500 by $3.20.

Kyle focused on gold and oil as the digits jittered in front of him.

Nahda Desert Region, Oman

Four Special Forces Humvees bounded across the Omani desert, invisible in the pitch-black night. The drop had gone well, they had all hit the drop zone, which was the good part; a couple of the guys got banged up on the landing, including the two NEST techs, with some scrapes and bruises, but no permanent damage. One of their Humvees landed on its back, though, which took them some precious minutes righting it before they could mobilize.

Humvees were about the most versatile vehicle in the world, with dozens of "configurations," from battle to utility. They were the Swiss Army knife of military apparatus. The lead Humvee, driven by one of the Delta Force combat drivers, was a straight-up cargo, troop carrier configuration. Kelso rode up front in that one, minding the terrain through his NOD (night optical device) goggles. One of the NEST techs and the Unit comms guy sat in the rear behind them.

The second Humvee was an ARMT (Armament Carrier) config. It packed a punch. It was up-armored and had a mounted M60 7.62-millimeter machine-gun turret atop. Three Delta Force ops rode in this one: a driver, a breacher, and one of the SAW guys. The third Humvee was similarly outfitted, also an ARMT config, the exception being that its mounted weapon was an MK19 automatic grenade launcher. Three Delta Force ops and the second NEST tech rode in that one.

The final Humvee was another cargo/troop carrier config, but with a pax top, which was a covered hard-top cargo area that held the team's supplies, gear, weapons, and ammunition—and had been readied with a small bay for an expected piece of cargo—the device—should they meet their objective. The four remaining Delta Force guys rode in that one: the combat driver, the two scout snipers, and the combat medic.

In the lead Humvee, the comms guy behind Kelso was monitoring a real-time view of the aerial overhead beamed from the CIA drone on a laptop monitor.

"Looks like over that next ridge. We're closing on them. They're about two klicks ahead of us now," he reported to Kelso.

"Stay in their wheel tracks, no line of sight," Kelso directed the driver.

"Copy, bro."

"What do we got ahead of us?" Kelso asked the comms guy, who also had the maps and images of the region they were in.

"Sand, scorpions, and a few berms. It'll flatten out more if we keep heading west," he answered.

"Any structures?"

"Negative. Could be encampments, fly-by-night bivouacs, that kind of thing."

"Right," Kelso answered him, and cautioned the driver, "the leveling's not good for us. Hang back more," he instructed him.

"You got it."

The world was an effervescing dark emerald green with an extra-wide field of view (FOV) through his NODs. Kelso noted the berms, along with the dipping wadis—ancient dried-up river and streambeds, which created an almost wavelike motion for the speeding Humvees as they rode over them.

"Where's this guy going?" Kelso wondered aloud. The NEST officer tapped Kelso on the arm.

"We need line of sight at some point, to reverify the target," he reminded Kelso. "I only need a few seconds, once in range," the NEST officer added.

"Copy that," Kelso replied as he continued to study the landscape.

"I'll think we'll have our shot in a few. Looks like the terra fans out coming up in about half a klick. We can prob gun it for a bit, get closer to him—quietly—and then drop back."

Operation 912 Task Force Center

Kazemi found Bob and Kate.

"Video's legit. Mossad verified, about a month old. They pulled some stills from it on the same hard drive, date stamps and all. The laptop owner was a known logistics operative. Add to that, the keyword hits for "Ras Tanura" in the background chatter keep increasing," he informed them.

"We know the logistics guy? See if they're in the brother's network." Bob paused and then remembered: "Oh, and this *Fadhil al-Hammadi*, make him the new central node for traffic analysis—we may have our mastermind."

"Update Mossad on the al-Hammadi hit. Our sources stay in the background," Kate reminded him.

A few minutes later, Bob and Kate were in the director's office.

"The threat to Ras Tanura appears credible. Increased traffic on that keyword is showing up," Kate reported.

"I think we need to start thinking about protection, air defense, get on with the Saudis, inform them there's a legit threat to their loading facility. Move some Patriot batteries over there," Bob suggested.

The director agreed. "Talk to the navy, too, see if we can get some Aegis ships." The director let out an annoyed sigh. "I have to do another round of updates now. DNI, POTUS, NSC." He wearily hung his head. "I spend more time just updating everybody than I do actual intelligence work."

Kate smiled at him. "Cost of the Patriot Act."

His face gave a ruddy beam, and his stomach shook with a quiet chuckle at the irony. He quickly became serious again and eyed the both of them.

"Remember, you guys have full authorization to take this thing out. That includes all couriers, guards, mules, whatever. They're in the desert now. Be as messy as you need to," he sternly reminded them.

Fortnum Bank Equities Trading Floor

Kyle juggled two phones, managing their customers' order flow. It was a few minutes after one p.m., and the floor was hectic. The Fed would announce in a little more than an hour.

Pete grabbed Kyle's arm and shook it. Kyle swiveled, as Pete was pointing at the crude oil chart on Kyle's monitor.

Crude oil was vaulting higher, up $2.30 to $94.00. Gold was moving, too, now up another $1 to $733.

"I'll call you back," Kyle shouted into one phone. "I gotta go," into the other. He begged Pete, "Why, what you see, anything?"

Pete hung up his phones, too, and shook his head *no*.

"Nada," he responded. And then he half stood. "Shit, look!"

A red "Breaking News" chyron flashed on the wall TVs, and the lower forty read, "US warships to deploy around Saudi oil facilities. Intelligence cites threat. US naval forces in Persian Gulf on heightened alert. Patriot missile batteries being moved to protect potential targets..."

The amplifying din narrowed Kyle's world. He peered back down at his charts: Oil was spiking, up $5.50 to $97.20, and gold soared $10 to $743.

"Shiiit," Kyle cursed.

"We just blew through both stops," Pete called out. He tapped his keyboard to get their fills. "We're done at seven forty-one, both orders," he informed. Since there was a gap upward, both their $734 and the $739 sell stop orders triggered at the next immediately marketable price, $741.

"Goddamn it!" Kyle exclaimed, pissed off. "Maybe more sellers will fill in here, add some downside pressure," he declared, in some denial.

"Vols expanding now, too, they'd been kind of muted before. Gold vol up to eighteen now, crude vol is closing in on fifty, dang. This is real," Pete said.

"Keep a close eye on gold. Negative gamma's gotta be over the horizon." He told Pete to stay alert.

"We're naked now, too, need to reenter our hedge," Pete fretted.

"Don't. I don't want to pay up and add to this buying panic. We're gonna get scalped ourselves. We need to get through the Fed first," Kyle said.

"You're the boss."

"Oil facilities? Why's the navy protecting? Aren't they escorting tankers?" Kyle wondered out loud.

"Don't know, but you saw it, said *facilities*, that means, like, refineries and pipelines again."

"Both of which they've hit already. So, then what are the Patriots for?"

"Ground-to-air missiles, ya know—remember them from the first Gulf War? That's how I'm in this business. I won my junior high's stock-picking contest because I had—what was that company—Raytheon, yeah, that fucker went—"

"Shut up, Pete."

"Sorry, a threat from the air. They shoot down incoming missiles and planes."

"So, what's by the sea—oh, hey, what's that huge oil terminal they have?"

"uh, Tanura, Ras Tanura—"

"*Ras Tanura*, yes, like the tankers float in and hook up to hoses."

"That'd be a big takeout."

"Major. Most of Saudi's oil gets loaded there. Ten million barrels a day."

Kyle and Pete exchanged anxious looks as they assembled the picture. They helplessly watched crude oil and gold futures blinking higher...

Nahda Desert Region, Oman

Surging out of a wadi, the desert leveled out and the lead Humvee accelerated onto the flat, closing the distance with the target 4x4 riding half a klick ahead of them.

"Maintain here," Kelso said. "This close enough?" he asked the NEST officer.

"Should be," the NEST tech replied as he prepped a more advanced neutron sniffer than the one Kelso had lugged through China. The NEST tech gripped it with both hands and pointed the lenses at their 4x4 target through the windshield.

Kelso reached above him and rolled open the roof hatch. He motioned to the NEST op to stick it outside instead. The NEST officer stood up, emerging out of the top of the Humvee, and steadied the sniffer on the roof. He couldn't both use his NODs and the neutron sniffer at once, so he flipped up his L-3s with a frustrated wave and lowered his sand goggles to deal with the blowing air at ninety kilometers an hour.

The tech tilted the device's screen upward and held it still with both hands for a few seconds. A small fiery-red object in the lower center of the monitor—the escaping 4x4—blazed as throwing off significant, greater-than-background levels of radiation and, more significantly, fast neutrons.

The tech closed up the sniffer and dropped back inside the Humvee.

"Lit up. Confirmed fast neutrons," he reported.

"Same package?" Kelso clarified as he slid closed the roof hatch.

"Hard to be any different," he confirmed.

"Drop back now," Kelso directed their driver.

"Hey, I may have something here. Look at this." The comms guy behind them indicated. He handed the tablet PC to Kelso, who flipped up his L3s and squinted at the darkened image on the tablet screen.

"Looks like an airstrip?"

"Good, I wasn't imagining it," the Unit op said.

"Nice eyes, soldier. Lock the coords on that. Bet that's where he's headed."

Operation 912 Task Force Center

Scanlon and Kazemi were drawing Kate's eyes around the site map, orienting her.

"They've identified a makeshift airstrip, here, apron here." Kazemi gestured. "We're watching to see if the 4x4 turns toward it. The map's a few weeks old, so there could be some tents and vehicles in this area," he went on, motioning.

"It's mostly flat, but there's some height, here and here," Scanlon picked up, identifying features on the grid. "Team can stage from just over these berms. They're three meters above the desert floor. Decent cover," Scanlon finished.

Kate checked her watch and assessed the landscape. "If there's not too many of them, this thing could be over in a few hours," she estimated.

Terry didn't reply to that, remaining more objective. And then Kate lowered her voice. "Remember, if there *aren't* too many of them, we want this thing, this gadget, these materials. Otherwise, orders are confirmed destruction," Kate said. She reviewed the map again. "What about air support? We gotta have assets all over here?" Kate noted its proximity to US-stationed air force bases in the region.

"JSOC secured two A-10s out of Al Dhafra. Will be configured for overwatch and close air support." Terry pointed to the air base in UAE they'd be flying from. "They can be in theatre in twenty minutes if the team needs 'em," he answered.

"Hey? Hey?" Carly called out to get their attention. They were all met by her exaggerated nod—which meant the 4x4 was turning into the airfield.

Nahda Desert Region, Oman

Kelso and the assault team were out of their vehicles and in full battle rattle. With their NODs engaged, they climbed the berm that was about a thousand meters to the north of the illicit, makeshift airfield. Reaching the crest, they dropped to their bellies, prone, and twisted their night-vision lenses to a ten-times-distance mode.

Kelso whispered details to the others: "Two light, fixed-wing, single engine aircraft. Four, maybe five, tents, about five meters a piece. At least six vehicles. A couple more 4x4s, maybe a PKM or two, maybe an RPG or two. I only count two live enemy targets. Any others must be inside the tents. If there's at least one for each vehicle, that's six, and we gotta figure as many as two dozen." Kelso paused and then requested, "NEST, where is it?"

One of the NEST techs was aiming the advanced neutron sniffer at the collection of trucks and tents. He maximized zoom so he could pinpoint the hot spot, struggling with the controls in the darkness.

"We're beyond range, I'm maybe getting a reading from one of the tents. Need to get closer for a decent confidence return," he reported.

"Let's assume it's in that tent," Kelso resolved.

They crawled back down from the ridge until they were below line of sight to the airfield, and they fell back to their staging area. Kelso commanded they huddle. The team closed into a tight circle around him as Kelso outlined their tactical assault plan.

"The berm is our decisive point. Our two snipers and I will position right here. The breachers will wire up the planes. We got overwatch from the high ground. Next, the team of four approaches from the east, flank the side of the ridge. One NEST tech will be with you. Confirm precise location of the gadget. You guys get into position first, you'll give us a single flash for an assault, a double flash is an all-stop." Kelso paused to let this stick. "The main assault will be with the Mike-sixty, full tilt, that will open us up. Snipers, you await the *go* signal, take out any targets as both teams approach. The rest stay here with NEST tech two, ready for reinforcements or when we give the all-clear sign." He paused again as the strike team listened intently.

"Couple standouts to keep in mind. One, hydrate. You know this turf, desert combat, but you dry up quick. Two, no radios, sat comms only. Our bad guys can pick up the radio chatter. Three, we're going in hot. You put rounds downrange, you take your guys out—and no fucking lasers. They stick out like flares in the desert night. You're iron sights guys, anyway. Four, we start taking fire, hear the whistle of an incoming mortar or RPG, spread the fuck out, get out of the kill zone. They'll take out more of us if we're bunched up. Final point, I saved the best for last, do *not* shoot up that southmost tent. I'd rather you guys take a fucking round to the gut than you hit that gadget by accident. This ain't no IED in the grass. This is a loose nuke. You hit that thing, you light up the entire desert from space, vaporize us all," he finished.

"Affirmative, sir," a number of them responded.

"We have the night. We can clean it up by first light," Kelso added.

The soldiers resumed their final checks. Most of them were so good, so well trained with their weapons systems, they could perform their inspections only by feel and sound. That satisfied Kelso. He knew these were the right guys for this objective. In any operation, there was so much randomness, and in any battlefield contact, there was luck, on both sides, good and bad. But the sharp training at least minimized the error factor for the good guys.

Fortnum Bank Equities Trading Floor

It was 2:29 p.m. EST. The Fed announcement was in one minute. Kyle and Pete exchanged nervous looks. They reviewed their screens, and each grabbed a phone handset to be ready. All markets were poised. The tumult on the floor braked to a dead quiet, and you could almost hear the proverbial pin drop.

The announcement came through squawk boxes and TVs, broadcast across the trading floor.

"The Federal Reserve Open Market Committee lowers the Federal Funds rate by fifty, five-zero basis points to four seventy-five—"

Shouts erupted. Phones trilled.

"Fifty, more than we thought," Pete commented above the racket. They watched their screens. Equities were rallying, up seventeen points already. Gold jumped initially, but then, exactly as Kyle predicted, it started to sell off. It showed back down to $735 at that moment. Crude was at $97, holding its level following the Persian Gulf threat.

"Keep a fucking eye pinned to gold," Kyle prompted Pete. "There's still buyers," Kyle commented, observing the tick behavior in the futures.

"How do you know?"

"I figured it should have sold off about fifteen or twenty handles. Most of the Fed should have been built-in already. Shirin gave me the stats for the average gold price move post announcement. It calculates out to fifteen or twenty handles, either way," Kyle explained. "Plus, that's what my gut says."

"So, where're these buyers?"

"Look at the dollar strengthening. Should be selling off, cheaper rates, cheaper dollar. Stronger commodities, anything priced in dollars. But they're not. Everything built in already. Let's let it all wash out here for a few." Kyle tapped Pete's screen, pointing to the gold tick chart. It had climbed back to $740.

"There's buyers in there," Kyle reemphasized.

"Shit, it's back to where it was. We're short here, you know?"

At that moment, they did a double take. Garner was standing behind them.

"Everything OK? I'm doing my rounds, see what's up, post-Fed, you know?"

Kyle and Pete both twisted around to him, but neither said anything at first.

"You know our positions, pretty light. Just been dealing with customer flow," Kyle finally responded, terrified Garner was there about the gold options trade.

"You see oil? I *told* you. I should be back on the desk. I got a sixth sense sometimes. I had a feeling about that. Glad you got out of that shit. Coulda been a nasty one," Garner said, all gloating.

He grinned with pride at Kyle and Pete and said, "Gotta go check on your boy, Sully, now..." as he strode away.

Pete and Kyle exchanged annoyed, but relieved glances.

"What a motherfucker! Now he wants credit for fucking us over for the year?"

"I shoulda clocked him with one of my phones," Kyle griped after.

"At least he still doesn't seem to know anything about the gold trade."

"Maybe I'll rat him out to the feds in my interview tonight," Kyle proposed, half joking but also half serious. Pete cracked up.

"Comedy. What would you tell 'em?"

"I'd say I suspected him being involved, and on the take. Maybe he is for all we know, he claimed prescience over the oil run-up." Kyle laughed.

"He's a spurious fuck. He panicked when he saw the numbers, and that's why he told us to close the position."

"*Spurious*, Princeton word. Yeah, I know. I could still make his life hell, though. Once you're on a list it's a difficult trick to get clean." Kyle chuckled.

They paused to glance at the charts. Gold was climbing higher again, back up to $745. Crude oil was range bound at $95.50, off its highs. Equities continued to rise, boosted by the Fed and cheaper rates.

The floor was still bustling but had started to subside when Sully appeared.

"How you guys doing?"

"Hey, man."

"Who let you out? Back to your hole."

"Garner come over and bother you guys?"

"Of course. He was a gloating motherfucker, too."

"Ha—about crude? Such an asshole. He's been riding me like a donkey all day. Does it every Fed. Tired of it. He's gotta be seen as doing *something* valuable," Sully ranted.

"He say something to you about our crude position?"

"He talked smack like he deserves the fucking Heisman," Sully told them.

"What a total dickhead."

"I'm definitely telling the feds about him," Kyle restated to Pete.

"Telling the feds about what?" Sully inquired, intrigued.

"Springer's got an FBI interview tonight," Pete blurted.

"Shut up, dude," Kyle scolded him and then completed the explanation to Sully in quieter tones. "Feds want to hear about my theories."

"Ha ha, you serious? Shit, how'd this come about?"

"Long story. We gotta catch you up."

"Damn right you do—"

"Hey, *Sully*?" Sully's clerk shouted at him over the din.

"Shit. I gotta go—hey, what you guys doing tonight? I'm busy after close 'til like seven or so."

"You're up whenever," Pete replied.

Sully made to go back to his seat but then half twisted back to Kyle.

"Hey, Garner ask about the gold trade?"

Kyle raised his eyebrows and shook his head, *nope*.

Sully returned a devious smirk. "I think you're home free," he said, and jogged back to his desk.

Operation 912 Task Force Center

Terry illustrated across the large map, updating Kate and Bob. "There are half a dozen tents, five-meter size, here," he started, sketching out small rectangles. "Another half dozen all-terrain civilian vehicles converted to light war-fighting capability, here. Might be some medium-heavy arms like RPGs and machine guns." He drew a few more boxes representing the vehicles.

"On the apron of this airstrip, we have two light, single-prop fixed-wing planes, Pipers or Cessna-types," he said as he penciled in two crosses representing the aircraft. "They estimate there could be about two dozen fighters. The gadget's location is most likely here, in this tent, but not confirmed," he finished.

"Stock terrorist training camp," Bob concluded.

"This has some funding to it, and support," Kate assessed, her eyes roving throughout the diagram.

"I think you're right. You've got at least six vehicle drivers. Probably a few pilots, a mechanic or two. Some guards, gunmen, logistics people, some mess people," Kazemi concurred.

"We ready?"

"They'll move shortly, conditions are good," Terry finished.

"Our drone up there?"

The JSOC officer nodded. "Streaming battlefield visibility to the strike team."

They said nothing, just quietly took their seats and faced the large projection monitor to watch the battle unfold in real time.

The overhead desert image strobed into focus. The landscape displayed as black background with small white profiles—people and lower-grade heat signatures from the cooling engines of the vehicles—dotting the rest of the camp.

Fighter Camp, Nahda Desert Region, Oman

Kelso counted the heat silhouettes downrange through his L3s, trying to assess the number of bad guys. He leaned to the Delta Force breacher next to him who was also surveying the camp and airstrip.

"Launch," he said evenly.

The Unit breacher didn't reply. He slid down the berm and jogged toward the rest of the staging assault team. He and his partner took off toward the aircraft.

Kelso followed the two breachers darting to the airstrip from the south side through his NOD binoculars. The parked aircraft were several hundred meters from the tents, and not guarded. The breachers split up, taking an airplane each.

"On scope," Kelso whispered to his Delta Force sniper who was eyeing the scene through his night-vision rifle scope. The sniper lined up his very deadly MK11 rifle, ready to zap any target who threatened his teammates. The gun fired a 7.62-caliber round at 2,500-feet-per-second muzzle velocity. With its sound suppressor on the barrel, and a range of a thousand meters, the target would be down before any noise arrived.

The breachers stole up to the airplanes. Each op removed two bars, 1.25 pounds of composition C-4. They bent the charges onto the engine blocks and affixed more C-4 to the wings. They rigged the charges with detonators and timers and ran back toward the covering ridge.

Kelso and the sniper tracked the breachers until they got back inside the wire. Kelso then swung his attention to the array of 4x4s by the tents. They needed to ensure the bad guys couldn't escape during the attack, so the vehicles needed to be neutralized next.

The second Delta Force sniper joined them on the berm, getting into position. His gun was the devastating M82, a .50-caliber cannon, classified as an anti-material weapon. A single slug from its long-barreled, heavy breech could take out a vehicle, even engage armor from over a kilometer away.

Kelso took a deep breath, focused the view through his binoculars, and snapped his fingers.

The M82 sniper squeezed his trigger. There was a blast from the powerful weapon, quickly eaten up by the desert night. Kelso eyed the array of 4x4s. The truck closest to the first tent jolted from the impact of the .50-caliber shell as it split its engine block into two with a pop and a small fireball that died as quickly and left a plume of smoke emerging from its hood.

The sniper found his second target and fired another round. There was the metallic noise of shattering glass from all its windows blowing out as the next slug smacked a second truck with an abrupt bang.

Fighters emerged from the tents and surrounded the trucks. The MK11 sniper went to work. The first terrorist was hit in the chest and flew backward onto the ground, where he lay motionless. A second terrorist ran toward the first and was met with a perfectly placed bullet through his temple and crumpled to his knees and pitched face-forward into the dust.

The M82 sniper swiveled his rifle aim to the next trucks. A blast erupted when he sent his next shot slamming into another 4x4. The bullet exploded the gas tank, igniting a tall, glittering red-and-white geyser that lit up the desert night for an instant and then closed itself into a dark column of smoke. His shot after struck a fourth 4x4 with a *clink* in a quiet kill of the vehicle.

Kelso lowered his binoculars and checked his watch. He squinted in the direction of the aircraft.

"Three. Two. One," he whispered.

Loud pops could be heard across the desert floor as both airplanes exploded in fiberglass and metal shards, casting debris across the airfield. The remnant wingless airframes capsized and quietly burned in the sand.

Kelso swung back to the tents. More fighters were streaming out. They had figured out the direction of the attack and were taking cover behind their killed 4x4s. The Delta Force snipers plugged rounds downrange at the emerging targets.

The bad guys returned fire. They intermittently popped up and got off bursts from their AKs, the resonant clatter skipping across the desert floor.

Next, on cue, the Humvee with the mounted M60 machine gun raced from the east side of the berm, flying toward the encampment. The Unit SAW gunner manning the M60 turret opened it up on the terrorists hiding behind the vehicles.

The heavy M60 rounds strafed the trucks, sparking and flinging debris into the night air. Kelso observed some of the fighters fleeing in random directions. A few were lying prone on the ground, and others hid behind vehicles, taking whatever cover they could.

"Take 'em out where you see 'em. We don't want them coming back on us with a suicide vest later," Kelso ordered.

His snipers pumped more rounds at the targets, dropping three more bad guys as they fled. Smoke and explosions and small fires were prevalent now, which was the bane of night-vision equipment, obscuring visibility and blending with human targets, making them more difficult to discern.

"Keep the cover fire. And don't shoot *us*," Kelso told the snipers as he slid off the berm and jogged to the rest of his Delta Force contingent readying the next wave. Kelso jumped into the front seat of a waiting Humvee, and with a second Humvee gunning, the two accelerated toward the camp. Their fourth vehicle would remain behind for backup.

Kelso flipped down his NODs as they charged the tents. His and the other Humvee both wheeled around to attack from the west side of the ridge, adding a "pincer" move with the M60 gun truck striking from the east.

The Humvee driving next to Kelso's was armed with a grenade launcher. The gunner manning that turret fired—*thunk-thunk-thunk-thunk-thunk*. The grenades lobbed out of the muzzle and bombed the encampment with a concussive force, rocking the vehicle husks and shredding one of the rear tents.

"Goddamn it! Watch that front tent," Kelso yelled, although the SAW gunner couldn't hear him. One of the grenades had exploded too close to the one they believed held the gadget.

As they approached, Kelso trained his focus on that tent, ensuring he didn't take his eyes off it—he didn't want them rabbiting with their objective.

Their Humvees came under fire. AK rounds smacked against the bulletproof armor as they rolled into the fight. Kelso calculated they had neutralized both aircraft, all six vehicles, one tent, and probably about half of the terrorist operators in the camp. They were five hundred meters from the tents, closing fast, when an explosion struck the first Humvee.

"Fuck!" Kelso shouted, averting his eyes from the bright flash. Their driver slowed their approach.

"I think they got RPG'd," the driver made.

Operation 912 Task Force Center

The center stared at the real-time combat feeds as Kelso and the Unit assault team took out the vehicles and attacked the camp.

"Shit!" Terry shouted.

From the drone's overhead view, they could see dozens of white objects descending on the battlefield—enemy vehicles approaching from both sides.

"There's two dozen of them," Terry fretted.

They all watched as an armada entrapped the three Delta Force Humvees. Kate and Bob, alarmed, reached for help.

"I'm on with Al Dhafra," the JSOC officer called out, already on his headset.

Others rushed to their stations in an attempt to recover the situation.

Fighter Camp, Nahda Desert Region, Oman

Kelso saw them—seven, eight, nine, more 4x4s bearing for them.

"Commander?" The comms guy behind them tapped Kelso on the shoulder and motioned to their right.

Kelso twisted to see. Another vanguard of trucks from the opposite side rifled at them, too. He spun back to the crippled Humvee. It had pitched onto its side, and he could see their teammates climbing out of it.

"The downed Humvee. Go, *go!*" Kelso shouted.

The driver ripped the wheel left. The third Humvee cornered after them.

Kelso ordered the comms guy, "Get us cover!"

"Radio, sir?"

"Radio!"

"We need a fucking storm of rounds. Rounds, rounds, rounds!" the comms op yelled into the radio as Kelso grabbed his sat phone.

"Get us those alpha tens, *now* now!" Kelso demanded on his sat phone, ordering CAS (close air support). He grabbed his MK16 SCAR assault rifle.

"We could have some down. Use the H as cover. Don't bunch up," he reminded his ops. He gave the comms guy a look and motioned to the NEST tech. The comms op knew he meant *check his protection*, so he ensured the NEST tech was helmeted and his flak vest was on tight.

"Swing to the left. We'll try to make it back to the berm," Kelso directed the driver as they approached the crippled Humvee.

The third Humvee started giving cover fire, throwing off an arc of grenade rounds at the oncoming vehicles. The enemy 4x4s were fast closing the distance. One grenade shell struck gold, a direct hit piercing the windshield. The truck blew apart with fiery fronds hurtling out of the windows. The vehicle reared and backflipped from the explosion. Shrapnel disabled a second riding alongside, and it skidded to a dusty halt.

The 4x4s gunning at them from the west fanned outward in angled paths to avoid the grenade fire as more shells punched into the desert ground, flashing in columns of fire and dust.

Kelso heard the AK rounds from the convoy of 4x4s closing in on them from behind. And that was followed by the deeper ratchet of PKM (machine-gun) fire. They were outgunned and would be pinned down. They had only seconds.

Kelso's driver jammed on the brakes as they slid up to the damaged gun truck. They leapt out of the vehicle and grabbed their teammates and the other NEST tech. Some were wounded or shaken up from the explosion that had hit them.

"This everybody?" Kelso shouted. The driver motioned to the Humvee—the SAW gunner was trapped inside. Kelso pulled his driver to follow him.

A 4x4 was blitzing toward them and strafing their Humvees with AK fire. They could hear the rounds hissing overheard as they ran. Kelso and the Delta

Force op returned fire, shattering the windshield and striking the faces of the driver and occupants. The 4x4 rolled onto its right wheels and knifed into the desert floor, plowing to a stop.

The SAW gunner atop the third Humvee kept up the grenade fire and had created a standoff barrier the enemy vehicles were avoiding.

Kelso and his driver climbed onto the rolled Humvee and heaved open its rear side door. Inside, they found their teammate crushed against the floor. Kelso grabbed handfuls of the soldier's jacket and pulled him up. He raised him above his head, enough so the combat driver could wrap his upper body with his arms and extract him from the rolled Humvee. The driver lugged his unconscious mate onto the ground.

AK fire was clattering all around them. Kelso stood and eyed two 4x4s approaching from their west flank. He raised his SCAR and pulsed several bursts into their grills. The first 4x4 skidded to a halt; the second swerved and exposed its profile to Kelso, who fired into the side, killing the driver instantly. The truck kept rolling past them on autopilot as the lifeless driver slumped onto the wheel.

They carried their fallen soldier to the waiting Humvee. The other Delta Force ops formed a phalanx, giving them cover fire with their HK416s as they all loaded inside the two remaining vehicles.

Another truck was gunning dead at them. Kelso aimed his SCAR when he heard a *chink* and saw a hole in the bad guy's windshield. He realized the Delta Force snipers on the ridge had taken out the driver with a .50-caliber plug. The 4x4 flipped toward the Humvees just as Kelso and the rest of the squad piled inside.

The two Humvees careened out of there as they took more AK and PKM fire from the 4x4s barreling at them. They pulled away in moments and raced back toward the berm behind them.

Al Dhafra Air Base, United Arab Emirates

Crews scrambled a pair of US Air Force A-10 Warthogs. Their pilots, call signs Bell Boy and Seeker, vaulted into their cockpits as crews shut their canopies. The A-10s pivoted onto the main air base runway. Their jet engines rose to a funneling roar, and they coursed down the tarmac and ramped into the air.

A-10s were legendary wicked ground attack and support jets. Shaped more like a flying cross than an aircraft, they were the tanks of the air, bad motherfuckers. With two large barrels for engines attached on the rear fuselage of the aircraft, they were nothing like the sleek USAF dogfighting jets, and yet they were among the deadliest in the Air Force fleet. Their pilots, the Hawg guys, took care of the dudes on the ground.

Armed under wing with GBU-38 guided bombs, air-to-ground Maverick missiles, and a diabolical thirty-millimeter nose cannon that shot DU (depleted uranium) bullets, the two A-10s screamed toward their fight in the Omani desert.

Operation 912 Task Force Center

The CIA officers watched Kelso's team get chased off the battlefield. The OPFOR (bad guy) vehicles now encircled the camp. It was a pummeling counterattack as more terrorists emerged from the newly arrived trucks and joined their brethren to pursue the Delta Force squad. Scanlon and the JSOC officer got on their comms to warn Kelso.

"Enemy rounding south side of the ridge. You must retreat," Scanlon ordered.

Kate and Bob exchanged worried looks. If they were driven from theater, they could lose the target for good. The broken arrow would continue to make its way to wherever it was headed, and they wouldn't have any way of tracking it.

"A-10s en route," JSOC officer reported.

"How long?" someone shouted.

"Fifteen minutes."

"They'll be dead in fifteen minutes."

Fighter Camp, Nahda Desert Region, Oman

"Negative, no retreat. *Where the hell are those Hawgs?*" Kelso demanded into the sat phone and flicked it off.

Their Humvees braked behind the berm. Kelso reached into the back seat and felt the pulse of the unconscious SAW gunner. He looked up at the others and shook his head.

"He's gone," Kelso said flatly.

The SAW gunner had been blown against the gun turret when the RPG shell hit them. The other ops saluted him and helped pull their fallen soldier out and take him to the combat medic, who removed his gear and zipped him up in a body bag. Kelso opened the roof hatch and emerged out of it to rally the squad.

"CAS is fifteen mikes away. Another dozen bad-guy trucks coming at us. If we leave our position, we lose this target for good and the package continues further west, where it can do some real damage." Kelso paused. "So, we stay and fight. We destroy this thing and we neutralize the bad guys. And we do it for our fallen man."

Kelso could hear "Fuck yeah, bro!" from the other soldiers as he exited the Humvee. He ordered all ops, except for his driver, to pack themselves into the other two rides. Kelso finished with the instruction, "Fly east until you're sure nobody's on your tail. Then turn back and reengage."

The two Humvees closed up and spun away, vanishing into the enveloping blackness. Kelso and his combat driver sat quietly in the remaining Humvee. Through their L3s they watched the approaching 4x4s closing the distance. They saw the blinking white puffs of AK and PKM muzzle fire as they shot at them.

"Sir?" the driver anxiously urged.

"What are you waiting for?" Kelso made clear to move, then asked him, "What do we got here?"

Driver pointed to two long guns in the rear seat. "Mike-eight-two," he answered as they accelerated off, referring to the powerful .50-caliber sniper rifle. Kelso grabbed it and rose through the roof hatch.

From the roof, Kelso gripped the breech, and picked a 4x4. His finger traced the arc of the trigger as he lined up the vehicle in the kill box. He squeezed it. A *bang*, Kelso rocked from the recoil. Miss.

Kelso tried again. He marked another vehicle, aimed lower this time, and clutched the trigger. *Bam!* The lead 4x4 exploded as the shell ripped through its engine block and split open half the truck, igniting its fuel lines. The burning husk caromed and rolled onto its side, out of commission.

"Good hit!" the driver yelled up at him.

But the 4x4s kept coming. Their Humvee was being hammered by PKM fire. Kelso ducked as he heard it dinging their armor and whistling overhead. This wasn't going well. The enemies were unfazed. Meanwhile, they were driving farther and farther away from the encampment. Kelso worried the fighters could use the distraction to escape with the gadget. He dropped back inside the Humvee.

"Start turning. Let's make our way back toward the tents," Kelso told him.

"They're gonna have the angle on us, bro, cut us off."

"I know, but I think we can drive 'em into the ridge if we time it right."

The driver bent the Humvee around, turning back east. The terrorist 4x4s were now cutting the distance even faster on a forty-five-degree jackknife angle at their vehicle. Rounds pelted their broadside as they floored it toward the encampment.

"What's the plan when we hit the camp?" the driver pressed.

"We're assaulting them again. Not a moment's peace," Kelso replied simply.

Crazy as it sounded, the driver smiled. "In-fuckin'-sane, sir," he responded.

Omani Border, 20,000 feet

The two A-10s hurtled toward the combat zone. The Seeker was the flight lead; Bell Boy, his wingman. The Seeker observed through his heads-up display (HUD) the ground below. He radioed over to Bell Boy.

"Bell Boy, comms, copy?"

"Copy, Seeker."

"Nothing but dark desert below us."

"Copy that."

"Eyes open, these are specs in the sand," the Seeker emphasized to Bell Boy.

"Danger close, copy that... Lower altitude?" Bell Boy requested.

"Affirmative. Descend to five," Seeker instructed.

Fighter Camp, Nahda Desert Region, Oman

Kelso tracked the outlines of the enemy vehicles in his green-amber night-vision. They heard the sudden, loud popping report of AKs, too close. A 4x4 was speeding toward them. Rounds struck their Humvee, battering their side armor.

"Shit!" the driver cursed.

Kelso grabbed his SCAR and rose through the roof hatch. He squeezed off several bursts, the bullets kicking up desert turf in front of the enemy truck as he fired short.

Kelso spied two more 4x4s descending on them. And in the back of the second truck was a terrorist readying a shoulder-fired RPG—steadying, aiming. Kelso ducked back inside, shut the hatch, and tightened the strap on his helmet.

"Incoming!" Kelso shouted and secured the strap on his driver's helmet for him as they swerved to throw off the RPG aim. The air trail lit up from the path of the RPG warhead as it whistled toward them. The desert pulsed in a bright-white flash that blew out their front left tire, warping their hood and grill.

The driver forced the wheel straight for as long as he could. Their helmets hit the seat back behind them and they slammed into the dash as the Humvee's engine was blown apart. The driver threw the wheel right to overcompensate, but the forces were too strong, and they plowed nose first into the dirt as they rammed to a sudden stop, their heads again impacting the dash.

For an instant, the world became silent, still.

The sounds of 4x4 engines getting closer and the riveting gunfire hitting their vehicle jolted Kelso back. He blinked and came to. He rocked his head to shake himself out of it.

"Fucked up," the driver uttered. He was shell-shocked, too, but his wits were still about him.

"Out this side." Kelso banged open the passenger-side door and held its weight enough to push himself out of the vehicle. The driver followed, tossing his weapon to the ground. They crouched beneath the raised side of the pitched Humvee for cover.

Some of the bad guys were running at them on foot and the strobing flashes from their muzzle bursts illuminated the desert floor in front of them. The driver sighted the oncoming terrorists through his scope. His vision was still hazy from the blow.

The driver stood and fired off a continuous volley, sweeping side to side to give them cover. Most of his rounds missed, but he watched the terrorist on his left flank trip and faceplant into the dirt, probably struck in the leg. The enemies kept firing, undeterred, and closing in. Kelso and the driver could hear the bullets impacting the dirt around them.

Kelso pegged one fighter coming fast on them and rattled off a chain of rounds at his chest. The bullets ripped him apart. Kelso swiveled to the other terrorists and plucked off the second one, hitting him in the legs and torso and dropping him into a pile. But there were too many.

Operation 912 Task Force Center

Bob spun around and yelled at the JSOC, "Damn it, *where are those A-10s?*"

The live overhead feed showed the ghostly white shapes of the downed Humvee and Kelso and the driver trapped behind it. And the center could clearly see the advancing enemy fighters—and the fleet of 4x4s behind them.

The other two Humvees were now racing back toward the battlefield from the reverse side, but they were still at least several minutes away.

The JSOC rep, on his feet, yelling into two separate phones, couldn't respond.

Kate nervously watched the targets in the upper left corner of the battlefield, where the tents were. She worried they could make an escape with the gadget in the din of the battle.

"Keep your eyes on those tents," she instructed Kazemi and another officer. "Track anybody who escapes this theater," she ordered, and drew a worried sigh.

Nahda Desert Region, Oman

Kelso panned his muzzle east and scanned the desert for any sign of the other Humvees but saw only empty night. The berm was about a hundred meters behind them. They could make a run for it and hope to get over the ridge. But he knew they would probably be cut down, shot in the back as they fled. Retreat was death. Remaining was death. They were caught.

The driver kept up his cover fire as the bad guys swarmed in.

"Too many," he shouted.

"Goal line stand," Kelso declared.

"Let's do this, bro."

"How much C-4 in the truck?" Kelso then asked.

"Some in the back," the driver replied, ducking incoming rounds. The shots were becoming more precise as the bad guys closed range. They could hear the sharp cracks of the rounds striking next to them. Kelso saw another shoulder-fired RPG fighter kneel on the ground and fire. The shell blasted out of the tube and screamed toward them.

"RPG!" Kelso warned.

The grenade overshot and hit the ridge behind them, exploding in a yellow ball. Kelso and the driver stood and returned fire. They saw the RPG guy reloading, fitting another shell onto his launcher. Kelso watched in slow motion. The RPG fighter squeezed the trigger.

There was a sudden, colossal *boom*! Kelso and the driver hit the deck. The ground thundered. The night lit up in a spectacular yellow and green flash, as brilliant as day.

Kelso's hearing went out. The world was a silent movie. He crawled to the front of the Humvee to get a clearer look. The RPG shell had not hit them. There was now nothing but a swirling smoke column as high as the sky and a gaping crater that had swallowed the RPG fighter, a dozen bad guys, and their 4x4s.

Kelso's hearing started to return. He heard the roar above and felt a vibration in his gut. That was an A-10. It had just fired one of its Maverick air-to-ground missiles that obliterated the terrorist fighters with its two-hundred-pound warhead.

"It's us!" Kelso shouted over to the Delta Force op. He was momentarily deaf, too, but realized when Kelso pointed skyward.

Above them, inside the Seeker's cockpit, the pilot looked down on the theater through the night-vision kill box—a white square on his monochromatic-green console that relayed a video feed from an underwing targeting pod. He saw an array of 4x4s that had braked at the Maverick explosion and were now fearfully reversing and accelerating in the opposite direction.

"Positive contact. Good kill, Seeker," Bell Boy radioed over.

"Copy that. Do we have a JTAC on ground?"

"Negative... Going in for a gun run, split these fighters," Bell Boy said.

"Give 'em some DU. Watch your friendlies."

Bell Boy lined up the train of 4x4s in his gun sights and pushed the stick forward in a quick descent and a thirty-degree angle of attack approach, his gloved thumb adjusting the trim.

Bell Boy's A-10 pitched downward and a fiery, pounding burst erupted from its 30mm rotary nose cannon followed by a torrent of hot metal shells that impacted the desert floor and shredded, one after the next, three escaping 4x4s.

Kelso and the driver watched from behind the damaged Humvee. Kelso swung his scope to the east and spied their other two Humvees arriving in the combat zone.

"They're here," he yelled over. He found his spotter and flashed it three times in quick succession at the Humvees. The Humvees curved in their direction, racing for them.

As the A-10s thundered above, vaporizing any remaining terrorist vehicles, Kelso and his driver rejoined their squad and rode to the berm where they could await the A-10s to finish their duty.

Fortnum Bank Equities Trading Floor

Equities rallied into the close. The floor had quieted down as the markets found their direction following the Fed announcement.

"Good day for equities," Kyle noted.

"I wonder how Sully did. Huge volume," Pete mused.

"Fifty bips'll get things moving."

"Crude's bid again. Gold, too. What we want to do here?"

Kyle pondered, his fingers carefully tracking the tick-by-tick behavior on his screens. Crude was now up a dollar in the new session to $96. Gold was approaching $750.

"Gold *is* behaving like there's buyers in it, not taking a break. Maybe it is Fed related, after all. Where does our gamma kick in, again?" he asked Pete.

Since they were short options struck at $800, they would need to hedge faster and faster as the price of gold approached $800. The option risk measure called gamma dictated the frequency and magnitude of those hedges. For option traders who were short volatility, like Kyle and Pete were in gold, negative gamma could be your worst nightmare, especially as the asset approached the strike price you were short ($800, in their case).

Pete punched some numbers into Scout and updated their risk exposures.

"If you believe the risk models then not until seven ninety at this rate."

"I don't believe our risk models."

"If it keeps climbing going into tonight, we probably need to flatten it out. I don't know, maybe another ten or fifteen, I'm surmising. Decay helps us tomorrow. But if it climbs all day tomorrow, like it did today, we're kind of fucked," Pete revealed the obvious.

Decay was a short option trader's best friend. As expiration approached, the probability an option could finish in the money (above $800), declined at an accelerating speed. It was the inverse of gamma, the flipside of the coin. Right now, with gold at $750, decay was on their side. But if gold kept closing in on $800, the negative gamma would overwhelm any decay that was helping them.

"I know," Kyle reluctantly agreed, "and we've got to reverse my short bet, too, take that loss. This is getting ugly. Garner might notice this," Kyle fretted.

"You serious? How?"

"He doesn't seem to see our OTC option position, but he can see us trading the futures, and it will be *a lot* of futures if we start approaching eight hundred."

"I forgot about that," Pete concurred.

Sully then appeared. They both turned to him. "Hey, man."

"Walk with me. I gotta catch a car to this thing on the Upper East," Sully said to Kyle, who got up and double-checked with Pete, "You got everything?"

"Of course," Pete cockily responded.

"Back in a couple."

Kyle and Sully talked as they exited the bank and walked its long esplanade toward the street.

"How'd you end up doing?" Kyle asked Sully on his S&P book performance.

"You can never catch everything, you know? I was long gamma down where it opened, and now I'm short up in here. I deflected a lot of bullets, though. Coulda been much worse," he said edgily, referring to the fact he had a good position where the S&P 500 started the day but then it got progressively worse as the market traded up, especially after the Fed.

"At least it's done now."

"Yeah, it's done. You doing alright with the gold trade? I saw it kept moving higher into the bell."

"Medium. I kinda played some scalping badly. I had it selling off after the Fed. I'm gonna eat that now and deal with it the next two days. Hopefully it doesn't get too much closer to eight hundred," Kyle remarked.

"I don't think it will. I think it stalls up in here. It's run up so much already," Sully enjoined.

"You best be correct," Kyle reflected and then asked him, "What time you done later?"

"I don't know, maybe like seven."

"I hope I'm done by then, too. If I remember being on the other side, these interviews usually last about an hour, give or take. The agents just want to get out of there. I know I always did," Kyle chuckled.

"Oh! You gotta catch me up. What are you telling them, again?"

"We think we found the account owner behind the gold trade."

Sully stopped walking for a moment and looked askance at him with surprise. "Shit, you for real? Who is it?"

"Some Middle Eastern guy. Terrorist name," Kyle joked.

"You kidding me? But there's hundreds of straight-up Middle Eastern clients. They're not terrorists, they're just degenerate gamblers. I've got like a dozen who hit me every week," Sully said, unconvinced.

"I know, I know. Maybe it's nothing..."

"It's nothing. Plus, you don't want to call attention to it, risk losing that sixty mil." Sully winked at him admonishingly.

"Trust me, I know how to play it."

They walked up Greenwich about half a block. The black car service sedans were lined up on the street all the way up the block and around the next. You could always tell an investment bank was in the vicinity by the long line of blacked-out sedans that accumulated on the street at the end of each working day.

"That one's me up there." Sully pointed to a car several back in the line.

"Call me when you're done," Kyle said as he left Sully, who had to weave through the congestion of several rows of cars to get to his.

"Back at ya," Sully said, waving as he got inside his car.

Kyle about-faced and headed back to the bank.

Boom!

Kyle was leveled to the pavement. Something behind him had exploded, and the shock wave knocked him onto his face. He felt his jaw. It was scraped up. His glasses were mashed. He slowly pulled himself to his knees, somewhat stunned, and bent his glasses back to normal.

People were screaming and running about. Car alarms were going crazy, set off by the blast. Shouts of "Call nine-one-one!" could be heard.

"Hey, man, you hurt?" Someone came up to Kyle who'd seen him hit the pavement. The man offered his hand, and Kyle wearily stood himself up.

Kyle stared at the guy and uttered, "Yeah, yeah, I think so, just bruised, I think—what was—?"

They both looked. One of the car service sedans was a burned-out wreck, windows blown out, frame blackened, on fire. Sirens were screaming as the rescue trucks approached.

"I don't know, like a car bomb or something," the stranger replied.

Kyle fit his glasses back on and focused in on it. "Sully!"

He realized the burning hunk was the car Sully had just gotten into. Kyle started toward it, but the stranger grabbed him. "Hey, man, don't get any closer!"

Kyle stood there, watching, in shock.

FBI New York Field Office, 26 Federal Plaza

Kyle sat in a chair outside an interview room at the FBI, on his cell with Pete.

"I know, man, it's fucked up. I don't know what's going on. And now Sully's dead. This can't have been an accident. That car was waiting for him... No, I came straight here. They want to talk to me even more now. Car bomb outside a bank in Manhattan is the real deal. Where are things?... futures selling off, crude flat, gold's up, how much? Seven-sixty? Shit. You cleared our short, right?... No, stay there. I'll call you when I'm done. Hang in there, man," Kyle snapped his phone closed. He took a deep breath.

Amy approached him. Kyle stood up, and they hugged each other.

"I'm so, so sorry, Kyle. How you doing?" she asked him.

Kyle nodded at first. "I'll be OK. Sully, man. This is so fucked up," he said.

She lowered her gaze. "I know, I'm sorry."

There was an awkward moment of silence, and then Kyle asked about the interview, motioning to the room.

"They want to take me seriously now?"

"There's going to be a couple more agents in there with you," she said. "Just tell 'em what you think you know. You remember how this goes."

Kyle forced a smile, not looking at her. "I remember."

"I'll wait for you out here?"

Amy disappeared and was abruptly replaced by a cadre of suited feds, one opening the door for everyone.

"Kyle?" The most senior agent offered his hand as they entered and sat down.

Seated across Kyle were seven agents and officers. The principal in charge, Special Agent Nunes, introduced everyone around the table. There were two counterterrorism agents, two field agents, an ADA (assistant district attorney), a US Treasury officer from TFI (Terrorism and Financial Intelligence), and Gabe, the CIA liaison officer, who was not introduced as such, but rather as a generic field agent to Kyle.

"I'm sorry about your friend, Kyle," Agent Nunes started.

"Thank you," Kyle replied solemnly, not making eye contact.

"I've lost good people over the years. It's never easy," he continued. Kyle only nodded. Agent Nunes paused and cleared his throat.

"You no doubt remember something of this process. It hasn't changed much since." He switched gears with a narrow smile. "Um, why don't you take us back a ways? Give us a bit on what you do, the bank, tell us about the players."

Kyle described the bank, the derivatives desk, what his job was specifically, and the role that he played at the bank, as the agents took notes. When they asked him how much he made, he hesitated, but then told them and watched as they discreetly exchanged glances. It was multiples more than any of them made.

"Thanks, Kyle. All this background will be very helpful," Agent Nunes started, but Kyle interjected, "You're going to look into this now? I mean, the—"

"Let's get into that," Nunes cut him off. "Tell us what led you to ask Special Agent Springer to investigate your client. Start at the beginning."

Kyle eyed Nunes, a bit irked, but went along. He took another deep breath and started, "About a month back, my junior trader and I—"

"Uh, Peter Graff?" one of the agents checked.

"Yes, Pete. Pete and I started to accumulate a large position in crude oil contracts, a short position," Kyle began.

"You were betting the price of crude oil would fall?"

"I had done research with the bank's analysts and all the macro—geopolitical factors—and crude oil supply situation indicated it would probably go lower, so we built up a large short position, yeah," Kyle explained. "The position was down small until Monday this week, when—"

"The pipeline attack in Turkey," one of the counterterrorism agents lodged.

"Right. The price of crude oil had been trading sideways, maybe a little higher, and then suddenly rallied on that event—went much higher," Kyle explained. "My position went from a gain to a big loss quickly—"

"How big?" the FinCEN officer asked.

"About thirty million against me," Kyle responded. "My boss, Ted Garner, global head of derivatives trading at the bank, forced me to close the position."

"Because of the loss?"

"And his view it would get worse. So, Pete and I traded out of everything, after which my book was down about fifty mil."

"And then what happened?"

"So, then a sales trader who works for us—"

"Samuel Bender?"

"He offers me an unusual trade—to sell gold options that expired Friday—*this* Friday, day after tomorrow. These are gold call options that pay off for the buyer if gold goes above eight hundred, way above eight hundred."

"You said unusual trade, why was that unusual?"

"Customers don't often make trades that large on such a short time horizon. That's only a couple days."

"Where was the price of gold when he offered this trade to you?"

"Was barely seven hundred," Kyle answered.

"And how much does gold go up or down in, like, a typical week?"

"Maybe ten or fifteen dollars, if that."

"So, the probability of this paying off for the bank's customer was very low?"

"Extremely low. Like it could really never happen low."

"And so, you sold him these options?"

"Not immediately, but, yes, I did the next day."

"Why'd you wait?"

"Do some research, understand the risk-reward better," Kyle answered. "It smelled funny to me. This customer was going to pay sixty million bucks on a lottery ticket—I mean, you have to understand, he was going to lose it, *lose* sixty million dollars if gold didn't go higher than eight hundred in three-and-a-half days. Nobody takes shots like that unless they're stupid or they know something."

"You were suspicious? Why didn't you raise it with your compliance team— or this—Garner guy?"

Kyle took an impatient breath. "I was suspicious, yes, but where was I going to go with it? It could have plausibly been a Fed bet—the Federal Reserve made their interest rate policy call today. Gold usually reacts to that." Kyle paused and then fessed up, "And I needed it to get out of my loss. If the trade won, I'd be out of the hole."

"So, you did the trade out of greed?" One of the agents butted in. He was met by Agent Nunes's scolding glance.

"Continue, Kyle," Nunes beckoned.

"Yeah, it would solve my problem. The one exception being if the buyer knew something. The research I did confirmed it was a manageable risk, so I sold the gold options. I didn't know much about the buyer."

"Is that typical? To not know who the buyer is or what their motive is?" the Treasury officer asked.

"Yes and no. Some clients you get to know well, even personally. The sales traders take them out, you know. But some clients want to be hidden. They come in through brokers. We're Chinese walled from knowing much. Most of the customer details are held by the clearing group at the bank, and we don't have access to their systems. You depend on the sales traders or brokers to have the relationships with the customers. Anyway, I put the trade on. Now, this part's critical. The trade should have triggered our global risk system."

"This Garner would not allow you to do this trade?" Agent Nunes clarified.

"The way it should have worked is my booking the trade would have triggered a risk flag in the global system. It would have alerted Garner, and he would have come over to me and asked me about it."

"Why did you put this trade on if you weren't supposed to, you knew it would be flagged?"

Kyle gazed up at the ceiling for a moment—at least they were following enough to grasp that.

"My plan was to bullshit Garner and buy some time until the trade expired on

Friday. If I did that, it wouldn't matter anymore, the trade would be history, the risk would be off the bank's books. I'd tell him something, like, it was a fat-finger error or something—" Kyle sheepishly but honestly explained.

Some of the agents exchanged suspect glances.

"What happened with this risk system, then?" the ADA asked.

"That's what's weird. Garner never came over—still hasn't as of this moment, because he never saw it. Something was wrong with the risk system..." Kyle trailed off, and added, more quietly, "Or it was deliberately overridden."

Agents exchanged glances again at that comment. But Kyle continued. "I checked with the risk group. They didn't see the trade at all, like it had been wiped from the database, which was *really* weird. But the trade cleared just fine—"

"But how can that—"

"Separate systems at the bank." Kyle anticipated that question. "Now you guys have to listen. The guy who owns that risk system, the only one who has the power to override a risk like the gold trade, is *Stephen Brooks*," Kyle emphasized.

"Right, the risk manager whose wife reported him missing," Nunes clarified.

"Reported to *us*?" one of the agents asked Nunes who didn't respond.

"You have someone on that?" the FinCEN officer asked him back.

"We do now," Agent Nunes told him.

"You guys find anything in his brownstone?" Kyle asked almost excitedly.

"We haven't canvassed it yet. But it's an active investigation, so we can't discuss it," the ADA commented.

"You have to get over there now!" Kyle said sternly, raising his voice.

"Easy, Mr. Springer. You're not an agent here anymore, remember?"

"You don't know what I saw," Kyle pleaded.

"Saw where?"

"There was—it looked like blood."

"Blood where?"

The agents were now thoroughly confused.

"In his basement, on the cement floor. Brooks's basement," Kyle revealed.

"Are you sure?" one of them asked.

"How did you see that?" Another was skeptical.

Kyle admitted, "I snooped, alright? I saw it through his basement window..."

"*What?*"

"I went over there to check it out. I may have trespassed a little, but I didn't break and enter, only approached, and peeked through the window. I saw this long smear, I remember bloodstains, especially recent ones. It looked just like that."

Nunes and the ADA frowned. The ADA lectured Kyle.

"You know the rules. If that becomes a crime scene, you might have tainted it," she reminded him, annoyed.

They were all half amused, half troubled by Kyle's behavior. But one of the agents conjectured, "Putting aside you possibly disturbing a crime scene, what do you think happened?" he asked.

"Maybe he was tortured or killed for the codes to the risk system."

A few of them chuckled but then quickly restored their professional mugs.

The CIA liaison, Gabe, the one person who'd been quiet thus far, leaned in a bit closer on that answer.

"Keep going with the gold trade," Agent Nunes nudged them back on track.

"That's sort of it. I mean, that's the setup." Kyle became flustered. "Since then, there have been more terrorist attacks in the Middle East, and crude oil has continued to go up, gold, too, like something's going to happen, something big. And Sammy didn't show up today, now he might be missing. Maybe he's dead, too," Kyle said as his focus rose to the agents who returned nothing but blank faces back at him.

"How do you know he's missing?" the ADA asked.

"A sales trader never, *ever* misses a Fed day. I think something happened to him, and now Sully." Kyle stopped himself, upset.

Agent Nunes put his elbows on the table and leaned in toward Kyle. "Kyle, from your description, your friend, Carl—Sully—didn't participate in this gold trade, is that accurate?"

"That's true, yes."

"So why do you speculate he was killed because of this terrorist trading?"

"I mean, he knew everything. He knew about the gold trade and Sammy. He knew all the details. We were friends, Pete and I told him all about it," Kyle said.

"Do you think—or do you know of, anyone he might have talked to about the gold trade?"

Kyle shook his head. "No, he doesn't—I mean, Pete and I are pretty much his only friends, besides all his girlfriends."

"Do you think he could have *reported* what you told him was going on to the compliance people at your firm?" the Treasury officer asked.

Kyle shook his head. "Doubtful...no, no way."

"Can we get to how you came to the name Fadhil al-Hammadi?" the CIA liaison asked him.

Kyle regarded him more favorably, glad for the direction change.

"That was the fluke in all this."

"What do you mean?"

"We don't have access to the systems to look up the customer's names. All that Know-Your-Customer stuff is done by the clearing house, so I had one of the sales traders try to look up the name for me. But this sales trader knew of a bug in the system and was able to get to the signature page of the ISDA sheet—that's the document that allows them to trade with us—and that gave us the name of a fund that provided credit for this customer. She happened to remember, from another bank she used to work at, this same fund name, and figured out then it was associated with this al-Hammadi guy," Kyle explained.

"How'd she do that?"

"Put two and two together."

More judgmental glances, but the CIA liaison paid even closer attention.

"You never directly dealt with al-Hammadi?" the other CT agent asked.

"God, no. Sammy hasn't, either. There's probably three layers of fund managers and brokers between us and him," Kyle explained.

Gabe then asked, "Tell me about the gold option trade. What do you think they're betting will happen?"

Kyle turned to him again.

"If they're not betting on the Fed, and it's not a hedge, it would have to be something, some event or attack, that is big enough to move gold more than a hundred dollars, past eight hundred—a huge move. And based on the other attacks and what oil's been doing, it could point to something even larger in the Middle East, like a major attack on oil facilities or something," Kyle answered.

"There's a lot of rumors to that effect?" the liaison clarified.

Kyle nodded forcefully, becoming a bit agitated.

Kyle then stood up, to their surprise, not sure what he was doing. "We can tell certain things from the options they purchased," Kyle started as he paced the room. The other agents tried to follow him, some turning in their chairs to pay attention, others wondering where the hell this was going.

"Any of you guys play poker?" Kyle asked the group but got mostly blank stares. He continued anyway. "The particular options they purchased are a tell," Kyle went on. "The first is the asset, gold. We know whatever it is, *if* they are front-running a terrorist attack, it will affect gold. Big terrorist attacks tend to make the price of gold jump. In fact, the bigger the attack, the bigger the price move. People and markets get scared. They buy gold." He did one lap of the room as he explained this.

"The next is the magnitude—the strike price of the gold options, eight hundred, way higher than the seven hundred gold started at when he purchased the options. So, whatever the attack, it has to be a big one. It has to be large enough to boost the price of gold past eight hundred. At these current levels, the Nine Eleven attacks didn't even move gold that much. So, it would have to be bigger than Nine Eleven." Kyle paused again.

"The last and most important tell is the timing. *This* Friday, expiration Friday. Whatever is going to happen must happen by then, or else this trade is worthless. They're out sixty million bucks, spent for nothing," Kyle declared emphatically and finally sat back down.

Some of the agents furrowed their brows, either annoyed or because they didn't follow.

"Kyle, we appreciate your coming in and telling us all of this. But, let me ask you—and I'm not judging—how do you know this isn't a bunch of coincidences? I mean, the gold option trade, large yes, but not unheard of?" asked one of the counterterrorism agents. "Or the risk guy just happened to let off some steam and not tell his wife. I mean, these things often have a habit of resolving themselves."

Kyle's face flushed at this—were they not listening? Kyle leaned back in his chair to calm himself.

Agent Nunes scanned everyone. "I think we have enough for now."

"Kyle, I know it's been a difficult day, and we thank you for talking to us under the circumstances. We have the background we need to start investigating some of these details over the next few weeks—"

"Next few weeks?" Kyle leapt to his feet again. "Didn't you *hear me*? *Friday—expiration Friday!* You have to investigate it *now*—tonight!"

One of the agents rose and laid his hand on Kyle's shoulder to calm and to potentially restrain him.

"Don't touch me." Kyle swatted his hand away. "You guys need to—"

Another agent approached Kyle, ready to grab him. Agent Nunes stood and admonished the others, "Sit down, sit down!" as tensions ratcheted.

"This is why Amy divorced him," one of the agents commented in jest to another, and—

Smack! Kyle punched him in the jaw.

The agent fell backward against a chair, losing his balance and tumbling to the floor. The other agents seized Kyle and pinned him against the wall, clutching his arms and throat. The agent who was struck recovered, rose to his feet, and faced Kyle with an upset glare, but he stood down as he angrily rubbed his jaw.

"We're done. Get him out of here," Nunes ordered. "Let us do our job, Mr. Springer, thank you."

They wrestled a struggling Kyle out of the interview room into the adjoining hallway. The agents shoved him into a chair, releasing him. They remained surrounding him to ensure he didn't get up and chase the agent he attacked.

Amy arrived to meet Kyle, catching the tail end of the scuffle, watching them all physically ditch Kyle onto the seats.

"What the hell's going on?" she yelled.

"Get him out of here. Take him home. Let him cool off," Nunes ordered.

He straightened his suit as the other agents, one by one, turned from Kyle and walked away. After a few minutes, only Amy and Kyle remained. Kyle slumped in the seat, breathing heavily, his temples pulsing. He didn't look up at Amy.

"Good interview?" she asked him with deliberate sarcasm to try to sedate him. After his no response, she watched him seethe for a few more minutes.

"Come on, I'll take you home," she offered.

Kyle finally replied with a half-hearted, "I'm sorry."

"I know. Come on, let's you get you home."

Operation 912 Task Force Center

Kate, Bob, and even the director, along with the rest of the center, watched the combat on the large monitor. The Delta Force team and the A-10s had gained the upper hand, and the enemy fighters were in retreat, scattered across the desert, being routed, and pursued on both land and from the air.

The room was more crowded as CTC officers joined following the FBI development. A liaison officer called out to Kate. "Ms. Harrison? You want to take this in your office," he hollered to her from his station.

The director joined Bob and Kate in her office. Reporting to them on speakerphone was Gabe, the CIA liaison officer who had been in the interview with Kyle. Gabe was a joint FBI and CIA desk officer, working on a CTC desk in the New York FBI field office and had been assigned to Task Force 912.

"I think you guys are going to want to follow up here. This may be a missing piece of this puzzle," he started. "There's a trader for a bank in New York City, his name is Kyle Springer. He's a veteran trader, and, funny thing, which we'll get to in a second, he was a former fed himself, left years ago and became a derivatives trader for the bank—"

"Which bank?" the director asked.

"Fortnum Bank. One of the largest US banks, huge operations. He's responsible for trading crude oil products, futures and options, those sorts of things, reported that from about two weeks ago, he started to see large trades being done ahead of some of these recent attacks, ya know, the Turkey pipeline and the Saudi refinery attacks?"

The three of them leaned in, their interest piqued.

"Go on," Kate ushered.

"So, he watched these trades happen, and he had a big position himself—he, uh, was betting the other way, that crude oil was going to fall, but kept seeing trades come in betting the price would go up, which it has been, but then he's asked to put on this very large gold trade—uh, a trade in gold *options*, actually."

"Gold? What does that mean?" Bob asked for clarity.

"When there's instability—fear, it's a big fear thing—the price of gold goes up. Instead of speculating with physical gold itself, you can buy options on it, which give you much greater leverage. So, there was this huge bet, and I don't understand it fully, but the size of this gold options trade, betting it would jump higher, of course, was so big, it wouldn't have ordinarily been allowed by the bank, and this Kyle guy took the other side of it, so he sold these gold options."

"So, then why was it allowed?" the director asked him.

"That's the interesting part. He described that something was wrong with their bank risk systems that should have ordinarily flagged this trade, but they didn't, and get this—maybe a coincidence but certainly seems worth a look—the risk manager for the bank, a guy named Stephen Brooks, the one guy with access to this system, went missing on Monday. There's an open investigation by the feds into his disappearance."

"Any evidence of foul play?" Kate asked.

"We don't know. Agency's been sitting on it," Gabe replied.

Kate gave the director a frustrated look. The liaison continued, "But get this, Kyle, former fed that he was, did his own snooping, swore he saw recently dried blood on the basement floor of this risk manager's New York brownstone."

"And the FBI's *not* looking at this?" Bob asked, with a tone of irritation.

"They said they would, but there was a little friction—I'll come to that—here's the kicker, Kyle, and I don't understand exactly how, was able to find out the ultimate customer behind this gold option trade—"

"Al-Hammadi," the three of them finished his sentence.

"Good guess."

Kate, Bob, and the director all exchanged sober glances.

"Are we sure about this?"

"Kyle's ex-wife is an active agent, at the New York field office with me here. When he discovered this name, and it was of course, layered, he passed it to her, see if this guy showed up on any lists. She entered it into the FBI's main system, and that's how we got the Sweeper hit."

"Dang it," the director muttered. "What are they doing about all this?"

"They are launching an investigation, but there was a little scuffle during the interview, and it ended early," Gabe explained.

"A scuffle?"

"I guess there's some history here with this Kyle guy. One of the feds insulted him and his ex-wife, and it got kind of physical," he continued.

"Kyle had a bit of a tough day—his friend, another trader at the bank—was killed in that car bomb in front of the bank."

The director bit his upper lip.

"This trader involved in this gold trade, too?" the director asked.

"Didn't appear to be, but he knew about it. Kyle's convinced it's related."

"He may be right," Bob commented.

"They looking into that, too?" Kate asked impatiently.

"They're on it, but no urgency. Kyle kept insisting Friday, Friday."

"Friday?"

"So, if I got all this, the gold options that al-Hammadi supposedly purchased, come due on Friday."

"Friday—*this* Friday, two days—day and a half from now?"

"The translation is that the wager on the price of gold expires this Friday. If the price of gold rockets higher, by some event, it has to happen by *this Friday*. Otherwise, al-Hammadi's out the price of the options, sixty million dollars."

Kate slowly shook her head, adding it all up.

"Is al-Hammadi behind those other trades, too?" Kate asked.

"We don't know. Certainly, something we should be looking at. Based on what I heard, if this is all legit, I wouldn't be surprised," Gabe replied.

"How credible is this trader—this Kyle?"

"Knows his shit. A bit paranoid, but maybe for good reason. His hunches uncovered the al-Hammadi connection, by an unexpected coincidence, I'd add, so, yeah, I'm giving this solid confidence."

"Gabe, pressure that case team, you got it?" the director instructed.

"Yup, I got it," Gabe replied.

"I want to talk to this trader, Kyle. Any legal concerns with that?" Kate asked, looking at Bob and the director.

"Should be clean if I'm there and an FBI lawyer," Gabe replied.

Kate looked to the director, who simply signaled, *do it.*

"Let's get him down here."

"I'll arrange something for tomorrow."

"No, now. Get him down here now," Kate demanded.

"Do it, Gabe. And I'll call the seventh floor, get them to up the urgency of this," the director requested.

The seventh floor referred to the floor at FBI headquarters where the senior brass and the FBI director were.

They hung up the phone. They couldn't render conclusions fast enough.

"We saw this kind of insider trading against target assets ahead of Nine Eleven, too," was the first thing out of Kate's mouth.

"We need to get covert banking on al-Hammadi ASAP, and—"

"Treasury."

"Treasury, too, a full sweep of everything. All transactions, all activity. There has to be more in there."

"Jesus. We need to shut this guy down."

"If they're planning to take out Ras Tanura with a stolen nuke, it will shatter global markets. This is all consistent with a major event—like a *nuclear bomb* attack on critical oil facilities. Crude oil and gold will jump much higher. It all fits with what we just heard."

"And we've got a broken arrow a stone's throw from Ras Tanura."

"We're close to securing that now."

"We need to focus on going after these guys, working up the chain."

"And we have to stop that device at all costs."

Carrick-On-Shannon Irish Pub, Lower Manhattan, United States

Kyle and Pete sat at the bar of a quiet and dark Irish pub, downing Guinness pints and commiserating about Sully.

"So fucked up," Kyle repeated, shaking his head and gulping his pint.

Pete stared into his ale and then followed, downing some of his and finally breaking his own silence.

"FBI say anything about it? Was it a car bomb?" he asked.

Kyle gazed absently across the bar at first and answered with some frustration.

"Didn't say shit. They were useless. Glad I left the Bureau, they really suck, you know? Had to be a car bomb. What else was that? Knocked me to my face," he said bitterly as he felt the scratches on his chin from scraping the pavement.

"I wonder what's gonna happen tomorrow. What'll Garner do?"

"Sully's got his junior guys. Big desk, they'll take over his book, manage it."

"You think Garner'll say anything?"

"He'd fucking better. He can't ignore this."

"Prob right, everybody's talking about it, they're scared. You talk to his brother yet?"

"Couldn't reach him. I called him a couple times. Can't leave a voice mail about that, ya know? I think the police will contact next of kin; I don't know. I can't think about this shit right now."

They downed more of their ale and sat silently on their stools, in their own thoughts. Pete then asked, "Why would they kill Sully? I don't get it. And the feds didn't say *anything* about it?"

"They asked some questions, just CYA shit. Something's definitely fucked up," Kyle said distantly, and then replied to Pete, more deliberately, "I'm with you, killing Sully doesn't make *any* sense. Why take him out?"

Pete motioned for the bartender to bring them another round as he gulped down and finished his. He went on opining.

"Let's say everything we've been seeing, all your theories are true—this Arab guy—whoever's doing all this, wouldn't have any reason to take out Sully. I mean, he knew less than we do."

"I know. I'm wondering if it was maybe meant for me."

"Shit, dude, don't say that."

"Ha—I know, sorry, don't worry it's a stretch because nobody knew I'd be out there."

The bartender pushed another pair of Guinness pints to them. Pete pulled his close, took a few swallows, and continued in between gulps.

"Maybe it wasn't meant for Sully at all," Pete rationalized.

"Could be. It was just meant to go off and keep markets on their toes."

"Gold did jump, you know?"

"I know. I thought about that, too. Maybe Sully was wrong place at wrong time and the thing was just intended to continue the attacks…I don't know."

"Makes more sense. Still, so perplexing. I just can't think straight about any of it, ya know?"

Pete tipped his mug to Kyle's. "To Carl."

"RIP, brother." They clinked mugs and drank with dejected gulps.

"Makes me feel like after Nine Eleven. We lost *so* many people. Crazy. I went to two funerals every day for two weeks."

"Don't think about that, man. Don't go back there."

"You're probably right," Kyle said as he gazed at the half-finished beer. "The funny irony is Sully is usually the dark one, bitter fuck that he was. I miss him, can't believe I'm never gonna see him again."

"Let's go back to talking about you being the target." Pete laughed morbidly and then gulped down his Guinness. "Actually, let's not because, otherwise, I could be next, you know?"

Kyle chuckled, too, and despondently offered, "It'd put me out of my misery."

They both laughed, and then were startled from behind.

"Mr. Springer?"

They spun around to see the FBI agent—the CIA liaison officer, Gabe—from the earlier interview; along with five other agents in tactical gear flanking him.

"Shit."

"We need to take you to Washington. There's a jet waiting for us at Teterboro Airport," Gabe said, with a pressing tone.

Kyle and Pete exchanged shocked glances, but Kyle hesitated. Then Gabe lowered his gaze to Kyle and repeated, "Come on, we need to go, *now*."

Kyle looked at Pete. "It's OK, go home. I'll call you."

Thursday, September 20, 2007

CIA Headquarters, McLean, Virginia, United States

A blacked-out Suburban with a flashing-lights chaser car raced down the desolate GW Parkway in Northern Virginia. Inside, Gabe and the other agents rode with Kyle to CIA headquarters in McLean. It was shortly after one a.m.

The passengers were quiet. Kyle stared out his window into the Potomac River gorge alongside the Parkway. He was mostly awake. He'd slept some on the forty-five-minute rendition flight from New York. As he gazed at the black river, Kyle was plagued by dozens of conflicting thoughts. His depression over Sully. His anger toward the FBI. His sharpened anxiety from the car bomb. His feeling of impending doom about what could happen Friday. His gold trade, and the money he expected to make if it worked out. His fear if it didn't. His daughter, Jill; and his ex-wife; and his goal to get his family back together.

"We're here," Gabe announced as they drove through a checkpoint.

"This really doesn't look like Pennsylvania Avenue," Kyle commented dryly, signaling he was aware they weren't at the FBI headquarters building in downtown Washington, DC. Instead, this was a treed Northern Virginia suburb, and another mysterious headquarters building they were now pulling up to.

"FBI has buildings all over the city and suburbs," Gabe responded, keeping up the charade, but they both knew where they were.

Kyle and the others entered a spacious conference room with leather seats and bottles of water on a glass table. A moment later, Kate and Bob entered, along with another FBI-CIA liaison, a TFI agent from US Treasury, and five more CIA officers—two attorneys, a desk officer from CB, and the other two from CTC.

Everyone sat down. The team stared at Kyle for a moment without a word.

"You want some coffee? Get him some coffee. And I'll take one, too," Kate started. "Thank you for coming all this way on short notice. I know it's late, too. We'll get you back home in no time," she added.

"Thanks," Kyle replied to her, appreciative of the respect.

"I hope you understand if we skip all the introductions and formalities. I think you get why you're here," Gabe said.

"All good," Kyle responded.

"I'm very sorry about your friend, Kyle," Kate offered. Kyle watched her and noticed how disarming she was, and he felt comfortable speaking to her.

"I appreciate it," Kyle replied.

"Tell them what you believe is going on." Gabe got right to it.

Kyle scanned the faces in the room looking at him. Having just done this for the FBI, he didn't want to repeat everything, so he jumped ahead.

"I think someone, this al-Hammadi, or whoever else, is betting—in the capital markets—on a large terrorist attack to happen this Friday," Kyle summarized.

"We've been debriefed on your interview at Federal Plaza. We know the details, what we want to understand, clearly, from you, is *why* you think these trades point to that," Kate elicited.

Kyle thought for a moment. He glanced across the array of faces impatiently watching him.

"You guys understand probability? I mean basic, like card-playing or casino-games probability?"

They all chuckled. "It's sort of our job, yes," Kate replied.

"Well, that's my job, too—probability. I trade options and, options are priced by probability—the normal, or Gaussian distribution, as math people call it, if I can get detailed about it. Asset prices like crude oil, or gold, or any stock, will, over a short time horizon, at least, stay close to where that asset's price is today. So, if gold is seven fifty, and you're asking where it will be in a few days, or a week, the *expected, statistical* range will be pretty narrow, like seven forty to seven sixty..." Kyle paused. He gazed down at the glass table to gather his next words and continued. "On Monday, when I was given this gold option, show, as we call it—I didn't trade the options until Tuesday—the price of gold was barely above seven hundred. This customer wanted to bet me sixty million dollars gold would be higher than eight hundred by this Friday."

"What did your statistical models tell you the range of gold would be in a week, or by Friday?" the Treasury guy asked him.

Kyle looked over to him. He was glad they grasped this.

"Seven twenty, seven thirty tops, and that was on an extreme move, too. We had the Federal Reserve interest rate policy announcement today, yesterday, now, and the price of gold can be sensitive to that, so we figured it was likely positioning in anticipation of the Fed. But the pricing range was *so extreme*, even a large, surprise Fed rate change couldn't have moved gold by that much," Kyle replied, "Gold just doesn't move that much, it has what we call low volatility."

"The strike price of these options is eight hundred dollars, is that correct?" the US Treasury rep asked.

"That's correct," Kyle replied, almost delighted.

"What does that mean? What happens if gold finishes below eight hundred, and what happens if it is higher than eight hundred by Friday?" Gabe followed up.

"If it doesn't make it, I keep the sixty million. Al-Hammadi loses the sixty million. If it goes above eight hundred, he makes fifty mil for every dollar above. So, eight hundred ten, he's up five hundred million, and so on," Kyle explained.

"If gold goes to nine hundred dollars?"

"He's up five billion dollars," Kyle said.

Kate and Bob glanced at each other.

"And the bank loses that?"

"Right."

"You have these pricing models for options—what's it called?"

"Black-Scholes. We have a lot of models, that's the one everybody knows."

"What did the models say the option was worth?" the Treasury guy pressed.

"Not even a penny," Kyle replied, glad someone finally asked that question.

"And this guy paid how much—per option contract?"

"A dollar twenty-five," Kyle said.

The officers at the table all exchanged wide-eyed looks at that.

"It implied an event probability of twenty percent. The option should have been worthless. Nobody should have *ever* paid that much," Kyle emphasized.

Kate took a swallow of her coffee. "I'm not sure I follow that." Kate sized up Kyle. "You play poker? Texas Hold'em?"

"I do, yes."

"Tell me in poker," Kate requested. Kyle was glad to play along.

"So, then, showing faceup on the table, there's maybe a two and a three of different suits—really tough to make anything out of—but this al-Hammadi guy's just bet massive through the flop, turn, and river, acting like he's got a four of a kind. He's filled the pot, each round."

"Got it. He's holding and he's not bluffing," Kate followed.

"He's betting he's *certain* he's gonna take this pot," Kyle added.

Kate, sharp as a tack, said, "Conditional probability."

"Exactly right." Kyle nodded vigorously. The others appeared more puzzled.

"Remember the Monty Hall three-doors game show? If Monty Hall revealed one of the doors, it paid to switch," Kate explained to them. They stared at her blankly, as they weren't old enough to have seen it. She clarified, "What's the probability of the prize being behind any of the three doors, if one of them is *not randomly* revealed to be empty?"

"Yes, it goes from a one-third chance to a much greater probability. What is the probability *given that* one of the doors is already known?" Kyle emphasized.

"So, that implies the customer behind this trade—Al Hammadi—knows something?" the Treasury officer clarified.

"The conditional probability is even higher. What is the probability gold moves past eight hundred *given* al-Hammadi's willing to wager so much on that event?" Kate responded. "I get it."

"What kind of event could move gold that much?" Bob probed.

"I did that research," Kyle said. "It would have to be a terrorist attack. And it would have to be big. I had one of our analysts do a regression on past attacks and the average move in price of gold. The larger the attack, either higher profile or infrastructure damage, the more gold moves."

"What do you think is coming, Kyle?" Kate asked him.

"My guess would be something huge against crude oil facilities, like in Saudi Arabia—this Ras Tanura loading point. If that were taken out, it would eliminate ten to fifteen percent of the world's crude oil supply overnight."

Kate looked at her colleagues in the room. She requested, "Will you excuse us for a few moments? I'd like to speak with Kyle alone."

The CIA attorneys exchanged uncomfortable glances and remained seated, but Kate regarded Bob with an insistent look.

"Come on, let's leave 'em." Bob motioned to the others, who also stood and followed him out the door.

Kyle didn't get what was going on. He didn't know how Kate fit in or what position she held or how senior she was. He knew she was smart and shrewd. He could tell that. She put the conditional probability thing together quickly. He liked that she was fast and got it. But he now eyed her with a bit of suspicion, unclear as to her motives.

The door shut. There was a moment of silence, then Kate asked, "You want some more coffee?" Kyle shook his head.

"Why'd you leave the FBI?" Kate probed.

Kyle drew in a breath, not expecting the question.

"I was an agent making fifty K a year, working narc cases, putting my life at risk, and all my friends were making five hundred a year and not getting shot at."

Kate regarded him without replying. Kyle felt the heat from her eyes, like it was an interrogation. He instantly felt compelled to answer more thoroughly.

"And my wife, she was a fed, too, we had just had a baby and we didn't want to have both of us at high-risk jobs."

She kept looking at him, through him. He couldn't stand it and finally broke.

"And I was a paranoid drunk who nobody wanted to work with. They kind of ostracized me. Sully got me onto the desk at Fortnum shortly after Nine Eleven."

Kate gave him a half smile of satisfaction at the honesty.

"When did the drinking start?"

"I don't know, it got much worse after Nine Eleven. I mean, I drank alcohol before then, but I didn't *drink*, ya know? I was an FBI agent, leading up to Nine Eleven, and I didn't, I felt like, I should have been assigned to something I could have done something about it, I could have spotted it, I could have figured something out, I—"

Kate gave him a flat, almost sympathetic smile.

"Kyle, you were dealing with it. We all were," she began. "You couldn't have done anything about it. Nine Eleven wasn't your fault. You can't harbor that."

Kyle had tears almost well up. He turned away from her and fought them off. He tried to give her a half-hearted nod of acknowledgment.

She went on, "I've got an entire agency—hundreds of officers and agents who feel the same way—like they could have done something about it, like they could have stopped it, reliving it, over and over."

"It killed my marriage, too, I couldn't, I just couldn't rationalize it all. It was too much," Kyle lamented.

Kate nodded in understanding and paused for a moment.

"Do you think you believe this terrorist insider trading theory of yours is because you're trying to correct your perceived failings from then?"

Kyle thought for a moment.

"My friends deride me about that. I can be paranoid, it's true. It's funny because it makes me a good options trader. You always think of the worst outcome, which is what you need to do." Kyle stopped for a moment. He reached for a glass of water, with Kate watching his hand as he drank some. "I've thought a lot about it, but... I'm pretty convicted about this. If I'm wrong, it's not because I'm being paranoid about it, that much I've decided. This trade stinks in some way. I might be paranoid, but the numbers aren't," Kyle said, with some sureness.

Kate studied him, unblinking.

"You've been on the other side, Kyle. You worked cases. You know our world is about probabilities, too, and risk. We make trades and decisions all day long, just like you do, often with little information, only discipline," Kate started.

Kyle didn't say anything but kept listening to her.

"You may have just given us a key piece of the puzzle," she added.

"I don't follow you."

"What I'm about to tell you is illegal. You need to have all sorts of security clearances and that sort of thing, and it also might fuck with your fragile mind, too, and my knowing you're an alcoholic risk-taker, and vulnerable right now after the death of your close friend, I'm not being very responsible, *but* I'm also an American and I defend this nation every day. I think that's something that will resonate with you, because that's why you felt so damaged from Nine Eleven. This is your pride," Kate levied.

Kyle was soberly following her.

"We're chasing a broken arrow. Do you know what that means?"

"Jesus Christ, yes, that's a loose nuclear weapon? *Are you kidding me?*"

Kyle put the pieces together quickly. She saw that in his eyes.

"I won't bother you with the origins or how it got out of state control, but we're pursuing it in the Middle East right now. It may be headed for that Ras Tanura, which, based on everything you've told us, appears to be consistent with the picture. I'm telling you for two reasons. One is selfish, that you knowing what the other part of the equation is might allow you to think and realize something additional that will help us stop this. The other reason is, well…may be for you. It might not help you now, but it could down the road. Your instincts were on the money, and you did something about it," she finished.

Kate dug into her pocket and pinched one of her business cards—CIA officers didn't really have business cards, per se, most listed their office as "US Department of State," as hers did. She wrote on the back and handed it to Kyle.

"My cell. You think of anything, you call me. And don't wait, either."

Kyle took the card and put it in his pocket. He shook Kate's hand, and they exited the conference room.

Nahda Desert Region, Oman

The pair of A-10s swooped over the desert, routing the tiny fighters scattering below. The bloodcurdling, almost electronic sound of the Hawg's rotary cannons and its subsequent echoes in the sky periodically rang out. Whatever vehicles were in the path of its steel rain that followed were decimated.

It was late morning, and the sun blared across the front. Kelso and the Unit soldiers had swapped their NODs for sunglasses and pursued the fleeing terrorists, both on foot and in their Humvees. The squad needed to sanitize the battlefield. They had to go vehicle husk by vehicle husk to ensure no bad guys remained lurking to ambush them before they finally got to their objective—the package.

Fortnum Bank Equities Trading Floor

Kyle slumped in front of his monitors, half asleep. Pete arrived, double-fisting two giant coffees for them.

"The antidote." Pete set them both on Kyle's desk.

"Thanks, man. Both for me? What about you?"

Pete revealed a paper demitasse cup skillfully placed in his shirt breast pocket that had survived the coffee run without spilling.

"Impressive." Kyle started on his coffee.

"Haven't used this trick in a while. I guess I've grown in the world." Pete looked at Kyle for a response to his joke, but Kyle clearly was still not present.

"How was it?" Pete broke the anticipation.

Kyle faced him with a dramatic pause.

"Dude, it was some scary shit. One day I'll tell you everything. Nightmares when I got home."

"I'm happy you're not dead. I freaked when I saw those feds. Fucking extraordinary rendition to some third world-country secret landing strip. I figured you'd have an electrified pole up your ass by now."

"No, that's Garner's office."

They both laughed.

"I think those folks actually knew what the hell they were doing, pretty good crew, not like our buffoons over at twenty-six," Kyle commented, referring to his FBI interview at 26 Federal Plaza.

Pete raised his espresso shot to Kyle in a mock *salud*.

"I gotta wake up," Kyle shifted. "Where is everything? Pretend I'm blind, because I am," Kyle asked as he drank more coffee. "Not kicking in fast enough."

Pete swiveled his leftmost monitor to face Kyle, tapped it as he pointed out charts of both gold and crude oil.

"Things have settled down. Gold's finally taking a break, down five bucks, seven fifty-five and a laugh. Gamma's evaporating quickly—we've got less than a day and a half left. If the futures stay around here, we can see the ducats dropping into our vaults. Decay's starting to accelerate, too. Crude's off about a handle, close to ninety-five," Pete finished.

"Calm before the storm," Kyle commented cynically.

"Dang, don't say that."

That decay effect was starting to kick in for them. Decay increased at an exponential rate the closer they approached expiration. And with the option still way out-of-the-money, far from the $800 level, the effect was quite in their favor. Meanwhile, the negative gamma, their worst enemy, was "evaporating," in Pete's words, which was great for their position, and meant the danger was dissipating.

"The break is good though. Let's hope it stays that way," Kyle replied.

They paused for a moment and then felt a presence looming behind them. They both turned to see Garner standing there.

"I'm sorry about Carl—*Sully*. I know you guys were friends with him." Garner extended his hand and shook Kyle's and Pete's.

"Thanks," they both replied.

"He was a great trader, too. I've got his clerks managing the book for now. We'll have a thing for him next week. You guys know when the service is?"

"We don't. We were trying to contact his brother, but I heard the coroner wasn't going to release the body until the investigation finished. I don't know when that might be," Kyle replied.

Garner peered at them uncomfortably. "I'm sure HR will know. I'll keep a line to them. Again, I'm very sorry," he repeated and then returned to his office.

Kyle and Pete shook their heads, insulted. Kyle's phone chiming interrupted the solemn pause.

"Kyle...hey, Shirin. Yeah, I'll stop by."

Kyle strode over to Shirin's desk with one of his giant coffees in hand.

Shirin had a forlorn look on her face.

"I'm sorry about Sully."

"He was a good dude."

"You scared?" Shirin asked him.

Kyle regarded her for a moment.

"I am, I admit."

There was an awkward moment, but Kyle let her out of it.

"What do you got for me?"

Shirin took a reset breath.

"You told me to keep an eye on things, let you know if I spotted anything else that fit the pattern."

"Right, and…?" Kyle responded, not fully paying attention to her.

"So, I'm seeing a lot in crude oil options now," she started.

Kyle stared ahead, half-listing.

"Not surprising," he absently replied.

Shirin shot him a puzzled look.

"Why would you say that? Don't you trade crude oil options, shouldn't you know this better than me?"

Kyle finally heard her and shook off his malaise. He focused in more.

"I—What patterns are you seeing?"

"Something quite odd about the order flow," she said, still unconvinced Kyle hadn't noticed them himself. "You sure you haven't seen this?"

Kyle shook his head. "I've been in a funk, and we haven't really been that active in crude since Garner made us level our position," he explained. "But show me what you got."

"Volumes in crude oil options are really picking up, but what's weird is the implied volatilities for the higher calls are starting to *drop*, and it's the opposite for the puts," she said.

Kyle started to pay attention now. "That could be. That's not such a strange thing, when the price keeps getting bid up, you can have call sellers and put buyers in case the direction suddenly flips back down. At some point, the price could reverse, so dealers are probably positioning for that," Kyle told her.

Shirin had expected that as crude oil prices were rising the last few days, the implied volatilities of the upside call options (upside bets) on crude should have been rising as well, but they weren't. Instead, the implied vols of those call options were dropping. And conversely, she also noticed that the implied volatilities of the crude oil put options (downside bets) were, in fact, rising, when they probably should have been dropping. Kyle pointed out this phenomenon may not be unexpected when the price rose quickly as traders could buy downside puts, anticipating a fast reversal, and thus bidding up their implied volatilities.

"But this—" she started but then noticed Kyle was not paying attention to her again. His gaze had wandered over to where the sales traders sat.

"Hello?" she demanded. Kyle rotated back to her with a sheepish grin.

"Sorry… Hey, can you send me what you're seeing? I'll take a look?"

Shirin only gave him a frustrated look.

"Fine," she uttered, annoyed, as Kyle tottered over to the sales area.

Kyle peered down the desk rows. Sammy's desk was still dark, untouched, undisturbed for the second day.

"Hasn't he come in?" Kyle called to the group. One of them swiveled to him with phone under chin and shook his head, *uh-uh.*

"He call in, or anything? Anyone heard from him?"

Another sales trader twisted toward Kyle. "We haven't heard shit." Then went back to her world, ignoring Kyle.

Pete saw Kyle returning with a perplexed expression. Kyle didn't sit down, he simply muttered, "Sammy still hasn't come in, two days. Nobody's heard from him. I told the feds about it yesterday, but they didn't seem to care."

"Yeah, so...and?"

"So? I'm gonna go check it out," Kyle said as he put on his jacket.

"Wait? What do you mean, *check it out?*" Pete put down his phone and observed Kyle, realizing his intentions as he fit his suit jacket on.

"No, not again. Come on, man—FBI renditions, car bombs—we lost our friend! This stuff's wigging me out... Shit," Pete pleaded.

Pete clutched Kyle's forearm, gripping it tightly. Kyle recoiled from Pete's forceful lacrosse grip.

"Hey?"

Pete pulled him close to his face.

"What are you doing, dude? We just lost Sully and now you're gonna go play detective at Sammy's—who might have, yes, *been killed,* too?"

Kyle, somewhat taken aback by Pete's sudden forcefulness, tried to reason with him.

"It's a piece of the puzzle. I can't not go check it out," Kyle insisted.

But Pete wasn't buying it.

"Half an hour. I'll be back, half an hour," Kyle relented in the negotiation.

Pete let go of Kyle's wrist. Realizing it was futile to stop him, Pete pressed, "Tell me where he lives so I know where to send the cops in *half an hour.*"

Kyle smiled.

"He's got a loft in Tribeca, a few blocks from here. Walks to work, too. Here's the address," Kyle said.

"You wouldn't know it from looking at him," Pete snidely commented about Sammy and then faced Kyle. "Half an hour."

Kyle backed away from Pete and walked off the trading floor.

"Again, fuck," Pete moaned, rapping his handset against his head, worried about this whole thing.

Operation 912 Task Force Center

Kate was pacing in her office. A million thoughts sped through her brain. She needed to go back through all those loose ends of the case, she reckoned. Kyle's revelation had been a huge help, and now they needed to figure out if al-Hammadi was responsible and fill in the rest of the missing pieces.

Kate mentally recorded the inventory: background intel on Sohn and his colleagues; the link between them and this terror cell, and then the connection of it all to al-Hammadi; and how this got all the way to Wall Street. The time target, possibly revealed by the expiration date of the gold option trades, was a great clue. They could use that to search for other operatives who might be moving into place and getting ready.

Next, she thought about this operation. There was sophisticated logistical support here. Someone with money was financing it all, which worried her, too. Most terrorist operations were shoestring, done on the cheap. They were funded with small drips, expendable bodies, and leveraged distributed networks. But this one had the fingerprints of a well-planned, choreographed concern. Was al-Hammadi funding it all, or was it someone else? She worried it could be a state actor—North Korea itself, Syria, Iran, or perhaps a combination, or even China.

Kate had not liked the long encroachment into China with little attention paid by them—that stunk to her. Might they be the nefarious puppeteers? Kate didn't trust the CCP for a second.

The use of corporate jets was highly suspect—which reminded her, she needed to check on the origin of the plane lease—another item for the list. Someone had pushed in at least eighty million already, including the gold option purchase, and that wasn't even counting the payment for the actual bomb itself. She couldn't estimate what that might have cost. Even if the Chinese weren't directly involved, it was their funding and enabling of the Kim regime that ultimately allowed this to happen, so they no doubt bore culpability, in her mind.

The SSO and his team were securing the Omani encampment and would shortly be in possession of the device—they would soon learn its yield, and the major calamity they had prevented. But there was something else lingering that more deeply troubled Kate—where was the second brother? Where had he disappeared to? She suspected he was headed to the Middle East, or was already there, having split off in China somewhere along the way. She calculated that he broke from his brother once they were en route, according to a predetermined plan. But the missing brother concerned Kate above all.

Kate couldn't sit still, not that she ever could. She huffed out of her office and down the hall.

Tribeca, Lower Manhattan

Kyle rounded a corner block and spotted Sammy's apartment, a top-floor loft in an old three-story converted brick warehouse. He strode toward the entrance but walked past it, pretending he was on his way elsewhere.

Kyle waited a few minutes for a deliveryman to appear at the building's front door. Kyle skulked toward him in anticipation. The deliveryman pulled open the door, grabbed his bags, and entered the lobby. And just as the door was about to shut, Kyle grabbed it and followed inside.

The deliveryman stepped to the elevator and pushed the call button. Kyle made a quick assessment of the lobby. He spotted a stairwell door, and swiftly vanished up the shaft.

Bounding to the top floor, Kyle entered the hallway and padded up to Sammy's apartment door. It was a tall steel door with two locks. He scanned the hall, listening intently. There were no sounds or signs of activity. And there definitely wasn't any visible evidence that the NYPD or FBI had been there. Kyle checked around him once more and then put his jacket flap on the door handle and tried it. To his surprise, it rotated.

The door creaked open as the knob latch rolled back with a sharp *clack*. Kyle flinched at the loud noise, hoping that didn't betray him. He pushed open the door and crept inside, closing it behind him. He twisted the deadbolt to locked.

"Sammy?" Kyle called out, but not too loudly. There was no response. It was still and quiet. He stepped along the floor into a narrow kitchen. All appeared normal in there.

Kyle next entered the master bedroom, where Sammy presumably slept. No Sammy lying dead on the bed, that was good—so he clearly hadn't died of a heart attack in his sleep, Kyle perceived. Clothes were strewn around the bedroom, but it was otherwise as expected.

Kyle turned to the expansive living room. In the center, there was a long sofa with a coffee table and a leather lounger with a side table, both facing an expensive fifty-inch flat-screen TV. Kyle was about to head toward the second, smaller bedroom when he did a double take. There was a dark-colored oval-shaped stain on the oakwood floor next to the lounger. Funny, he'd seen something similar through the basement window of Brooks's townhouse.

He bent down to inspect the stain. Straightening back up, he exhaled, troubled. It didn't look right. He needed to report that right away. Kyle turned to leave the apartment but heard the front door handle rotate. Kyle froze.

The door was pushed inward but couldn't open because Kyle had locked the deadbolt. There was a pause from whoever was trying to enter. Kyle's heart jumped. Adrenaline flooded his chest. Who was it? Sammy returning? Did Sammy have a housekeeper? Was it the super with the FBI? But there was no knock or announcement.

Kyle heard a key slide into the front door's upper lock. The bolt turned over. Kyle leapt into Sammy's bedroom. He spun around—where to hide, *fast*? Under the bed was too narrow. The closet—he dove inside.

He couldn't see but he heard footsteps in the entryway. The footfalls resonated in a slow, deliberate, and skeptical pace—they hadn't expected the door to be locked—now they were on guard. Kyle tried to calm himself by slowing his breathing. The footsteps grew louder as they approached the bedroom. Kyle had a blurry view of the bedroom entrance between the jackets he was under. He watched a pair of legs appear. Black pants, black sneakers, a form emerged. Plain gray shirt and black leather jacket. This figure was too svelte, too tall, to be Sammy. And then he saw it—in his hand, a silencer-tipped pistol drawn.

Kyle glimpsed the man's face—expressionless, emotionless—goddamned sinister. He had a swarthy complexion with a sharp, curving nose. Kyle knew an assassin when he saw one.

The Hawk-Nosed Man approached Sammy's bed. Kyle tightened up. He would have to fight this guy if discovered. Kyle tugged a few more clothes over him. The Hawk-Nosed Man walked over by Sammy's bedroom window and scoped outside onto the street.

The gunman then approached the closet. Kyle held his breath. He got ready to leap out, go for the gun first. The Hawk-Nosed Man half slid open one of the closet doors with the silencer drum. He glanced inside, up and down, and jangled a few of the hangers. He didn't inspect the heap of clothes on the floor. Satisfied, he exited the bedroom and walked through the kitchen and could be heard checking that out, too, opening doors and inspecting hiding places.

Kyle let out a long puff of relief. He remained absolutely still, silent, blended in with the pile of clothes—never was he so happy that Sammy was a slob. Concentrating, he could hear how far away the assassin was from the floorboard creaks. Kyle thought about making a dash for it. He could rush out of the bedroom and out the front door before the gunman could react.

Kyle's phone started vibrating. *Shit!* He clutched his pocket. It kept rattling. He felt inside his jacket. *Fuck!* His finger searched—find the On-Off button—was that the right one? He pushed it in. The vibrating stopped. Kyle held his breath to see if the gunman had heard it. There was silence. Kyle noiselessly exhaled.

Kyle heard the gunman pause in the living room. There was a quiet interval for a few moments, and then his footsteps returned to the kitchen with more purpose. Kyle heard the rush of faucet water briefly. He knew what was happening. He cursed himself as he heard the Hawk-Nosed Man return to the living room followed by the squeaks of wiping sounds. The Hawk-Nosed Man had spotted the bloodstain and was cleaning it, removing the evidence.

Then the footsteps grew louder, coming closer. The Hawk-Nosed Man was back at the bedroom. He entered. He swept the room and approached the closet.

The Hawk-Nosed Man eyed the few hangers that were still swinging from when he had jangled them minutes earlier. Kyle tensed his muscles. The Hawk-Nosed Man's pistol was fortunately holstered, for now. The gunman grabbed the swinging hangers to stop their motion. He did another visual sweep and stepped back toward the apartment entryway.

Kyle heard the front door open and close. He exhaled and felt the sweat on his forehead. His heart pounded through his shirt. Kyle didn't stir. He remained as fucking still as furniture, in the same place, under the pile of Sammy's dirty laundry and discards, for what felt like a half hour. The image of that assassin strobed in his mind. He'd never forget that face, that nose—a look of pure evil.

Finally emerging from the closet, Kyle steadied himself and shook off the muscle cramps. He tried his best to step without making the floors squeak.

At the front door, he twisted the door handle, simultaneously leaning against the door itself so it wouldn't lurch open when the throw latch popped. Kyle inched the door open and peered out for a split second and then ducked back inside. The hallway was empty. He flung open the door and rushed out.

Kyle jumped through the stairwell door, letting the door slam behind him with a crash. He didn't care. He leapt down the stairs at a clip, shortly landing on the ground floor, he flew across the lobby.

He burst outside, crashing down to the sidewalk, and recovering, strode onto Reade Street as if nothing had happened. Kyle swung around and scanned the neighborhood. He saw no sign of the assassin.

Kyle reached the corner of Reade, and his thoughts turned to who he could call to relay all of this. He may have just witnessed Sammy's killer, and very likely the risk manager, Stephen Brooks, too, and maybe even Sully.

What the fuck to do now? Kyle thought about making an anonymous call to the police, which might force the FBI's hand in a single action. He also thought about calling Amy, but wasn't sure what her reaction would be, especially after last night's fracas. Plus, he didn't fully trust the FBI. They should have been all over that apartment already, and Brooks's place, too. He also thought about calling the CIA officer, Kate, but was unsure she even had jurisdiction or would be able to do anything about it. Kyle crossed the street, his cell phone remaining in his pocket, as he pondered what to do. He turned down the corner and continued briskly back to the bank, peering over his shoulder every half block.

As Kyle paced ahead, a block away, concealed behind a parked car close to Sammy's apartment entrance, the Hawk-Nosed Man stood watching him. He had seen Kyle exit the lobby. He coldly marked Kyle, studying him, eyeing him as the trader strode toward the intersection at the end of the street. And then the Hawk-Nosed Man emerged from behind the car, and he tailed Kyle...

Fortnum Bank Equities Trading Floor

Kyle barged through the trading floor doors, haggard and sweaty, and beelined for an empty conference room, pulling out his cell.

"Amy, it's me... It's been crazy—I'm OK. Hey, listen, I need you to listen to me, for real. I was just over at Sammy's... The missing broker... Don't *worry* about that. I saw blood, on the floor, no body, but I'm sure there is one somewhere... Anyway, I was inside the apartment when this guy entered... I don't know... Shit, woman, listen to me!... He wasn't friendly... No, I didn't *talk* to him, I was hiding... Listen to me, Amy! He had a pistol, with a suppressor... Yes, the real deal, this guy was fucking scary looking... I don't know, maybe Middle Eastern, Eastern European, that kind of thing. Had this heinous birdlike nose... *Now*, I was *just* there, half hour ago... Amy, forget about that! Calm the fuck down for one second. Somebody's killed Sammy, and probably our risk manager, too... weren't you guys gonna check it out?... Yes, get some people over there, like now... Tell them the living room floor, by the lounger, ya got that?... No, I'm at work, at the bank. Yes, here, safe... Thanks."

Kyle snapped shut the phone and slumped in a chair, exhausted. He glanced through the glass walls at the trading floor and the global clocks. He saw how late it was, after three p.m. already, prompting him to jump up and head to his desk.

"Where the fuck you been?" Pete glared at him as Kyle finally reappeared.

"Back of a milk carton."

"Fuck you," Pete snarled back. "You said *half an hour*! I called you, and was about to call—"

"There's some shit—"

"I can't be your wife, man. I can't worry about you like this. I was scared shitless, dude, like, urinate-on-the-floor scared," Pete lectured him.

"I know, I'm sorry. It took longer than I expected. And something happened."

"What does that mean—something *happened*?"

"Fucked-up shit, man. There's definitely something going on."

"What shit? Stop jerking me around. You gave me a slow heart attack the last couple hours—at least give me some payoff here."

Both their phones trilled, interrupting them. The break reminded Pete. "Oh yeah, Shirin keeps calling and IMing for you, she's been over here like five times. Something ain't right, look," Pete said as he tilted his leftmost monitor toward Kyle, showing him where markets were.

Kyle took a closer look. Gold had surged higher while he was at Sammy's. It was now up $10 from earlier to $765. Crude oil was also up, $2 to $97.

"Dang! Gamma kicking in? We need to hedge?"

"Clock's still on our side. Only a day left now. I did hedge a little, though."

Kyle nodded in approval.

"Order flow in crude is crazy, too. I haven't really done anything, but I've taken a ton of shows. But *size*, both ways," Pete added.

"That is a big move in gold. And no news?" Kyle asked, the magnitude of the lift only then sinking in with him.

"Not that I can tell. You probably know more than anybody right now," Pete cynically called him out. *"So?"* Pete looked at him anxiously.

"At Sammy's..." Kyle paused and leaned over to Pete. "I saw blood on the floor. And I saw this guy walk in with a handgun," Kyle revealed.

"You *shittin' me*?"

"I think they killed him. Probably Brooks, too, and I bet Sully. I wished I coulda jumped up and killed him with my bare hands, Pete, but I was scared, fucking scary moment," Kyle confessed.

"Fuck me. You tell—?"

"I called Amy," Kyle replied, anticipating Pete's question. "They had better check it out now."

Pete was about to press Kyle further when Shirin came stomping over.

"You don't give a fuck about me?"

"There she is." Pete motioned to Shirin.

"You're not so innocent either, Graff, I told you to—"

"I *told* him you were looking for him," Pete protested, and off her skeptical look, begged, "I did, I'm not joking." Pete laughed.

"Let's go," Kyle said, and as they headed to her desk, she began to unload.

"Something really weird's happening in crude," she launched.

"Yeah, Pete just told me the flow's been nuts."

"But it's where the flow *is*. Remember what I told you this morning?"

"About the skew inverting?"

Skew was option trader lingo for the relative asymmetry of the call prices versus put prices. Basically, it showed how "tilted" the demand for upside bets versus downside bets was in the options.

Shirin had pointed out to Kyle earlier that morning that she saw the skew for crude oil starting to invert, meaning that the puts were becoming more bid than the calls—unusual for crude oil, given that it was a supply-side commodity. The inverted skew indicated there were many more downside bets than upside, which wasn't consistent with what was happening in the markets, as crude had been pushing steadily higher.

"But now it's *really* inverted. I've never seen it like this. And crude oil price keeps going higher, but the skew keeps inverting," Shirin said fretfully as they arrived at her desk.

"Look," she continued, showing Kyle her analysis. She presented several charts of the crude oil skew over the past few days. Kyle studied them. She was right, the skew was becoming more and more negative—which projected option traders believed the price of crude oil was going to collapse, not keep climbing.

"I see what you mean," Kyle replied as he scanned her charts. "This doesn't make any sense," Kyle puzzled, half to himself.

On his mind was what Kate had told him about the broken arrow in the Middle East. The option price action Shirin was showing him did not jive with the sudden, impending doom Kate had revealed to him.

"I know. That's why I'm *showing* it to you," she scolded him.

"No, I mean—" Kyle stopped himself. He obviously couldn't mention what Kate had told him.

"Can we analyze the order flow? Like, from each option trade, can you tell the buyers and sellers?" Kyle asked her.

"I can sort of see that, yes. I mean, for electronic trades, at least. I can't see floor and I can't see OTC. And I can't see actual accounts, either, but I can see give-ups and I can tell which way they were," Shirin explained.

A give-up was essentially the bank or brokerage firm that a customer was executing from. They might use Lehman to execute their trades, but if their accounts were held at Fortnum Bank, they would "give up Fortnum" on a trade.

"How long will that take you to do?" he asked her.

Shirin checked her watch. "Couple hours maybe."

Kyle, flustered, nodded at her.

"You owe me so much," Shirin said, off his nod.

Kyle wheeled and staggered back to his desk.

He was about to sit back down when Pete told him, "Amy's on three."

Kyle picked her up.

"Hi… Yeah, I can…" He glanced at his watch. "I'll be over in about fifteen." Kyle hung up and tossed his handset back on his desk without sitting down. He looked at Pete. "I'm going back to Federal Plaza. I don't know how long I'll be. An hour maybe—anyway, go home once you're done here. Be careful getting home, you got me? Watch your back," he said to Pete, with stony eye contact.

Pete looked back at him, worried, as Kyle added, "Call me once you get there, so I know you didn't end up like Sammy."

Nahda Desert Region, Oman

Darkness had returned to the desert. Kelso and the Unit warriors had cleared the combat zone. A few 4x4 skeletons continued to burn. Immense craters from the A-10 bombings smoldered. The team had collected and organized the terrorist bodies and inventoried their weapons and armaments. The A-10s had since departed and the CIA drone continued overwatch above.

Kelso, the NEST techs, and the two breachers prepped to enter the suspected tent with the gadget. The NEST ops geared up with all their PPE and detectors. The breachers would also act as EOD (explosive ordnance disposal) techs.

The five of them appraised the tent from a hundred meters. One tech eyed the tent through a neutron sniffer. The second tech scanned different quadrants of the battlefield with another sniffer. The first tech lifted from his eyepiece.

"Commander, that's our tent. It's hot as it can get," he reported.

Kelso eyed the tech without replying. He had worried in the fog of the battle that some of the fighters would try to remove the package and it would slip from their grasp again.

"Let's go." Kelso started for the tent, but the techs exchanged flustered looks.

"Commander? We need to keep you and the other soldiers at a safe distance in case there's a fissile event, you understand?" the first one said to Kelso.

Kelso gave him a rare smile.

"I believe I do understand."

"Once we secure the device, whatever form it might be in, and inspect it, we may need to neutralize it if it's unstable. We'll wave over if we need EOD."

Kelso was about to respond when two other Delta Force ops approached them dragging a body—one of the fighters.

"Amir al-Khonari," the first op announced.

Kelso's attention turned to observe the body, and face, of one of their sought-after mules. He consulted an image of Amir on his tablet and compared it to the mired face of the corpse.

"That's him," Kelso confidently assessed. "Where?"

"Was in one of the trucks, probably taken out in a Hawg gun run," the second op replied. Kelso merely eyed him, "Bag him, we'll take him back with us."

The ops dragged Amir's body away and Kelso turned back to the NEST techs.

"Don't destroy it unless you absolutely have to. Command wants the thing preserved as much as possible, intact."

They nodded to Kelso. And reminded him, "No radios in vicinity."

The NEST techs stumped off for the tent. Kelso and the breachers minded them lugging all their equipment. Kelso opened the front passenger-side door of the Humvee and grabbed his sat phone.

Operation 912 Task Force Center

Scanlon relayed the call to Kate.

"Sitrep from our man on the ground. Field's clear, and confirmed Amir al-Khonari, EKIA. He's ordered the NEST team to secure the device. The squad has formed a thousand-meter perimeter, safe distance, in case there is a detonation or a fissile event," Scanlon updated.

"If this is a fully wired warhead, could it be detonated remotely?"

"We don't believe it's assembled or even armed, but, yes, if it is and there's any sort of radio actuator as part of it, or even a timer for that matter, it could be live," the NEST rep informed. "They've given radio-silence orders. Our officers also have jamming equipment they can enable, but they need to be within a few meters of the device," he added.

"What's our ETA here?" Kate asked, checking her watch.

"Depends on what we're dealing with. Disassembled warhead, it'll be a few hours as they gain access to its container and then analyze each component and ensure it is not a ready, armed device. And if it is…"

"And if it is?"

"They may end up destroying it in the neutralizing process, ma'am."

Kate stood, unconvinced, and addressed the NEST liaison.

"I don't want that thing damaged or destroyed unless we're talking about an imminent twenty-kiloton bang," Kate stared him down for emphasis. He was a bit surprised by her demand.

"We might not have..." The NEST officer trailed off, unable to complete his sentence nor maintain the standoff with her.

Kate resumed with her coterie of analysts and officers. She was about to continue gathering reports when Gabe, the FBI liaison, pulled her aside.

"Seems our New York City options trader did more snooping and may have actually run into one of the terrorists himself *in Manhattan*," he whispered to Kate.

"What?" Kate looked at him, half shocked.

She waved Kazemi over and called Bob, too, to hear this.

"There are two possible victims from the bank who may have been used and eliminated—the risk manager, Stephen Brooks, and a broker on the same desk as Kyle, named Sammy Bender," Gabe informed them. "Brooks went missing early Tuesday. Sammy, the broker, was reported missing Wednesday. Our trader, Kyle, left work a few hours ago and went over to this Sammy's apartment."

"Wasn't the FBI supposed to investigate?" Kate gave him an indicting look.

"They hadn't gotten there yet," Gabe submitted.

"Bullshit, but keep going," she urged.

"Kyle managed to gain access to the apartment, and spotted blood on the floor—then, get this, was actually inside when the killer, or what appeared very likely to be the killer, returned to the apartment, probably for a final cleanup. Kyle hid, saw this guy was armed, and then got out of there after he'd left."

"Shit, he get a good visual?"

"He did and seems we might know this guy. He shows up in multiple databases in Europe, Mossad has him, too, got a dozen aliases, has this identifiable nose, like a bird's or something, really curved."

"Connection between him and al-Hammadi?" Kate asked for the obvious.

"I've got a guy on that right now," Gabe replied.

"We can get CTC all over this," Bob told Kazemi, too.

"Please tell me the FBI has now gone to both locations," Kate pressed Gabe.

"Confirmed blood at both sites. Expect DNA labs shortly," Gabe revealed.

"Is this guy on clean-up duty?" Bob asked.

"Would appear the case, which would mean, one or both of our VICs knew a lot more."

"Or didn't, but were compelled to participate," Kate added, then asked, "What about the car bomb and a connection to this *Sullivan* trader?"

"Still working that out."

Kate tilted her head to Bob. "There's something that bothers me," she started. "Well, there's a lot that bothers me."

They chuckled morosely. "If we follow Kyle's trail, everything he was aware of—al-Hammadi purchased a warhead off the NKs to destroy a big Saudi oil field and bet on it in the financial markets—the roles of Stephen Brooks and the broker make sense, but the car bomb doesn't. Why take out this Sullivan guy? Unless that was in error or he was collateral damage?"

"We have to assume collateral damage," Bob concluded.

Kate called Kazemi back over.

"Where do we think al-Hammadi is now?"

He shrugged his shoulders. "We're searching. He's got palaces and properties all over, yachts, you name it, some are obvious, in his name, others totally off the grid. He could be anywhere," he said.

"Sorry, go back to the assassin," Kate said.

Bob looked at Gabe. "What do you guys have on this target?"

"If it is who we think it is, he's a nasty guy, real fundamentalist killer. He's personally killed scores, if not hundreds. Langley probably has a lot more in the drawer on him than the Bureau does. He doesn't usually operate in the US. He shows up in Europe and he's all over the Middle East. He's on a bunch of lists, and he got over here *somehow*. They're looking into that, too."

Kate frowned on hearing that. She walked back over to where the analysts were meeting, and she grabbed Sarah and Dr. Ahn and pulled over Carly, the NRO officer, as well.

"So, we have one brother confirmed dead in Oman. Have we *found* the second brother yet?"

They collectively shook their heads.

"NSA's on a traffic search, too. Nothing," Sarah lamented.

"What about along the original van path?"

"Negative. We've been over every inch of film, plus the GPS tracking device," Carly said.

"Show me, show me where," Kate requested, bringing them over to the map of southern China and the Yellow Sea that Sarah had originally created.

Dr. Ahn pointed to the orange magic-marker van path down the east coast of China, culminating at Hong Kong. The path switched colors when the van was ditched for the SUV but otherwise evolved in a continuous path.

"Here's the firefight." Dr. Ahn tapped, referring to the failed attempt to take the gadget on the Chinese road. "We had visual confirmation from on-the-grounds through here." She drew her finger down the coast. "Last confirmed visual was probably here. And here's where the SSO witnessed Amir ditching the van." She dithered that distance with her fingertip. "We had birds through here, that means the brother could have split anywhere in this region," Dr. Ahn finished, swiping her finger over a narrow stretch on the highway.

"What is this, about fifty klicks?" Kate asked.

"Eighty. And we don't see any drops, halts, or jogs," Carly told her.

Kate reviewed the trail. She traced the path with her own finger.

"Can you get me those films?"

"Will send them to Sarah now," Carly obliged.

"I'll go back to my old days." Kate smiled at them.

Fortnum Bank Equities Trading Floor

It was after hours. The trading floor was empty except for Kyle and Shirin, working at her desk, and a few custodial staff doing their rounds.

"I was able to pull the transactions, here, individually, that's each one." Shirin paused and looked at Kyle.

"I got it, yes, each one."

"That's like, thousands of trades, tick-level data." She stared at Kyle expectantly. "This is a fucking Picasso," she demanded.

Kyle laughed. "Tell me what the masterpiece says."

"This is what doesn't make sense. I've got over two hours in this zone here." Shirin motioned to a tick chart of the crude oil price. "About fifty trades, with crude moving up, but there's, like, thirty trades, maybe more, that are buying puts. And they're taking the offers, just seizing whatever's on the book. This is what was driving the skew so negative for crude today," she explained.

Taking offers meant the buyers were grabbing any puts available, at whatever prices that were offered, usually an indication of aggressiveness, like when a house buyer pays over asking.

"Let me see that?" Kyle leaned in for a closer inspection.

Shirin pointed out the row of individual trades.

"Shit, these are all lifting offers everywhere, a mania. They're driving up the vols. That's what's twisting the skew," Kyle realized as he scanned over the trade log Shirin had assembled.

"Exactly. Why would they be doing that? Why would you be in such a hurry to buy so many puts, any of them, all of them?" she asked rhetorically.

Kyle studied the detailed readouts. His eyes rose from the tables, in thought.

"Something's not adding up," Kyle audibly whispered. The concern in his tone was clear. Kyle was reacting to this in the context of the loose nuke Kate at the CIA had told him about. Shirin nodded in agreement—obviously unaware of the broken arrow but perplexed, nonetheless. Kyle continued.

"Unless the market wasn't believing this run-up in crude prices. Funny, this is exactly the position I had on that Garner made me unwind. But all these buyers are in a big hurry. Like they know something's going to happen. Very soon."

Kyle kept examining the data.

"And most of these are incoming paper? So, these are banks and dealers taking the other side?" Kyle asked.

"The customers are either clearing out the top-of-book passive orders or being very aggressive and pushing up the market-maker quotes on the screen or the floor, cleaning out their inventory, forcing them to repost higher and higher prices. Look at this one period, here. They come for thousands of puts, over and over. They push up the vols by eight points. In an hour," Shirin said, astounded.

Kyle concurred, lifting his glasses to more clearly read the small type. "Yeah, that's not normal, that's behavior that you..."

He lowered his glasses and peered at her, and she finished his sentence.

"That you know something." She paused in reflection. "But what could you know that would cause a sudden drop in crude oil prices the next day? That's the part that doesn't make any sense."

Kyle sat down at the trading desk next to hers. The lights on the trading floor dimmed, darkening the entire floor and illuminating their faces with computer glow from Shirin's screens. The custodians had finished their rounds and were exiting, turning down the lights. Neither Kyle nor Shirin really paid attention, though; they were both deep in thought about the data before them. Kyle rapped the desktop with his fists as he pondered.

FBI New York Field Office, 26 Federal Plaza

Amy was packing up her things, stuffing her purse, and getting ready to leave for the evening when Special Agent Jim, and two other agents, walked up to her.

"Where's Kyle?" Jim asked with some urgency, "Turns out your ex may have been right, forensics found blood in both places," he informed.

"I thought you guys just finished with him, didn't he go back to his office?" Amy responded, half paying attention. Then things sort of sank in.

"Wait, *both* places, what do you mean *both* places?" She now faced them.

"And this guy Kyle saw, he's the real-deal, serious assassin. Both places, I mean, the first guy, Brooks, that risk manager, found his blood on the basement floor, was his, DNA match. And that Bender guy, blood on the floor of his living room, was his, too. Both places, and both vics are probably dead. We need to—"

Amy shot him a look, suddenly spooked. "And Sully, too," she realized.

Amy fished into her purse, yanked out her cell and dialed as she continued talking to the agents.

"We should probably get Kyle in here, for protection," Jim told her, but she had already concluded that.

She was again only half paying attention to him, now more alarmed and focused on her call. She checked the phone's reception, frantically, several times, as it didn't seem like anyone was picking up.

Amy opened her purse to make sure her Glock was inside. Her face turning white, she impelled Jim.

"Send some agents to find *Pete Graff*, Kyle's colleague. Get him in here ASAP. I'm gonna find Kyle. And get me some tacks to this location like *now* now!" she fired off, scribbling the bank's address on a note and handing it to him.

Amy had already dashed down the hallway, throwing open the stairwell door. Jim didn't have a second to react. "Amy, wait, take—" He stopped. She was out the door. He handed the agents Kyle's office address.

"You heard her."

Outside, Amy raced toward the bank, the building and car lights around her turning into stripes as she ran. Her Glock was in one hand, her cell in her other.

"Come on, Springer, pick up…"

Fortnum Bank Equities Trading Floor

Kyle's suit jacket was hanging on the back of his trading desk chair. Inside the pocket, his cell phone vibrated and vibrated, fluttering the jacket lapel.

Over by Shirin's desk, Kyle and Shirin continued discussing the crude oil option data. Kyle was too far away to hear his cell phone activate.

"What expiries are these?" he asked her as they continued their analysis.

"Most are like your gold options, Friday, *tomorrow* Friday," she answered.

Kyle looked up to the ceiling tiles and the dimmed recessed lights. A faint glow came in through the west wall windows from the city lights outside the building. Kyle thought again about what Kate had told him, what he couldn't mention to Shirin, the nuclear bomb making its way through the Middle East to attack an oil target.

But he couldn't think of an oil target that would cause the price of crude oil to *drop* suddenly. Destroying or damaging pretty much any crude-oil-related target would make crude oil more *expensive*, not cheaper. These traders, whoever they were, were betting the price of crude oil would collapse tomorrow. That could only happen if the market were to be suddenly flooded with crude oil. Kyle wasn't getting the math here.

"Who are these accounts? Can we see that?" he asked.

Shirin shook her head. "Can't really tell. Because these are exchange-traded options, most are executed through regular brokerage or FCM accounts. One thing I *can* see is that it doesn't look like these put buyers are commercials, ya know, oil producers and oil majors hedging. They're mostly hedge funds," she said.

"Pete seemed to say the same thing. We've been getting desk shows for this order flow. Most of the shows are from brokers who rep funds, fast money. Can we tell if it's only a single account? Or at least a smaller number of accounts?"

"I can look at the give-ups, at least, see how many there are."

She clacked at her keyboard, interacting with the scripting code editor on her machine. After several moments of her entering SQL commands into the prompt, the screen dropped down with a new result set.

Shirin slowly shook her head again in suspicion.

"There aren't many, only like half a dozen. And who knows, these could all trace back to the same entity."

Kyle soberly raised his eyebrows in response. He stood again and started to pace behind her, mentally processing.

"What I keep coming back to is the sudden expectation," he began his supposition. "Let's say you knew about the attacks on crude oil infrastructure—the Turkish pipeline, the car bomb at the refinery—and you'd bought a bunch of calls on crude to front-run those attacks? And now those trades paid off. You'd either close those out or let those expire in the money?"

"You'd cash out."

"Could this be that?" Kyle proposed. "They're just exiting their original trades? And that the action is bidding up the downside of crude oil, inflating the price of the puts?"

"Could be," Shirin reasoned with him. "But then the volumes aren't consistent with that. Look at the call buying here, leading up to the attacks. There's some, but there's not a lot. But now look at all this put buying the last few days. There's *tons of them,* I mean, *size,* as you traders say. This would mean, if someone was originally front-running the earlier attacks, they're unwinding a hell of a lot more trades than they did in the first place," Shirin explained.

"You're right, doesn't add up. Also, unwinds probably wouldn't push up the skew that much, would more depress the calls than anything."

Kyle stopped his pacing for a moment.

"They're betting oil will collapse tomorrow. What would cause that?"

"You know crude oil better than I do. Really, the only thing that causes a sudden price collapse is a price war, ya know? The Saudis open up the pumps, push a ton of crude onto the market, which…"

"Which is unlikely now, given the market fundamentals. It's in the Saudis best interest to let it ride higher," Kyle said.

He resumed pacing, and then Shirin snapped her fingers in realization.

"What if this whole thing was a head fake?"

"What do you mean?" Kyle paused his back and forth, turning to her.

"Isn't that what you sports guys call it?"

"Maybe. What are you saying? The first two attacks were misdirections? And the real trade all along has been a collapse in the price of crude oil?" Kyle started following her logic.

"Something like that. Let's say they are in bed with these terrorists, and they're front-running these attacks. You have a really big thing that will cause the price of crude to collapse—I don't know what—but you want to inflate the price of crude first so you can put your bearish bet on."

"Pump-and-dump scheme," Kyle reflected as a graver look came across his face. "Or if you wanted to throw people off about what was really happening?"

"What do you mean by that?" Shirin was now not following Kyle.

Kyle's face went white.

"What did you tell me about the Nine Eleven attacks? All their bets paid off except one, the crude oil bet?"

Shirin replied vigorously, "That's right. They miscalculated, thinking that the price of crude oil would jump because it was terrorism related, that the market would always associate terror with increased crude oil prices."

"But it didn't, it fell."

"Because the attack on the US homeland meant a reduction in general business activity, a recession, which—"

"Which would decrease the need for oil and depress the price."

"Maybe they're betting on something that could do that."

"But what would do that?"

"Something would have to instantly shake the large economies of the world, Europe, Japan, the US, the major crude oil importers and consumers."

"The gold trade would be consistent with that, wouldn't it?"

She thought. "Depending on what it was, I guess it would," she reckoned.

And then it hit Kyle like a two-by-four across the face.

"It's coming here."

Shirin looked at him, confused. "What? What's coming here?"

Kyle ran to his desk.

"Kyle...? Kyle...?" Shirin called after him as he fled to his row.

Kyle fumbled through his coat and grabbed his phone and then dug into his pants pockets for Kate's card. His hands shaking, he retrieved it, barely keeping it steady as he dialed.

Operation 912 Task Force Center

Sarah, waving a phone handset, shouted at Kate, "Kate, line two."

Kate was involved in a conversation, and absently replied, "Who is it?"

"Some guy named Kyle from New York. Insists to speak with you, says it's urgent. Says he'll wait."

"Kyle from New York?" Kate puzzled briefly to herself. "Ah, the trader, Kyle." She replied to Sarah, "Yes, hang on, I'll take it."

Kate walked to her desk and picked up her phone.

"Hi... OK... What?—I don't understand. What does that mean, it's coming here?... Head fake?—"

Fortnum Bank Equities Trading Floor

Kyle, on his cell with Kate: "...the trades all show a big bet on crude oil prices suddenly collapsing tomorrow, along with a huge spike in the price of gold, which means, they're not attacking oil facilities in the Middle East. It's a ruse, Kate. It's coming here, to the US, a city—"

Blam! Cap-cap-cap!

Kyle's cell phone exploded next to his ear. Bullets zinged past him. Shirin screamed from over by her desk. Kyle dove below the line of monitors and into the trench between the trading desk rows.

Cap-cap! Monitors fragged as more bullets flew, blowing them apart, their innards sparking and fizzling. Shards of metal and plastic burst over the desks. More shots pummeled Kyle's area.

From down on the floor, Kyle tried to make eye contact with Shirin, but couldn't. She was one row over and probably cowering below the desks, too. Kyle shimmied along the floor to the next row.

It was difficult in the dim lighting, but from his new spot he could see Shirin. Her glasses were off, and she was staring at him, crouching, as well, below the desk level, shaking with fear. He waved to indicate he was OK and reassure her. Meanwhile, he could hear the attacker stalking the floor, getting closer.

Kyle knew he was a dead man if he remained in that spot, and he needed to get Shirin to safety. He saw Shirin was closer to one of the exits, which was two desk rows behind her. He could create a distraction and she could run for it.

The stalker's footsteps grew closer. Kyle could hear the attacker's breathing. Kyle reached above his head to within the trading desk wiring canal—where all the computer wires ran—and yanked out several of the monitor cords. The fourteen-inch flat-panel monitors that were on every desk also detached easily from their mounts. The gunman was now just one row away.

Kyle waved to get Shirin's attention. Making eye contact with her, he motioned for her to run to the exits behind her. She didn't understand at first and then peeked over her shoulder and back to Kyle and nodded to him, *I got it.* Kyle pulled two of the monitors off their mounts and jumped up. Like frisbees, he flung them at the attacker—and realized it was the assassin, the Hawk-Nosed Man!

The Hawk-Nosed Man saw Kyle pop up from the desks and spun around, aiming his automatic pistol just as the first monitor struck him in the arm, jarring him aside. The second struck him squarely in the chest, knocking the Hawk-Nosed Man off-balance. Kyle signaled to Shirin, *run!*

Shirin bolted for the exit behind her. In the dim light and without her glasses, she slammed into desks and chairs. The Hawk-Nosed Man turned to the noise and fired at her, *cap-cap-cap!* Bullets shredded the corner desk and shattered the glass wall by the exit. Shirin screamed as glass rained down on her. She slipped behind the wall and out the door. She'd made it out.

Kyle, using Shirin's escape as a diversion, ran along the desk row toward the opposite side of the trading floor, ducking and keeping below eye level. He made it to a more secluded area behind a back row of desks. He needed a plan to get himself out of there. His one mistake was that the Hawk-Nosed Man was now in between him and the exits.

Kyle rose a hair above the desk line and peeked over it. He saw the Hawk-Nosed Man sweeping side to side, searching each row, machine pistol leading the way. Kyle eyed the weapon. It appeared to have an extended clip, as many as fifteen or eighteen rounds. Kyle calculated he'd already gotten off about half that. His mind raced. *Think!*

Outside in the hallway, Kyle heard the elevator doors open. Heels clicked on the short span of marble between the carpeted elevator landing and the entrance to the trading floor.

"Kyle...? Kyle!"

It was Amy calling out for him. Kyle shuddered.

"Amy, get down!" he shouted.

Cap-cap-cap! The Hawk-Nosed Man turned and fired at Amy as she entered the trading floor.

Amy dove below the front row of desks as two rounds ripped through the walls behind her, vaporizing the glass door and showering her with glass shards.

Amy rose, and leveled a volley at the Hawk-Nosed Man.

"FBI, drop your weapon!" she shouted as she fired. Two of her nine-millimeter rounds—*whap-whap!*—smacked into the desk next to the Hawk-Nosed Man, and almost hit home. Kyle jumped in between two desk channels and ducked down again to give himself cover.

Operation 912 Task Force Center

"Kyle...? Kyle...? Kyle?" Kate yelled into her phone.

The line was cut. Kate didn't know what to make of it. She thought she heard a gunshot before the line went dead.

"Gabe!"

Gabe hustled to Kate.

"I was just on the phone with Kyle, the trader in New York. I swore I heard gunshots in the background before the line went dead—"

"Shit!" Gabe grasped it and got on the phone to HQS.

Kate looked up at the overhead projection screen monitor, still displaying the terrorist battlefield in the Omani desert where the Delta Force team and NEST techs were now in the process of securing the nuclear device. Kate focused on the tent where the device was sitting, where NEST officers were now working.

"Tell me what it is. What's in that package?" Kate yelled to the NEST liaison.

"They're in the process of inspecting it. I told you that. It might be a while," the NEST officer responded impatiently.

"No, now. Tell them to open the thing up. What's inside?"

The NEST officer gave her an irritated look.

Kate went to Terry's desk.

"Get him on the line," she demanded.

"Get who on the line?" Terry and the others regarded Kate, perplexed.

"The SSO. I need to speak with him."

"Direct contact with a SOG rep is—"

"Just do it, get him on the sat phone for me, now."

Scanlon complied, dialed, handed her the phone, and she grabbed it, waited for it to connect.

"Hi, who's this?... Hi, Commander, this is Kate Harrison at CIA in Washington. I'm the control officer for nine-one-two. You currently have NEST technicians inspecting our target device, yes?... Good, I want you to join them. I'm ordering you to open and disassemble that device, and report back what you see, right away... Thank you, Commander." Kate handed the phone back to Terry.

Fortnum Bank Equities Trading Floor

Kyle kept low. He imaged, in his mind, where he, Amy, and the Hawk-Nosed Man were on the trading floor. He was at the far north end. Amy was close to the entrance, and the Hawk-Nosed Man was virtually in between the two of them, a bit closer to Amy. Kyle needed somehow to get to Amy. And they needed to neutralize the Hawk-Nosed Man.

That gave Kyle an idea. He could use himself as a decoy again, which would give Amy the opening to fire at the Hawk-Nosed Man, and hopefully take him out, or at least wound him, he thought.

Kyle leapt up and vaulted over the first row of desks, clattering and smashing monitors he kicked on his way over. The Hawk-Nosed Man fired a single shot at Kyle and moved to the wall to get a clearer vantage.

Kyle hurdled over the next row and dove down in between the desks. Another shot struck the back of a chair next to him, spinning it around.

Amy stood and, *pop-pop-pop!* Fired off three shots at the Hawk-Nosed Man, her rounds pounding and zinging and tearing into the wall behind him. The Hawk-Nosed Man reversed back to fire at Amy, *cap-cap!* She ducked as his shots exploded the flat-screen televisions above her.

Kyle again leapt over two more rows of desks. He was now in the same row as Amy. He signed to her, motioning to where the Hawk-Nosed Man was.

Kyle scrambled along the floor and made it over to her.

"You hurt?" he whispered.

"This is the guy who killed Sammy and Brooks. Both dead, high confirm," Amy whispered to him.

"Shit. Probably Sully, too."

"More feds are coming. We just need to hold him off—"

Their position was betrayed.

Cap-cap! One bullet went clean through the desk, almost hitting Kyle. He fell back from its impact, knocking into the side of the desk.

"FBI. Give yourself up. More agents are on the way," Amy shouted at him.

She rose and fired—*pop-pop!*—as the Hawk-Nosed Man returned fire, *cap-cap!* Both shots struck Amy. The first hit her in the forearm, the second hit her in the collarbone. Amy was twisted sideways and flew backward against a chair, coming to rest on the floor, her head against the roller of a chair wheel.

"Amy!" Kyle lunged for her. He cradled her head and felt for a pulse. She was still alive but unconscious, losing blood, fast. Kyle found the wound on her collar. He pushed it in, applying pressure. He heard the Hawk-Nosed Man running toward them. Kyle realized the Hawk-Nosed Man knew he'd hit her. He was coming in to finish the job.

Kyle groped for Amy's Glock, grasping and reaching everywhere. He couldn't find it! He scanned around them, the floor, underneath the adjacent desks, as fast as he could. The Hawk-Nose Man's stomps were almost on top of them.

Kyle's hands grabbed for anything with a grip. He felt all over; both Amy's hands were empty. It must have fallen out somewhere. She was hit when she stood and fired, she was up higher. Kyle looked on the desktop—there it was, her Glock, resting on the keyboard. Kyle grabbed it—as the Hawk-Nosed Man turned into their row. Still on the ground, Kyle rolled and fired, *pop-pop-pop*!

The first shot stunned the Hawk-Nosed Man. Almost hit him in the forehead and sailed above his head. The Hawk-Nosed Man fell backward. His feet rucked against the carpeting, and he struggled back to a stand as Kyle's two following shots whizzed by the small of his back. The Hawk-Nosed Man retreated behind an adjacent length of desks.

Kyle clutched onto Amy and held her. His left hand pressed into the wound on her shoulder. He pulled her closer to him, beneath the overhang of the closest trader desk, to give them the most cover. In his right hand, he held the pistol out in front of him, waiting for the Hawk-Nosed Man's next try. Kyle knew he'd come back. Kyle rocked Amy as he held her tightly. "Come on, Amy, hang tight. Stay with me," he mouthed.

Kyle's hands were bloody, and he could feel the stickiness of the drying blood on the palm of his gun hand and on the Glock's pistol grip. Kyle's adrenaline pounded his chest and body. He held the Glock out at the ready.

"FBI, drop your weapon!" Tactical agents stormed onto the trading floor.

Kyle partially stood. He saw half a dozen officers with long guns in tactical gear advancing into the room.

The Hawk-Nosed Man leapt over a row of desks and sprinted for the west-side conference rooms. Automatic weapons fire erupted, disintegrating the glass-walled meeting rooms, blowing the windows out, and spraying glass onto the street below. The Hawk-Nosed Man raced into the conference room remnants and bounded out one of the shattered windows. Agents chased after him, halting at the edge and staring down below.

There was a row of bushy trees and grassy ground on the Hudson side of the building. The Hawk-Nosed Man had crashed through the trees, which had broken his fall. He staggered up to his feet and hobbled up the West Side Highway.

"Shit, we got a runner," one of the agents cursed into his radio.

Kyle flagged the agents. "Agent down. Agent wounded!" he shouted to them. They rushed over to Kyle and to Amy.

Minutes later, EMTs hoisted Amy onto a stretcher and hustled her outside to a waiting ambulance.

Nahda Desert Region, Oman

Kelso ran to the tent where the NEST officers were. He burst inside. They turned to him, startled. Kelso spied bedding mats with laptops sitting on them, a couple of AKs leaning against the tent's supports, and a makeshift table of a board and two chairs supporting it. Three lanterns hanging from the tent poles lit the interior.

"Hey, we told you—you can't be in here. It's not safe," one of the NEST agents protested.

Kelso saw the still-closed transporting case in front of them. The NEST techs had distributed their instruments and were prepping to perform a non-invasive scan first.

"This is a radioactive device, you're endangering your—you're not shielded. We can't protect you from an acute radiation dose," the other NEST officer pled.

"Change of plans. New orders," Kelso said urgently.

"What change?"

"Open the case," Kelso ordered.

"What do you mean, open it?" the first NEST officer asked incredulously.

The two Delta Force breachers entered the tent, following Kelso. The breachers inspected the case. It had one padlock on the side of it. Kelso gestured to open the case. The breacher hesitated at first, looking to his partner for help, but then he walked up to the lock with a pair of bolt cutters, and—

"Hey!" from one of the NEST officers. "We need to measure the radiation of the contents before—"

The Delta Force op ignored the tech and compressed the bolt cutters, and the padlock shackle snapped. He yanked the torn lock out of the away. Kelso used the muzzle of his SCAR rifle to gingerly lift the wide, wavering lid. He knew, if the thing was booby-trapped, they'd all be dead now.

The five of them exhaled in relief when it didn't cause an explosion. The NEST techs actively measured the rads as Kelso raised the lid. So far, everything was safe there, too. Kelso then flung the lid wide open. They all peered inside.

There was a secondary, shock-absorbing harness of suspended rubber and a partial, smaller case within it. Kelso motioned to the NEST officers to inspect it. The first tech unlocked its two latches with his radiation-shielded gloves and opened up the interior case. The second tech hovered a Geiger counter over the smaller box as the needle bounced around, indicating very high radiation readings. He tilted the meter toward Kelso so he could see.

They pushed the smaller lid all the way open. Inside, there was more molded foam, nestling half a dozen metal canisters, each about the size of a soda can.

"This doesn't look like a warhead or even a fissile device," one of the techs appraised. Kelso motioned for the other tech to inspect one of the canisters.

The first tech positioned his thick, lead-lined gloved fingers atop one of the canisters and with his other gloved hand gripped the bottom of it. He pushed downward into the foam to be able to grasp the canister and extract it.

"Seems like aluminum casing—odd, not at all protective," he noted.

The NEST tech delicately removed the canister and lifted it to about eye level. The canister had a flip-top lid. Handling it with the very clumsy gloves, he managed to push open its lid. He eyed inside the canister. Stacked within it appeared to be several coins or buttons each about the size of a quarter. They all exchanged puzzled looks.

The NEST agent moved toward the makeshift table with the canister and rotated it upside down to extract the contents onto the wooden board tabletop. He gave the back of the canister a tap to ensure it emptied. A dark pewter-colored disk dropped with a *thunk* onto the wooden board. He gave another tap on the back of the canister, and a second dull-looking, heavy metal coin fell out.

The second NEST officer inspected one of the disks with his gloved hand, lifting it, holding it to get a clearer look but also ensuring it was an arm's length from his face. He held up the Geiger counter to it, and the needle flattened all the way to the right, the highest reading.

"Plutonium buttons," he announced. The first tech concurred, feeling the weight of the disk in his gloved hand.

"What is that? What does that mean?" Kelso demanded.

Both NEST agents answered him, "No bomb."

"What do you mean, *no bomb*? What have we been chasing? What have I been detecting this whole time?"

"This." The first NEST officer tapped the case.

"These could become a bomb, but not without a lot of work," he said.

"These are pieces of plutonium. Plutonium buttons, we call them."

"Weapons grade?"

"Looks like it, definitely."

"How much is here? Is this enough for a bomb?"

The NESTs more confidently grabbed each remaining canister and emptied them onto the table. The rest of the buttons clunked onto the board. There were about twenty in all at the end of it.

"Maybe, barely. You need about two and a half kilograms of high-quality plutonium-238 to have enough for a bomb."

The second tech had already produced his electronic scale and proceeded to weigh one of the buttons and multiply by twenty, given they were of uniform size.

"This is only two kilos, not enough to produce a bomb," he said definitively.

Kelso cursed under his breath.

"And even if this was enough, you'd need to machine it, form it into a fissile core. Like the size of a softball. That would take specialized equipment and plants and handling. You need trained machinists and metallurgists, physicists."

"What else is in there?"

The two Delta Force breachers stirred the rest of the foam with the muzzles of their rifles. Foam padding was all that remained in the container.

"But we can see this with all your detection equipment? The readings were always off the charts."

"Yes, it's weapons grade plutonium, so will give a high return from a neutron sniffer," the first tech answered.

"So, from a distance, there's no difference between this package and a fully functioning nuclear warhead?" Kelso asked indignantly.

"If the warhead was plutonium based, that's correct. They both have about the same detection profile, similar signature," the second tech acknowledged.

"And you said this wasn't enough for one bomb, but is close to that quantity?"

They both pursed their lips in agreement.

Kelso spun, furious.

"Son of a bitch!" he yelled.

He wanted to fire off his SCAR rifle.

Kelso stomped the bomb case with a powerful boot, irate. They all jumped back, looking at him, astonished, even the two Delta Force ops.

"This is a goddamned decoy!" Kelso fumed.

He grabbed his sat phone and flew out of the tent.

Operation 912 Task Force Center

Kate, Bob, and even the director coursed desperately about the room. Scanlon, with phone in hand, called to them.

"Commander Kelso on sat," he announced what they were all waiting for. They rushed to their phones and headsets.

"What do we have, Commander?" Kate was the first one to ask.

The room fell silent as they all fixed on Kelso's report.

Then Kate dropped her phone. In slow motion, it fell, clattering to the desktop. She ran over, searching for Sarah.

"Sarah…? Sarah!"

The room exploded in a frenzy as the center became an instant beehive, everyone spinning to sitrep their offices. Amid the din, Sarah made eye contact with Kate.

"Yeah?"

"Do we have those South China films from Chantilly yet?" Kate shouted.

Sarah frantically waved for Kate to come. Kate hustled to Sarah's desk and sat down beside her as Sarah loaded the videos on her monitors.

They sped through the overheads. The images were nighttime infrared heat renderings of the highway routes in South China that the target van had traveled through. The fuzzy white squares and rectangles (infrared images of vehicles) against a black background flew through the films in accelerated time. Occasionally, a red circle appeared surrounding one of the white rectangular moving blobs.

"That's our van target," Sarah pointed out.

Dr. Ahn joined them, watching over their shoulders.

"What time is it there?"

Sarah pointed to a time ticker in the upper right of the films. "Here."

"And we're pretty certain the brothers are still together as of this time?"

Sarah confirmed, "Yeah. The firefight had just happened, back here, so highly unlikely they could have made any sort of change-up if they'd just fled the scene."

"Pretty even path," Kate commented as they watched the little white blob flowing down the highway, uninterrupted, in a smooth trajectory.

"I know this part of the country. We can probably skip down to the next set of towns," Sarah offered and sped up the film even faster. The images blinked by as the white bead whizzed through each frame.

In one sequence, there was a brief blink as the white bead disappeared but then reappeared a short space later down the image.

"Hey!" Dr. Ahn pointed to it.

"*What was that?* Go back." Kate saw it, too.

Sarah, with the younger eyes, hadn't caught it. "Where?"

"Back there, go back a bit, a few minutes before," Dr. Ahn directed.

Sarah reversed the reel and rewound a few minutes.

"Start from here. Go slow, frame by frame," Kate prompted, as they all leaned in toward the screen.

Sarah inched through the footage. She zoomed in several more levels, and the white bead inflated in size, becoming fuzzier. In the next frame, the van is seen advancing down the highway. Sarah clicked forward, and the van continues to move along the road. And then it vanishes for several frames, disappears—but the clock continues to tick, uninterrupted. A dozen frames later, the white box reappears at a location farther down the road.

"What's going on *here*?" Kate asked.

"This is where it was." Dr. Ahn rapped the screen.

"What's the scale here?"

Sarah put her hand to the screen and referenced a scale key in the lower right. "Looks like about twelve meters, thirty to forty feet, maybe."

"Back up a couple frames," Kate asked, as Sarah scrolled her mouse wheel.

The fuzzy white box leapt in reverse, back up to the top of the screen again, skipping the large segment of road in the center, like it had entered a wormhole at that point on the highway.

"Do we have a missing section of film?"

"Did we switch lenses or birds?"

Sarah referred to the frame count with time stamps. "No, this is from the same source. Appears pretty continuous," Sarah responded.

"It's like the van jumps about forty feet. Simply disappears and then reappears forty feet later," Kate said, baffled.

"And takes about a minute—no, two, to do it?" Dr. Ahn added a key detail.

"Calcs to about two minutes, yeah. No missing film, either," she verified.

"What's the van's velocity here, before this disappearance?" Kate drew her finger across the upper right segment of film.

"Looks like..." Sarah did a quick calculation. "It's slowing down, too. Comes in at about sixty miles per hour and then is down to about thirty before it disappears," Sarah calculated.

"And then what about when it emerges from this gap?"

"Let's see..." Sarah scrolled through the frames and recalculated. "Weird, sort of does the opposite. It's only about fifteen miles an hour here, and then a few moments later, it's back to sixty."

"It's like it's slowing down and speeding up through here," Kate noted.

Dr. Ahn snapped her fingers with a eureka.

"There's something there. Give me the land coordinates, there, this blank spot. Where's that NGA analyst?"

Sarah gave her the coordinates, and Dr. Ahn bolted to the NRO desk with Carly and the NGA team and returned some moments later with a physical map and daytime overheads of that same area.

"Here. Look," Dr. Ahn pointed out excitedly as she splayed the daytime overheads of the same spot onto the desk in front of them.

Kate and Sarah saw it at once. There was a bridge, an overpass, at that spot.

"Motherfucker!" Kate exclaimed.

"It stopped under here," Sarah said the obvious.

"The analysts missed that."

"Everyone missed that."

"The van emerges here. He's beneath the overpass for a few minutes."

"Could it be a bio-break?"

"Could be, not a bad explanation, but—advance the film again until this area is almost out of view."

Sarah scrolled further through the frames as the white box representing the van dropped down the screen.

"And zoom out, to give us the widest angle."

"We might lose some acuity," Sarah advised.

"It's fine, we won't need it. But let's see what we have."

Sarah zoomed out and the image narrowed on the monitor. The white van shrank to nearly a dot.

"Play it here."

They watched as the scene evolved forward at normal speed. The target van continued south as the bridge/overpass rose to the top of the screen with the satellite's aperture sweeping southward over that area.

"Slow it down *right* here," Kate requested.

Sarah jogged it more slowly.

"Look!" Kate said in horror.

The films showed a second fuzzy white dot emerging from the underpass after the van had left. That vehicle heads south as well, trailing the van. The second vehicle remains in view until the satellite aperture sweeps beyond its range.

"That didn't come in with the van. It was waiting there," Dr. Ahn emphasized.

"And transferred some contents into that second vehicle. This was planned," Kate added gravely.

"Stopped for two minutes, which would be just enough time to come to a screeching halt, jump out, move some cases into the other vehicle, hop in, and start it up," Sarah estimated.

"Son of a bitch, son of a bitch!" Kate cursed, and then asked, "Do we have any films of this area after this bird's flyby?"

Sarah shook her head. "I can check with Carly, but I don't think so. We were lucky to get this equipment, and it was trained on the van target."

Kate inhaled deeply in thought. Her mind jammed with all the possibilities. And she arrived at something.

"Let's say they both headed to the same destination. They just split their arrival times, by a few hours, maybe. Enough to throw us off."

"You're saying the second brother flew out of the Hong Kong corporate terminal, too?"

"I'm saying, let's check that possibility. Can we get security video?"

"I'll talk to Hong Kong CIB. I'll get manifests, everything," Dr. Ahn headed back to her desk.

"What are you thinking? They moved the *actual* bomb into this second vehicle, and it flew?"

Kate, with a slow nod, replied, "That's unfortunately what I'm thinking." She searched the room. "Where's the director?"

NYU Downtown Hospital, Gold Street, Manhattan, United States

Kyle leaned against a wall in the ICU corridor, his face buried in the crook of his elbow. Pete was sitting in a nearby row of chairs. Amy's sister sat next to Pete with Jill on her lap, and a pair of FBI agents next to her. NYPD Hercules counterterrorism officers guarded an ICU room across the hall, where Amy was.

Pete came out of his seat and approached Kyle.

"I can't believe all this is happening," Kyle grieved, lowering his arm, his eyes red with tears.

"I know, man. I'm sorry," Pete offered. "Was it the same guy?"

"The same fucking guy who killed Brooks. Same guy who killed Sammy, same guy I saw in Sammy's apartment and who tried to assassinate me tonight, probably killed Sully, too, and now shot Amy." Kyle paused, his hand in a fist. "I want to fucking kill this guy, Pete, whoever he is."

Kyle slammed his fist through the hospital wallboard with a thud. Amy's sister, the cops, and the agents all startled at the noise. Pete pulled Kyle away from the wall, steering him farther down the ICU corridor.

"Come on, man," Pete urged. "Think about Amy. She's gonna get through this. You have to think about *her* right now."

"There's a bomb coming, Pete," Kyle spat. "What good is her recovering if we're all fucking burned to death when the thing goes off?"

Pete looked down, "Look, we don't know—a *what?*"

Kyle shot him a nasty look.

"I know it's gonna go off tomorrow. We're all fucked. This has just been one big buildup. I want to find that guy and fucking kill him, Pete." Kyle motioned like he was strangling the Hawk-Nosed Man.

"Feds looking for him? Wait, go back to the *bomb* part—*what?*"

"He escaped. Everybody's looking for him. You shoot a fed, they're gonna find you. This guy's at the center of the whole thing."

Pete leaned against the wall, rolled his head back. "This is nuts. I can't believe he attacked you."

"Amy saved my life. He would have taken me out, Shirin, too. He'd come after you. This whole thing is shit. Someone's trying to cover all trace of this thing so the bomb'll go off, markets will go berserk, whoever's behind this will make a ton of money, and all history of that will be erased," Kyle railed. "And we could have stopped it. We could have stopped it—just like Nine Eleven, all the tells were there—everything." Kyle shook his head, upset. "The gold trade. I fucking fell for it. How could I have been so *stupid?* Of course, it was a rotten trade, fucking front-running terrorists. I'll kill 'em all!" Kyle shouted with clenched fists, his voice ricocheting down the hallway.

Pete stayed with him as he ranted. Kyle calmed down after a few minutes.

"I get it, man," Pete soothed. "Go back to the bomb, again."

Amy's sister came over holding Jill.

"I'll take her home now," she said as she set Jill down in front of Kyle.

Kyle grabbed Jill's hand and drew her away from Pete and Amy's sister. He hoisted her up to sit on a counter, so she was eye level with him.

"Will mommy wake up?" Jill asked sadly.

"Mommy's going to be fine, OK?" he reassured her. "Mommy's tough. She's an FBI agent. She's a superhero," Kyle told her.

Jill started to cry.

"It'll all be OK. Be tough for me, Jill, like mommy, be tough."

"I'm tough," Jill uttered, as her fists clenched. And tears continued streaming down her cheeks.

Kyle pulled her to him and picked her up. He carried her back over to Amy's sister and passed her over to her. An agent motioned for a pair of NYPD officers to escort Amy's sister with Jill out of the hospital.

The corridor was quiet after they left, only Kyle, Pete, the FBI, and Hercules guards remained.

"What are we gonna do now?" Pete asked.

"I don't know. Amy's already had two surgeries. One bullet's lodged close to her spine. They said she's stabilized, but she's got another surgery tomorrow." Kyle shook his head wearily. "I don't know."

"She married you, she can brave anything." Pete gave him a lighthearted dig.

Kyle chuckled.

"And tomorrow's expiration Friday," Kyle added. "I'm terrified. Like, I want to get out of here," Kyle said anxiously.

"I get it, man, so about this *bomb*?" Pete grabbed his arm.

Kyle pulled Pete into an empty berth. He revealed to Pete what Kate from the CIA had told him. After that, Pete sank into a chair, the wind knocked out of him.

"So, that's what this is all about."

They said nothing for a few minutes, both in their own thoughts, only to be interrupted by one of the suited FBI agents. "Hey, sorry to bother, your friend, Carl Sullivan, how old was he?"

Kyle and Pete exchanged puzzled glances. "He was the same age as me, thirty-six," Kyle answered.

The FBI agent appeared confused. "Something's strange, then."

"What do you mean?" Pete asked, looking at Kyle again, perplexed.

They exited the berth, and another, more senior agent joined them.

"You witnessed Mr. Sullivan *in* the vehicle that exploded?" he asked Kyle.

Kyle emphatically nodded. "He got into the car, shut the door. Then I turned around and headed to the bank, and it exploded. I got up and his car was blown out and on fire."

"We found two charred bodies in the wreckage. One was the driver, who's been identified by his wife and dental records. The other was a passenger we *believed* was Mr. Sullivan, but the body is actually of a much older male, in his sixties, maybe seventies," the agent explained.

It didn't register with them. "What are you talking about? There was another passenger with Sully?"

"No, that *was* the only passenger. Unless Carl was in his sixties, he wasn't *in* that car. We have no body for Mr. Sullivan," the junior agent clarified.

Kyle and Pete exchanged intransigent looks. "That's impossible," Kyle said, and Pete added, "There's gotta be some mistake. Are you saying he's *alive*? Then where the *fuck is he*?"

The agent shrugged his shoulders. "That's what we wanted to talk to you about. If he wasn't killed in that explosion and not injured, there were four other people injured, and we know all of them. Carl Sullivan should be alive and well, and we need to talk to him."

Kyle was about to get pissed off at the agent. "Hey, I saw Sully get into that limo. I heard it explode and I saw it burning, with my friend *in it*. And Sully's been missing ever since that exact moment. Check your information again."

"We *did* check it. Those are the forensics. Our techs reviewed it repeatedly because we didn't believe it, either. We thought Mr. Sullivan died in that car, too."

Kyle wanted to punch the agent. He held back. Pete took a calmer approach.

"I'm sorry, we're not talking on the same level here—if Sully wasn't killed, or even injured in that explosion, then where the hell *is he*? I mean, he hasn't been back to work since that moment. He didn't just vanish."

"We don't get it either, Mr. Graff. Agents have been to his apartment. His cell phone isn't registering on the grid. We're trying to figure it out, too, which is why we need to speak to him."

Kyle shook his head. This was all crazy, he thought. "So, according to the FBI, Sully is *alive*?"

"If you guys don't know where he is—he has to be somewhere…"

"Of course, we don't know *where* he is! If he was never in that car, he would have come right back to work. He would have been hanging out and drinking with us and none of this crap would be happening!"

"Hang on a second, hang on," Pete persuaded the agent. "Give me a couple minutes with him."

The agents regarded them and then retreated to the seating area.

Pete and Kyle walked farther down the hallway.

"Kyle, did you *actually* see him get into that car?"

Kyle clutched Pete by the collar. "I fucking saw him get inside that car!" He let him go. "I remember, I saw him close the door, too, and then I turned to the bank, and the explosion happened and sent me to the fucking ground—no, I didn't *see* our friend get blown to bits and cooked on fire, if that's what you're getting at?" Kyle paused. "You think he made it out of there, and this Hawk-Nosed Man got to him? Kidnapped him—you think they *kidnapped* him?"

Pete shook his head and leaned against the wall. "No…I think I get what the FBI is asking now."

Pete gave him a penetrating look that Kyle finally picked up on.

"You think the FBI suspects Sully's mixed up in this plot? Like, from the bad guy's side?" Kyle laughed in disbelief.

"Then where is he? Where's our friend? *Kyle?* You *turned around*. How long was it between when you saw him get inside that car and the bomb exploding?"

Kyle thought for a moment, the world not making sense.

"I don't know. I don't know—thirty seconds, a minute, maybe. Seemed like it was instant, but maybe, I don't know—fuck, I don't know anything."

Kyle only stared at the floor, unable to process it. And then Pete crossed that line. He regarded Kyle, flatly serious. "Who subtly pushed the gold trade on us? Who kept telling us it would be fine? Who kept telling you that you were paranoid about your theories?"

"I can't believe—"

Kyle's fist was already in midair.

"Don't punch the wall again!" Pete cringed, ducking. Kyle stopped short of it.

"My fist already hurts," Kyle refrained and leaned against the wall, too. "Pete, he can't be mixed up in this thing? He can't—I mean, he can't…I think they took him. That's the only explanation."

"Maybe. You know him much better than I do."

"This is beyond evil, though."

"This is about money. You pull this off, you make *a ton* of money. Maybe that's all it's about. Ideology is only something *he* hijacked," Pete proposed.

"We gotta, we got—my head's spinning, too much. I'm not thinking clearly."

Kyle glanced back toward the FBI agents. He put his head in his hands in exasperation and shouted, "It doesn't make any sense!"

Pete pulled him over to a pair of hallway chairs, where they sat.

"Tens of billions of dollars makes *a lot* of sense," Pete said.

"He's your friend, too, why are you betraying him like this? You seem so fucking nonchalant about it."

"Look at everything. Why was he asking us all those questions about the crude options market the week before? Why has everyone involved in the gold trade been killed or attacked? And where *is* Sully? What else makes sense?"

"No, it doesn't make sense. I don't believe it."

"Then explain it for me. You said it yourself—Sully shoulda been at a bar drinking with us that night. Where the fuck did he go?"

Kyle pondered for a moment, his eyes searching the hallway.

"Then how the *hell* did he get his hands on a nuclear weapon?"

"I don't know. He probably didn't. He's probably using some terrorist ring, that al-Hammadi guy, or whoever. Maybe they're working together. Sully provides the trading expertise, al-Hammadi gets the nuke and supplies the thugs. I don't know," Pete speculated. "Plus, Sully was always bitter at the bank. Remember, he wanted to run the prop desk you now run. They passed him up for you, remember that? The veteran trader lost out to the former FBI agent crossover who'd only been trading a few years, and who *he'd* brought in. I know he always resented that—and quietly resented you for it. Maybe he wants revenge."

Kyle was silent for a moment and then acknowledged him. "He was, it's true. He was upset for a long time about that. He never showed it, but you could tell. Sully always was a dark motherfucker, but come on, to get involved in something like this? Betray your country, kill *thousands of people*? I mean, that's a one-way chute." Kyle looked up and out into distant space again.

"Maybe they're blackmailing him, forcing him to do this," Pete offered.

"That's the only thing that makes any sense. So, what do we do now? I mean, like, tomorrow?" Kyle anxiously wondered.

Pete, now being more the voice of reason, advised, "We gotta forget trading—the gold trade, the bank, even forget about Sully. You have to focus on Amy. Give her your attention, man, make sure she rebounds, and take care of Jill. She's little, she doesn't get this, she's scared. She needs her daddy," Pete insisted.

Kyle grinned at the ironically wise words coming from Graff at that moment. Kyle looked over to Amy's room. There was a pause, and then Kyle jumped up and jogged over to it. Pete chased after him, unsure of what he was up to. Kyle got a nod from the NYPD to enter, with Pete following him inside.

Amy lay on the bed, asleep. IVs and EKG wires were rigged to her with the regular tone of her heartbeat.

"Kyle, man, come on. Let's leave her be. Let her rest," Pete whispered, trying to pull Kyle back into the hall.

"We've got to get her out of here," Kyle insisted in a stronger whisper.

"Wait—what do you mean, get her *out of here*?"

"The bomb's coming here. I'm not having her die here, I'm sorry," Kyle protested as he frantically searched beside her bed.

"Stop! What are you *doing*? You can't just *pick her up*. She's in IC, we can't move her."

"She's not dying here!"

A frenzied Kyle circled the bed several times, looking to unhook wires. Pete followed him around as he scoped the console area at the head of her bed. Kyle then dropped to the floor, searching for the plugs.

"How do you know the bomb's in New York? It could be anywhere."

Kyle halted for a moment and leered at Pete.

"Where would you put it? Ninety-three, they tried to knock down the towers with a truck bomb. Nine Eleven, they collapsed them with airplanes. They're not gonna stop until New York City is in ruins," Kyle retorted, crouching below her bed again. "We'll get her into an ambulance and get outside of the city to Long Island or someplace," he said, continuing his search for ways to disconnect her.

Pete half-heartedly searched around the bed, identifying the cords and plugs. "If it's coming here, at least New York real estate will get a lot cheaper. I'll finally be able to afford something," Pete cynically quipped.

Kyle appreciated his black humor and chuckled from underneath the bed. "If it only took that."

Then Kyle shot up. His eyes darted back in forth in sudden thought.

"Pete?"

"Shit. What now?"

"We might be able to figure out where the bomb is going."

"Huh?"

"You just joked New York real estate would take a bath if a nuclear bomb goes off in Manhattan. If you knew that, you would short New York properties—"

"Because they would—"

"Let's say Sully *is* involved in this, I can't bring myself to, *but*—whoever is doing this trading *knows* what they're doing. They know the markets, they know derivatives. The trading has all the fingerprints of a pro."

"Yeah, *so?*"

"Sully's a great trader. Again, him, or someone like him, wouldn't leave any alpha on the table. It's sacrilege. Plus, I'm sure there's a lot of people involved, people to pay off. That means they need to make as much money as they can."

Kyle eyed Pete expectantly as the understanding registered on his face.

"Holy shit. We might be able to—"

The two of them burst out of Amy's IC room.

The FBI agents watched as they dashed down the hall.

Kyle and Pete found an empty orderly's room. Kyle flipped open his cell.

Operation 912 Task Force Center

An emergency call was in progress. With the CIA team on the conference were the secretary of Homeland Security; the APNSA (Assistant to the President for National Security Affairs), who was representing the NSC (National Security Council); and two senators from the Homeland Security Committee.

"My God, and what are we talking about here?" the APNSA asked, dismayed.

"Looks like a twenty-kiloton plutonium-based warhead. Basically, a Fat Man knock-off," Kate described.

"And we think this is in one of our cities now, and is going to detonate tomorrow? Are we hearing that right?"

"That's the intel we have, yes, high confidence," the director answered.

"Christ!" exclaimed one of the senators. There was silence.

"What's the potential casualty estimate?"

Bob took that one. "A dense city, like New York, we're looking at about a mile radius of near-total destruction, heat and blast and fires for another three miles out. That would translate to about half a million killed instantly, another one million from injuries, and then another million in a cancer cluster that goes on for decades after…and an economic collapse."

There was silence again, not even gasps. The dread was the loudest thing on the call. Then the Secretary of Homeland Security spoke.

"We don't know where this thing is; we're going to have to prioritize. New York, Los Angeles, Chicago, Washington, and Miami. We'll distribute resources across those. Start to get NEST teams out ASAP, close bridges and tunnels going in and see if we can coax people out of the big cities."

"Has anyone spoken to the president?" the first senator asked.

"I've updated both vice and POTUS. We'll convene an emergency meeting at the White House at eleven Eastern with the full National Security Council," the APNSA told them.

"We need resources, but we need to keep this tight; if this leaks out, there could be mass panic and hysteria, something we just can't control," the second senator demanded.

"My God, you'll have anything you need."

"Let's regroup after we've briefed the NSC. HS is now lead agency, absorb the CI Operation 912 Task Force and direct any DoD resources. Joint Command at Nebraska Avenue. I'll recommend we move the terror alert level to yellow and we go to DEFCON 3," the APNSA advised everyone.

They all hung up. With the call ended, Kate, Bob, and the director exchanged distressed looks. The director leaned back slowly in his seat.

"What can we do here? What loose ends are we still chasing that can help us—could help us—prevent or forestall this?"

Kate thought and then rattled off several items.

"We're still combing through video footage to see if we can locate the second brother. If we can find him at HK International, we might be able to narrow the flights he boarded—and the destinations. Also, CB still tracing all these wires, figure out how it all gets back to al-Hammadi," Kate assessed.

"What about this assassin in New York? The one that's been killing everyone at the bank—and he shot an FBI agent, right? How's he doing, by the way?"

"She," Kate corrected him. "Amy Springer, she's the ex-wife of that bank trader who's been giving us the insider trading info. She's stable last report I got," Kate explained. "Yes, there's an FBI BOLO on him—trust me, they're on him."

"He *must* be a key lead. We find him, we'll probably find the bomb," the director noted.

Kate's cell phone rang. She glanced at the display.

"Speaking of which, it's that trader, Kyle."

"Put him on, here," Bob requested.

Kate forwarded the ring, and the director switched on his speakerphone.

"Kate?" Kyle asked for her.

"Hello, Kyle. You have me; Bob Stalfort, whom you met before; and the director of Central Intelligence on. How's Amy doing?"

"She's stable, but not out of the woods yet, thanks for asking. Kate, I think we might have an idea, but I need your help," Kyle began, somewhat excitedly.

"Go on," Kate offered.

"I don't know if you heard, but our friend Carl Sullivan might be involved in this—he wasn't killed in that car bomb, after all."

"Your trader friend in the limo outside your office, *Sully*, that one?"

Kate raised her eyebrows at the revelation.

"Wait, the one in the car bomb—wasn't he killed?" Bob was confused.

"No, the FBI informed me a few minutes ago he wasn't. Someone else was inside that car. He must have slipped out—it was meant to look like he died. But he's been missing since then—"

"Wha—the FBI looking into that?" Bob asked.

"Yes, but that's not why I'm calling," Kyle answered.

"That is the point, that's a key lead—*if* he is involved," Bob argued.

"No, that's not the lead I'm talking about," Kyle protested.

Kate tapped Bob's arm to let Kyle continue. Bob looked at his watch, annoyed. The director sat quietly, listening.

"Tell us, Kyle."

"We don't know for sure if Sully's involved, if he's being coerced or if he's dead. I get that. But I know Sully better than anyone else. I know his trading style. All the positioning to date, the gold bet, the crude oil head fake, it's all followed Sully's trading style perfectly—or else it's someone who's a pro and knows exactly what they're doing, working with this al-Hammadi guy." Kyle paused.

The three of them started to listen more intently.

"Keep going," the director enticed.

"This was an expensive operation. You guys know that more clearly than anyone. Even I can see that from where I sit. One part of Sully's trading, maybe a strength, but also a weakness, is that he'll never leave money on the table, we call that edge. If he knows there's edge to be had, he'll put a trade on to try to capture it. But also, to finance this operation and pay off everyone involved—"

"We're not following the connection," Bob urged.

"You recall the Nine Eleven trades? There was that handful of trades that especially stood out—the puts—bets that a stock price will drop—on American and United Airlines?"

"Yup, sure, you mentioned those, too, when you were here before."

"Those trades stood out, statistically. They implied a negative event against those two airlines, and/or air travel. Looking at the entire set of trades, you could tell there was information being transferred to the marketplace that something negative could occur to air travel, *and* to those two airlines, specifically."

"But that was never proven, and something like that could—" Bob started, but the director put his hand up for him to shut up.

"Finish, Kyle," the director urged.

"So, if there were assets that would be negatively impacted by this bomb, Sully, or whoever, would be thinking about those. They would be positioning to take advantage of that."

"Kyle, we're still not following. Can you give us an example?" The director was growing impatient, too. But Kate started to follow him.

"I think I know what he's saying," Kate realized. "Give them a for instance," she told Kyle.

"Yes, so if the terrorist financiers behind Nine Eleven went after American and United because they knew those stocks would be hit, and that that could have alerted us to an upcoming action against those airlines, there could be similar type trades, like this gold option trade, but more specific. Let's say you knew the bomb was going off in New York City. It would devastate assets that were linked to or based on New York locations and proximities, New York real estate, for example. They could place a ton of downside bets on what we call REITs, real estate investment trusts, that specialize in the New York area—also, companies headquartered or with major operations in New York would be hit, all the large investment banks, certainly. My point is, we could look for those trades. Those fingerprints might be there. And that *could*, *might*, give us a hint to the assets that will be impacted—and then we could triangulate any geographical commonality to those specific assets." Kyle paused, a bit winded.

The three of them exchanged knowing glances and nods, finally seeing what he was proposing.

"Kyle, what would you need to do this?" the director asked.

"I have an analyst I work with at the bank, Shirin. I need her, given some protection so she can get to me, but I need access to other bank's trades. I can only see ours. If I could see what all the other banks were doing, really what their customers were doing, we might be able to put the pieces together and identify these statistical anomalies across markets. I know Treasury and the Federal Reserve have access to these."

They pondered but needed to confer. "Hang on one sec, Kyle," Kate requested and put him on mute.

"We can have White House authorize a task force under Treasury," the director said.

She took him off mute.

"Kyle, where are you now?"

"Hospital, downtown New York, with a bunch of feds," Kyle replied.

"Kyle, have the FBI take you back to 26 Federal. We'll get this Shirin over there, too. You guys can set up there. We'll talk to Treasury and have someone meet you at 26 Federal, OK?"

"Yup, I got it. Thank you."

They hung up.

The director checked his watch. His admin chimed onto one of his lines, and he put her through.

"Director, motorcade is waiting."

NYU Downtown Hospital, Gold Street

Kyle hung up and raised his eyebrows to Pete indicating they were on. In the hallway, the lead agent was already beckoning, *let's go*, with a field officer in tactical gear next to him.

"Let me see Amy, first," Kyle said as he hustled back into her room.

Inside, Kyle watched Amy's chest rise and fall with her breathing as he sat on her bed. He stroked her cheek. "I'm sorry all this happened. We'll get through it. I have an idea," Kyle whispered to her.

Kyle gripped her hand as she lay there. He kissed her forehead and exited her room, nodding a *thank you* to her NYPD guards. Kyle and Pete, two FBI agents, and two tactical agents with long guns entered the elevator and descended.

The six of them boarded an FBI SUV in the hospital's garage and drove up the ramp onto Gold Street where the hospital was.

"No, don't go that way—Brooklyn Bridge traffic. Swing around the block and go up Beekman," the first agent said to the second, who was driving.

The driver steered the SUV around the block, as Kyle gazed out the window and checked his watch.

"Shirin meeting us there?" Pete asked.

"Yeah, FBI's picking her up. I hope she's OK. I haven't talked to her since we were almost killed. She's probably still freaked out," Kyle worried.

The SUV's lights and sirens flared as it weaved and sped through the nighttime traffic. It slowed down at an intersection to ensure it didn't hit any crossing vehicles. Two motorcycles pulled alongside them, one on either side, as the SUV slowed through the intersection.

Kyle watched the bikes with sudden attention, as did the tactical agents. Motorcycles were frequent terrorist assassination instruments because of their agility in traffic. The motorcycles sped up and accelerated past them as the SUV glided through the intersection. Kyle breathed a sigh of relief.

They were halfway to Federal Plaza, about to turn onto Church Street. The windshield popped open with a bullet hole, and then another and another. Bullets struck the driver. He slumped against the dash. The SUV careened to the left.

"Brace!" someone shouted out. The tactical agent in the front seat grabbed the wheel and stabilized the SUV and rocked it back onto four wheels.

"Get down!" the agent in the back yelled, forcing Kyle and Pete to the floor.

"Where is he? Where's the target?" one of the tactical agents shouted.

"Is he down?" an agent shouted about the wounded driver.

"Get him out of the seat!" another yelled. The tactical agent in the front pulled the driver out and shoved him into the passenger seat. He was unconscious and bleeding. The agent squeezed into the driver's seat as the pings of more shots hitting the SUV's grill and hood rang out.

The tactical agents were armored, with helmets and ballistic vests. The agent now driving floored it, and the SUV took off, lurching onto the straightaway.

"Where the fuck is he?" the driver shouted.

"Just drive!" another agent yelled.

"Son of a bitch! They're shooting at us!" Pete yelled to Kyle from the floor.

"Stay down," Kyle shouted back at Pete.

Kyle peered above him at the tactical agent driving and at the wounded agent slumped in the passenger seat. He spied a Colt M4 Carbine resting by the wounded agent.

The driver's side window exploded as bullets ripped across the broadside of the SUV. The driver clutched his left arm and screamed out in pain.

"I'm hit. Goddamn it!"

The SUV swerved again as the driver tried to control it at high speed with one arm. They struck a compact and then sideswiped a van. Out of control, they caromed across the road, rotating a half spin, and slammed into a short median wall. The SUV rolled onto its side and skidded to a halt down another block.

Everyone inside was thrown to the right and sandwiched against the side doors of the SUV as the side became the floor and scraped and screeched to a stop. A second of silence, all stunned, in shock. Kyle's eyes blinked open. He could feel his head hurting and his shoulder felt dislocated.

"Hey?" Kyle cried out. "Everyone OK?"

There was no response. He heard voices outside the SUV.

"Holy shit, get an ambulance!" someone yelled, and then the gunfire returned. Loud, concussive reports of automatic weapons strafing. The few bystanders screamed and ran. Slugs exploded, impacting the undercarriage of the SUV, which was now perpendicular to the street.

Kyle realized the attacker was running toward them. He couldn't see much. There were bodies on top of him. He pushed one agent off him. Kyle hoisted himself to a crouch. He found Pete. He was coming to. Kyle slapped him a bit to bring him along.

"Stay down," Kyle instructed.

Pete was woozy but appeared to comprehend. Kyle recalled where the special weapons agent laid down his Colt M4. It had dropped somewhere when the vehicle rolled. Kyle searched for it. He groped with his hands, prodding anything that resembled a rifle.

He heard footsteps outside striking the pavement, growing louder, closer. More shots rang out, clanging the undercarriage and ripping into the transmission. The other agents started coming to.

"What the fu—"

Kyle touched what felt like the cold muzzle of a long gun. He gripped it and hefted it up, rolling over one of the agents who was draped on it. Kyle wrenched the gun free. He looked above him—the left side of the SUV was now the roof. Kyle rammed the barrel into the windowpane. It shattered, raining glass bits on top of them. He hoisted himself out of the window opening, rifle first.

He saw the Hawk-Nosed Man bearing down on them, about thirty yards away, an AK in his hands. Kyle steadied on the roof of the SUV and, *click*—safety! Shit, these motherfuckers had it on safety. He pressed in the safety latch, and—*k-k-k-k-k!*—sent a burst of rounds at the Hawk-Nosed Man.

Kyle ducked back inside, waiting for return fire. The Hawk-Nosed Man got off a burst. The shots were grounders. The bullets sparked off the pavement, flashes on the nighttime street, and punched into the underside of the SUV.

Kyle rose out through the window opening again and fired. More accurate shots this time, the volley whizzed by the Hawk-Nosed Man's shoulder and, *crack*! The Hawk-Nosed Man's AK splintered apart before him. One of Kyle's bullets had struck the breech and shattered it.

The Hawk-Nosed Man was stunned for a moment. He eyed the fragments of weapon in his grip. He looked up, panicked. Kyle gripped and steadied for another burst. The Hawk-Nosed Man leapt off the street, over the rock wall, and sprinted up the adjacent road. Kyle lost him behind the edge of the block's corner building.

Sirens swarmed them as NYPD and ambulances arrived. Kyle heaved open the left-side SUV door, and helped officers climb onto the SUV to pull everyone out of the vehicle.

FBI New York Field Office, 26 Federal Plaza

Pete sat at a long twenty-seat table in a conference room holding an ice pack to the back of his neck. An FBI aide brought him a cup of coffee.

"How you feeling?" Kyle asked him.

Pete scoffed at first.

"I'm not injured, thanks," he finally replied and then asked, "Did we get the son of a bitch?"

One of the FBI agents who drove with them answered. "He escaped."

Kyle added, "They'll find him. Everybody's looking for him."

Shirin, who was sitting at the long table with them, interjected with some ire.

"Who is that guy? Needs to be caught and—" she spat, stopping herself before she said something nasty.

"Terrorist hit man. We have an agency-wide BOLO on him," another of the agents answered.

Agent Nunes, the most senior agent from Kyle's original interview, was in the conference room with them. Kyle and Pete also noticed there were a bunch of new faces sitting around the table, all with wide, stern eyes trained on Kyle. Agent Nunes spoke up.

"Kyle, these people are going to help you out. They're part of an emergency task force under the US Treasury Department." Agent Nunes indicated each person as he introduced them. "Steve, head of the Markets Desk at the New York Federal Reserve; Kacie, also from the New York Fed, Central Bank and International Account Services; Abby, from Treasury, TFI, Terrorism and Financial Intelligence; Nitin, from Treasury, TFFC, Office of Terrorist Finance and Financial Crimes; And lastly, Jon and Terra, both from Treasury, OIA, Office of Intelligence and Analysis," Agent Nunes paused. Kyle and Pete gave a *hello* nod to each of them. "They've all been briefed, and they all have authorization from the top to help you and give you whatever you need. They also have all the requisite clearances, so don't filter anything you need to say." Agent Nunes moved toward the back of the room.

Kyle's eyes followed his. He noticed there were PCs and monitors arranged with a stack of encrypted laptops at the other end of the conference room table.

"We set you up in here. You should have access to the main Treasury and Federal Reserve databases." He motioned to all the computers. "Let us know ASAP if you need anything or hit any snags," he finished.

Kyle and Pete regarded Agent Nunes and the Treasury and NY Fed teams, and then Shirin, and all the computers. Shirin was already up, walking to the far end of the table.

"We can't waste a second." Kyle got up and joined Shirin.

Joint Tactical Operations, Department of Homeland Security, Washington, DC, United States

The CIA team arrived at a sprawling, arena-size control center. Arrayed throughout were operators and analysts seated at eight banks of consoles, all facing twenty immense overhead monitors projecting a multitude of live data—everything from the status of the nation's electricity grid to run-time blotters of local police reports coming in from different municipalities around the country to grids of dozens of live television broadcasts from all over the world.

A tall figure approached the CIA contingent. He was dressed in a dark-blue uniform, with all the brass and accolades of the United States Navy.

"I'm Rear Admiral Beringer, undersecretary for tactical response... Kate, Bob," the admiral introduced himself and shook their hands and then turned toward the large operations center, his arm in a broad, circular motion over it all. "Welcome to Omaha," he presented.

Since the Department of Homeland Security was formed in 2003, their headquarters had emerged in this byzantine complex on Nebraska Avenue. Members had nicknamed it Omaha, in part for Omaha, Nebraska, and in part for Omaha Beach on D-Day, as it was *the* new beachhead in the War on Terror.

Beringer swung back to them and started to point to different sections around the operations floor.

"FBI and local law enforcement there, all mobilized, hunting for this bastard killer and anyone else on the ground." He motioned to a bustling group closest to the monitors. "Next up, Secret Service working to get VIPs in DC to safe, undisclosed locations." He rotated to another section. "Here, national communications system and infrastructure protection. And there, the Nuclear Incident Response Team, along with FEMA, getting ready for it," he said with sobering gravity. Lastly, he pointed to: "And you already know the busiest, the NNSA, they're out there looking for it, this moment."

Beringer walked them over to a section with empty seats. "Langley team, you're here. You're working to find the fucking owners of this thing, and anything international. It's all configured for you," Beringer informed and then finished, "I'm right here, I'm also the tallest jerk on the floor. Come get me with whatever you need." And then he looked them in the eyes, "And with whatever you find."

Beringer returned to his seat, a tall perch, rather like a ship captain's chair that was elevated and could swivel around with line of sight to anyone in the space.

The CIA team dispersed into their section, grabbing seats and logging on to their terminals. Kate sat down and drew in a deep breath as she got oriented to this environment, and her computer, a bit uncomfortable, but she didn't care. She yelled out to her team, "Any update from Kyle in New York?"

A Treasury Department liaison from a nearby section answered her, "They're just getting started."

She didn't reply, simply waved back and leaned to Sarah, seated next to her. "Make sure we get the locations behind any accounts they find suspicious or linked to any of the trading that they see, got it? We need leads to where al-Hammadi or this *Sully* might be."

Across the floor, Brent Lowry from the NNSA called out, "Admiral, Miami's ready to sweep."

"Do it. Stop talking to me and get those birds up there," Beringer yelled back.

Some of the monitors flickered to overhead shots of Miami. Peripheral screens displayed the downtowns of the other selected cities. Beringer demanded, "Brent, status on other targets."

One of Brent's logistics engineers shouted back, "Still mobilizing, another couple of hours."

"Move it. We only have hours here."

"Yes, sir," they responded in unison.

Beringer swung back toward Brent and the NNSA desk and commanded, "Let's go to Miami."

Miami International Airport, Miami, United States

Two Sikorsky helicopters, each with mounted detector pods on their landing skids, blades buzzing, lifted into the night air over Miami. Once at altitude of a few thousand feet, the lead helo swung around and flew north. Its partner sprinted south as they divided up the city.

Inside the first helo, a radionuclide physicist, squished in with two other scientists, pushed his laptop screen as far back as it would go against the pilot seat in front of him. On his monitor was a glowing green Aerial Measuring System (AMS) map of Miami. It displayed hued contours that represented the changes in background radiation of the neighborhoods below. The radioactivity measurement units were in mR/hr (Milliroentgen per Hour).

Most of the Miami background AMS map registered about eight to twelve mR/hr—an actual reading was 0.008, but physicists quoted it as "eight," which was illuminated on the map in a bright-green color. In certain spots, usually where there was more concentrated bedrock (rare in Miami), or collections of buildings that utilized terra-cotta roofing tiles (a lot in Miami), the background color would be in the twelve to fifteen, or even eighteen, mR/hr levels, which was rendered as a mustard-yellow color.

A radioactive source, the kind they are looking for, jumps to levels in the sixty mR/hr range, or even a hundred and into the hundreds very quickly. Those levels would appear as orange and deep-red zones. If they got a red or orange hit, it didn't necessarily mean it was *the* target, as there were many false positives, such as hospitals, with radiological equipment, or other legitimate industrial radioactive sources, that could trigger a higher return. Usually, those civilian sources had been established from the AMS mapping exercise, unless they were new, which would then need on-the-ground verification.

The first helicopter banked east and began raking a grid pattern over southern Miami. Their stretch was the area from Kendall, and then up and east to Miami Beach. The second helo would scan from that parallel up to Fort Lauderdale.

The physicist looked down at his screen. Already, there was a glowing orange-red spot forming in the Coral Gables neighborhood.

"Hey, *hey*?"

"What do you got?" the lead technician crammed in next to him asked.

He tilted his laptop screen to him and tapped the red spot. The tech shouted to the pilot and navigator.

"A hit in Coral Gables, not on the AMS map."

The helicopter plunged a thousand feet and arced over the Coral Gables neighborhood, swooping in for a closer reading.

The physicist watched the numbers as they bounced and steadied into time-weighted averages of the mR/hr readings. His screen painted mostly green all over—acceptable levels. He enlarged his real-time readings over the AMS map, squinting at the colorations. He shook his head *no*.

"False reading. There's nothing here," he shouted.

The technician tapped the pilot and motioned with his thumb skyward. The pilot took the helicopter back up a few thousand feet. The helo banked again and resumed its sweeping pattern, back and forth, up and down, over southern Miami.

FBI New York Field Office, 26 Federal Plaza

Kyle directed the team of Treasury Department and Federal Reserve analysts and data programmers. They now had access to all the trades of major money center banks and clearinghouses. They could see everything, along with all exchange-traded data, the only exception being OTC option trades done very recently and not yet submitted into clearing systems.

"Start with all public exchange data. If we can get anything from this set without going into the OTC world, all the better," Kyle charged. "What we're looking for are statistical anomalies versus historical averages. We're going to concentrate on equities and their options. Outlier option volumes will stick out in less liquid names a lot more than liquid names."

Abby raised her hand. "Abby, just yell it out."

She dropped her hand and asked, "Give us an example, so we can write the sequel—so we can write the code—in the best way."

Sequel, which was the pronunciation for SQL, or Structured Query Language, was the lingua franca of the database world. All major database systems used or understood SQL and its respective queries.

"Let's say they put the bomb in Detroit. The terrorists might have purchased puts on the major auto companies, like Ford and GM. We would want to look at the average daily volume of put options on Ford and GM, and then look to see if recent put volume exceeded those averages," Kyle explained.

"So how many of these equities with options are there?"

"Probably about three thousand," Shirin replied.

The analysts appeared stressed at that. Shirin began circulating to assist.

"We can divvy it up. Here's a list of all the optionable stocks—companies that have options on them," she started. "We each take about five hundred to start, and then we can pull them together. I can help with the sequel."

She distributed the lists, and they delved in.

Kyle and Pete walked to Steve and Kacie, the Federal Reserve team. Steve was the head of the Federal Reserve's Markets Desk, and a former quant trader himself. The Markets Desk was responsible for transactionally implementing Fed policy in the open markets—the actual buying and selling of US treasuries, futures, mortgage-backed securities, or others to add or subtract liquidity from the marketplace. Kacie was an accountant at the Fed and had access to all major banks reporting their OTC deals.

"You're going to do something similar, looking at the trades at banks. We want to find any sudden change in trading in particular stocks, like, if the Lehman trading desk usually doesn't trade a lot of Home Depot options, but then suddenly traded a ton in the last month or so, we want to see that."

Steve grasped it quickly. "And we want both listed and OTC trades?"

"OTC, especially," Pete told him as Steve and Kacie dove into their laptops.

Pete pulled Kyle over to a quieter section of the room.

"It's about midnight," Pete said. "The doctor said I needed to sleep, but I'm not, cuz I know the long-term damage is worth it if we figure this out. But I need some alcohol."

"If you want to drink now, I know you're feeling better…this is such a long shot, I don't know if we can even pull this off," Kyle admitted.

"Shit, we gotta try something," Pete encouraged. "Plus—if Sully is involved in this shit, he'd be trading as many names as he could." Pete sat, his expression taking him elsewhere. "Let's play some things out. Let's say it *is* him—"

"Are we saying it's him?"

"I don't know, but it strangely makes more sense than the alternative."

"True."

"Plus, if Sully is involved, it could help us. Let's think like him. Nobody knows his trading style more than you, Springer."

"No, I agree."

"If you were a goddamned wicked evil motherfucker planning all this, what would you do? How would you set this up? What time is this all going down?"

Kyle paused, in thought, reflecting, understanding Pete's questions.

"I see where you're going with this. There's some practical reality to this thing, some thinking and planning." Kyle and Pete continued thinking out loud. "He can't wait too long, can he? The bomb would have to go off pretty early. Markets have to open, so after nine thirty Eastern. And then he wouldn't want it too late, not too close to the close, cuz—"

"He wouldn't get the real bang out of the moves," Pete finished his sentence.

"Especially on an expiration Friday."

"On a *triple witch* expiration Friday."

"And we have to assume the exchanges would halt very quickly after the detonation. He wouldn't be able to trade out or realize any gains that quickly. He'd want to lock in the spectacular plunge, first."

"So, bomb goes off—I can't believe I'm saying this—there's a delay because people don't know what's really going on, but it gets reported, gets into the system in a few seconds, markets collapse—"

"Markets collapse."

"And then they either hit exchange circuit breakers or the feds halt trading."

"That's a narrow window to get everything traded out, a few minutes at best."

"He'll probably have his orders ready."

"All his OTC stuff will have to pay out, legally, financially settled, with the opposing banks. So, he's not going to be worried about those."

"No, it'll be the listeds—equities, options, futures, treasuries—he'll try to realize as much gain as he possibly can before the door gets shut on him."

"And that probably means he triggers the thing before noon."

"Sometime late morning, exactly. That's his window."

"That gives him enough time. He trades the open, prices move around. There'll be the usual positioning and gamma trading ahead of expiration. Triple witch after a Fed lower, liquidity will be great—shit, he really thought this through, probably picked the best month to pull this off." Kyle paused and processed for a moment. "The more we work this out, the more it feels like Sully if you think about the setup. Shit."

"You *see*? Yes, just after Fed, active September trading, lots of hedging unwinds and positioning, a ton of liquidity. That fucking bastard."

"We get a froth of trading going before everyone goes to lunch, then things slow down a bit, and he blows it."

"Markets crater."

"He exits his shorts, locks in his puts, and he's done."

"And then things shut down, and the world's suddenly different."

"And he's up thirty billion."

They both came to the objective conclusion in their out-loud thinking.

Kyle had a sarcastic but satisfied grin. "You come up with all this on your own? We should give you a concussion more often."

"Hey, we've got the first list, here," Nitin interrupted, calling to them.

Kyle and Pete looked to see Shirin also waving them over. They approached and stooped to view Nitin's screen. There was a list of a couple dozen stocks.

Shirin pointed to them. "All these had a two hundred percent or greater put volume in the last month versus the average of the previous year," she detailed.

"That's good, that's a good filter," Pete figured.

Kyle read over the list of names. His brow wrinkled a bit.

"I don't see a pattern. Big-cap companies, small-cap companies, tech, industrial, consumer cyclical, some oil companies based in Houston, a paper company based in Pennsylvania. What's this telling us?" Kyle rubbed his cheek in thought, at a loss.

Shirin reminded him. "We need to do all three thousand stocks. This is only the first batch, and then we can compare these baskets. Some of these could be telling us something, but without statistical confirmation from the whole population, we can't say. But thirty companies down from five hundred is a good set size to work with. If we get that many from each batch of five hundred, we're in good shape. That will be a much easier population to deal with."

"Second set, let's go, let's go!" Abby, the Supervisory Financial Analyst from TFI, badgered the group.

Joint Tactical Operations

"Kate? Bob? Get over here." Sarah and Dr. Ahn beckoned with anxious gestures. Sarah displayed security camera footage from the corporate air terminal in HKI.

"Hong Kong International gave us the tapes from their security cameras," Sarah announced.

"Took us a while to digitize them. We have the twenty-four hours before and after Amir's arrival, but look at this," Dr. Ahn motioned to Sarah's screen displaying a replay of the sequences.

"This is from about two hours before the taller brother and our team arrive."

"Two hours *before*." Bob stomped his foot, shaking his head in consternation.

"Here, slow it down."

The view on screen was from the camera covering the business terminal's main entrance. In grainy, striped video, the shorter brother, Farouk, appears, dragging two large cases behind him.

"Shit, is that him?" Kate cried.

"*Two* cases?"

Dr. Ahn affirmed, and the video continued. The limited footage showed the shorter brother approaching security and queueing. He then disappears out of the camera's range, exiting onto the tarmac.

"That's two cases—*two* cases. Am I seeing that right?"

"Yes, two, so more confirmation this one has the *actual* warhead."

"Shit."

"And we saw no sign of him when we tagged the taller brother?"

"No. And based on his path through the terminal, appears he flew before."

"That narrows the number of possible flights he could be on."

"This is where somebody tells me we're getting the manifests of all the aircraft that departed in this time window." Bob glared at the team.

Room, Somewhere

Inside a plain, dimly lit room with unpolished wooden floors stood a sturdy, four-legged dining table. On the table was a large spherical device, about three feet in diameter. It was encased in a machined, matte aluminum shell that appeared to be assembled from sectionals, eighths of a sphere. Each sectional was edged by a flange that fit flush with its adjacent sectional. The flanges were tightly fastened to each other with bolts and wing nuts.

Terminating in an electrical contact on the external surface of each sectional were wires that fed into a central control box on the table. The box was about four inches by four inches with three plastic buttons and a metal toggle switch on its face. There was also a thin master switch on the base of the sphere with a digital display and a short black antenna.

Scattered around the table was a mess of tools, screwdrivers, pry bars, drills, glue guns, pliers, wire cutters, a claw hammer, lots of pieces of cut wire, and discarded foam packing material. Two opened and emptied carrying cases lay on the floor behind the table.

The room was otherwise bare. There was a single door, shut, and there was one window with its blinds closed. Little to no light came in from outside. The room was lit only by a small desk lamp on the table, casting its cone of light across the room and projecting dusky shadows of the sphere onto the floor.

Across from the table was a metal fold-out chair. And in front of the chair, on a short prayer rug, the missing Syrian brother was prostrated with his forehead on the wood floor. He rose, whispering prayers, and bowed again, his warped shadow lunging across the walls...

FBI New York Field Office, 26 Federal Plaza

"Where's the next set? Where is it? How many names?" Kyle demanded.

The team banged away at their keyboards.

"Here, here!" Kacie yelled out.

"Looks like about twelve names, twelve companies," Nitin tabulated.

"That makes about forty-two, total?"

"Any patterns?" Kyle pressed.

Shirin assembled both lists. She shook her head *no*. "Doesn't look like it, not yet. Need more names. Still too broad of a cross section," she said.

"Next set, come on, come on!" Kyle clapped. "We've got a thousand done, still two thousand to go."

Kyle turned to Steve and Kacie, and Terra, who was now helping them. "How we doing over here?"

Terra didn't look up, she kept keyboarding. "Trying. Nothing yet. The data's a mess. Banks have no standards reporting their OTC trades. I have to clean it all first and then compile," she complained. Steve and Kacie were nose in, too.

Kyle eyed his watch: twelve thirty a.m. Pete stared at him, on edge.

Joint Tactical Operations

"Come on, flight logs!" Kate shouted at Sarah and company.

Sarah gave her a *thumbs down* in response.

Frustrated, Kate swiveled back to Bob. "What about all of al-Hammadi's locations? Who's looking into those?"

"Kazemi—"

"Hey?" Kate shouted at Paul before Bob could finish his sentence. She waved him over. Kazemi and another officer came up to her.

"Al-Hammadi's locations?"

"We're still scouring dozens of—he's got offices, palaces, villas, mansions, apartments. They're all over the Middle East, Europe, the UK, but we need to get eyes on the ground at each, and we need to do it almost simultaneously, so he doesn't move from one to the other," he fussed.

"Any of our friends helping us?"

"Everybody, everybody's helping; Mossad, the Saudis, we've got MI6, BND. We thought we had him in a penthouse in the Czech Republic. They stormed it, and it was empty. He's gotta be somewhere," he tallied.

"We need to get him in the next twelve hours," Kate said directly.

"I *know* that," Kazemi shot back and skulked to his console.

"And nothing from New York yet?" Bob asked Kate.

"Not that I've heard. It's a long shot, anyway. But we need irons in as many fires as we can get. And the NEST teams are zeroes so far." She looked over at Beringer and the sprawling AMS maps of cities on the projection screens.

FBI New York Field Office, 26 Federal Plaza

"I got something!" Terra yelled to Kyle as Pete arrived gripping a bunch of coffees for everyone. He passed them out and joined Kyle by Terra, Kacie, and Steve.

"I got a list of about a hundred names. These are all stocks that had large OTC put trades on them with the major trading houses. I don't really see a pattern, though," she said with some distress.

Kyle and Pete visually scanned the list of stock tickers and company names.

"You see anything?" Kyle asked Pete, who shook his head. "No, pretty broad list, too. Nothing common I can see."

"Save this. We might be able to cross-reference against later," Kyle requested.

"Accounts," Pete reminded Kyle.

"Yes—can you see the accounts behind all those trades?"

"We can get that, yeah. It'll be about a few dozen probably. But I can find that. Give me a few," Kacie offered.

"Thanks," Kyle encouraged them and prompted the Treasury crew, *"Hey?"*

"We got next set. There's like forty names from this batch," Abby said.

"What does that make, total?"

"About eighty now. Eighty-two, to be exact."

"Dang, that's too many. We need fewer names, not more."

"Shirin?"

Shirin shrugged her shoulders, furiously banging on her keyboard.

"No, no real commonality, maybe a slight bias to large caps in this latest set, but, still pretty vague. Jon's running them against fundamental databases, see if there's anything we're not seeing," Shirin reported, not looking up.

Sky Over Miami, South Florida, United States

Inside the second NEST helo, the one covering the northern half of the Miami-Dade area, physicists monitored real-time streaming data from the ground below. The lead tech was consistently getting measurements in the nine to fifteen mR/hr range—all normal background readings.

"I've got nothing over background," he reported to the lead physicist. He nudged the navigator and gave him the *cut it* signal.

The navigator got on the radio. "This is Miami-two, we've found nothing above regular background, copy?"

An NNSA rep from Joint Tactical Operations replied over radio, "Copy that, stand down. Return to MIA. We need the equipment in Chicago ASAP."

"Copy," the navigator replied and signed for his pilot to take it down.

Joint Tactical Operations

Brent Lowry rose and reported to Beringer.

"Admiral, Miami's negative. We're starting on New York City."

"What about Chicago and LA?" Beringer demanded.

"The Miami team is headed to Chicago. They'll be there in a few hours. LA, we've had some equipment trouble. We're having a late start, behind schedule."

"Hurry the hell up, those are all big cities. A lot of people."

"Yes, sir."

Sarah ran up to Kate and Bob with a printed list in her hand.

"We have the destination logs from Hong Kong International. There are thirty-seven cities on it. It might not help us, I'm afraid."

"Thirty-seven?"

Kate snatched it and read the list of cities out loud. "New York, Shanghai, Chicago, Los Angeles, Tokyo, Los Angeles, New York, London, Beijing, Beijing, Dubai, Singapore, London, Sydney, Tokyo, Beijing—shit." She didn't even finish reading the list, just tossed it back to Sarah.

"We're really fucked if it went to Europe, you know?" She looked at Bob with an almost hapless expression before replying to Sarah.

"Miami's not on that list. At least it agrees with us ruling out Miami." Kate chuckled morbidly.

"Keep that on hand. We may need to refer to it again," Bob reminded her.

"This is giving me a big fucking headache," Kate said.

Sky Over Manhattan, New York, United States

A Sikorsky helicopter with the mounted detector pods swung over the mash of skyscrapers and building canyons of midtown Manhattan and leveled out into a north-south beeline. A second Sikorsky shadowed the first, but from a lower altitude, and from an offset distance of a few thousand feet.

Inside the lead helo, a NEST tech monitored his laptop, surveying the readings versus background levels. The baseline AMS for New York City was higher than most cities, as there were more naturally occurring sources of radiation, typically in the fifteen to twenty mR/hr range.

New York was also a complex city to scan and monitor. Not only was there a great deal of stonework in the building facades, which was a source of naturally occurring radiation, but there was also the more difficult aspect that a simple overhead scan—how the team scanned Miami and D.C.—was not possible. A sixty-story building would only register the readings of the upper floors from an overhead perspective, which frustratingly masked the lower floors.

The NEST teams had to instead use a technique that combined overhead scanning with side scanning, which was why two helos had to do the sweeps simultaneously. To deal with the height, there were also multiple teams on the ground in specialized vans driving up and down the avenues. Those teams would perform independent ground-level sweeps. The ground teams also had the challenging task of scanning the New York City subway system, as the terrorists could easily stage it in one of the tunnels. New York would take a while.

"Tell the pilots of NY2 to keep their eyes on the buildings. Don't crash, that won't help us at all," the tech called out to his navigator.

He squinted at his laptop balanced on his knees as he watched the green, CAD-like, wire-frame 3D image of New York City.

"Starting scan."

Inside a nondescript dark-blue van trolling downtown NYC, two NEST techs sat in the rear, monitoring their own ground-level readings. Their driver announced over his shoulder.

"Yo, I'm on the grid. We're going into Battery Park City now," he said.

"Got it," the first tech replied, not looking up from his laptop.

Battery Park City was a residential neighborhood in Manhattan, but also headquartered a number of major banks. And it was where Kyle lived, and the Fortnum Bank office was only a few blocks north of Battery Park. That area, along with the Federal Reserve of New York building in the Financial District nearby, made Lower Manhattan a prime target. They had to scan it slowly and thoroughly.

"*Hey?* Wha-what's that?" the first tech noticed, showing the orange highlight in an area of Battery Park City as they rolled by.

"Slow down here," he shouted at their driver, who let up on the gas.

The van slowed to a coast. The techs scrutinized the digital profile of what appeared to be a parking area amid residential apartment buildings.

"I see it, elevated readings. What is that?"

They both stared at the digital rendering of a parking area in front of a high-rise. The lot was blazing orange where cars were parked along a curved part of a private neighborhood access road.

"Stop, *stop*," the lead tech begged the driver. "I want to get out and look at this. You think this thing could be in a car?"

"Let's check it out," the second tech agreed.

The van braked. The techs jumped out the rear doors, waving handheld detectors. There was a set of stairs that led up to where the cars were parked. As they ascended, their detectors blazed out max.

"Over sixty here."

"Me, too."

"That might not be high enough for fissile material, but still."

"What is this?" the first tech asked, tapping on the solid stair wall.

It was dark so it was difficult to see the material that the stepped landing was built from. The first tech removed a penlight and illuminated the wall. An almost mirrored, marble-like sheen lit up their faces.

"Fuck! I knew it."

"What?"

"Son of a bitch! This triggers a lot."

"What is it?"

"Rose granite, full of uranium. Goddamn it. Must be new, it's not on the background scans. Shiiit."

The techs hastily scanned the cars behind the rose-granite wall just to confirm it was, in fact, a false positive and hustled back to their van to resume their sweep.

FBI New York Field Office, 26 Federal Plaza

"We're up to two thousand now," Nitin called out.

"How many filtered?"

"About one fifty."

"Is that enough?" Kyle looked to Shirin.

"That's enough, yeah. Send me the list. We should be able to find patterns from this group now."

One of them hurriedly emailed Shirin the list. Shirin ran the filtered columns of stock tickers through their fundamental databases to match geographic commonalities. The results emerged on her screen. "Dang it! I'm not seeing anything. They're all over the place, *still*. Mostly big-cap companies," she carped.

"Maybe it's not here at all. Maybe we're looking for nothing," Pete said what nobody wanted to contemplate.

"I don't believe that. There's gotta be some fingerprint," Kyle rebutted.

Kyle paced uneasily, trying to keep to an uninhibited train of thought. "We need to narrow the list more. Can we filter by, like, way out of the money put trades? The bigger, the better."

"We don't have that time," Abby complained.

"We have to keep trying—anything!" Jon parried.

Shirin, ignoring the bubbling frustration in the room, kept clattering on her keyboard, her brown eyes through her green glasses laser sharp on her screen.

"Shut up, people. I can try something like that. Hang on," she said, entering commands into her editor and waiting the few seconds for the result set.

"Yes—brought it down to like, a hundred." But she shook her head. "Still a lot that don't make sense, though. Like, here's 3M…"

"3M's in Minnesota. Hard to believe they'd attack there."

"What else?"

"I don't know, another one is AT&T."

"Where's AT&T's headquarters? Or their operations center?"

Shirin banged in a few commands to retrieve. "Uh, looks like Dallas, Texas."

"Shit, *Dallas*? Dallas could be a target."

They all exchanged fearful looks they'd missed something.

"I wouldn't rule it out."

They helicoptered over Shirin.

"How many other Dallas-based companies?" Kacie demanded.

Shirin beat out more commands, and then replied after a collectively held breath. "None, that's the only one."

The group dissipated with some relief. Kyle resumed his laps around the long conference table.

"Dallas is unlikely, then."

"They're probably buying those because it's part of the broader economy, if it's even them," Pete pointed out. "It's a distraction for us to look at it."

"And you're running these against headquarters locations?"

"Maybe we could try the reverse—query a city and see how many of this set come up," Terra suggested.

Shirin listened to them.

"Or maybe this is too blunt a query, looking at the cities. I mean, these companies have operations everywhere. They could have headquarters in one city that's just a bunch of suits, but their manufacturing and real valuable operations are somewhere else," Steve said.

"That's true, I agree, but I keep coming back to the perception. The reality, yes, but the trade will be against the perception. That always does the most damage," Kyle said.

There was a collective pause as they all thought. Pete then interrupted.

"Let's try Terra's idea though—let's try New York," he urged.

"How many in New York?"

Shirin quickly tapped away and stared at the screen as it logged the results.

"There are a few, but not many. Same with Los Angeles, only a handful, and those companies aren't very big, either. Small market caps, internet companies, a few others," she reported.

"I think you're right, we still need to cull the names, then," Kyle said, trying to get everyone back onto their original method.

Kyle craned to see Terra. "Terra? Send your list now. Let's compare what you have, take the intersection."

Terra emailed her list to Shirin, who uploaded it and then pasted the names into spreadsheet columns and sorted the combined lists to isolate the differences.

"That helped. With the block trade filter from the OTC accounts, we're now down to about thirty companies with huge put trades on them."

The group regathered around Shirin.

"Good, that's good, who do we have now? Just read them out," Kyle pressed, dabbing the sweat from his face.

"Still looks like a random list, uh...Chevron?"

They shrugged their shoulders.

"Oil company, I don't know. Go on..."

"Another is Wells Fargo."

She paused. The group blankly looked at each other.

"A bank, what else?"

"Cisco Systems...Yahoo...Google?"

Kyle turned away, frustrated, searching the walls and ceiling.

"I'm not seeing it," he implored them.

Nitin then said, almost electronically, "Those are all Bay Area companies."

Everyone turned to Nitin. Nitin looked back at them and added, "I used to work for a dot-com in the Bay Area. You know, San—"

"San Francisco!" everyone shouted.

Kyle lunged for his cell phone—

Joint Tactical Operations

Kate, with phone in hand, furiously swatted at Sarah.

"What, *what*?" Sarah looked at her, confused.

"Give me—where's that flight list—out of Hong Kong?" Kate desperately demanded, still holding the phone to her chest.

"It's here. What do you want from it?"

"Is there a San Francisco area airport on there?"

Sarah flattened her eyes to the list and drew her finger down the column of three-letter airport codes and times.

"Yes—*yes*! Right here, SFO, San Fran International. In the window, too—"

Sarah stopped herself. She glanced up at Bob, who shot a look at Kate.

"Holy shit!" Bob exclaimed.

"Admiral?" they yelled.

Beringer barely had time to look when shouts of "San Francisco!" erupted from the CIA team.

"You gotta be kidding me?!" Beringer exclaimed.

In less than a second, half the center had turned to face Beringer, and the active din suddenly hushed. The conviction and the urgency in the CIA team voices only further confirmed it.

Beringer swiveled to all the massive screens in front of him. His eyes reviewed each one, New York, Chicago, Miami, Los Angeles, there was nothing geographically close to northern California.

"Son of a bitch!" Beringer yelled, his call echoing to every corner of the control center. Then he ordered, "All assets to Bay Area, full stop!"

DOE and NNSA officers thronged the admiral.

"Sir, my closest teams are scattered over Los Angeles—it's going to take us"—Brent referred to his watch and quickly calculated—"four hours to get them over there!"

"Just get 'em there! As fast as you can!" Beringer commanded.

He swiveled to the FBI team. The NNSA and DOE officers scattered back to their stations.

"We need the largest tactical team—" he started and wasn't even able to finish before the lead fed interrupted him.

"It's underway," he replied, already on with local field offices.

Beringer next found the FEMA groups and beckoned an NNSA officer over and then waved for the CIA team. As they encircled him, the admiral started asking the ugly, pointed questions.

"What is the destructive power of this thing?" he asked Bob and Kate.

"Best of our intel, about twenty kilotons, maybe twenty-five."

"What's that translate to, blast radius?" Beringer looked to the NNSA rep.

"About a mile, hard, ground zero, pretty much everything gets wasted, vaporized. Another two to three out, you have severe blast wave, fire and radiation destruction," he listed.

"At full boat, downtown San Fran, what are we talking about?"

The FEMA rep approached, but before they could reply, Beringer ordered his assistants, "And put San Fran up there on the screen."

"We could be looking at—if everyone from their commutes arrives at their jobs—probably half a million casualties, upwards of a million," she started, then continued, "We can work to mitigate—"

An analyst handed them a folded-up map of the San Francisco greater Bay Area. The FEMA rep unfolded it and drew a circle with her finger on the peninsula that was downtown San Francisco.

"San Francisco is sort of like Manhattan, it's a commute city—a lot of people come into work from the surrounding area. We can mitigate casualties by limiting access into the city, here, here, and here." She pointed on the map. "There's the Golden Gate Bridge here, the Bay Bridge here, and then there are several key routes into the city from South San Francisco," she said as she pointed along the map's perimeter.

Beringer studied her and tacitly agreed with a firm nod.

"Not a word of this gets out," he started, looking directly at each of them. "Make it very localized, a road problem here, a temporary closure there, you got it? These are one-way doors. Let them out but don't let them in. It's nighttime now. Get on with the mayor and governor, get their help. It'll be at least until morning commute starts before the media figures out we're staging a coordinated closure," he instructed. "That'll buy us time to work out a way to quietly evacuate the city while our boys search for this fucking thing," Beringer finished. He shooed them off and turned to the NSC (National Security Council) officials.

"Time to wake up the president," he requested and grabbed a telephone handset that was thrust in his face.

FBI New York Field Office, 26 Federal Plaza

Kyle and Pete stood alone in a hallway at FBI headquarters, staring at each other.

Pete broke the silence. "I want to sleep."

Kyle peered down the hall for a moment and back to Pete.

"Remember what we were talking about earlier—Sully's damage window— when he might set this thing off?"

"Yeah?"

"I have an idea. We might be able to help them," Kyle offered.

He opened up his phone. He dialed Kate again.

"Kate? It's Kyle. I have an idea, but I need your help, only you can help get this done," Kyle started and paused, and took a deep breath. "Get me out there, Kate, to San Fran."

Pete shot him a look that he was mad. There was a pause on the other side of the line, but Kyle jumped in before Kate could respond.

"I think I can help you guys. I might be able to stall when this thing could get triggered, which could buy you some time, *if* Sully is behind this thing, or part of it, I know how he thinks. I know how he'll trade this, how he'll set things up to maximize his gains. We can use that to our advantage—*and possibly* manipulate him. But I need to be out there, be on the ground, see the developments with my own eyes so I can know what's real and what's a bluff—and when we can get away with bluffing *him*," Kyle persuaded, and went on with more details. "I need Pete on the Fortnum Bank trading floor with the authorization to use the bank's capital to trade and drive the market in certain directions." Pete shot him another look that he'd gone off the deep end as Kyle pitched all this to Kate.

"We can delay the bad guys, maybe enough to give you time to find the bomb *and them*," Kyle, already on the thinnest limb, finally finished. "But I need to be out there, in communication with you and with Pete on the bank's trading floor."

Kate could be heard responding to him over the phone as Kyle listened intently. "Thank you, yes, got it," he answered her and hung up.

"She's going to speak to some people about it and call us back."

"You're *fucking crazy*, you know that?" Pete lambasted him. "You can't leave it alone. How hard is it? My God, think about Jill, and Amy, and *me*!" Pete yelled.

"I am thinking about them, and everybody else, which is *exactly* why I have to do this."

Kyle held his cell in his hand, watching it. It rang, and he opened it up...

Expiration Friday, September 21, 2007

FBI Department Cessna Citation X, Flying Cross-Country

Kyle awoke with a jolt. He'd been having a nightmare. He was disoriented and, for a moment, didn't know where he was. He peered around. The rushing-air noise of the pressure cabin gradually returned his awareness. The corporate jet's narrow interior was darkened. Others were catching a few winks, too. On the flight with him, were FBI agents and NEST techs who had been with the New York City teams and were now flying out to San Francisco to provide more support.

They were arcing across the country aboard a lightning-fast FBI Cessna Citation X, the fastest civilian aircraft in the government fleet. Kyle checked his watch; it was almost seven a.m. East Coast time. He set it to Pacific time, four a.m. Adjusting his watch also made him realize that they would have a time-zone advantage, which they could leverage. Sully, or whomever else, might not have fully appreciated that when they planned everything, Kyle thought.

For Sully and the bad buys to get the biggest "bang," the optimal time for them to detonate the bomb was late morning East Coast time, like eleven a.m. or eleven thirty, just before traders took their lunchtime break. And Kyle realized, that time frame raised a problem if you were trying to inflict maximal damage on a West Coast city. Late-morning East Coast translated to eight or eight thirty local time, with rush hour underway, but that was also before everyone was in their offices. Kyle knew the 9/11 attacks happened at 8:46 a.m. and then 9:03, the first and second planes hitting the Twin Towers, respectively, and many people, thank God, were still on their way into work. The Pentagon attack happened at 9:37 a.m., and the fourth plane crashed in Pennsylvania at 10:03 a.m., all local time.

If al-Hammadi was trying to replicate an attack in this time frame, in the local time zone, they would be smack in the middle of the lunch break on the East Coast, which would mean fewer hands at the wheel of the markets. And once they crossed that lunchtime period, Sully would have a closing window of opportunity, markets-wise, and would likely start to get more desperate, Kyle calculated.

Kyle had downloaded much of his plan to Kate before he took off. She had been on the phone with the FBI, Homeland Security and Treasury. They had tentatively approved Kyle's plan, and had agreed to get him out to San Francisco, as well as grant him, Pete, and Fortnum Bank all the appropriate legal and financial permissions to utilize firm capital to essentially manipulate the market— under the direct supervision of the US Treasury and Federal Reserve, of course.

Early light reached inside the cabin. They would be landing in half an hour. The FBI counterterror agents started to organize their gear. The NEST techs and scientists conferred with each other, studying maps of San Francisco.

Kyle leaned back in his seat and gazed out the window. He saw the tiny lights below, flickering on as dawn broke and people inside those little homes arose.

Joint Tactical Operations

Joint Tactical Operations was noisy and anxious. A giant digital clock read 7:45 a.m., Washington, DC, local time. Pacific time was 4:45 a.m.

Admiral Beringer helmed from his perch. He read reports as they were handed to him by incoming analysts from the different departments. A giant map of downtown San Francisco was projected on the main monitor. Beringer swiveled in his seat and called out for operational readiness from each of the stations.

"FBI Special Weapons," Beringer started.

"Go," an agent yelled back.

"NEST."

"Go."

"FEMA."

"Go."

"Treasury, Fed, and markets."

"That's a go."

"Eyes in the sky."

"Go."

"Signals."

"Go," the DoD rep yelled back.

Beringer swung back to some of the nearby techs.

"Do we have local video feeds?"

"Not yet, teams are rolling them into place. Another half hour or so."

Over at CIA desk, Kate and Bob were back to pinpointing where al-Hammadi, and possibly Sully, could be. They knew if they could locate them first, they might be able to abort any sort of fissile event, if they were within the control wire.

Kate had a theory she was working. Some of the 9/11 investigators from the FBI teams had told her they were able to trace leads backward in time to determine when they potentially met up with key leadership figures. An effective intelligence technique, sort of like rewinding the video to see if there was a common starting point among all the different players. That's how investigators identified Hamburg, Germany, as a key operational staging point for one of the 9/11 hijack teams. Kate and Bob were following that same technique using, as their leads, the two Syrian brothers and the Hawk-Nosed Man, as well as al-Hammadi's last known locations, and any travel Sully might have done.

"Sarah, Paul...*hello*?" Kate impatiently blared at them.

They scrambled to gather up papers and rushed to Bob and Kate. Dr. Ahn joined them a moment after.

"Looks like an intersection in Tokyo, about six months ago," Sarah began.

"Tokyo?"

"Six months is too far back," Bob criticized.

"Maybe, but we have an interesting crossover there. Both Sully and al-Hammadi were there at the same time. They overlapped by about a week."

Kate and Bob leaned over to see, intrigued.

"That's enough time to interact and to plan everything out."

"It's also geographically proximate to where things began. *If*, in fact, they *are*

252

working together and they did meet up there, it's possible they could have met others there, too, especially some of the North Koreans involved."

Bob looked to Dr. Ahn, who confirmed, "There were several North Korean attachés in Tokyo at that time—including one Colonel Cho, high up in their nuclear program—preps for six-party talks," she added.

"Can't all be a coincidence," Kate noted.

"We talked to Kyle about Sully's visit, too, he remembers it. He said it was a trip for Fortnum Bank to train the Tokyo office derivatives traders. He was there about two weeks."

"Getting warmer. What about vacations or other travel since?"

"Yeah, there's this, about three months ago. All the traders have to take an annual two-week mandatory compliance vacation. They can't come into the office, can't be near it. It's a regulatory thing for that world to see if they're hiding trades or anything like that. Kyle said Sully hung out with them in the evenings on Sully's first week, but then he disappeared the second. He said Sully told them he was visiting his mother in Florida, but he didn't buy it, said they all thought Sully was with a girl. That could have been easy cover for an overseas trip, too."

"*And*, get this, I have a verified sighting of al-Hammadi in Lisbon that week."

"Lisbon?"

"No travel records from Sully to Lisbon?"

Paul shook his head *no*. "But he's a guy of means. He could have slipped the grid and popped over there somehow, borrowed somebody else's passport, gone by water from London or something. Lisbon's not a tight net."

"Easy jump from North Africa, too. Syrians could have made that trek."

"Exactly."

"It's possible Sully never interacted with those guys, more likely al-Hammadi or his henchmen did that."

"And we do have some good intel from the Saudis about these Syrian brothers. Turns out they were in Spain at the same time."

"This is definitely not all random."

"Can't be. Let's narrow the al-Hammadi property search to anything in *that* area, Iberian Peninsula, Western North Africa," Kate ordered, eagerly. "We're gonna find this little fucker."

Her bevy of analysts quickly went back at it.

"Terry, Terry?" Kate pulled Scanlon over.

Terry arrived with an expectant look.

"Keep him moving *west*," Bob ordered. Kate's eyes reinforced the directive.

Fortnum Bank Fixed Income Trading Floor

Pete appraised the rows of trading desks, his eyes searching above the tops of flat-panel monitors. He had an odd feeling. He stood there, almost still, at the very same desk that he occupied on the lower trading floor, the equities floor, that was now closed off due to it being a crime scene and damaged from the Hawk-Nosed Man's attack the previous night. Fortnum Bank IT and operations teams had worked triple-time overnight and crammed everyone onto the bond trading floor, which was, to any outsider, an almost perfect facsimile of the equities floor.

Surrounding Pete were clerks and assistant traders assigned to him. Shirin sat to his left, and on the other side of his row were the teams from Treasury and Federal Reserve they had worked with overnight at the FBI.

Pete, Shirin, the Treasury, and Fed teams, and a few key interagency liaison officers, were the only ones in the know. Fortnum Bank's global head of trading had also been informed. But Garner, and many of the other local desk heads, were in the dark. As far as they all knew, and the instructions that had been given to management, Pete was to be given full latitude to deploy the firm's balance sheet, working in concert with the New York Federal Reserve Markets Desk, to be able to implement a series of market-stabilizing moves whenever necessary. The two entities would work in concert, directed by Kyle on the ground in San Francisco, to buy and sell, driving major markets in the direction they needed.

"This is exactly like *our* floor, strange," Shirin echoed Pete's feeling.

"I know, surreal. I feel at home but out of sorts at the same time," he confided.

Pete sat on the edge of his chair and scanned the markets on his screens.

The Nikkei, the major Japanese equity index, had closed down two hundred points, which had triggered a sour mood in Europe. Those indexes, the FTSE 100 (UK), CAC 40 (France), and DAX (Germany), had followed the Japanese markets lower and were down substantially ahead of the US market open.

"It's funny, the markets can sense it. Or maybe it's just me," Pete commented, gauging his array of charts.

"Equity futures are down twenty already," Shirin added. "And gold's up fifteen dollars, seven eighty," she added, worried.

Pete realized, "Crude, too, up almost two bucks." But then he noted, "This is not a great opening setup for them. They don't want equities to go much lower. It's kind of risky in here," he said, tactically, but it also induced an ominous feeling between them.

Private Office, Somewhere

In an expansive office, half a dozen traders, each wearing a traditional keffiyeh, an Arab headdress, sat before sleek flat-screen monitors on opulent, gold-trimmed wood and leather desks. The rich private trading floor was quiet, with occasional mouse and keyboard clicks.

It was an elegant, high-ceilinged room about forty meters broad with floor-to-ceiling windows on the south wall facing a breathtaking view of an aqua-colored ocean. The entire space was lavishly appointed. Antique Persian rugs were spread throughout. The coffered ceilings and moldings were all gold-leaf trimmed. Three large flat-screen TVs, encased in mahogany, mounted on the east wall broadcast US, European, and Middle Eastern news and financial channels.

As the traders clicked away, two figures entered through a pair of gold and cypress wood-paneled doors at the head of the small trading floor. The first was an urbane Saudi, in a chocolate pinstriped silk suit, impeccably tailored. He also wore a keffiyeh, black-and-white checkered. His hands were encrusted with an array of twenty-four-karat gold and turquoise rings on most fingers, along with a thick Patek Philippe watch on his right wrist. This was al-Hammadi. The second figure, more plainly dressed in slacks and a collared shirt, entered alongside him...Sully.

They strode in and sat down on two plush, pillow-adorned sofas at the back of the room, overseeing the traders.

Al-Hammadi turned his wrist and glanced at his watch.

"All of Europe is lower. And US markets open in minutes. I don't like where things *are* right now," al-Hammadi scowled at Sully.

"Let's be patient and cross the open. It's expiration, which creates a lot of volatility. We can push things around more easily. Equities might turn around, and we can drive it the other way. We want to play this just so," Sully responded with cold confidence.

Bayshore Freeway, San Francisco, United States

First light broke over the Bay Area. In the distance, the iconic skyline with its thin pyramidal tower poking above the surrounding buildings shone before the fading purple dawn. It was looking like a clear, cloudless day, no fog.

A winding freeway stretched through the faint light and disappeared into the downtown cluster of office buildings. The freeway was quiet and mostly empty of traffic, except for a long column of vans and box trucks racing toward the city. Some of the vehicles were plain white, while others had delivery or service provider branding on them. Leading the convoy was a long blue utility truck.

Inside the "utility truck," hardened FBI Special Weapons agents lined the interior, checking their gear and weapons. There were two command figures at the head, the FBI counterterrorism commander, and the Nuclear Emergency Support Team lead. The CT commander juggled a map and radio as he conferred with the NEST lead.

At the back of the truck, Kyle stood watching out the rear window as the formidable convoy got closer and closer to hell. He was outfitted in FBI tactical gear as well, sans the hardware.

Kyle dialed his cell.

"Pete, how things looking?" He listened to Pete summarize an inventory of the various markets. "Thanks. Remember, you're my eyes and ears... I agree with you. This market start isn't great for them, but if equities fall too much at the open, they might get spooked and set it off early... Yup. Start buying S&P and treasuries, try to take it toward unch going into the opening bell. That should give us some breathing room. Call me after you've driven things up a bit." Kyle snapped closed the phone.

He approached the command team.

"Commander, markets are a bit dicey right now. We'll be exposed if things go any lower from here. There's a chance they get spooked and trigger early. We're trying to lift it, give us at least another hour," Kyle reported to the CT commander, the lead officer in charge of the San Francisco operation.

The CT commander checked his watch.

"It'll be at least a half hour before we can get the NEST units on the ground searching. We've got *some* aerial coverage, but we're not getting much from them yet. When again do you expect the danger window?" he asked Kyle.

"My best guess is about three hours from now," Kyle replied. "But that could change quickly with market behavior."

"That's eight thirty to nine, local." The NEST lead eyed the CT commander.

"Three hours is nothing. We're barely going to be past staging then. We need to get lucky," he said.

The CT commander clutched a fistful of Kyle's jersey. "You let us know the *second* you think otherwise."

Kyle met him, nose to nose almost. "We'll do our part," he assured.

The CT commander let him go and told the NEST lead, "Double reminder for complete radio silence."

"Yes, sir, everybody knows."

"We have to assume they're watching. That they've got eyes all over the place. If they sniff us out, they'll…"

The commander didn't have to complete his sentence; they understood.

All the NEST techs were also disguised as delivery personnel, SF utility workers, or average commuters. They had to be totally incognito, as they had no idea what sort of detonation trigger the bomb had.

Fortnum Bank Fixed Income Trading Floor

Pete clutched his handset against his chest as his eyes trained with intense focus on the ticking of the markets. He abruptly called out to his team.

"Spoo December, and ten-year, start entering size bids just below the market," he directed, paused, and then added, "If it rises away from us, walk up your bid levels with it, and lift some offers, but not too loud. Clear?" He panned his vicinity, eyeing all the traders and clerks around him as they got busy. Pete exchanged knowing looks with the Treasury and Fed teams across from him. The clamor across the desks rose. Pete had put a floor under the market, and traders and brokers were responding.

The S&P bumped higher. It climbed five dollars in a few minutes, now down only fifteen handles. Treasuries rose, too, sending interest rates lower and adding an additional accelerant for equities.

Private Office, Somewhere

Sully stood over the traders, watching as the futures lifted. The S&P was now down about eight points.

"We're higher now. Should be a smoother glide into the open. After that, we'll have to see how it trades," he told al-Hammadi.

"Good," al-Hammadi replied and approached the bank of traders.

"How's the city looking?" he asked one of them.

The leftmost trader dialed up a matrix of real-time views of downtown San Francisco. Traffic was beginning to increase, although still a bit light. People were emerging from houses and starting their commutes as the sun rose over the bay.

The trader tapped the images on his screen.

"Looks pretty normal. Not seeing anything suspect. A bit light, traffic-wise, for now, but I wouldn't read anything into it," the trader replied.

Al-Hammadi strolled back to Sully.

"I'd like to sell some more here as it rises into the open," he instructed Sully.

Sully looked back at him and then down to the screens.

"We're almost at unchanged. I think it works higher after the open. We can sell some there," Sully replied, turning away from al-Hammadi.

Al-Hammadi didn't like Sully's reply and impatiently watched the screens.

"What about crude? Can we short more here?"

Sully eyed crude oil. It was at the same place from earlier, up two dollars, sitting at ninety-nine. He nodded slowly.

"We got some room. We can short more," Sully approved, finally eliciting a smile from al-Hammadi, who gestured to the desk traders.

Joint Tactical Operations

"Shit!" a DHS comms rep yelled.

Beringer swiveled toward her.

"We've got a blogger posting online that it's strange there are simultaneous road closures at all access points into San Francisco."

"Shut that blogger down. And pull the site," the admiral ordered.

"It's on the web already, I mean, it's out there."

One of the communication team leads hustled over. She picked up the phone.

"We're on with the ISP now, requesting they disable that site."

"Watch for more of this shit. We're on borrowed time here," Beringer warned.

He swiveled to the overheads displaying maps of San Francisco scored into grids and shouted to Brent, "Where are the aerials? I don't see anything."

"No, sir," Brent yelled back, "and we're too high up. To keep out of sight, we're scanning from higher altitudes, which lowers confidence."

Beringer sagged in his seat and muttered to himself, "Means we may have already overflown the thing." He hollered back, "What about our ground teams?"

"Approaching, yes."

"They should be all over that city by now!" he fired back.

Beringer regarded the clocks, now nine a.m. Eastern, six a.m. Pacific.

Sarah and Kazemi approached Kate. They shoved a real-estate contract written in Spanish in her face, to her annoyance.

"No joke—look at this. We've got two places, both interesting. The first is an office tower real-estate investment partnership in Malaga, Spain. It's on the southern Mediterranean coast. Al-Hammadi, through partnerships and other entities, looks to have the controlling interest in this property here," Kate started to pay closer attention. Bob also came over to listen. Kazemi added further color.

"The second, also suspicious," he said to them, pointing to a map, "is a palatial estate overlooking the Atlantic coast outside of Tangiers."

"Tangiers...*Morocco*, Tangiers?"

"That's the one. And this property isn't directly connected to al-Hammadi. Looks like it's owned by a theoretical associate we don't think exists, a cutout."

"Get eyes on the ground on both targets immediately. Confirm any activity— vehicles, lights on, smoke from the stacks, anything," Bob ordered, and slapped his watch, "and we have, like, no time."

Sarah and Kazemi dashed back to their seats.

Kate called over to Terry, "Western Med, you understand?"

Terry replied to her with a shallow nod.

Bayshore Freeway, San Francisco

Box vans and light trucks broke off from the main convoy and multiplexed into downtown. A "utility truck" vanished into the Mission District. A "postal van" swung into Forest Hill, and another pair of "delivery vehicles" bent toward the lower Haight and Design Districts. Dozens more fanned out behind those.

Inside the lead command truck, the CT commander faced his troops.

"Listen up. We're in trolling mode here. We're just a utility truck until there's an actionable order from our NEST guys," he said.

The Special Weapons troops inside the long van rechecked their equipment.

Kyle flipped open his cell and dialed.

"Pete, where the hell are we?"

Fortnum Bank Fixed Income Trading Floor

Shirin watched the wall clock tick from 09:29:59 to 09:30:00.

"Ding, ding, ding," she uttered as the equities markets breached the open.

Pete, on the phone with Kyle, called the race out of the gate as the equities markets blew through its unch level and rallied higher.

"Equities up ten. We're not actively buying. We goosed it already. Gold is softer, seven seventy. Crude's only up a buck and half, under some pressure... Start buying crude?... Yup, got it."

Pete tossed the handset and directed his team, "Crude oil, front month, plus options, now that we have some liquidity, start taking it up. Lift offers where you see 'em. Don't be shy."

Private Office, Somewhere

Al-Hammadi loomed uneasily behind the traders.

"Crude oil's going up again," he said, fidgeting.

"Let it. We'll continue to sell into the strength."

"And the market is open. Let's do it...now."

Sully shot him a disapproving glance.

"No, way too early. We'll miss out on too much here."

"Remember, you're not in charge. I decide *when* this happens," al-Hammadi reproved under his breath.

"Fine. You want to do it now? Go ahead, light it up," Sully shot back.

He stared down the Arab. Al-Hammadi pulled a satellite phone from his suit pocket and turned it on. He gave Sully a look and then paused.

"No, you're right. Let's wait a bit more, but not too much longer."

Sully replied with a grin as a servant pushed a tray of tea in front of him.

"No tea," Sully rapped.

Sully patrolled the traders' desks, peering at the markets, and glancing up intermittently to check the newswires on the wall-mounted screens. All appeared normal, if not a busy or hectic expiration trading day, from his perspective.

Then a crude oil price alert began to flash. Crude was lurching, now up $3.30, to $100.30, and moving higher. That caught Sully's attention.

"Look, look!" al-Hammadi cried anxiously. "Crude keeps moving higher. Are you sure we're OK here?" he worried.

"We are on a mark-to-market loss now in crude," one of the traders reported. "We could get squeezed if it goes much higher from here," he added.

Sully ignored them, squinting at crude oil ticking higher, not liking it.

Fortnum Bank Fixed Income Trading Floor

Pete stuck his finger in his ear to seal out the swelling trading floor noise so he could hear Kyle. He had to shout into the phone to give him a report.

"Equities are up but losing steam. Same with bonds. I can't push crude any higher. We're buying everything in sight, but offers keep filling in. Feels like things are starting to go the other way now."

Streets of Downtown San Francisco

Inside the command truck, Kyle was on cell with Pete, concentrating to hear him as they trolled the narrow, hilly San Francisco streets.

"We need to focus on crude. It's their Achilles. If we can blast it above a hundred, they'll be in a pain trade and probably sitting on losses... No, I don't think he'd pull the trigger on that alone. He'd double down first, but he *will* start to sweat. I know him, it'll get him steaming, throw him off his game. It'll fuck with him. Let's think. Crude's about a hundred now. How can we bully it higher?"

Fortnum Bank Fixed Income Trading Floor

Pete held his handset in thought, with Kyle hanging on. His eyes flashed around the floor as he pondered, and he pulled the phone back to his ear.

"I have an idea," Pete said simply and hung up, and shouted out to the entire trading floor:

"Word of a coup underway in Saudi Arabia! A *coup* in Saudi Arabia!"

An onslaught of yelling and screaming followed. Crude oil shot higher in almost a single trade, punching through $105 a barrel.

"Nice," Shirin shouted over the din to Pete.

"Buy it. Buy it big!" Pete ordered all the traders.

The floor swung with the sudden turn.

Steve, the head of NY Fed Markets Desk, eyed Pete with disapproval as more capital and liquidity were being sucked from their reserves in this buying spree.

Private Office, Somewhere

Al-Hammadi and his traders panicked as the chart of crude oil exploded higher.

"We're getting killed! We're getting killed! *What are you thinking?*" al-Hammadi shrieked.

Sully didn't reply. He remained cool, but his eyes narrowed suspiciously at the boards. Then the alert painted the newswires and TVs, "Rumored coup underway in Saudi Arabia."

"Look!" one of the traders shouted, pointing to the Arab-language network TV channel broadcasting the report.

"We're losing too much money now!" another trader blurted.

"We're detonating! If we detonate now, oil will fall," al-Hammadi demanded.

Al-Hammadi started dialing the satellite phone. Sully clutched it, grasping al-Hammadi's fingers in a tight grip.

"Not yet...It's bullshit. This is a head fake. It'll start selling off again, just wait," Sully stated with disciplined calm as he eyed the crude chart. He was right. Crude oil topped out at $109, and then, in an instant, started dropping in gaps.

"Sell some on the way down. Hit bids where you can. Pound it back down," Sully's voice rose with his confidence. He let go of al-Hammadi's fingers.

The Saudi traders worked quickly to sell more, and they calmed down as the price started to subside. Al-Hammadi returned the sat phone to his pocket.

Sully vexed at the TVs and the blinking price of crude oil.

"Nice try, guys," he reproved under his breath.

Fortnum Bank Fixed Income Trading Floor

Pete was back on with Kyle.

"He's taking some damage but the market's wising up."

As that left Pete's mouth, he watched the words "Saudis issue a statement denying coup rumors" flash on the TV.

"Fuck! That didn't last long... Kyle, we might have a problem. This thing's doing a one-eighty."

Pete looked down at his chart of crude oil. It had already fallen back below $103 and was now crashing.

"We might have an inversion," Pete cried.

Streets of Downtown San Francisco

"Dang it! You need to support it at ninety-eight, OK?" Kyle shouted back to Pete.

He snapped closed the phone and looked at the CT commander.

"Anything?"

Both the CT commander and NEST lead replied with a *thumbs-down* signal.

"We're at least in every neighborhood now," the NEST officer said.

"Good, because we may have a problem," Kyle revealed as he stepped toward them through the crowd of tack troops.

"What the hell does that mean?" the commander demanded.

"I'll know in a few minutes. The price of crude oil is dropping. That could get them to trigger early if it falls too far, too quickly. We're trying to support it. I'll get you an update," Kyle explained.

"Shit."

Joint Tactical Operations

Brent Lowry threw off his headset, stood, and shouted, "Admiral, we could have an imminent detonation."

His words rang throughout the operations center.

Beringer jumped out of his seat and was at the FEMA desk in a second.

"Emergency centers ready?"

They were all on phones and headsets. The agency director had a fatalistic expression as he replied, "I've got two hundred EMT vehicles on standby. National Guard staged. This won't be pretty."

Streets of Downtown San Francisco

NEST vans, box trucks, and SUVs were sweeping the streets as fast as they could. Overhead, there were a dozen aerial assets scrubbing the city, too.

An unmarked dark-blue van rose and fell with the San Fran hills as it scanned the Chinatown district. Inside, four NEST techs sat before their opened laptops, their eyes dilated, unblinking, watching every little blip from their instruments.

The tech closest to the driver complained to the others, "This is dark. This is all dark. This entire neighborhood. There's nothing here."

"We have to stay on it, methodically," another tech insisted.

The driver half twisted around, overhearing, looking for direction.

"Keep on the grid course," the lead tech admonished.

Frustrated, they returned to their laptops just as a red flash blazed on one of the tech's screens.

"Hey...*hey*! Stop, stop the van!"

The driver tapped the brakes.

"Look," the tech called excitedly, hitting his laptop. A three-story house they just rolled by shone in bright red, significantly exceeding background radiation.

One of the other techs leaned over and inspected. "Not super high, but definitely worth a look," he confirmed to the rest.

The lead tech fitted on his jacket, a flower shop smock.

"I'll check it out. Where's the hit, precisely?" he asked as he frantically fumbled for a handheld radiation detector. Another tech passed him one as the "flower guy" jumped out of the van.

"Yo?" one of the techs tugged his smock and handed him a dozen roses.

"Thanks," he said as he juggled the detector with the flowers.

The flower guy advanced toward the house, a classic three-story pointed-roof Victorian. He had only one arm in his smock, hurriedly fit on, as he balanced the handheld trying to conceal it within the rose bouquet.

He stepped across the short front yard while observing the detector. The readings were declining, now just at background levels. He reversed to the van and shook his head at one of the techs watching him through the front passenger window as the tech vigorously pointed to the south side of the house.

The flower guy responded with a surreptitious nod and shifted his approach. There was a narrow, flagstone walkway between this house and the adjacent one. He stalked to the end where it opened into a backyard. There he came upon scores and scores, even hundreds, of potted plants stacked on wooden racks.

"Can I help you?" a squat woman with a watering can in hand rotated to him, surprised and suddenly defensive.

The flower guy startled and almost dropped his detector.

"Oh, hi, I'm sorry. Nobody answered the door…uh, flower delivery."

Suspicious, she eyed him. The lead tech's heart started to pound. He looked down at his detector again. It was going wild. The concentration of the terra-cotta planters was driving the high returns.

"I'm sorry, I'll leave them here." He set the roses down on the flagstone path.

"But I didn't order…"

The flower guy had already turned out of the alleyway and jogged across the street. He hopped back inside the van.

"Fucking false positive. Bunch of pottery."

"Let's go. We're behind our grid schedule. This cost us ten minutes."

He shut the rear van door behind him, and they screeched off.

Joint Tactical Operations

Beringer glared at Lowry.

"False positives everywhere, all over the city. It's a mess, it's slowing us down," Brent pled.

Beringer eyed the clocks: ten thirty a.m. Eastern, seven thirty a.m. Pacific.

"Get 'em to move faster," Beringer ordered. "Do we have every possible asset we can get on that city?"

"I'm tapped out. I even got an amateur crew out of Sandia Labs; two dozen separate trucks, seven aerial assets," Brent complained.

Beringer grimaced and swiveled toward the FEMA and counterterrorism teams. He called them over. He also beckoned the joints chiefs and NSC reps.

As they gathered around him, Beringer fired off the dire orders.

"Get on with NORAD. Take us to DEFCON 2. Move the terror threat level to red. Hostile surface nuclear detonation in a major metropolitan area is imminent," he started. "Let's get the president in the air, and enact the continuity of government plan… FEMA, notify all emergency facilities in the Bay Area, and get 'em ready at the other cities, too, in case we're wrong here. And move our troops to Force Protection Condition Charlie."

Everyone dispersed. Beringer called over the CIA team.

"What the fuck is this intel? NNSA is coming up empty. If this is a head fake, we're all really fucked. We've got almost *all* our eggs in the San Fran basket."

Kate and Bob exchanged worried looks, showing a bit of fear for the first time. Kate composed herself and shifted her glasses.

"Highest confidence, Admiral. We stand behind the intel," she reaffirmed without batting an eye.

"This isn't something we can be wrong about. We're not finding *anything*, and we have maybe an hour, hour thirty, tops—*what the fuck?*" he yelled.

Bob kept his calm, too, being used to angry brass and politicians.

"Admiral, keep the NEST teams on their routes. They'll find it. It's only a matter of time—I know we have precious little of it. We'll see what we can do with the New York traders to buy us more time," Bob offered.

Beringer studied them for a moment and relented a bit. "Get me anything, anything you can. Even ten minutes helps us."

Streets of Downtown San Francisco

Kyle made eye contact with the NEST lead, who shook his head again.

"Only false positives," he shouted to him. Kyle's cell rang and he answered.

"Kate... No, not shit on the ground here. We're doing what we can in crude oil and stock indexes. We think that's bought us a little time, but I bet they start to get anxious shortly... You want to buy *more* time?... I get it, I get it. We don't have much ammo left, and anything we do now could actually accelerate their end game... I'll try something." Kyle shut the phone.

Angered, Kyle punched the wall of the van, denting the metal. Kyle thought. What more could they do at this point? He rang Pete.

Private Office, Somewhere

Sully inspected the markets, pacing behind al-Hammadi's traders. A sliver of a smile betrayed his confidence.

"I like where we are now. Equities are steady, gold's up, ready to pop, and crude is on a downward turn," he assessed.

Al-Hammadi, unable to contain his anxiety, approached Sully.

"What do you think?"

"I'm thinking we trigger on crude at ninety dollars or eleven thirty a.m. Eastern, whichever comes first," Sully responded with a cold sneer.

An eminent smile spread across the Saudi's face as he caressed his sat phone.

"Good," he replied plainly.

Fortnum Bank Fixed Income Trading Floor

Pete watched the screens with dismay. The trading clock read 10:55:35. Gold was higher, back to $780. Equities were also higher, but not by much, up $10 on the S&P. Crude was the real problem, though. It was still falling, now down to $97, below their support threshold.

"Buy it! Buy crude, get those bids out there!" Pete screamed.

The line traders hollered into their turrets, relaying buy orders. Steve from the NY Fed pushed his way over to Pete. He grabbed Pete's arm and got in his face.

"We don't have much more available liquidity. We're going to need to sell bonds to free up cash if we keep buying shit," he yelled at Pete.

Pete looked him in the eye. "If we sell bonds here, it will take us exactly in the direction we don't want to go!" Pete yelled back.

"Kyle on two," Shirin signed to Pete.

Steve let go of Pete's arm as he answered the phone.

"Kyle, it's not looking good. The tide's against us here. I'm deploying more and more capital, and crude's not budging. Gold's looking like a tinderbox, too"—Pete glanced at Steve—"plus, the Fed guys are telling me we're running out of bullets. What the fuck—tell me what we can do."

Streets of Downtown San Francisco

Kyle lowered his cell, thinking. He peeked out the rear window of the command truck. Morning sunlight was flooding across the bay. It was eight a.m., and the streets were now full of cars and the blur of workers racing to their coffee shops and jobs. He raised the phone back to his ear.

"If prices get to where they want them, they've accomplished their goal, right? I mean, I think it's time to spell it out... I said: *Spell. It. Out.*"

Kyle hung up.

"Commander?" Kyle shouted across the truck. "Get ready for mayhem."

"Shit, Kyle. What'd you do? Son of a bitch!"

Fortnum Bank Fixed Income Trading Floor

Pete tossed his handset. He gauged the trading chaos. He swallowed a big gulp of air. And then climbed up and stood on his trading desk. Shirin eyed him, as did the Treasury and Fed teams—*what was he doing?* There was a momentary lull in the cacophony as the floor's attention turned to him. And then Pete shouted out, *"There's a nuclear bomb in San Francisco!"*

A split second of silence reigned for a beat that seemed like an eternity. And then came an eruption. Like a spreading shock wave blowing across the trading floor, the panic sells exploded.

Shirin and the Treasury and Fed teams watched him in shock. In a moment, it was hard for anyone to see several feet in front of them. Everyone was out of their seat, screaming. The interagency heads started toward Pete but could barely push through the frenzied crowds.

Markets exploded. Gold rocketed to $850. Crude oil cratered to $85 and then to $83 and lower. Equities nose-dived in a total rout, down a hundred points in the S&P almost instantly. Every stock was in the red.

Joint Tactical Operations

Beringer leapt off his chair. "What the *fuck*?"

The giant monitors displayed the free fall in the markets. Their phones and boards lit up, blaring with calls from every agency and government official.

Kate and Bob incredulously shouted, "Jesus Christ!"

Private Office, Somewhere

Al-Hammadi and traders gaped at the monitors as the announcement came across.

"And now there's another rumor quickly spreading among the New York trading desks, that—this is only a rumor, folks—there's a loose nuclear bomb somewhere in the city of San Francisco..."

Al-Hammadi shot Sully a horrified look and pulled out the sat phone.

"They know!"

He started to dial, but Sully slammed shut his phone again.

"What are you *doing*? You heard them. They know! It's only a matter of time before they find it now. We have to detonate it," Al-Hammadi protested.

Sully stared at the markets, all the markets, now going their way, huge.

"Look at the power of fear," Sully remarked in rapture.

"We are up over twenty billion dollars now," one of the traders delighted, with a huge grin on his face.

Streets of Downtown San Francisco

The CT commander and NEST lead watched the sheer panic in the city unfold through the front windshield. Their van was now stuck in the middle of their current street. Horns blared as cars rode up onto the sidewalks. People screamed and poured out of homes and buildings into the streets.

"Motherfucker!" the CT commander yelled. "Go lit."

The driver engaged the sirens to urge the van through the jam. As the agents dealt with the traffic, Kyle got back on the phone with Pete.

Fortnum Bank Fixed Income Trading Floor

Amid the pandemonium, Pete struggled to hear Kyle.

"We might have bought us some time, but we started a financial meltdown. You gotta bail us out real soon..."

Pete eyed the markets.

"Gold's closing in on nine hundred. Our gold trade is real fucked now," Pete said with a macabre chuckle. "S&P is down almost five hundred points, and crude's at eighty. If we don't have a better plan, the Fed boys are going to intervene," Pete warned him.

Streets of Downtown San Francisco

"Hold them off as long as you can. Once they lower rates, that'll drive things back up quickly, and I'm sure Sully triggers the bomb. Let things drop. I know it's scary as shit, but I figure we've bought us another half hour or so. I bet they're jumping up and down right now, those fucks. That'll last for a bit, and then they'll want to pull the trigger…yup," Kyle shut the phone.

"Springer, goddamn it! This is a real mess you got us into here. You jammed up all our vans!" the CT commander rebuked.

Kyle ignored him and watched the gridlock out the rear window.

Room, Somewhere

In an oasis of quiet, the short Syrian prostrated on his prayer rug in the light-starved room. He rose and bowed in a rhythm mouthing soundless litany. Behind him, the bomb, assembled and ready, stood on the table, awaiting its commands. A cell phone lay on the table next to it…

Private Office, Somewhere

Beaming grins around the opulent office.

"We are up more than forty-two billion dollars now!" a trader glowed.

Al-Hammadi strode up and down his row of traders, relishing and high-fiving and checking the markets as everything went their way.

Sully sat on the sofa, taking a short break.

"I think we let it move for a while," Sully called out to al-Hammadi, who half paid attention to him, too engrossed with his P&L at that moment. "The risk is the Fed may intervene and lower rates, which will send things the other way."

But Sully's admonition fell on deaf ears.

Downey Street, San Francisco

A white NEST vehicle dressed up as a cable van banked onto Downey Street, a normally placid Haight-Ashbury neighborhood lane with trees and classic two- and three-story Victorians.

Inside the van, the NEST techs were glued to their laptops, scrutinizing the radiation returns as they drove by.

"This is a dead street. Let's speed up and move to the next one over," the lead NEST tech ordered the driver, who stepped on the gas.

As they accelerated up the steep street, an escaping sedan reversed out of its driveway, smashing into their right front grill and headlight.

"Ah shit! Just what we needed. Goddamn it," the driver cursed as he braked.

Outside, the terrified woman driver of the sedan hopped out and ran toward to the "cable van driver."

"Can we still drive?" the NEST lead asked his driver.

"I think so. We just have some front grill damage," the driver replied.

"So, drive around her."

"I think her car is stuck to our bumper. We have to pry it apart."

"Shit."

"Plus, we have to deal with her. Look."

They peered out the front windshield at the hysterical woman banging on the van door.

"Get out! Look what you did!" she yelled at the NEST driver.

The NEST lead motioned to the driver. "Fuck. Go and help her. Just get her car off the van and give her the basic government info," he griped.

The NEST driver and a tech jumped out of the van.

The woman confronted them, screaming incessantly in their faces.

"See what you did? I need to get out of here. Get your van off my car, now! Did you hear—? They're gonna blow us up, the terrorists!" she shrieked.

The NEST driver and tech exchanged glances—*this woman's nuts.* The NEST driver head-motioned to the tech to push on the front of the sedan so he could work simultaneously to dislodge its back bumper from the van's fender.

"Yes, ma'am. Please give us a moment. We'll have you on your way."

The NEST tech, dressed in his cable guy uniform, jogged to the front of her sedan as the woman chased him around the car, yelling at him.

"You guys are going to pay for this. I've seen the other cable drivers in this city. They're crazy. Just like you, and, and—your phone is buzzing in your pocket," she interrupted herself. "Answer your phone!" she insisted, unable to deal with the mess *and* his phone ringing at the same time.

The NEST tech regarded her questioningly. He didn't even have a phone on him; it was in the van.

"In your pocket there, your phone. *Why don't you answer it?*"

The NEST tech looked down inside his shirt. He realized his body radiation detector was registering something and was buzzing. There was radioactivity from somewhere close by.

He froze. The hairs on the back of his neck stood up. He peered behind him at a set of three adjacent houses. He eyed the house and driveway of the three-story Italianate that this nutjob had just backed into them from.

On the left side of her house was a plain two-story Victorian sandwiched in between hers and another three-story house. But the two-story house had shades drawn on every window, no cars in the driveway. His heart started to pound.

"Hey, come on, lift!" the NEST driver yelled over to him.

"See, even your driver's telling you to hurry up... Hurry up! He can't drive for shit, but he knows we're all going to *die* if you don't move it!" she blared.

The NEST tech, shaking, barely able to focus, inhaled and looked back at his driver. He leaned on the hood of the sedan to push it forward as the NEST driver pried the van's fender off, freeing the sedan.

"You see, there!" she yelled as the car became unstuck.

The woman approached the driver and demanded their details. As she was doing that, the NEST tech took a few furtive steps up the block and pivoted toward the two-story Victorian. He glanced down inside his shirt pocket and watched the mR/hr reading ratchet up as he got closer and faced the house. His shaking worsened. These were high readings, eighty to a hundred mR/hr, significantly over background. The levels kept rising the closer he got to the house.

The tech peered up and down the street. Downey was a classic, super-steep San Francisco street. They were about in the middle of it. The street kept rising from where they were and crested at the top of the steep hill.

"Hey, come on. We're *really* behind now!" the driver shouted at him, jumping back into the van.

The woman scrambled into her sedan, steered over the curb with her busted-up trunk, and sped the opposite way, disappearing down the hill. The techs hustled back inside their vehicle. They shut the rear door, and the driver restarted the van.

"Hey, hey!" he yelled at the lead, slapping his arm to get his attention. "*Listen* to me carefully," he ordered the driver. "Go slowly. Move *very slowly* up the hill. I want to see something," the tech demanded.

"We can't really do *anything* slowly right now," the driver yelled back.

"Just do it."

"Fine."

The van steadily labored up the hill as the tech watched every tick on his laptop, his eyes unblinking as they trolled past that two-floor Victorian.

"Come on, come on. *Where was it?*" the tech complained out loud. "It was right there. I know I wasn't imagining it," he griped.

"What are you talking about?" one of the others pursed.

"Let's go. We're wasting our time here. Speed up to the top of Downey, to the top of the hill. We'll figure out where to go from there. We can't waste any more time. That stupid crash set us back four blocks at least. We need to catch up."

The driver sped up.

"No. *No!*" the tech yelled at the driver to slow down again, but he wouldn't. He sped up and they rolled past the Victorian.

"Holy shit! *Did you see that?*" one of the other techs exclaimed, furiously pointing at his laptop.

"See what?" the lead tech impatiently scoffed.

"What do you want me to do, speed up or slow down?" the driver yelled back.

"Back up, back up!"

"I can't, the hill's too steep. We'll roll all the way the fuck back down."

"Then stop! Stop the van!"

"Stop the van!" the NEST lead finally yelled.

"You saw it, *didn't you?*" the one tech demanded of the other.

"I got a *huge* return on my handheld when we were pulling that woman's car out, eighty to a hundred."

"I saw something as we passed by that Victorian house. It blazed hot, like red hot—in it or close to it."

"Yes, *yes*, the Victorian."

"You guys aren't shitting me?" the lead tech challenged.

"Can you rewind the readings as we drove by?" another tech asked.

"We can, yeah. Hang on…" The tech dialed it back a few seconds.

As he did that, the laptop monitor displayed a silhouette of the house that appeared in a ghosted outline against a black and hued, mostly green, shaded background. As they went frame by frame, the images corresponding to when the van passed by the house lit up orange and red.

"That's real!" the lead cried out. "Get me the sniffer—now!" he ordered.

One of the techs pulled it down from an inside shelf and switched it on. He waited for it to calibrate and then passed it to the NEST lead.

"Pull up to the curb," the lead ordered the driver. "Make it look like we're doing a cable call for real."

"Got it," the driver replied, edging the van into the curb, and yanking up the emergency brake on the steep hill.

"You can get a good shot out the rear window," the one tech motioned to him.

The lead tech shuffled to the rear of the van, exited and aimed the neutron sniffer at the north side of the target house. The neutron count lit up like an exploding firework, almost to ten.

"My God. Whatever's in there is throwing off all kinds of fast neutrons. This is not naturally occurring," he said excitedly. He rushed back to the van, "Where's the data from the target? Get the profile. We need to comp this," he ordered.

The other techs clambered all over their laptops to retrieve the radioactive signature profile from the target they were chasing. The CIA worked closely with NNSA to capture and store radiation profiles for many of the warhead types in the world for exactly these radiological forensics.

"Got it, got it...from a distance of fifty to one hundred meters, minimal shielding, profile should be in these fast-neutron ranges above background...here," the tech read out.

The NEST lead dropped the sniffer and jumped over to look at the profile graph on the laptop. He then referred to the data from the sniffer and looked back and forth several times comparing the two.

"What do you think, about...?"

"If it's that north front corner of the house, within fifty meters, yes."

His gaze rose from the computer.

"Goddamn it. This is a dead-on match. Call this in, now, *now*. Send these profiles to HQS, too—no radios—*now*! Fuck, fuck, fuck, *now*!"

He surged to the rear of the van and peered out the back window.

"And let's get out of here. We've been sitting here for too long," he worried. "We're gonna raise suspicion if we stay."

The driver started up the van, and they climbed to the crest of the hill, where they turned right and came to a stop, out of any line of sight from the Victorian.

Joint Tactical Operations

"Admiral—target, target, target!" yelled the FBI and NNSA stations.

Beringer was already over by the NNSA, looking up at the main screens as they were instantly painted with an aerial of the suspect street and house.

"Tacks are getting into place," shouted an FBI agent.

"What's confidence? What's the confidence on this hit?" Beringer demanded.

"Highest. This is the target. Matches all profiles. Something in that house is raining fast neutrons. That means *this* is our gadget," Brent replied.

"Block off the streets around this house, four-block radius. Let's get some real-time overheads in place...quietly," Beringer commanded.

"Copy, Admiral," the FBI supervisor yelled back.

"And start jamming signals all around that spot. I don't want a cell tower ping, radio wave, nothing to get in. You got it?"

"Yes, sir, we're on with half a dozen carriers. We're shutting down the cell towers. We've got an EC aircraft getting into place overhead now," he reported.

Counterterrorism Command Van, San Francisco

Kyle opened his cell, about to call Pete—

"We have a target. We have a target!" the commander yelled. "Hot spot, Frederick and Downey, three blocks over. Go, *go*!"

The driver rolled the van hard right, jumping a curb and bouncing into the street with a tire screech.

Kyle was thrown against the rear doors as the rows of hardened tactical agents were flung side to side. As soon as they'd stabilized, the CT commander caught his balance and faced the troops.

"Listen up. This is op-go. This is real-world. You guys know the assault profile, breachers provide entry and we clear whatever resistance is there. NEST teams do the rest," he announced.

"And total radio silence. We're gonna start jamming all signals in this area…everyone at condition zero," he finished.

Condition zero meant all weapons off safety and rounds loaded into chambers. The order was followed by a chorus of clicks and weapons being cocked.

The commander stepped to the rear toward Kyle. "You probably have another minute or so—if you need to call out, do it now. We're gonna start jamming everything," he said to Kyle, who immediately dialed Pete.

"Pete, where is it?… Got it. Listen to me, keep the Fed out of it for another few minutes. We need that. You hear me? It may be a little while before I can call you back," Kyle told Pete and hung up.

One of the troops tossed Kyle a bulletproof vest.

"Thanks," Kyle replied and strapped it on.

"No gun, though. I'm sorry." He smiled and winked at Kyle.

The troops adjusted their armor as the van accelerated up the street.

Fortnum Bank Fixed Income Trading Floor

Pete's eyes ricocheted among the markets. Everything was spiraling out of control. Gold was now at $920. S&P was down almost 750 points, unprecedented. And crude oil futures were plummeting to $70 a barrel.

"I got Fed governors calling me. They want us to lower, fifty, and then another fifty," Steve shouted to Pete.

"No! We can't, we need more time. Just a few more minutes!"

Steve sharply shook his head *no*. "The board of governors is meeting now. They'll issue a statement shortly," he said.

"You have to stop them!" Pete slammed his phone and ran to the other side of the trading desk. He grabbed Steve by the shoulders.

"Kyle told me, *specifically*, hold off the Fed. You *can't lower yet*. You'll set this thing off!"

"I don't have any choice. It's out of my hands."

"You've got to be able to do something to stop them."

Steve didn't reply, just squinted angrily at Pete. Pete released him.

"Shit!"

Pete ran back and dialed Kyle. Busy. He hung up and tried again. Another busy signal. Pete, desperate to reach Kyle, banged the handset on the desk.

"Come on, Springer. *Pick up!*" he yelled. *"Fuck!"*

"We're done," he said despairingly to Shirin, who returned his panicked look.

Sky Over San Francisco, 10,000 Feet

An Electronic Combat (EC) aircraft, a light fixed-wing plane with a single propeller circled over the Haight-Ashbury district. Its single engine was quiet, almost soundless.

Inside, there was a pilot and an electronic warfare officer (EWO). The EWO was cramped in front of a short bank of black consoles packed with dials and control switches. He serially flipped on each lever.

"We're engaged. Pretty much blocking most of the spectrum, with the exception of a few long-wave frequencies," the EWO reported into his headset.

Downey Street, San Francisco

FBI sniper teams fell into positions on rooftops encircling the two-story Victorian. Each team, a sniper, and a spotter, prone and camouflaged, set their scopes to target the windows and doors of the home below.

From a third-floor bedroom in the house directly across the street, two plainclothes agents and two NEST techs crept toward windows with line-of-sight to their target. Remaining out of view, one of the techs configured a detector dish attached to a long boom and pointed it precisely at the lower left wing of the suspect house.

He switched on a viewing monitor connected to the scope. It produced an infrared heat-signature view of the corner of the Victorian. Its optics were powerful enough to see through walls and could isolate the locations of heat sources—the human beings inside the structure *and* radioactive objects.

The monitor displayed two high-contrast forms in that section of the Victorian, in what appeared to be a room on the front-facing corner of the house. Two objects radiated as heat sources. The first was a spherical return, somewhat off the ground, and appeared like a dim star in the infrared rendering. That object was less "bright" than the second target, which was vertically shaped, a human's form, and was moving about the room.

"That looks like the target device, there." The tech whispered, pointing to the spherical heat signature on the monitor. "This looks like a human operator. We don't see any others in this structure. Can we take him out from here?"

The agent studied the image. "Possible with a fifty cal, we can fire through the wall. Risky because if it hits anything, like a pipe inside the wall along its path, it could deflect and miss. And we'd probably only get one shot at him."

"And that might trigger him detonating," he replied to the agent in charge, who shook his head, *no way.*

"Let's do this up close and personal, then," the lead agent decided.

Private Office, Somewhere

The Saudis were enjoying the boon. But Sully's veteran eye had noticed the acceleration slowing.

"Do it now," Sully directed, turning to them.

Al-Hammadi looked at Sully. "What, now?"

"Detonate it."

Al-Hammadi was ironically surprised by Sully's sudden insistence.

"You sure?" he questioned. "Everything's going our way. This is good."

"The Federal Reserve is probably going to intervene shortly. When that happens, it'll reverse fast. Don't fight the Fed, as they say."

Al-Hammadi turned back to the markets and double-checked each of them.

"I see your point," he said directly as he removed his sat phone from his pocket and dialed. He listened but then lowered the phone.

Al-Hammadi frowned at Sully. "It's busy. I'm getting a busy signal."

"Try again," Sully urged.

Al-Hammadi dialed again, heard the same busy signal. He handed the phone to Sully who listened, a rail of concern forming on his forehead.

"Do we have another way of reaching your guy on the ground?"

One of the traders swiveled around to him. "We can text him through here."

"Do it," Sully ordered without hesitation.

Downey Street, San Francisco

The command van braked at Downey. The hardened Special Weapons troops poured out of the rear. More vans and SUVs arrived, their doors flying open and the vehicles emptying as dozens more troops joined. Kyle jumped out. He suddenly felt good, safe, his feet being on the blacktop. The commander and NEST lead hopped out behind him. The target house was two hundred yards uphill from where they were staging.

A specialized NEST van rolled in with a screech of its brakes. Its rear doors swung open. A tech emerged wearing a darkened suit, like a chemical warfare suit. On his back were two side-by-side tanks, like a scuba rig. He wielded what appeared to be a double-barreled long gun connected to the tanks by a hose.

He was a NEST nitro specialist or *can man*. His pack was a set of tanks (cans) filled with liquid nitrogen. One of the tricks NEST used was to neutralize, or brick, bomb components by freezing them to temperatures a few hundred degrees below zero. That rendered electromechanical parts inoperable, at least for a few minutes, giving bomb techs enough time to remove detonation elements from the device.

The troops stalked up the sloping street toward the Victorian, hugging the adjacent houses, keeping to the blind spots. The can man trailed closely behind. The tacks took positions in recesses, below windowsills, and behind cars. A full assault team of thirty agents and NEST techs, in addition to the rooftop sniper cells, was poised and in place surrounding the Victorian.

The CT commander and NEST lead, along with Kyle, directed the action from the front yard of a house three doors down from the Victorian.

"Stay with us. Don't move from here," the commander ordered Kyle as they all peered at the front of the house where the assault was about to go down.

A "delivery man," who was the tactical breacher, skulked up to the Victorian and crept onto its front porch. He craftily stuck several bars of C-4 explosive to the threshold of the door. He wired them up in seconds and sprang away, accomplishing his crime in the blink of an eye.

Four Special Weapons troops flanked either side of the front door, crouching below windows and ducking into shadows.

The front-most assault agent, at the corner of the Victorian, and with line of sight to the CT commander, peeked at him over his shoulder. The counterterror assault team was a coiled spring, everyone on hair trigger readiness.

The snipers and their spotters, from their positions on surrounding rooftops, lined up their assigned windows and doors in crosshairs. They settled their postures, and collectively inhaled.

Overhead, the jammer plane circled, providing blanket coverage, and blocking signal transmission into or out of a thousand-foot bubble over the house.

Inside the Victorian, in the dimly lit room, the short Syrian approached the window. He craned his neck to squint through the downward angle of the closed blind slats. The street was quiet as far as he could see or hear.

He returned to the table and inspected the bomb, running his hand over the sphere and tugging on each of the sectional detonator wires. He checked his watch. And he depressed the arming switch. A red light illuminated on the detonator box.

The Syrian was about to sit down but opened his cell phone first. He noticed zero reception bars. He also reviewed the small digital screen on the base of the bomb—zero reception bars there, too. Something was wrong.

His eyes shot around the room. He waved his phone about, checking it again, but there was no change in reception. He circled the room holding the cell out in front of him but still didn't see any improvement. His eyes lifted from the phone, now suspicious. He stepped to the adjoining hallway door and turned the door handle, opening it slightly and poking his head out.

He eyed his cell again, still nothing. Then he did a double take. A shadow curved above him on the hallway ceiling. He froze, observing it. The shadow stopped moving and held still. The Syrian placed one foot into the hallway, tentatively, so as not to cause the floorboards to creak. He watched the shadow again from a better angle. It shifted, elongating farther down the hallway ceiling.

The Syrian's eyes widened. He realized. He lunged for the bomb.

Outside, the CT commander signaled with his fingers to all the assault team, *two...one*, and squeezed his hand into a fist. The tacks averted their eyes—

The breacher depressed the fire control switch.

Blammm!

The C-4 blew. The street filled with a blinding yellow-and-white double flash. The front door and entire porch of the Victorian exploded in a burst of wood and smoke. The door flew off its frame and twisted through the air into the house. The front windows shattered from the pulse.

The tacks stormed inside. Leading the charge was the NEST can man, his nozzle piercing the smoke-filled entryway. Flanking him were two six-foot-four armored agents with suppressed AR-15 assault rifles, followed by a half dozen more tacks charging into the house behind them.

Their boots thundered onto the wooden floor into the hall. The Syrian had been knocked to the floor from the blast. Covered with bits of Sheetrock and wooden splinters, he scrambled to stand, his hands and feet rucking the dust- and debris-covered floor. In a split second, he was up, and he half turned to the hole in the front of the house. Rushing at him with the flooding sunlight he spied the armed troops storming in.

The Syrian clambered to regain his balance and stretched to the bomb. He reached, clawing for the detonator box. His hand dug into the table as his other hand found the box. His fingers pinched the detonation switch.

The nitro gunner surged through the curtain of smoke into the bomb room. He lasered onto the gadget on the table and saw a short figure through the smoky haze grabbing at some device.

He leveled the nozzle at the figure and gadget and squeezed the trigger.

Two white rod-shaped jets of liquid nitrogen blasted out of the nozzles. The Syrian depressed the detonation switch just as he and the bomb were painted in liquid nitrogen. The nitro gunner fanned the nozzle side to side and up and down, blanketing the table, the Syrian, the gadget, the detonation box, and all its wires.

The Syrian stiffened into a statue-like paralysis. His body and expression froze in a moment in time with a determined but fearful look on his face, his mouth opened in strain. His right arm, all the way down to his fingers pinching the detonation switch, were petrified in mid-action, caught perfectly in between contacts. The scene in the room became utterly still, glistening, everything held in an instant stasis like someone had hit the pause button.

The front of the gadget gleamed and darkened with a sheen of aluminum being brought hundreds of degrees colder. The other components, the wires and the table, were all coated in a thin layer of the ultracold liquid nitrogen.

The can man blinked from behind his goggles, assessing the state of the bomb. Behind him, the tacks ran in, pointing and leveling their weapons about. The lead agent opened fire at the frozen Syrian. Several other agents discharged rounds at the Syrian's paralyzed figure.

The volley of shots shattered his ceramic-like body into hundreds of shards, each hit an explosion of vapor. As pieces of his solid form were blown apart, the structure of his frozen body was compromised—it collapsed under its own weight, teetering, it plummeted to the floor, smashing into a million pieces.

"Hold fire. Hold fire!" a NEST tech shouted.

"Cease fire," the tack lead yelled.

The second NEST tech rushed through the group of agents. He wielded an axe-like weapon, raising it high into the air as he lunged forward. He chopped the wires between the control box and the bomb.

In the background, shouts of "Clear!" could be heard as agents secured the house. More NEST scientists and techs hurried into the room. They bullied their way through the hulking CT agents and shone an array of instruments and probes at the gadget.

One of them performed a 360-degree walk around the device, with a radiation detector and a density scanner. The CT officers were shoved to the periphery as a crowd of bomb techs inspected the device and all of its wires and components.

"Jesus, this is the real thing," one scientist remarked.

"We need to get this out of here. It's still technically live," another of the bomb techs warned.

The CT commander and the NEST lead entered.

"Commander, this is the real deal. This thing's twenty- to twenty-five kilotons," he said, his hand waving over the device. "It's still capable of a detonation, so we need to get this as far outside the city as possible. Fast."

"Copy that. Air evac team landing now," the commander motioned.

The NEST lead turned to the other techs. "Let's get the litter to haul this thing out of here," he shouted.

A few moments later, techs entered wheeling what resembled an ambulance stretcher. They jostled it and forced it over the debris.

"Hey, clear us a path!" one of the NEST techs yelled to the agents.

The CT troops, in their armor, gear, and guns, started to sweep away all the debris and clutter, clearing a smooth path from the table to the outside doorway.

Ten NEST and bomb disposal techs delicately protected the gadget. They wrapped it in several layers of linen cloth. They rolled the litter up to the table and gently worked the gadget to the table's edge. The team gingerly lifted and shifted the hundred-pound device onto the litter, where it rested on a padded bed.

This was all done to minimize shocks to the high explosives that surrounded the plutonium core of the device. The high explosives were very sensitive and could be easily detonated.

"Let them through!" yelled the CT commander.

The techs eased the gadget on its specialized gurney out of the room and down the hallway. They awkwardly hoisted and carried it over the damaged front porch steps and set it down onto the short walkway.

A NEST van pulled up in front. The teams worked to transfer the bomb into the van's bay where it would be driven up the hill to the top of Downey Street. They would meet the rendition helo at the intersection where it was flat enough to land safely. The helo was already circling overhead, preparing to set down.

Kyle jogged to the front of the Victorian. He witnessed the device being wheeled out of the house and loaded into the van.

"Holy shit," he uttered.

He looked to the CT commander, who flashed Kyle a *thumbs-up*. Kyle responded with a grin. He flipped open his cell phone but remembered when he saw the zero bars that they were being jammed.

"Hey? Where is outside the jamming zone? I need to make a call," he asked one of the nearby tacks.

"Top of the hill, intersection with Frederick, right up there. You should be able to get some coverage, but heads up, we're landing a bird there."

Kyle hustled up the steep street. He watched his cell, eyeing his reception bars. Two hundred yards up, there was still no coverage. The hill was quite tall, and he didn't want to huff all the way to the intersection, but he needed to call Pete ASAP to confirm the Fed. He climbed another hundred yards and finally saw one bar appear, good enough. He dialed. Through very staticky reception:

"Pete, we got it... Yes, confirmed. Get the Fed to move, and start to take it back up," he told him.

Fortnum Bank Fixed Income Trading Floor

"Holy shit, you serious? Awesome!... You got it. You're a fucking hero." Pete tossed the handset.

He waved to Steve and gave him a thumbs-up.

"We're good?" Steve confirmed.

"A quarter-point definitely, fifty if they can."

"We're on it," Steve responded and was already on the phone.

Pete turned to the traders.

"Lift it. Buy in size. Go, *go!*"

Shirin looked at him for affirmation. Pete winked back at her.

Private Office, Somewhere

Sully kneeled next to one of the traders, anxiously watching their screens. Markets were reversing, and the Saudis weren't happy. Al-Hammadi, working with the trader trying to contact the Syrian in San Fran, looked at Sully.

"We've lost contact," he shouted, alarmed.

Sully stomped over to them.

"What does that *mean*, you've *lost contact*? We can't detonate the thing?"

"It means we can't get through to him, yes!" al-Hammadi spat.

"Shit!" Sully stormed in a fury. He started hounding the traders.

"Cut our positions. Take profits, as fast as you can," he ordered.

"I think they might have it," al-Hammadi fretted.

"We're fucked if they have it!" Sully agonized and badgered the traders again, "Come on, cut our positions, fast!" he yelled at them again.

At that moment, they watched the news flash on the screens and monitors, "Federal Reserve intervenes with emergency 50 basis point cut."

"Shit!" Sully raged. "Buy us back. Get us out!"

Markets lurched in the opposite direction. The S&P rocketed three hundred points higher in a second. Gold dropped $30, plunging back to $890. Crude oil jumped $2 to $72.

The traders scrambled to enter orders but were not quick enough. Markets were moving too fast; there wasn't any liquidity for them to exit.

"Fast!" Sully pressed. He looked to al-Hammadi, who looked back at him.

"Something's happened..." al-Hammadi confirmed.

"Again, what the fuck does that mean?"

"It means I need to call insurance man," al-Hammadi cryptically replied.

Sully rolled his eyes at that. "What the *fuck*, man?" He scowled at him and implored the traders, "Buy it in, whatever you can, *now!*"

Downey Street, San Francisco

Kyle heard the incoming whoops of the angel flight that was landing at the crest of the hill. The helicopter grew louder as it rattled the air around him and touched down on the intersection. Its blades kept whirring so it could take off as soon as the bomb was loaded.

Kyle reversed and started back down the hill toward the command truck and the rest of the teams. They were packing up, throwing gear and weapons into their vehicles. Kyle watched as the NEST van carrying the bomb gassed up the steep hill and labored past him toward the waiting helicopter.

And then Kyle froze. He did a hard double take.

Unmistakable. It was the face he would never, ever forget—in the passenger-side seat of that NEST van—the Hawk-Nosed Man.

Kyle swallowed. He tried to shout. His throat was paralyzed. It dried up. He couldn't utter anything. He searched downhill and desperately waved to the CT troops. They were busy loading gear. Nobody saw him. He watched the van ride past him in slow motion.

He turned and sprinted after it. The van had almost reached the crest, a few hundred yards uphill from him, approaching the helicopter. Kyle kept running.

"No, *no!*" Kyle finally shouted.

He ran as fast as he could. He watched the van brake at the helicopter. The helo pilot jumped out, and the van's driver and the Hawk-Nosed Man exited with two NEST techs. They pulled open the rear van doors and removed the bomb. The techs rolled the gurney up to the side of the helicopter, and they all transferred the bomb into the rear seats of the helo, and strapped it in.

Kyle yelled downhill, "Help! *Help!*" A few tacks peered up in his direction but couldn't tell what he was saying. He tried to signal for them to come—*fast.*

He turned back to watch the Hawk-Nosed Man remove a pistol from inside his jacket. "The van guy! The van *guy!*"

Cap-cap-cap-cap! The Hawk-Nosed Man, in half a second, shot the NEST driver, then the tech in the van. The helicopter pilot froze with fear. The Hawk-Nosed Man swiveled around and—*cap-cap!*—shot the pilot twice in the head. The pilot spilled onto the front of the van, crumpled to the street, and rolled into the front yard of a nearby house.

The higher-pitched sound of the gunshots penetrated through the thump of the helicopter blades, and some of the other CT agents alerted at the recognizable noise. They looked uphill. It was hard for them to see that distance. But they saw at least two bodies and Kyle, running toward the fray.

"*Commander?* We got action up the hill!" one of the agents yelled.

The commander ran over. "Go, *go!*" he hollered for everybody to race up there. The tacks took off.

The sounds of the helicopter blades whirred faster and louder. Kyle bolted toward the helicopter as the Hawk-Nosed Man shifted into the pilot's seat and pulled the door shut. The Hawk-Nosed Man unhooked the chopper's landing lock. The agents were only halfway up the hill.

Kyle reached the helicopter just as it lifted off the ground. In desperation, he threw an arm around the right landing skid and grabbed his wrist with his other hand, locking himself around the skid as the helicopter rose into the air.

The Hawk-Nosed Man, at the controls, the bomb sitting in the rear seat row, boosted the helicopter higher. He was unaware that Kyle was dangling from the landing gear, outside.

Kyle clung on for dear life. His arms were interlocked around the skid tube.

The rush of air and helicopter blades deafened him. He didn't dare look down as the rooftops diminished below.

He saw he was eye level with the taller buildings in the city. He knew he was high up and rising. He couldn't let go. Death was no option. There was one thought in his head that swelled more than any other. He wanted to kill that Hawk-Nosed Man once and for all. He wanted to crush his skull.

Kyle kicked his legs up, to no avail. He struggled against the momentum of the helicopter's g-forces. The speed of the air was prying off his grip. The insanely loud racket of the blades was killing him.

He swung his right leg up. It missed. He tried again. This time, his foot caught the cross brace. He gripped it with his foot and gained some leverage. Kyle rotated himself around the skid tube, pushing down with his thigh. He jerked his other leg up and wrapped his foot around the cross brace. Like a constrictor, he coiled tightly around the skid tube, arms and legs, hugging it securely, perilously.

The Hawk-Nosed Man ascended further. They were a thousand feet above the city of San Francisco. Inside, the Hawk-Nosed Man leveled it out. He peered through the windshield at the sky above him, his focus inclining upward. He spotted the one-engine prop plane flying circles overhead. His fixing lowered back to the horizon, and he thrust the pitch level forward. The helicopter zoomed ahead.

The sudden acceleration knocked Kyle loose. The helo leaned into a forward angle, and the skids tilted downward. Kyle's legs fell off, and he slid down and impacted against the cross brace, jolting his hold, and almost casting him off. He grimaced from the pain and the pressure of the blasting air.

He struggled, inching himself back up the skid. The downward angle made it easier to get his legs around again, and he swung his feet onto the cross brace in one try. He squeezed himself higher along the skid tube and was again tightly lashed around it with his entire body, gripping it with all his strength.

Kyle felt the chopper level out again. He kept his grip as firm as he could. He had to think about his next move. His only hope, he thought, was to get inside the cabin, somehow. He looked above him. He noticed the rear cabin side door had an external door handle. And it appeared like it wasn't fully shut, not flush with the helicopter's skin. It probably hadn't been closed properly in the attack, Kyle surmised…and *hoped*. He was dead otherwise, he reminded himself.

Kyle wormed his way toward the rear of the skid. He locked his arms together around the rear cross brace. He glimpsed up. There was the door handle. He looped his right arm through the skid cross to give himself some leverage. And freeing his left arm, he groped along the helo door toward the handle to see if—yes, he could reach it!

Joint Tactical Operations

Confusion and commotion came from the FBI sections. Beringer rotated to them.

"What the fuck is going on?"

The lead FBI officer, on two phones, faced Beringer.

"The bomb's been hijacked."

"What the fuck does that mean, *hijacked*?" Beringer thundered.

They all pointed at the monitors. Their closed-circuit drone cameras were now filming the events. They strobed to focus on the helicopter ascending over the city. Gasps. Everyone saw the lumpy shape on the landing skid.

"That's a person!" someone shouted out.

"My God!" Bob exclaimed.

"Keep the jammer on that bird like a fly on shit."

"On it," Brent yelled back.

"And let's shoot that thing out of the sky. Can we get a gunship up there?"

"On the way, sir. Ten minutes," a DoD rep responded.

Fortnum Bank Fixed Income Trading Floor

Pete directed the traders to keep buying. Markets were going their way, returning with a vengeance. S&P was down only 200 points now, rallying back from down 750. Gold had dropped to $850, and crude oil was closing in on $80 again.

Pete had a grin on his face and regarded Shirin with widened, confident eyes. And then the FBI liaison grabbed him. It was hard to hear over the noise.

"We have a problem," he reported.

"What?"

"We have a problem, a serious *problem*!"

"What do you mean?"

"The bomb has been hijacked. We're not in control of it."

Pete stared at him. For a moment, he thought the officer was joking but then noticed the almost sad, resigned expression on the agent's face. Pete's eyes searched the floor. He reviewed the markets and where they were trading at that moment. All prices were going against the bad guys. He instantly calculated.

"They're going to detonate it," Pete pronounced.

Private Office, Somewhere

Al-Hammadi watched the markets rip past them. Sully was beside himself, furious. He continued yelling at the traders to close their positions, which they weren't having much success doing.

"Markets are almost back to flat. We've given up most of our gains," one of the traders announced.

Al-Hammadi glanced at his phone.

"We're in control again," he said simply.

Sully shot him an angry look. "What the fuck, man? Can we detonate or not?"

"Yes, we have the bomb."

He confirmed from his phone. "And we have connection."

Al-Hammadi dialed the detonation sequence.

Travis Air Force Base, Fairfield, California, United States

On the airfield tarmac, crews scrambled two US Army Reserve AH-64 Apache gunships. Their pilots and weapons officers boarded and fired up their engines.

Each helo was armed with thirty-millimeter chain guns, seventy-millimeter Hydra rocket pods on their stub wings, and a pair of AGM-114 Hellfire missiles.

Their blades whipped around, and the two birds rose off the airstrip, ascending to a thousand feet. With their nose guns angled to attack, the Apaches sprinted over the desert hilltops toward San Francisco.

Sky Over San Francisco, 2,000 Feet

The Hawk-Nosed Man pressed the stick forward, and the helicopter shot toward the Financial District. He looked upward out the windshield, trying to locate the jammer plane. He spotted it in the southwest quadrant and watched as it fell behind him.

Several thousand feet above the hijacked helicopter, the pilot and EWO in the one-engine EC plane frantically looked for the helicopter. Their electronics only had a limited jamming range to block signals, so they needed to stay close to the helicopter to keep it within the jamming bubble.

"There he is," the EWO cried, pointing at the fleeing helicopter below them. "He's out of range right now."

"Descending," the pilot affirmed as he pushed the yoke into a dive.

The one-engine craft was nimble. It lowered its right wing and spiraled after the helicopter, quickly dropping a few thousand feet. In seconds, it had caught up to the target. The EWO's monitors lit up, indicating they were jamming an incoming satellite-based signal.

"Shit. They're trying. We barely covered that attempt. Sat signal," he said.

The Hawk-Nosed Man marked the jammer plane, irritated it had gotten too close again. He ripped the helicopter hard left and took it back in the opposite direction.

Outside, Kyle reached up and tried to grab the door handle just as the helo rolled left. The torque threw his free arm out into the air, almost pulling him off the skid again. He fought off the centrifugal force and pressed his hand back around the tube. His forearms were tiring, and he had no respite as the helicopter straightened out, smashing Kyle again into the forward skid cross.

Recovering, Kyle worked himself along the skid tube toward the rear cross again. Reaching that, he wrapped his right arm in a half nelson around the joint, to help give himself a little more height in extending for the cabin door handle.

Kyle knew that, with his right arm twisted through the cross brace, if the Hawk-Nosed Man banked sharply again, the g-forces would probably break his arm. Kyle focused. He freed his left arm and groped above him, feeling along the smooth door. His hand found the depression of the door handle. He also felt that it was a lift mechanism, and he was going to have to pull it upward, quickly, a motion that from his position would be awkward and he would have little power with which to accomplish it. He also knew that if the door did open, the Hawk-Nosed Man would see him and would probably roll the helicopter to try to dislodge him. He'd only have a few seconds, at best.

Kyle peeked toward where the Hawk-Nosed Man was flying. They were back over the Haight-Ashbury neighborhood. A sudden acrophobia came over him.

Kyle's mind spun. He felt like letting go. He felt his arms weaken. He was only brought back by the horrendous, deafening roar of the helicopter blades. He shook it off. Kyle realized the Hawk-Nosed Man would probably bank again in another few seconds. This was his chance, he knew.

He unwound his right arm from its half nelson around the skid cross. He was now unsteady. This was dangerous as shit. The winds battered him. The thundering of the blades distracted him. His grip was tenuous. If he missed, he'd probably lose it and plummet to his death. In a swift move, he flipped up the door handle and pulled it as hard as he could. It swung open.

Kyle glanced up and spotted an inside door bar. He extended and stretched as he let go of the skid and grabbed onto the door bar, praying it wouldn't rip off from his weight. He squeezed enough of a grasp and hoisted himself upward and into the helicopter. His foot found the edge of the open door, and he wedged himself against it to finally gain some leverage. But the door swung open with his motion as he clung to it.

Kyle was half inside the helicopter, stuck to the inside door bar, his foot pressing against the door as his right hand clawed hopelessly at the fabric of the rear seats in the cabin.

The Hawk-Nosed Man heard the sudden wind rush of the open door. He eyed over his left shoulder and saw the opened door and Kyle scaling through the opening. The Hawk-Nosed Man's eyes widened.

He yanked the helo hard left, banking at such an angle, Kyle lost his footing on the door. His legs flew out as the Hawk-Nosed Man tried to dump him out of the cabin. Kyle was again dangling, clinging to the inside door bar while gripping the lobe of the rear seat. He hung on as the helicopter was almost flying on its side.

But the Hawk-Nosed Man couldn't keep the helicopter banking at this sharp angle for too long. Forced to, he leveled it back out. Kyle held onto the door as the helicopter rocked upright, and he leveraged the rotational force to his advantage and propelled himself inside the rear cabin. He slammed into the bomb, cutting his lip and cheek on the aluminum sectional flanges as he flew into it and dropped onto the floor below the rear seats.

Kyle regained his balance and reached for the door, which was waving open and closed with the helicopter's rocking. He grabbed the inside door bar and pulled it shut for good. The Hawk-Nosed Man drew his pistol and awkwardly tried to point it at Kyle over his shoulder to get a shot off.

Cap! The bullet widely missed and blew a hole through the left rear window. Kyle grabbed for the pistol as the Hawk-Nosed Man pinned the control stick between his knees to get a better angle to shoot him.

Fortnum Bank Fixed Income Trading Floor

News channels had started to broadcast from the ground in San Francisco. The out-of-control helicopter wrenching above the city rooftops was now live on TV.

The trading floor wall monitors all displayed this real-time sky drama. Traders' attentions had shifted from the markets to the TVs. They watched the human dangle and hoist himself into the helicopter.

"Holy shit, was that *Kyle*?" Shirin shouted, appalled.

Pete couldn't even react; he grabbed the lead FBI agent by the collar. "Is that the hijacked helicopter? Is the bomb in there? Is that Kyle hanging from it?" Pete screamed at him. The agent just looked at Pete and nodded tightly.

Private Office, Somewhere

Sully, al-Hammadi, and the traders watched the same events broadcast on their TVs. Sully couldn't believe his eyes.

"Why isn't the bomb detonating?" he yelled at al-Hammadi.

"They're jamming the satellite signal. We have to keep trying," he griped. And he started to dial again.

"Give me that!" Sully grabbed the satellite phone and dialed himself.

Sky Over East Oakland, 4,000 Feet

The two Apaches raced toward San Francisco. The point of the Transamerica Pyramid emerged on the horizon, reflected in the pilots' visors.

The first pilot, behind his darkened face shield, centered on their objective. "Opera House? This is Silver Wolf. Two mikes to theater, copy?"

Joint Tactical Operations

The large monitors splayed out the twisting helicopter over San Francisco to the entire operations center. Everyone was on their feet, eyes unblinking.

DoD reps turned to Beringer.

"They keep trying to detonate the warhead, Admiral. This is not good. We've blocked three incoming signals now," one of the officers reported.

"Where are those birds, *goddamn it*?"

"Still two minutes out."

"Two minutes? They can fire a missile at them from that range."

"Sir, we're over a civilian area. Do we have authorization?"

"We're trying to stop goddamned nuclear detonation over a civilian area. *Yes,* you have authorization. Shoot the fucking thing down!"

Kate and Bob exchanged worried looks.

"Kyle's on that helicopter. You saw him. I wasn't imagining that."

Bob returned a vacant expression. "What can we do?"

Kate stared at him, intense and frustrated. Bob felt her eyes burning into his head but didn't turn to her. In the tense moment, Sarah appeared next to Kate.

"We're inside," Sarah reported, but Kate didn't respond, too incensed at Bob.

Sky Over San Francisco, 2,500 Feet

The Hawk-Nosed Man bent around and—*cap!*—fired again as Kyle ducked, the bullet blowing a hole through the fabric of the left rear seat. The helicopter jostled, and Kyle grabbed at the pistol, clawing into the Hawk-Nosed Man's right hand, who yanked it away from the sudden pain. The helicopter lurched forward, and the gun flew from his hand, ricocheting off the inside windshield and clattering onto the floor and under the empty navigator seat.

The Hawk-Nosed Man angled to find it, but the gun was far enough under the seat he couldn't spot it. He groped around just as Kyle landed a strong blow to the left side of his head.

The Hawk-Nosed Man was pummeled against the right window, momentarily stunned. He slumped over the control stick, and the helo pitched forward, accelerating and launching Kyle backward against the rear seats and bomb. The back of his head slammed into the bulkhead, and Kyle was dazed, too. Kyle shook it off as the Hawk-Nosed Man recovered and steadied the helicopter.

Kyle glanced at the bomb. It occurred to him to open the right-side passenger cabin door and push the bomb out with his feet, but he didn't know if that would set the thing off. Also, he had to unstrap it, which would take precious time and give the Hawk-Nosed Man the advantage.

Kyle saw his opponent reaching for the gun again. Kyle lunged at him and grabbed his head, putting him in a secure headlock. The Hawk-Nosed Man struggled, grasping at Kyle's arms, punching backward. The blows hit Kyle like kicks, but he held and compressed his arms around the Hawk-Nosed Man's neck.

As Kyle was taking the blows, the helicopter rolled and then swung upward, into a high-pitch ascent. Kyle did a double take through the right windshield—two military helicopters barreling for them. He forced the Hawk-Nosed Man to bank it left. The Hawk-Nosed Man also saw the Apaches and actually helped Kyle, yanking the stick hard left with him.

The lead Apache opened up on them with its thirty-millimeter cannon. They heard the rounds scream overhead as their erratic helicopter flopped right and left. In the rocking, Kyle lost his hold of the Hawk-Nosed Man and fell backward into the bomb. He staggered upright as his nemesis took control again.

The second Apache curled around and lined them up.

"Down, down. Take it down!" Kyle yelled as he lunged forward, shoving the Hawk-Nosed Man into the control stick, forcing the helicopter downward. Kyle glimpsed the Apache's cannon muzzle aflame, churning rounds at them.

Their helicopter dove toward the San Fran rooftops as the bullets flew past them. One round smacked through the left landing skid with a loud clang. Their helo plunged a thousand feet as both Apaches revolved around for a second run.

The Hawk-Nosed Man pulled the stick straight back into his lap, sending Kyle slamming into the rear bulkhead again. The helicopter reared and climbed back up to five thousand feet. The Hawk-Nosed Man searched outside through the windshield. A mile to the east, he spied the single-engine jammer plane.

The Hawk-Nosed Man thrust the helo forward, a beeline for the plane.

Fortnum Bank Fixed Income Trading Floor

Pete stared at the wall monitors broadcasting the fumbling helicopter. His hands were sweaty. He couldn't pay attention to his charts. The trading floor and the markets were now swinging with every hairpin turn the helicopter made.

Sky Over San Francisco, 5,000 Feet

The EC pilot and EWO watched in panic as the helicopter charged right for them.

"What the fuck is he doing?"

"Dive, dive!" the EWO shouted.

The pilot shoved the yoke forward.

The small aircraft pitched into a descent and plummeted.

The Hawk-Nosed Man angled the helo, keeping them on a collision course.

"Jesus Christ, he's gonna collide with us. Bank left, *left!*"

The pilot threw the plane left, narrowly missing the helicopter as it blared by. The helo rotated in a tight 180 and darted after the EC plane. The pilot and EWO tried to look over their shoulders to find him.

"Where is he? Is he chasing us now?"

A horrendous rattling roared by them as the jammer plane narrowly avoided being shot up by one of the Apaches.

"Son of a bitch! They're shooting at us!" the pilot yelled.

"They're shooting at them. We're getting in the way."

"Let's get out of here!"

"We can't—you see the signal trying to get through—they'll detonate that thing! We can't leave!"

"I'll take us down, then!"

"We've got to be over them, at a higher altitude."

"Climbing!"

The pilot pulled the yoke to take the plane back up.

Inside the helo, while the Hawk-Nosed Man was distracted trying to chase the jammer plane, Kyle groped the floor underneath the front seat with his left foot for the pistol, but no luck, he couldn't feel it. The Hawk-Nosed Man tried to reach behind him and grab Kyle. Kyle blocked his arm, grabbing it with his left hand and punching the Hawk-Nosed Man with a swift right jab in the jaw. The Hawk-Nosed Man jerked from the strike, blood ejecting from his long nose. He sagged—he appeared knocked out.

Kyle glimpsed out the windshield and saw an Apache hovering, lining them up for another shot. Kyle reached the stick in time, sending their helicopter pitching nose down again as more Gatling fire whistled overhead.

The Hawk-Nosed Man recovered and realized they were diving. He wrestled, fighting off Kyle, deflecting him with his left elbow as he pulled the stick, swinging the helicopter from a roller-coaster plunge and back into a steep climb. They were heading directly for the jammer plane again.

The Hawk-Nosed Man straightened out, level with the EC plane. As he did that, they both heard the metallic rattle of the pistol on the floor. It had dislodged and slid into the front footwell. The Hawk-Nosed Man saw it first and dove for it. Kyle lunged for it too, but the Hawk-Nosed Man beat him to it. He grabbed it and twisted around, and—*Cap! Cap!*

A shot grazed Kyle's left shoulder. He screamed out in pain as blood splattered against the ceiling of the cabin and the bullet ripped through the bulkhead behind them. The second shot hit Kyle square in the chest, like a sledgehammer, slamming him against the left rear door. Kyle's wind was knocked out of him, but he was saved by the Kevlar vest the tacks had given him. Kyle gasped, coughing to recover. The Hawk-Nosed Man glanced at Kyle, tried to twist for a kill shot to Kyle's head, but he couldn't get the angle.

Inside the jammer plane, they could see the helicopter flying right at them again.

"He's there. Son of a bitch!"

"Banking east," the pilot parried, as he squeezed it left. The plane's left wing dipped, and it flung toward the Bay just as the helicopter flew into its airspace.

The EWO's components lit up.

"Shit. That was another signal. They're really trying to light this thing up. We're almost level with them. They're exposed! Climb more, climb!"

The pilot swung the plane back around and took it up to seven thousand feet.

Private Office, Somewhere

"Markets crashing," one of the traders shouted.

"We're positive again. A few billion," another reported.

"Good. Everyone's watching this. It isn't good for confidence, and we're going to turn San Fran into a Roman candle in a second," Sully said, evilly.

"Our man is getting us out from under that jamming plane. Keep trying."

Al-Hammadi gestured, and Sully dialed again.

"Son of a bitch, Springer. You want to play this game? Let's see what else you got," he said as he angrily jabbed the phone's buttons.

Sky Over San Francisco, 7,000 Feet

Kyle grabbed for the pistol as the Hawk-Nosed Man awkwardly aimed it, trying to shoot Kyle with one hand while pulling the control stick back to a climb again after the EC plane.

"The gunships!" Kyle yelled, pointing out the windshield. The Hawk-Nosed Man looked to his right—it was a bluff—no Apaches. Kyle grabbed the gun and dug into his gun hand. *Cap!*

The pistol fired a shot, shattering the pilot's left side window as they wrestled for it. Kyle gripped the gun, and the Hawk-Nosed Man pulled the trigger again and—*click!*—they both eyed each other in recognition. Empty. The gun was useless now. Kyle slugged the Hawk-Nosed Man in the temple. He screamed in pain as Kyle landed another square punch on his nose, breaking it.

Blood streamed down the Hawk-Nosed Man's face, his eyes blurry with tears. Kyle leapt into the empty front seat, striking the Hawk-Nosed Man with a fierce elbow, twice in the face, and in his broken nose. He shrieked in pain.

Kyle grabbed the stick and thrust the helicopter to a lower altitude, but the Hawk-Nosed Man, his face bloodied, gripped Kyle's arms, fighting against him.

The helicopter teetered, its tail swinging wildly as Kyle and the Hawk-Nosed Man dueled for control. Kyle gained the upper hand for a moment and forced the stick forward into the dash, nose-diving them again. But the Hawk-Nosed Man battled back and knocked Kyle off and swung the helicopter into a climb.

Their helo was on a roller-coaster track, rising and dropping. It made it difficult, fortunately for them, for the Apaches to get a solid lock on their target.

The Hawk-Nosed Man rammed Kyle into the windshield, but he let go of the stick. Kyle grabbed the Hawk-Nosed Man's neck and swiped for the stick with his other hand. The Hawk-Nosed Man punched him hard in his gunshot wound. Kyle howled. The Hawk-Nosed Man punched him again in the same spot, knuckles out.

"Son of a bitch!" Kyle wilted, writhing in pain in the left pilot seat.

The Hawk-Nosed Man grabbed the advantage and pulled the helicopter into an ascent, aiming right at the jammer plane again.

Kyle got ahold of himself. He faced the Hawk-Nosed Man.

"You piece of shit, I'll kill you!" He grabbed the Hawk-Nosed Man's neck and strangled him. The Hawk-Nosed Man struggled, grasping at Kyle, scratching at his hands, and grabbing his hair, anything. The Hawk-Nosed Man tried to kick, but each thrash jolted the control stick in a random direction.

The helicopter jerked side to side from the melee going on inside, like it was a toy being shaken on the end of a string.

Inside the jammer plane, the pilot and EWO watched the out-of-control chopper twist dangerously close to them. It briefly leveled itself, only to roll over again.

"Let's get clear of this thing. Get us up more, higher!"

"I think you're—"

The jammer controls lit up again as another detonation signal was blocked.

"Hurry!" He banged on the blinking instruments.

The pilot drew the yoke backward, rocketing the plane into a climb.

The two Apaches swiveled, scissoring into a figure eight to chase down the helicopter and line up a final kill shot. The lead Apache bent around in a wide turn and straightened out. It rose into a climb to line up with their target helo.

A burst of Gatling fire erupted from its nose cannon. The laser-like bullets needled through the air, narrowly missing the unpredictable helicopter as it jumped about the sky.

The second Apache banked in the opposite path and emerged, lining up dead-on with the helicopter. The second pilot thumbed the trim, his finger tapping the trigger. Through his gun sights, their target was still difficult to lock onto. The Apache was in a shallow climb, nose gun aimed in an upward angle.

The target helicopter swung into and out of the Apache's kill box. The pilot kept his focus aligned, and his hand steady on the control stick. Watching his target's rhythm, the gunner didn't hesitate. He counted the next pendulum swing.

And he depressed the fire trigger.

The cannon unleashed a volley of rounds. A fiery plasma ignited around its spinning muzzle as it discharged. The Apache pilot looked up at the target for visual kill confirmation just as the helicopter yanked in a head fake left and then dropped from his kill box, revealing, directly behind it, the tail of another aircraft in a climb, the wrong target—the EC jammer plane.

The thirty-millimeter shells ripped through the aircraft, piercing its thin skin. The small plane exploded into searing debris of metal and fiberglass that rained down over San Francisco.

Fortnum Bank Fixed Income Trading Floor

They stared at the televisions, mouths agape.

"Holy shit!" Pete shouted.

The floor erupted in a panic of sells.

Pete hit Shirin. "That wasn't Kyle, was it?"

She shook her head and pointed at the wobbly helicopter that was still in the air. "No, Kyle's in that one."

Pete turned to the market action, snapping out of it.

S&P was down five hundred points again. Gold was above $900, and crude oil was dropping, back down to $74.

"Everything's their way."

"I think that plane was protecting them. I think it was preventing the bomb from being detonated," Shirin fretted. "I think it's going to explode."

"Come on, Springer. Be alive, goddamn it," Pete prayed under his breath.

He shifted helplessly. He needed to do something, but there was nothing he could do now. He looked to the Fed team.

"Can we do another intervention?" he shouted at Steve.

"We're out of bullets," Steve responded.

Pete hopelessly watched the televisions.

Sky Over San Francisco, 7,000 Feet

Kyle and the Hawk-Nosed Man both watched the dimming fireball in the sky and the cascading, smoking tracks of the plane's debris falling to the ground below.

The Hawk-Nosed Man laughed out loud.

"You're dead," he said amid his chuckles.

Kyle seized him and put him in a headlock. With a sturdy grip, he rolled him into the navigator's seat. The Hawk-Nosed Man struggled for breath and clawed at Kyle's strong forearms around his neck. Kyle flexed and contracted his hold in pulses, tightening his embrace. He felt the Hawk-Nosed Man's body go limp as he passed out from lack of oxygen in the sleeper hold.

The helicopter spun with no one at the controls. Kyle glimpsed outside, at the two gunships swirling above him, lapping for a final kill shot.

Kyle grabbed the Hawk-Nosed Man's body by whatever handles of clothing he could, and hurled him into the rear seats, where he slumped to the floor.

Kyle shifted into the pilot's seat. He knew what he had to do. Kyle plowed the stick forward, jamming it into the dash.

The helicopter plunged toward the city. Gatling fire crackled around him, barely missing as he dove. The Apaches barrel-rolled after him.

Joint Tactical Operations

Everyone was speechless, watching the plummeting wreckage from the jammer aircraft. The cameras were now on the bomb helicopter rolling into a nosedive.

"We shot our EC out of the sky!" an officer yelled.

"Goddamn it. We killed a friendly."

"Just shoot that helo out of the air!" Beringer yelled. "Now. We have about three more seconds before a detonation signal comes through!"

Fortnum Bank Fixed Income Trading Floor

Pete watched the helicopter in a nosedive as it plunged straight for the ground.

"Kyle, what are you doing?"

Shirin and Pete exchanged fatalistic looks. Pete said with a deep breath, "He's taking one for the team."

The markets dropped, along with the helicopter.

Sky Over San Francisco, 2,000 Feet

Kyle, in a vertical dive, the rooftops fast approaching, put all his weight on the stick. The Hawk-Nosed Man came to in the back and saw what Kyle was doing.

"No!" The Hawk-Nosed Man shouted, lunging at Kyle.

Kyle opened the left-side pilot door just as the Hawk-Nosed Man lurched over the seats. He yanked up the stick and shouldered the Hawk-Nosed Man out the open door. The Hawk-Nosed Man was thrown off his balance, and desperately grasped at anything he could. Kyle banked the helo to the left, dumping the Hawk-Nosed Man out of the cab.

The Hawk-Nosed Man shrieked in defeat, swiping and batting as he fell from the helo, plummeting to the rooftops below.

Kyle pulled shut the door and leveled out the helicopter.

He glanced above and saw the Apaches bearing down on him.

Private Office, Somewhere

Grins emerged on the faces in the posh office. As they observed the dust and smoke cloud from the jammer plane shot out of the sky, they all calculated and knew—the next call would get through.

Al-Hammadi beamed and looked over at Sully, who was holding the phone.

"Gotcha, Springer."

Sully dialed the number, and his thumb was about to hit Send when the satellite phone shattered into pieces.

Sully jerked backward. Al-Hammadi puzzled at the vaporized phone. Sully curiously eyed a small, leftover plastic fragment of the phone in his hand, and looked up at al-Hammadi, confused.

There was a loud *snap*. One of the traders' heads exploded in blood and bone onto his monitors with pieces of fabric from his keffiyeh.

Sully and al-Hammadi, stunned, twisted to the origin of the sound. The tea servant removed his keffiyeh—it was Commander Kelso, leveling a suppressed HK MP5.

"Greetings from the U S of A," Kelso uttered coldly.

Kelso sprayed the traders, dispatching them in seconds with a pounding of bullets that ripped through them, shredding their flesh, and fizzling their monitors.

He turned to the paralyzed Sully and al-Hammadi, whose eyes were as wide as saucers, totally frozen with fear. The white muzzle flash from Kelso's MP5 was the last thing they ever saw.

Joint Tactical Operations

As the Apaches lined up to take out the helicopter, Kate and Bob shouted:

"We have control! We have control!"

"Call it off!"

Beringer stood and yelled to the DoD station.

"Guns down! Stand down, *stand down*!"

Sky Over San Francisco, 3,000 Feet

The first Apache pilot, centering Kyle in his kill box, overheard, "Silver Wolf? This is Opera House. Stand down, stand down! Copy?"

The pilot returned the cannon to standby.

"Copy. Disengaging."

Kyle, guiding the helo with the stick between his knees, kept it level but didn't know how to get it down. He glimpsed out his right-side window and saw one of the Apaches pull alongside. The pilot hand-signaled to follow him. A voice came over the radio.

"TH Pilot? This is US Army Specialist Scott Henry, aka, Silver Wolf. I'm going to talk you down."

Kyle turned to the Apache and saluted him in acknowledgment.

Fortnum Bank Fixed Income Trading Floor

Pete was the first to put it all together.

"Buy it, *buy it*! *Buy everything!*" Pete suddenly shouted. "Take it back up. It's over. Buy 'em sloppy!"

The markets reversed on a dime. The trading floor exploded as traders and sales traders grabbed whatever offers they could.

Pete stared at gold which tumbled, down to $840, then $815, and finally finding a bottom at $765. He slumped in his seat and cracked a wide grin.

Golden Gate Park, San Francisco, United States

The three helicopters descended, the Apaches directing Kyle to a grassy flat in Golden Gate Park. Kyle kept the controls even and followed their instructions as he watched dozens of FBI and emergency vehicles race onto the green below him.

Kyle dropped the helicopter onto the field, cutting its lift as it bounced and skidded along the grass and came to a jolting halt, its skid points lodging into the dirt. Kyle was slammed into the dash, striking his head. He came to and threw open the door, the blades still whirring at speed.

Emergency personnel rushed in. Several battle meds pulled the wounded, exhausted Kyle from the half-crashed helo. Another tech shut down the bird, its engines finally slowing and coming to a stop.

A military transport helicopter landed on the grass next to them. NEST teams encircled and, in moments, had removed the bomb and placed it onto another litter, and hustled it over to the airlifter.

As EMTs hoisted Kyle onto a stretcher, he watched the NEST techs load the bomb onto the rendition helicopter, its invisible spinning blades forming a circular halo above the craft.

The transport helicopter, with the bomb secured, lifted off and ascended into the sky in seconds, where it was joined by the hovering Apaches. The three helicopters sprinted past the San Francisco skyline and out over the Pacific Ocean where they disappeared from sight.

Afterword

Kate Harrison

Kate worked tirelessly but unsuccessfully to convert the intelligence gleaned from the captured North Korean warhead into a political windfall in the six-party talks. While its possession helped the DIA (Defense Intelligence Agency) render a detailed image of the North Korean weapons program and its technical level of progress, the dividends, unfortunately, stopped there and did little to thwart the steady advancement of the NK program in the years following. Successive administrations were also reluctant to confront China with the evidence.

Kate spent her next ten years convincing lawmakers of the existential threat the CCP (Communist Party of China) posed to the United States. She knew, because she was paid to be the expert, how they had organized to defeat the United States and become the world's most dominant power. They were postured for war along many dimensions, and the United States just didn't perceive that. She saw the threat from the nefarious, totalitarian regime coming from a mile away, but it took her years to convince the nation's leaders to understand what she did. Finally, policy started to catch up, and subsequent administrations and Congress began to act to protect the United States from the CCP. It wasn't remotely enough, but it was a start.

In 2015, Kate was promoted to head of the DI (Directorate of Intelligence), where she served until 2020. Following that, she left the Company to join the NIC (National Intelligence Council), the body that bridges the intelligence community with policymakers, where she is today. In her role at the NIC, she continues her push to address the threat from China.

Kate was awarded the National Intelligence Cross and the Distinguished Intelligence Medal.

Kyle and Amy Springer

Amy recovered from her gunshot wounds and, after four months of rehabilitation and physical therapy, returned to her position at the FBI. Kyle took care of their daughter, Jill, while Amy recuperated.

After persistent convincing by Kyle, he and Amy reconciled, and they've been living together as a family since. Although Amy refused to remarry Kyle, common law did catch up with them, and they are, in fact, legally married again. Jill is now twenty-one, attending NYU, studying criminology, looking to follow her mother's career. Amy continued with the FBI, where she still works today as assistant special agent in charge (ASAC) in the Counterintelligence Division.

Wall Street moved past the Scare, as it came to be called, with most in the industry chalking up the market volatility of that week to the Fed and expiration and to the increasingly worrisome subprime mortgage market. Any curiosity into what had really happened, industry or other, was quickly erased by funding liquidity problems in the subprime mortgage market and its respective custodial banks. Not more than six months later, the trading house, Bear Stearns, collapsed, accelerating the financial crisis of 2007 and 2008 and culminating in the bankruptcy of Lehman Brothers almost exactly a year later. Fortnum Bank was acquired, as many other banks were, following the Lehman Brothers bankruptcy.

In 2009, a year after the financial crisis, Kyle was approached by the US Treasury to become an officer in the Treasury's TFI (Terrorism and Financial Intelligence) service. He joined but also kept his Wall Street position so he could remain "connected." Today, his cover role is head of an electronic options market-making desk at an investment bank that cannot be named while he serves as an officer in the US Treasury, TFI group.

In private ceremonies, both Amy and Kyle were awarded the Presidential Medal of Freedom. Kyle additionally received the National Intelligence Distinguished Public Service Medal and Amy was awarded the FBI Star.

Commander Ken Kelso, USN, Retired

Commander Kelso continued operating in the shadows for the US government as an officer in the CIA's Special Activities Division, which later became SOG (Special Operations Group), for another five years. Following that, Kelso first semiretired from field service but remained involved, providing training, logistical support for ops, as well as other "practitioner assistance."

In 2017, Commander Kelso retired from the CIA for good to study traditional Japanese carpentry. He is currently an apprentice for a teahouse carpenter in Kyoto. He and his wife now have a little boy, Kentaro, who is eight. Once Kelso completes his apprenticeship, he, and his family plan to return to the States to open a Japanese carpentry business.

Commander Kelso was awarded the Distinguished Intelligence Medal and the National Security Medal.

Pete Graff and Shirin Abedi

Pete was quick to ask out Shirin after the Scare. Shirin and Pete dated for several years, but Pete remained hesitant to pop the question. Shirin finally "enforced her position," and Pete paid up for a ring and they got married in 2011. They are currently arguing over whether to start a family or not.

Shirin is now the head derivatives trader for the Biotech/Pharma Desk at the bank. Pete left the bank in 2015 and joined a boutique broker-dealer where he trades pre-IPO private equity.

Pete and Shirin were each awarded the Presidential Medal of Freedom.

Sarah Sussman, Dr. Clare Ahn, and Paul Kazemi

Dr. Ahn continues at the CIA today. She is one of the nation's experts on the North Korean nuclear program, and she has written several books on North Korea, the Kim regime, and its weapons program in the years since.

Paul remained at the CIA working his way up the DA (Directorate of Analysis, formerly the DI) in the Office of Terrorism Analysis. He left the Company in 2017 and joined a global disarmament NGO where he works today as an advocate against nuclear weapons and WMD proliferation.

Sarah left the CIA in 2012 and joined a Wall Street investment bank where she is today in fixed-income research.

Sarah Sussman, Dr. Clare Ahn, and Paul Kazemi were each awarded the Intelligence Medal of Merit.

Made in the USA
Las Vegas, NV
21 May 2024

90208398R00164